Praise for *The Lies* [illegible]

“Noelle Salazar has an unerring instin[illegible] n big hearts. Flight nurse Kate Campbell [illegible] tal tour in the Pacific: keep your emotions locked down, your [illegible] your patients, and leave everything else behind as soon as the combat plane leaves the ground. But an injury sends her back stateside and then to the thick of the European front, where a blue-eyed soldier tempts her with promise of a softer future—if a deadly secret from Kate’s carefully hidden past doesn’t destroy everything first.”

—Kate Quinn, *New York Times* bestselling author of *The Rose Code*

“Perfectly compelling from first page to last. Here is an expertly researched work of historical fiction about how the crucible of war so often burns away the temporal and immaterial and shows us what we really desire and have convinced ourselves we need—and what we’re willing to do to win it. It’s the WW2 story you haven’t read and need to.”

—Susan Meissner, *USA TODAY* bestselling author of *Only the Beautiful*

“Suspenseful, adventurous, and romantic, *The Lies We Leave Behind* took me on a twisty World War II journey from the Pacific to England and then right into the heart of the enemy. I couldn’t put it down. This is a book that reminds us how resilient and courageous the human heart really is.”

—Elise Hooper, author of *Fast Girls* and *Angels of the Pacific*

“This book has my heart. An emotional yet hopeful journey, with so many twists and turns I did not see coming, *The Lies We Leave Behind* feels like an instant war-time classic. Noelle Salazar’s latest is sure to be a favorite for 2024 and well beyond.”

—Jenni L. Walsh, *USA TODAY* bestselling author of *Unsinkable*

“A story of triumph and heartbreak in equal measure, *The Lies We Leave Behind* is an incredible journey of a novel. Salazar deftly takes us from the jungles of the Pacific to the English countryside to the bombed-out streets of Hamburg, immersing the reader in a complex web of lies, and leaving us no choice but to fall head over heels for Kate and William. Hold onto your heart for this one!”

—Sara Ackerman, *USA TODAY* bestselling author of *Radar Girls*

Also by Noelle Salazar

The Flight Girls
Angels of the Resistance
The Roaring Days of Zora Lily

THE LIES WE LEAVE BEHIND

NOELLE SALAZAR

MIRA

MIRA™

ISBN-13: 978-0-7783-6961-5

Recycling programs for this product may not exist in your area.

The Lies We Leave Behind

For questions and comments about the quality of this book, please contact us at CustomerService@Harlequin.com.

Mira
22 Adelaide St. West, 41st Floor
Toronto, Ontario M5H 4E3, Canada
MIRABooks.com

Printed in U.S.A.

For the nurses.

The women.

The unsung heroes of WWII.

1

William

Seattle
2003

IT WAS THE kind of day my wife had often written about in one of her novels. The kind of day when, in my younger years, I'd have grabbed a couple of beers from the fridge and headed to the beach for an afternoon of swimming, lounging, and sunning myself. Or, in my not-quite-as-young years, pulled a few towels from the linen closet, grabbed a plastic bucket and shovel from the garage, and whisked my daughter and wife out the back door, across our lawn, and through the little gate with its little bell to our stretch of rocks and sand, the navy blue water of the Puget Sound stretched out before us. We'd play in the sun until our noses and shoulders turned pink, and then pack up our things, and tread tired but happy back up to the house.

It was the kind of day when, should I allow it, I could be taken back to another time and place. A too-brief period that came now only in flashes of faded memories brought about by particular scents and sounds. The smell of the earth and wildflowers, the wind rustling the leaves on the trees, the warmth of the sun pressing against my skin. And the heat of the day undulating, almost visible, but not stifling—thanks to a breeze happening by to lift the hair from my head and cool my skin with a quick kiss of relief before flitting away again.

It was the kind of day you took notice of. Appreciated. Didn't take for granted as you lifted your face to it, eyes closed, a small smile as you took in its simple perfection.

"Magical," a voice from the past whispered in my ear.

A memory.

A ghost.

I grinned, lost for a moment as I allowed my mind to take me back. Just for a minute. I wouldn't let myself stay there, or else the guilt would come. I'd had too good a life to let myself get pulled into the what-ifs and why-nots. But sometimes I liked to travel back. To imagine. I felt I owed it to the man I was.

I felt I owed it…to her.

"Dad?"

A hand pressed on my shoulder and I started and turned in my chair, looking up into the concerned golden-brown eyes of my daughter, Elizabeth. Lizzie. Named for her mother's all-time favorite literary character.

"You okay?" she asked, her dark brow furrowed. "I was calling you."

I chuckled and pressed my hands to the worn navy blue arms of my favorite deck chair. So many times Olivia, my wife, had wanted to have it repainted. But I liked it this way. We had bought the pair of chairs soon after we'd moved in many decades ago now, and while she'd had hers sanded and painted several times over the years, I liked that mine had weathered with me, each of us showing our age, my body forming to it, or perhaps it forming to my body. Who could know. Regardless, it was mine, and I liked the way life and age had changed it, as both had changed me as well.

I got to my feet and pulled my daughter into a hug, dropping a kiss on her head.

"I'm fine. Just enjoying the weather." I stepped back and gestured to the familiar view she'd grown up with. Below the large deck where we stood, a pristine green lawn with flower beds bursting with color gave way to the Puget Sound beyond. It was an idyllic spot, perfect for long, lazy evenings in the warmer months, cozy fires at the firepit during the long-lasting gray months, and raising a family.

"Where's Emma?" I asked, looking past her for my granddaughter.

"She just pulled up. But she was on the phone so who knows when she'll grace us with her presence." She shook her head and then turned, staring inside the French doors I'd left open to the boxes stacked against one wall of the living room. "You sure you want to donate them all?"

"It's not what I want," I said. "It's what she wanted."

The boxes were filled with books. Her books. From the very first to the very last, spanning five decades. Somehow, despite an aggressive cancer diagnosis, she'd managed to stay alive long enough to finish edits on her last contracted book, see it launch, and then pass quietly in her sleep a week after it hit the *New York Times* bestseller list.

"I did it again," she'd said, her voice barely more than a whisper as she'd held up her phone with a shaking hand to show me the text from her editor.

"Of course you did," I'd told her.

They all hit the list, and deserved to. She told stories like they were real life. Women and men alike saw themselves in her characters. She had a way of pulling you in, breaking your heart, and then building you back up with love and magical moments that, as one popular morning show host said, could feed you for weeks.

I'd often found it ironic that losing her could not be described. For a woman whose career depended on words, her death left me speechless. There wasn't any one word that could express what it felt to lose her presence. The absence of her laughter ringing out down the hallway when she'd written a clever sentence. The way she'd side-eyed me when I took an extra-large helping of ice cream. The way her hand felt in mine.

It had taken months for me to stop calling out her name with a question on my lips. My sleep was often interrupted as my leg drifted toward her side of the bed and found it lacking the warmth that used to be there. I couldn't seem to remember I was the only one drinking the coffee, and still, even now, a year later, made enough for two in the morning.

And her smell…the scent of lavender and vanilla…had all but ceased to exist in the house, time slowly stripping it, stealing it—and her—away.

The front door opened and shut with a small bang that sent a tremor through the walls. Lizzie shook her head and gave a little laugh.

"Apparently, Emma has decided to join us."

"Hey, kid," I called out to my granddaughter who, at thirty-six was still as much of a whirlwind as she'd been at six.

Like her grandmother, she was an artist, but her stories had always come in the form of dance. I had loved watching the two sit together over the years, the elder and the younger, one with a pen and paper, the other twisting her body like a pretzel as they chatted about the art of storytelling.

"Hey, Old Man," she said, entering the room, her long dark hair in its ever-present ponytail, her willowy silhouette all grace and fluidity.

She'd been the prima ballerina at the San Francisco Ballet for a decade, hanging up her shoes only four years ago to take a job as lead choreographer for Seattle's Pacific Northwest Ballet Company. How it thrilled us to see her featured in the newspaper, appreciated for her "fresh take on old classics, while honoring those who had come before."

She was a star. A star who, at close to forty, still had the impish look of the girl she'd been three decades before, and a mischievous streak to match.

"You start that job I tasked you with?" she asked, narrowing the blue eyes she'd inherited from me. It was the only physical trait that linked us. But the mischief she got from me too.

"I got close," I said, raising my hand and holding my forefinger and thumb an inch apart.

"Old Man..." she said, shaking her head. "I'm disappointed in you."

"But the longer I hold off, the more likely you are to come around and check that I did it, providing me with much needed company."

"You're not fooling anyone."

She winked and then turned to her mother and the two headed toward the boxes stacked against the wall. There were hundreds of books. Author copies Olivia had held on to for giveaways, for friends and family, and donated to women's shelters and local charities. To go with the novels there was also the swag. Book bags with her book covers emblazoned on them, pins, buttons, pens, stickers, bookmarks, and mugs. There were a handful of custom bobbleheads we had made when one of her characters became so swoon-worthy, she'd given him his own series of books. There were fleece blankets, candles, and a tin of mints for a novel that had come out fourteen years ago.

Much of it was destined for the trash bin, some would be sent to her publisher and agent for special gift sets they were putting together for her most rabid fans, and the rest would be given away, Lizzie, Emma, and I keeping only what we couldn't bear to part with.

While the women discussed who was taking what where and when, I threw on my favorite worn-in cardigan and ambled down the hallway, my slippers scuffing across the hardwood floor as my gaze skimmed over the family photos lining the walls, the most recent at the start, the oldest at the far end. Memory Lane, Olivia had dubbed it. On these walls, one could document nearly our entire life together as a couple, starting from the night we met, thanks to a mutual friend having a camera on hand. We met moments before the flash went off, and then spent the rest of the night talking tentatively, both of us carrying pain we could hardly bear, but not wanting it to rule our lives.

Olivia was a salve. Funny, kind, and determined to not let herself dwell in the past. And I was a distraction. Maybe not what she was used to, but someone she came to rely on, trust, and eventually fall in love with. We often told those who asked that we saved each other. Right time. Right moment. Right person.

I stopped for a moment in the doorway of her office. It had always amused me that such a sunshiny woman did her work in a space so dark. But she'd insisted on the deep blue wall color, the plush plum velvet couch, and dark wood desk.

"I need to be in a cave," she'd said. "I need to sink down and disappear into my stories. Light and bright will just distract me."

Sometimes I'd join her, slipping quietly from my office across the hall while she typed away, her glasses perched on her nose as she leaned toward the screen to peer at some word or sentence. I'd sit in the corner of the couch, a book or sketchpad in hand, and be a few dozen pages in before she noticed she wasn't alone. Rather than be startled though, she'd just grin, give a happy little sigh, and get back to work.

My eyes took in the familiar sights of the room that was hers and hers alone. This was where one came to find the real Olivia. This was the room where all her barriers came down.

Where she didn't pretend to be anyone but herself. Not wife, not mom, not even *New York Times* bestselling author Olivia Mitchell. She was just her. Silly and ruthless and perfect.

"This is where I let the kid in me out to play," I'd overheard her tell a friend once as they perused the comics she'd clipped from the newspaper and tacked to a bulletin board. Three stuffed doggies took up the corner of the couch opposite the one I always sat in, dolls she'd found while traveling sat on shelves along with numerous other knickknacks and images she'd found funny or quaint or inspiring and had stuck here and there all over the room.

I sagged against the door frame. It seemed impossible that it had been a year. A year and six days exactly since she'd said my name, held my hand, or brushed her fingertips across my cheek. A year and six days since those warm brown eyes had closed to me for good, taking with them her opinions on what glasses looked good on this old face, the hand that reached for that last bite of toast I may or may not have wanted but would always give to her regardless, and her side of every story we were ever part of together.

I sighed and turned, staring into my own office where a large box of photos sat on top of the trunk I used for a coffee table, a catch-all, and a footrest.

I'd been circumnavigating the box for a week, and steering clear of the room altogether if I could help it. It wasn't hard, the only work I did anymore was consultations, and I could do my daily allotment of word games from anywhere in the house with the shiny silver laptop Olivia had bought me two Christmases ago. At one point I'd even shut the door. But I'd always loved how the light that poured in from Olivia's office met with the light that poured in from mine, meeting in the middle of the hallway. Shutting my door had cut off the joining of our lights, making me feel lonelier than I already did, so I'd opened it again, leaving me with no choice but to just keep ignoring the large box of photos of my wife at all her many author events through the years. I'd been tasked with going through them. Disposing of some, keeping others, and gathering a pile to send off to her publisher.

I took a seat on the sofa and slid the box toward me, glancing down at the old trunk it sat on and running my hand over its smooth surface.

Olivia was the only person, aside from myself, to ever see the contents of the trunk I'd hauled stateside from Europe. It had been covered up, shoved into the shadows, forgotten and found again, and then finally placed in this very spot several years ago by my late wife who'd claimed it was an important part of my story, and she hoped one day I'd share it with our daughter and granddaughter. But like so many others who had served, sharing that part of my life was the last thing I wanted to do, and so it had stayed locked, its contents unseen and unspoken about.

The night Olivia had seen its contents was the one time early in our relationship that I'd stood her up for dinner. Rather than accept such treatment, she'd driven to my house, marched up the muddy front path, and banged on my door, ready to give me a piece of her mind. But when she'd seen the state of me, drunk and red-eyed from crying, she'd immediately dropped her purse to the floor, slipped off her mud-splattered heels, and led me to the couch where the trunk sat open, what was inside on full display.

She took a beer from my fridge, sat beside me, and asked careful questions about the comrades standing beside me in one photo after another. After a while, I felt a glimmer of hope for my future. This woman wasn't daunted by my pain, my sorrow, or the photo of a pretty young blonde woman staring into the lens of my borrowed camera with obvious love in her eyes. She'd run a gentle finger over a sprig of dried bluebells she'd found pressed within the pages of a book. She'd smiled gently, understanding my agony. She knew what it was to have loved and lost.

After she'd finished her drink, she'd helped me place the memories back inside the trunk, lock it up, and set fresh cans of beer and two bowls of spaghetti I cooked for us on top. I never opened the trunk again, and she never asked. But a few weeks later I woke in her bed to find her watching me. Hesitantly, she handed me a small velvet bag.

"What is it?" I'd asked, watching her cheeks redden.

"I hope it's okay," she said. "I just thought..." She shrugged and bit her lower lip. "It's okay to remember."

I gave her a quizzical look and then untied the string and turned the bag over, watching as a small but heavy dome of glass fell into my palm. Inside it were the bluebells.

"William?" she said after a minute during which I'd sat in silence. "Are you... You're mad. I'm so sorry. I just thought—"

I'd met her eyes, my own filled with tears, and reached for her hand.

"Thank you," I said. "It's beautiful."

Over the years, that little bit of glass had found itself in the silliest places. A plant pot, an Easter basket, a candy dish, beneath the Christmas tree, out in the yard, brought there by our old dog Charmer. It once went on vacation with us to Hawaii, a road trip down the Oregon coast, and had even made it into the pages of one of Olivia's early books.

And now it was in my granddaughter's hands as she stood in the doorway of my office, watching me.

"Were the flowers special to Gran for some reason?" she asked, smoothing a long, slender finger over the top of the clear dome of glass. "I just realized I've never seen bluebells anywhere else in the house. Did you pick them for her?"

"No," I said, reaching my hand out and smiling as she handed it over. "And this wasn't hers. It's mine."

Her mouth opened as if to ask more, but I cut her off, the scent of food wafting down the hall toward us.

"Your mom cooking?"

"Lasagna. You won't go hungry for at least another week."

"Thank God. I was starting to worry."

We laughed. Every week Lizzie came over and made a week's worth of food, claiming it was an accident.

"How does one accidentally make enough food for a small squadron?" I'd ask, but she'd just shrug and get back to work.

The doorbell rang then and Emma pushed off the door frame.

"I'll get it," she said. "Probably the guys coming to pick up the books."

As she wandered off down the hall, I slid the glass sphere into the pocket of my sweater and pulled the lid off the box of photos.

"Here goes nothing," I said to myself as I grabbed the first envelope.

The photographs inside were from one of her last in-person events. There she was sitting on a tall stool, one of her author friends beside her on another stool, microphones in their hands. There she was signing books. Laughing with a reader. Giving the photographer a silly smile as she posed with a wall of her books the bookstore hosting her had thoughtfully displayed. There she was with me, her head resting against my chest, me proud as anything as I held her latest novel up. Her and Lizzie. Her and Emma. Her and—

"Grandpa?"

I startled, not because I was surprised by the voice, but because of what she'd called me. Emma didn't call me Grandpa unless something was amiss.

"What's wrong?" I asked, meeting her eyes and noting the little crease between her brows.

"There's someone at the door for you. A woman."

I sat for a moment more, watching her, and then got to

my feet. As I passed her in the doorway, she reached out and squeezed my hand.

"Love you, kiddo," I said, kissing her forehead.

"Love you, Old Man."

Shoving my hands in my pockets, I grasped the glass piece I'd forgotten was there and then reached for the handle of the front door and pulled it open, finding myself staring at a face that looked strangely familiar, though I was positive I'd never seen the woman before.

And then I noticed her eyes. A shade of pale blue reminiscent of another time, long ago.

Neither of us said anything for a long moment, and then I chuckled, embarrassed at myself and my lack of manners.

"I'm sorry," I said and shook my head. "Can I help you?"

A breeze lifted her shoulder-length blond hair, blowing it gently around slender shoulders. My breath caught as a memory tried to force its way forward.

"It is for me to apologize," the woman said in a rich French accent, her voice low and husky. "I am sorry to intrude at dinnertime. But...are you William Mitchell?"

"I am," I said, looking for a name tag or a bag of some sort with whatever product name she was trying to sell me emblazoned on it. But there was nothing. Just a large but tasteful handbag hanging from her shoulder.

"My name is Selene Michel. I am wondering if you knew a woman named Gisela Holländer?"

I frowned and shook my head.

"No. I'm sorry. I've never heard that name."

She seemed to expect this, nodding, her eyes searching mine as she took in a deep breath, let it out, and then said a name I hadn't heard in nearly six decades.

"And what about Kate Campbell?"

A million tiny moments flashed through my mind, a song long forgotten playing its tune in my head. I looked down at the bluebells in my hand that I hadn't realized I'd removed from my pocket, and then back at the woman.

"Yes," I said. "Yes. That's a name I've heard before."

2

Kate

Somewhere in the Pacific
Summer 1943

THE METAL FRAMES of the bunks clattered in the cavernous metal belly of the plane as it hit a pocket of air and jerked us upward before dropping us several feet. The contents of the medical box in my hands rattled violently as the men strapped to their bunks groaned.

"Hang in there, boys," I shouted.

I looked through the pale strands of hair now marring my sight at the handsome pilot grinning at me over his shoulder. The last amber light of the setting sun burst through the windshield in a fiery display, bathing him in a golden glow. If I were the kind of girl who swooned, that image of him would've done it.

But I wasn't. At least not for a guy like Mac.

I'd met Mac my first day on the job. After he'd asked me

out, his grin more leer than smile, and I'd promptly turned him down, we'd developed a brother-and-sister kind of relationship that none of the other women on base could understand.

"But he's so dreamy" was the oft-touted opinion as they stared at his well-built physique, wavy blond hair, and pale green eyes.

But to me he was silly. A caricature of someone he'd probably seen in a movie once, studied, and tried to emulate. He was all seductive leans, slow grins, and piercing gazes. While the others fanned themselves in his presence, I had a hard time not rolling my eyes. Men like him would never turn my head. They were all show, no substance. I'd grown up around men like that. Slick specimens using their good looks and charm to persuade, lie, and manipulate. They were not to be trusted.

After my quick shutdown of Mac's proposed date after we'd first met, he'd realized I'd seen through his game and immediately showed me another side to him. One I liked infinitely more. He had a quick wit, big heart, and was known to throw himself in the line of fire to protect his comrades. I respected him, even while still detesting the romantic methods he used on my friends.

"You good?" he shouted to me now.

I looked from him to the nineteen men lying in their bunks, bandaged, stitched, and in some cases their wounds left open due to infection or to relieve the pressure of flying on their stitched organs, muscles, and skin. None of them were okay, but no one seemed in any more pain than they'd been in before the turbulence.

"All good!" I yelled back over the noise of rattling metal.

As fast as it had started it stopped and I took in a long deep breath and closed my eyes for a moment, lifting my face toward the warmth coming through the window and stretching its way across the cold, rigid floor toward me. Despite being in the Pacific, where temperatures on the ground were often sweltering, it was always freezing at this high altitude. The cold seeped beneath the layers I'd pulled on earlier this morning in preparation for the cold ride. The pool of sweat between my breasts from two hours ago was now freezing. Regardless of the physical discomfort, and recognizing how minor mine was compared to what the men laid out before me were experiencing, I allowed myself to take in the moment of stillness. These were the moments I waited for. The reprieve from what came before, and what would surely come after. The breath that filled my body, slowing my adrenaline.

"Got some smoke up ahead," the copilot, a man called Wes, warned. "Might get a bit bumpy again."

I sat up and looked out the tiny window beside me, but all I saw was blue sky.

"What kind of smoke?" I asked, undoing my buckle and making my way to the front of the plane to have a look. I scanned the horizon for a glimpse of the base. "Is it us?"

"Not us, doll!" Mac said.

I made a face. I was not one of Mac's dolls and took offense to being called one.

"Don't call me that. You know I hate—"

But the last part of my sentence was drowned out as a loud bang erupted somewhere outside the small plane, and my bones shuddered along with the stacked beds in back. Ahead of us a plane swooped toward the earth, another on its tail.

"What are they doing out here?" I asked, hanging on to the back of Mac's seat.

Most of the action was back in Guadalcanal, where we'd just loaded the men.

"Dammit, I don't know!" Mac yelled, pulling us higher as another plane came into view. "Get back in your seat!"

Holding on to what I could, I moved unsteadily to the back of the plane again, noticing as I went that one of my patients was pulling at the bandage on his arm. An arm that had been partially amputated.

I let go of the wall and moved as fast as I could, grasping hold of the bed frame as the plane tilted to one side.

"Hey," I said, wrapping my free hand around the man's remaining one, my eyes going to the name that had been fastened to his gown. "You need to leave it, Thompson. The stitches are fresh and you don't want to pull them out."

But he shook his head, confusion in eyes clouded with pain medication as he looked down, searching for the missing appendage.

The plane shook violently and my grip slipped, one knee hitting the edge of the bunk below before slamming into the floor.

"You okay?" Mac shouted.

"No!" I shouted back, feeling my leg, my hand coming away with blood on it. "Get us out of here!"

"I'm trying. I'm trying."

I got to my feet again and took the patient's hand as I looked at his bandage. There was a little blood staining the fresh wrap and I wondered how many stitches he'd managed to get to. Hopefully it was just a bit of seepage from the wound and nothing that would require him to endure even more pain.

"We'll be on the ground soon," I said, wincing as the initial ache in my knee subsided and a stinging sensation from the skin being ripped away set in. "Hang in there, okay? Just a little bit longer and we'll be on the ground."

The air began to warm and I realized it was quieter again, the shaking of the beds lessening.

"We clear?" I yelled toward the front of the plane.

"All clear. Our guys got him. Buckle in for landing."

With a last squeeze of the soldier's hand, I let go and hurried to my seat, strapping in and watching out the tiny window at my side for the familiar sight of palm trees rushing by, the telltale sign we were home.

A few minutes later we touched down hard, the wounded bodies on the beds across from me rising for the briefest of moments before settling again, several of the men wincing as they were violently shifted.

"Jesus, Mac!" I shouted.

"Hey! You're alive! What do you say?"

I rolled my eyes. "Thank you, Mac."

"That's better, doll."

I scowled over my shoulder at him and he winked back and then steered us across the pavement.

"Whatcha got on tonight, Lieutenant?" Mac asked as he opened the side door and then stood aside as several nurses and doctors hurried across the runway with foldable litters to collect the wounded. "Wanna get dinner in the mess? Maybe have a drink and play some cards?" He patted the bag slung over his shoulder, the sound of glass bottles clinking against one another.

I shook my head as I unhooked an IV from where it hung and helped move the soldier it had been connected to before kneeling to help the guy on the bunk below.

"Sorry, I'm beat. Plus, I'm hanging on to my winnings from last time."

He laughed. "You cleaned me out."

"You were drunk as a skunk."

"You took advantage of my delicate state."

"Damn right I did." I did a quick check of a stomach wound and then covered it again before standing aside for the patient to be taken.

After all the men were unloaded, I grabbed my bag and limped beside Mac across the dusty, pit-riddled runway.

"I don't know how you do all that," he said, nodding toward the makeshift hospital the patients were being loaded into. "Some of those wounds make my stomach turn."

"Not all of us can be as delicate as you, Mac."

He elbowed me and I smacked him on the arm.

"Lover's quarrel?" a female voice asked.

A pretty brunette leaned against the hood of a truck, dressed in a pair of military issued trousers and a button-down top with the top few buttons undone. And not because of the heat. I glanced at Mac who was also taking in the scenery.

"Hey, Char," he said.

Charlene Newcomb was one of the women I bunked with on the little island of Espiritu Santo in the New Hebrides, and one of my best friends. There were four of us who hung out regularly together, sharing two sets of bunk beds at one end of a cramped, dusty, canvas barracks named Burlap Flats, where the air inside was so thick and stagnant, we often worried we'd suffocate in our sleep.

Charlene hailed from San Diego. Tilly from Savannah. And Paulette and I were from the East Coast. Manhattan for me, Boston for her. The four of us couldn't be more different if we'd been born in different countries, in different eras, and in separate universes. Yet somehow we got on like we'd known each other for years, rather than only months.

"You playing cards tonight with us, Kate?" Char asked, her gaze straying to Mac, whose shirt was damp and sticking to his chest, before taking in the state of me. "Shoot. What happened to your knee?"

"Mac's flying."

"Hey!" he said, his face turning red as he looked to Char.

I shrugged. "It got a little precarious up there. Mac kept us safe though." I patted his arm. "No cards for me tonight. I'm tired."

"Mac?" she said, taking in a long breath, the action pushing her breasts forward.

"I could probably be persuaded," he said.

I shifted my bag on my shoulder, trying not to smirk. The two of them were ridiculously obvious. They'd been playing a game of cat-and-mouse for weeks now, but so far Char had held off on going all the way.

"I like to make a guy work a little to get all this," she'd said one day, giving her ample breasts a squeeze and causing the rest of us to erupt in laughter.

"You two have fun," I said, giving them a wave as I hobbled off in the direction of the barracks.

Exhaustion set in as I walked, the heat weighing on me, pressing down around me, making my body feel heavy as sweat trickled down my spine. Spring on Espiritu Santo had been almost unbearable. Summer was indescribable.

"Hiya, Kate," a soldier called out as I passed by the makeshift hospital.

I glanced at the familiar face and clean medical scrubs. At this time of day, the only reason he was wearing clean clothes was because the last ones had been bled on. A lot.

"Hi, Chuck."

"You look like you could use a little tending to yourself for once." He pointed to my leg and I stopped, realizing my wound probably did need to be cleaned and I had nothing to do the job in our barracks.

I nodded, hitched my bag higher on my shoulder, and limped toward him.

"How was the flight in?" he asked as I followed him inside, took a seat, and carefully pulled up my ripped pant leg to reveal my skinned knee. I was more worried about the pants than the injury. We only had so much room for clothing, which meant I didn't have much in the way of backup options. I'd have to sew these up as best I could, or find a patch to cover the hole. Most of the patches around these parts were for patching people though, not clothing.

"It wasn't bad," I said, sucking in a breath as he cleaned some grit from the delicate pink skin that was seeping tiny pinpricks of blood.

Good flight. Bad flight. Not bad. Coulda been better. It was how we asked without asking, answered without answering. It was an unwritten rule among those of us who tended to the wounded. We did the job when on the job, but we left it behind us as soon as we left the tent or stepped off the plane. Doing it any other way could make one unfit for the job, and no one wanted to be the one who quit on the wounded.

"Well, the good news is," Chuck said, taping a small square piece of gauze onto my knee, "I think you're gonna make it."

He patted my other knee and held out a hand, helping me to my feet.

"You're a lifesaver, Chuck."

"That's what they tell me."

He gave me a wink and then hurried off, his shoulders carrying the weight of the world.

I walked up the two steps to the glorified tent I shared with nineteen others and opened the door, doing a quick scan of the dimly lit space. As usual, there were several women asleep in their bunks, a few others reading or writing letters, and two playing a card game.

Noting my bunkmate's empty bed below mine, the duffel she used for work missing from the footlocker, I slid my own bag from my shoulder and stored it in my locker before stepping carefully on the frame of the lower bunk and pulling myself up to check for uninvited creatures hanging about. It was a common occurrence to find any manner of bugs, snakes, and other unwanted animals in our beds when we didn't occupy them for a night.

"It's like they watch us and wait for us to leave," Paulette said one day after she'd gone screaming from our tent after finding a rather large grasshopper in her bed.

Satisfied my bunk was clear, I threw on a fresh shirt, brushed my hair and pulled it into a ponytail once more, then headed for the mess hall for dinner.

My presence was instantly noticed as I walked in the room. With so few women on base, we stood out like beacons of something the men missed, desired, or ached for. It wasn't so much that they wanted *us*, but more that we reminded them of home. Of girlfriends, wives, sisters, and mothers. Our mere existence provided comfort. Soft voices, soft bodies, long hair and, except when straight off a plane after a mission, nicer smells. It was disconcerting. Uncomfortable at times. The need coming off their persons palpable. And as a woman who tended to keep people at an arm's length at all times, it was even more awkward.

I pasted on a smile and made my way to the food, grabbing a tray and plate and perusing the evening's choices. The scent of fresh-cooked food made my mouth water. I was starving, my last meal eaten in a hurry as the sun rose this morning before loading injured men onto the plane. I grabbed two rolls, spooned a pile of potatoes on my plate, some chicken, corn, and piece of pie before circling back to grab two more rolls.

"Where you gonna put all that?" asked a soldier at the opposite end of the table where I sat.

I shoved a huge forkful of potatoes into my mouth and smiled. I hated being underestimated.

A loud crack of laughter echoed throughout the room and I glanced at a table at the far end. Mac was holding court, gesturing wildly as he told some story, probably of his own heroism, while Char sat beside him, a coy grin on her pretty face. She may have been obvious in her desires for him, but she was also in on the joke.

"Oh, I know he's obnoxious and incredibly high on himself," she told me in private one day when I woke to find her sneaking back into our tent after curfew. "But when he stops talking and gets down to business, he really knows what he's doing."

I'd wrinkled my nose at that and she'd laughed and climbed into her bunk fully clothed.

She caught my eye from across the room now and gestured

with her head to join them, but I gave an exaggerated yawn and she nodded her understanding before turning her attention back to Mac's antics. I stared down at my plate of food and pushed the potatoes around, images of the day before seeping in from the place in my brain where I hid them at the end of each mission. They always found me no matter how hard I tried to forget, haunting me in the quiet hours, which was easily done in my constantly exhausted state.

I took another bite, but the food was tasteless now. I was tempted to throw it away, but for the two things stopping me: guilt for wasting and the idiot who'd challenged my ability to eat my weight in food. Sighing, I shoved a forkful of potatoes in my mouth.

After finishing nearly everything on my plate, I dumped the scraps and made my way through the dark along the familiar path back to the barracks. Most of the women in attendance were asleep, a few with lanterns hanging above their bunks as they wrote letters or read books.

I changed into a pair of pajamas I'd purchased in the men's department of Bloomingdale's, as everything offered in the women's department had ruffles and lace and long, flowing sleeves that ended in elastic at the wrists that irritated my skin. The men's options were far cozier. Wide legs, roomy tops, and fabrics that were soft, not satiny. I'd bought three pairs of men's pajamas in the smallest size they had, and every one of the women I bunked with had commented with envy about them.

"I still can't believe no one's swiped those from you."

I glanced over my shoulder to the woman in the bottom bunk next to the one I shared with Tilly as I climbed up to mine.

"It's not like they could hide it if they did," I said, pulling back the covers and checking under my pillow for creatures before tucking the mosquito netting around my mattress.

"I'd put them under my nightgown," she said and I laughed. Paulette was a no-nonsense kind of soul. The kind of woman my aunt would say spoke "from the gut." She wasn't mean or harsh, just said whatever she was thinking, and was honest about it.

"Well," I said, "if I find any of them missing, I'll look up your skirt first."

She grinned.

"How'd today go?" she asked.

"Fine," I said and she nodded and went back to the book she was reading while I lay back and stared up at the ceiling of our large tented home and debated if I wanted to pull out my own book, kept beneath my pillow.

But as my eyes blurred with tiredness, I decided against it and rolled onto my side, pulling the thin sheet and blanket I slept with over me and mulling over the word *fine*.

"A word to mask what you're really feeling, because all you feel is numb," my aunt once told me after I'd given the word as an answer to how my first day at my new school had gone.

Some days it was all one could say though. No one had died on my watch, but there had been near misses. Moments when I thought I might fail the men in my charge. Seconds I thought the plane might go down, killing all of us.

Good days weren't ever truly good. They came laced with small miracles, and battles fought and sometimes lost. And no matter how well a flight went, there was always the possibility that we wouldn't make it through the rest of the day or through the night. So *fine* was all we got. And fine I would take, because it was a gift that I got to say it at all.

I drifted off to sleep then with the hope that tomorrow would be fine as well, the distant sound of gunfire like a lullaby in the background.

3

I WOKE TO a scream and sat up, my face hitting the net that had sagged in the night under the weight of the humidity.

"Get it out!" someone screeched from the other side of the barracks. "Help!"

In the dim lighting I watched for a moment the scuffle to catch a rat with a shoe and a box and then lay back down and rolled over. Rats were common visitors, especially when the river rose. And, by the sound of the rain battering the canvas roof above me, it most likely had. The rats, pushed from their homes, came looking for a dry spot to harbor in. Mosquito nets weren't just for bugs, they were also supposed to keep the rats out of our beds. Most of the time it worked. Sometimes it didn't.

The next time I woke it was due to my bed shaking. Squinting in the sliver of light shining through one of the plastic windows someone had exposed an inch of, I shoved my netting aside and leaned over to look at the woman below me.

"You just get in?" I asked, taking in Tilly's haggard appearance through her own net.

Her skin had a yellow tinge from the Atabrine, the medicine we took to keep from getting malaria, and there was a faint smear of blood in her wispy blond hair that she'd probably tried to wash out but hadn't done a good job of in her haste to get to her bed to sleep. We were always in a state of mostly clean. Water conditions could change in the blink of an eye. Sometimes the shower was too hot, sometimes too cold. Never something you wanted to stand and luxuriate in. And a lot of times it was just two to three women sharing a bowl of water to splash over our faces and under our armpits with a little bit of soap. It was only when we had to keep soldiers alive that anyone cared about our cleanliness. And only our hands at that.

Tilly yawned and nodded.

"How'd it go?" I asked.

"Fine," she said.

Fine.

I nodded, not needing to imagine the ravaged faces and bodies I knew she'd seen, or hear the wailing and moaning and blistering tirades she'd heard. I knew them only too well. All while the plane we'd boarded shook and rattled and threatened to succumb to the gunfire and bombs discharging nearby, making us wonder if we'd make it out alive physically, mentally, and emotionally—the damage to our minds and hearts possibly too great.

And yet I did it without complaint, even thriving on it. If I thought they'd allow it, I'd ask to be sent out twice a day, the job not so much a calling as a deep-seated need to try and make amends for something I knew I wasn't responsible for, but felt guilty about regardless.

"You out again today?" Tilly asked, her blinks getting longer.

"Yeah."

"Stay safe, buddy."

"I'll do my best, buddy."

She was asleep then and I rolled onto my back once more and stared between the netting to the ceiling. My body ached from head to toe. I was stronger than I'd ever been, but my skeleton felt bruised. My bones weary. And yet I pushed myself up, pulled the netting free of my mattress, and hopped down to the floor to do it all over again.

"You taking me in?" I asked an hour later as I entered the little building sitting at the edge of the runway.

At the front desk was Gus, one of the dozen or so pilots I'd flown with since landing on Espiritu Santo four months ago. Gus was what the younger men called seasoned. He was older, wiser, and didn't take crap from anyone. A man of few words, he was incredibly efficient, and the rumors about him were numerous. Feats of bravery, men he'd saved… He never admitted to any of it, but there was a look in his soulful brown eyes. A sadness I'd seen in others who had experienced what was considered courage, but wore on a human soul. Regardless of what he had or hadn't done, whenever I flew with him, I felt safe. There was a quality about him that reminded me of a dad. Not my father, who'd never been anything but cold and standoffish. But someone's dad. And the kind of dad I'd always wished I'd had.

"It's you and me, kid," Gus said before grabbing a clipboard and heading out to do a last check of the plane transporting us. "See you onboard."

The flight in was easy. I sat in my seat, eyes closed, arms wrapped around my torso as the plane rose and the temperature dropped. I dozed for most of the trip, waking every now and then as we hit a pocket of air that set the empty bunks rattling, and then as we entered the war zone, Gus doing his best to dodge bullets that had missed their mark and were zipping our way.

But we landed safely and he laughed as he always did when

he swung open the big door to let me out and I squinted in the bright light after napping for two hours.

"Watch your step," he said as I tripped over a rock.

"Shut up," I said, making him laugh harder.

"See you soon, sunshine," he called after me.

The hospital was swarming with doctors and nurses, the smells and sights enough to make one's stomach turn. There were seeping wounds and bandaged body parts every which way I looked.

"Morning, Lieutenant. Gonna be a doozy of a transport today."

I glanced over at the head nurse who had just sunk down on a stool on the other side of the counter from me, his face weary.

"You say that every time, Percy," I said.

He gave me an apologetic look.

"We got a fresh truckload in a couple hours ago and..." He trailed off. A fresh truckload meant wounds that hadn't had much time to be tended to. And a high likelihood that not all of the men onboard would make it. But I'd be damned if they were lost on my watch.

"How many?" I asked.

"Twenty-one."

"Well, twenty-one just happens to be my lucky number."

"I thought sixteen was."

"That was two days ago, Percy."

He gave me a sad, tired grin. "Let's hope you're right," he said and hurried off, his shoes squelching on the bloodstained floor.

Each patient loaded onto the plane came with his own set of instructions, pinned to his shirt, his pants, or the sheet covering his body. Some were unconscious and would only require a periodic glance, others had lost limbs, their wounds wrapped but not necessarily cleaned yet as there had been no time.

Some would need help shifting in their cot to ease discomfort, others needed pain medication to be administered at different times and in different quantities, oxygen might be a necessity depending on elevation levels, and then there were the stomach wounds.

Doctor Fischer, the man in charge, pointed to a soldier with a thick bandage around his torso. "Keep an eye on this one as you climb."

"Yessir."

"You're aware what could happen?"

"Well aware, sir."

Stomachs had a penchant for expanding if the plane rose too fast, bursting stitches and causing a wound to become life-threatening—and messy. On a plane filled with men in excruciating pain with only one nurse to tend to them all, it was best not to have to perform a surgery onboard. To counteract such issues, the stitches had to be cut and then redone as soon as it was safe to do so.

I'd only heard of one incidence of that happening since arriving at Espiritu Santo, and thanks to the gory details, I swore to myself it would never happen on one of my shifts. Poor Carlotta had returned the following day looking as though she'd seen a ghost.

"There was blood everywhere..." she'd said, her voice trailing off as she stared through the rest of us.

In addition to the stomach wound I'd have onboard, I also had a soldier with a brain injury.

"Is he coherent?" I asked Percy, who'd returned to help load the patients.

"Not exactly. He's mostly quiet but sometimes babbles nonsense. He's been here for a couple of weeks. We thought he was getting better. He had some other minor injuries so we kept him here, but those healed. His head hasn't."

"Non-aggressive?"

"Benny? Nah. He's harmless."

"And he'll stay in his bunk without a fight?"

"Definitely. He's happy to just stare at the wall, maybe at you because you're pretty, and jabber on about nothing, sing, or just be silent. He won't give you a lick of trouble."

"Anyone else I need to know about?"

He went down a small list and I made some notes for myself, and then the two of us, Doctor Fischer, and three other nurses helped load the troops carefully into the plane.

As I helped one young man across the tarmac, his uninjured arm around my shoulder, he cracked jokes about his missing arm, which had been blown off by gunfire, along with a chunk of his left thigh.

"I was just looking for a quick way home," he said. "And some cute girls to flirt with."

He gave me a wink and I tried not to laugh. He was eighteen but looked younger, with freckles smattered across his face and a mop of red hair.

"Well, I hope you find some," I said as I helped him into his bunk and strapped him in.

Once all the patients were onboard and in their bunks, I went about double-checking that they were secure, tightening straps as needed, checking IVs, and placing a gentle hand on arms, fevered heads, and an exposed shin or foot to comfort—and to check temperatures. Several of the men were slick with sweat, shaking from cold despite the heat.

I tucked blankets, adjusted pillows, and peeked beneath bandages, all the while murmuring words of reassurance.

"You about ready?" Gus asked, poking his head in.

"Give me two minutes," I said, glancing toward the man with the brain injury and the guy with the stomach wound in the bunk across from him.

"You got it," he said and shut the door, taking what breeze there was with him and leaving me in suffocating warmth and the overwhelming smell of sweat and urine.

"How are you doing, Benjamin?" I asked the man with

the bandaged head. His chart listed him as Benjamin Wells. I kneeled beside him, my eyes on his, but his gaze didn't meet mine, instead moving all around my face, landing here and there but never lingering in any one spot.

"He goes by Benny," the man in the bed above him said.

"Benny, huh?" I asked, watching his big brown eyes glance off my nose, my chin, and my hair. "Well, it's nice to meet you, Benny. I'll come check on you again later."

He mumbled something and I leaned in.

"He said Lila," the man below him said.

I looked down at a face held together on one side by dozens of stitches.

"Who's Lila?" I asked.

He shrugged. "No idea, but it's the only word he ever says."

I stared at Benny and then reached out and gave his arm a squeeze.

"Lila," I said. "We'll try to get you home to her soon."

I moved on to the soldier with the stomach wound then, glancing at my list of names and injuries to identify the soldier and his reason for being on my plane. He was unconscious, having been given a large dose of pain medicine for the ride, but his face showed that regardless of what he'd been given and the deep sleep he was in, he knew he didn't feel good.

I undid the belts securing him, lifted his blankets, and then his bandage. The stitches were fresh, the skin beneath red and angry and swollen. I sighed. Out of all the injuries onboard, this one worried me the most.

"We're off in one!" Gus shouted from the front of the plane. He was standing behind the pilot's seat, giving his passengers a quick once-over.

"Warn me if we have to climb fast," I said, leaving the injury exposed so I could keep watch on it from my seat.

"You got it."

And with that, he slid into his seat and began throwing switches.

"Buckle up!" he shouted as the engines kicked in.

I hurried to my seat, buckled myself in, and stared across the belly of the plane at the stomach wound. Crossing my fingers, I prayed to whoever or whatever might be listening that we all made it through this flight with no problems.

"Here we go!" Gus yelled.

With a lurch, we pulled out of our parking spot and turned onto the runway. I winced as we bumped over rocks and dipped hard into the divots sprinkled across the crude pavement, watching the patients that were awake squeeze their eyes shut and grip their beds. There was a slight pause, the motor loud and echoing through the fuselage, and then the plane started rolling, lumbering at first as it hit yet more holes in the tarmac, causing the beds to shake and rattle, the noise almost suffocating in its intensity, and then the road smoothed and we were in the air.

While we ascended, I breathed. Deep, slow breaths, filling my lungs with the stagnant air, holding it, and then blowing out. I wasn't afraid of flying, or even being shot down. What did push that extra rush of nervous energy through my veins was knowing it was only me to tend to the twenty-one injured on board. Should more than one start to bleed out, I was almost guaranteed to lose a man.

I turned my attention to Miles and his stomach wound. He was still out like a light. He'd be fine so long as we didn't have to go too high. But just as I thought it, the plane tipped sharply, pushing me back in my seat.

"Hang on!" Gus yelled.

A loud explosion nearby reverberated off the metal of the plane and I pressed my hands to my ears to try and block the sound, my entire body buzzing from the blast.

"We're gonna have to get higher!" Gus shouted again as the distinct sound of gunfire discharged nearby.

I exhaled and nodded, undoing the latch of my buckle and getting unsteadily to my feet. Holding on to the harness, I grabbed my medical bag and unzipped it, feeling around until I found the case holding my scissors. Shoving it in my pocket, I made my way toward my patient.

I could see from several feet away that Miles's stomach was already expanding as we quickly ascended. I stumbled and fell, just missing the knee I'd injured the day before.

"You okay?"

I looked up at a soldier staring down at me from a top bunk.

"Fine," I said, hurrying to my feet and to Miles.

"Shit shit shit," I said, staring down at the flesh that was tearing around the stitches as the stomach ballooned. I grabbed the scissors from their case, not caring as it fell to the floor and slid out of sight. "Hang on, buddy. I've got you. I'm not going to let you bleed out."

Bracing one hand against the man's hot flesh, I began to cut as quickly and carefully as I could so as not to do further damage. As I moved down the line of crude black thread, I watched the skin pull back, exposing fatty tissue and muscle below. Grabbing the bag of supplies I'd secured to the foot of his bunk before takeoff, I pulled out a clean gauze and draped it loosely over the wound before securing it with tape. I checked his pulse and exhaled. He was still alive.

Sagging against the frame of the bunk, I glanced over at Benny.

"You doing okay, Benny?"

He stared at my cheek, my ear, my chin.

"Lila." I saw him say the name but couldn't hear it over the noise of the engine.

I nodded.

"Lila," I said, and felt the plane level. With a sigh of relief, I bent down to retrieve my scissors case and then began to make my rounds to the other patients.

4

"YOU COMIN'?"

I glanced over the side of my bunk at Char, who was wearing mascara that was already leaving black smudges beneath her eyes from the humidity, and a tight-fitting red dress that clung damply to her ample breasts.

It was our day off and as usual she was itching for some action. The kind that didn't involve dodging bullets or keeping someone from bleeding out. She'd told me once, the first time she'd donned one of her rather risqué dresses, that she could handle any wound or close call so long as she could get some male attention after to "keep the balance." I'd never identified with a statement less. For me, the balance was survival. Both mine and my patients'. But to each her own.

"Is Mac going to be there?" I asked, watching her wipe away a bead of sweat sliding over the narrow edge of her collarbone.

If Mac was going to be wherever she was headed, I'd opt out. It never failed that the two of them always wandered off.

It was fine if it was more than just she and I, but more often than not it wasn't and I ended up getting left behind to find my own way back to base. Thankfully, we were never too far away, the nearest town less than two miles away. But walking alone was never encouraged. Day or night. Because you never knew what kind of desperation you might cross paths with.

"Nah," Char said. "He flew out an hour ago."

"I hope you sent him off with a smile," a nurse called Debbie said from two bunks over.

"I always do!" Char shouted back.

I gave her a look and she had the audacity to blush.

"He wasn't smiling *that* big," she whispered and I laughed.

"You are an awful tease, Charlene Newcomb."

"Actually, I'm quite good at it."

"That poor man's balls must be so blue they're the color of the night sky by now."

Her eyes went wide and she clapped a hand over her mouth. I laughed and rolled onto my back, trying to ignore the pleading face she was now giving me.

"Ugh," I said, rolling my eyes and sitting up. "Fine. I'll come. Where are we going?" I held up my hand as soon as the words were out of my mouth. "Never mind. Don't tell me. I'll probably change my mind if you do."

Char had a knack for finding her way into some of the dingiest little places in Luganville, the nearest town to base. But while she found diversion flirting with drunk soldiers for free drinks, batting impossibly long lashes and making empty promises, I only felt the sense of sadness hanging over the men's heads. They laughed and joked and teased, but the laughs were hollow, the jokes often didn't hit, and the teasing came tinged with a longing that physically pained me. There was a palpable feeling of dread among them, as though they knew their time was nearly up. They couldn't keep narrowly escaping death forever. Not in this place.

"Should we wake Paulette?" I asked, looking at the sleeping form of our friend. She'd gotten in a few hours ago but mentioned she might want to go out if we did.

"Shh!" Char said, pressing a finger to my lips, which I batted away. "What did I tell you both? Never again. She scares all the boys away."

She wasn't wrong. Paulette's sharp tongue, while sometimes warranted, had a way of turning an easy conversation into something awkward.

"I still haven't forgiven her for what she did," Char said, glaring at her.

I pressed my lips together. I knew Paulette did it because she was bored and looking for a reaction. She also just really enjoyed ruining whatever game Char was playing. But even I had been shocked when, during a conversation about the pains of war with three men, one of whom Char was heavily flirting with, Pauline had burst out with, "You know what's really painful, bending over to resuscitate a patient while on your menstrual cycle."

The look of shock on the men's faces was nothing compared to the wide-eyed disgust on Char's.

"I will never forgive you," she'd said under her breath as the man she'd been talking up excused himself to the other side of the bar—and never returned.

And she hadn't. Even two months later. In fact, she brought it up anytime she got a whiff of Paulette being interested in joining us, which wasn't often as her days off rarely fell on the same days as ours.

"How long until we leave for whatever godforsaken place you've found for us tonight?" I asked, grabbing a wrinkled navy blue dress.

"You can't wear that!" Char said, grabbing it and tossing it back into my footlocker. "It looks like it got run over by a tank. Twice."

She opened her own locker and pulled out a pale pink number I'd seen her wear half a dozen times. If I remembered correctly, and I did, it had a neckline that dipped into the indecent territory. I'd have to wear my white Midgie cardigan over it, despite the wretched heat. With a sigh, I took the pink dress and lifted my shirt over my head, smiling as Char turned her back to give me privacy.

It was amusing to me how modest some of the other women were, hiding their bodies behind bunks and blankets. Even Char, who put her body on display as often as she could, was a bit of a prude when it was time to change clothes. I'd never had the luxury to experience modesty in my young life. It had been stripped from me, literally, by my mother, who had expected me to keep up appearances at all times and surveyed me for what she deemed "unnecessary weight." I wasn't allowed to bathe unattended by her until I was sixteen. Which was the age I left her house and never returned.

I caught myself, shuddering as I shoved those memories aside, and reached for my brassiere.

The establishment Char had picked out was one we'd been to before. Cramped, dirty, and loud. My heart sank as her eyes widened in excitement at the possibilities she somehow saw laid out before her. There were only two other women in the room besides us and a few dozen men, a ratio Char referred to as a "buffet of opportunities."

"I don't know why she gets so excited," Tilly said on a rare night the four of us got to go out together. "She doesn't put out. She barely even lets them get a feel. Unless of course she's with Mac."

"She likes the game," Paulette had informed her. "The power of hooking them, reeling them in, and then leaving them wanting more."

I'd found it fascinating watching the other three navigate the scene. Char was all big eyes, delicate hands touching strong arms, a push of her breasts to keep the men engaged if their eyes began to wander, and that deep, sexy laugh of hers. Paulette, plain but pretty in her own right, was usually half scowling, half amused, and scaring any man who got within two feet of her with the piercing stare she gave over the rim of her glass. And then there was Tilly. Soft, quiet Tilly, with wisps of blond hair forever falling in her face, pale gray eyes wide and wonder-filled, and blouse buttoned as high as it would go to cover as much skin as possible. Most of the men thought she was too young to be in such a place, her youthful, demure appearance giving the illusion she was closer to sixteen than twenty-six. It boggled my mind that she'd chosen the kind of work we did. Until I'd seen her in action. Tilly, despite her innocent looks and demeanor, was unfazed by blood, severed limbs, and the sound of gunfire. She was precise, noticed everything, and moved quickly.

"She frightens me," Char said once. "She's the kind that could walk in a place and not gain a second glance—and then blow it all to bits."

I'd laughed at the time, but she wasn't wrong. Tilly was a quiet force and I admired her for it—and loved having her for a bunkmate. She felt like a mystery, peeling back layers of herself as time went on. Letting us in bit by bit. I understood her more than I let on. I had my own secrets. But no one here would ever be privy to them. Mine were the kinds of secrets that incurred judgment. Oftentimes before an explanation could be given.

"I'll get us drinks," Char yelled over the noise, pulling me from my thoughts. "You get us a table."

But I shook my head. Getting a seat, much less two, would require something I didn't possess—tolerance of the opposite sex openly and thirstily eyeing everything below my jawline.

"I'll get the drinks, you get the seats," I said, and headed for the bar before she could change her mind.

"Whatcha want, love?" the bartender asked.

"Couple of beers," I said, and he nodded and grabbed two glasses.

While he poured, I surveyed the room. It was a far cry from the bars I'd frequented in New York before boarding the boat for New Hebrides. It was just as loud, the men just as obvious, but while this place gave off the feel of a good time, one could see the fear behind each man's eyes. As much as I hated it, I couldn't blame them for their staring and obvious ways. They were men possibly on the verge of death. And they wanted to forget.

"Here you go," the bartender said. I eyed the sudsy overfill slopping over the sides of the glasses, handed him some money, and turned to see what Char had found for us, inwardly groaning when I saw the two men who had let her join their table.

It wasn't the men themselves that were the problem, it was that there were only two of them. Which meant when Char decided on the one she wanted, I'd be stuck trying to make conversation with the other for the remainder of the night. At least when there were three or more, they could still talk among themselves if I didn't join in the conversation, and often did. But that wouldn't be the case this time.

"There you are," Char singsonged, taking a beer from me.

She made introductions and I smiled and nodded, taking a seat and surveying the situation. Clearly, she hadn't made her choice as to which man she wanted to spend her evening flirting with yet, so I politely engaged in conversation with both men and tried to keep my eyes from glazing over as they boasted about being in battle and how many kills they'd made.

After a few hours of idle chitchat, warm beers, and lackluster flirting, Char finally called it a night, her interest in both men waning as they got drunker and stupider and we, in response, sobered and became less tolerant.

"That was…fun," Char said as we walked back to our barracks after catching a ride with a couple of friends from base who had shown up halfway through the evening.

I made a noncommittal noise, words for how the night had gone failing me.

"I know. It was awful." She laughed, linking her arm through mine. "Thanks for coming with me though." I rested my head on her shoulder. As much as I dreaded these nights out, I knew she needed them. For survival.

"It keeps me hopeful," she'd told me one night when we'd walked home after she'd had a particularly flirtatious evening. "The thought of finding love. Or even just companionship while I'm here."

I'd nodded, understanding, but not feeling the same. For me, the thought of finding love out here would only complicate things. Would give me more to worry about. I didn't want or need the distraction a man would provide. Not that the idea of having someone hold me after a particularly harrowing day in the air didn't sound appealing. But knowing I could lose them within moments of saying goodbye wasn't something I was willing to risk. I needed to keep my wits about me so that I could not only keep my patients alive, but myself as well.

Morning brought rare June storm clouds and wind, the flapping of the canvas door, whipped free of its ties, slapping against the bunk frame nearest it and kicking up the ever-present sand and dust on the floor.

Char made a sound from her bunk beside me and I looked over to see her bury her head under her pillow.

"Someone shut the damn door!" Paulette yelled from where she was huddled beneath her blankets.

"I'm trying!" someone else yelled back as several other women shrieked at both the noise and the wind causing the sides and roof to billow and snap, the netting around our beds working its way loose.

"What is all the fuss?" Tilly said from below me. "It's just a little wind."

But it wasn't. This was the kind of tropical storm I'd been warned about when still stateside.

"I thought this shit only happened in the winter months!" Char shouted over the noise.

"Welcome to the Pacific," someone said. "If the malaria doesn't get you, the surprise storms will."

Less than an hour later, every one of us was dressed and damp, securing what we could as rain pummeled down outside, the noise thunderous against the canvas and whipping inside in small, violent bursts through the flimsy door.

"Shit," someone yelled as a small family of rats scurried down the center of the barracks, followed by a stream of water trickling in from a small tear in the roof. "If you have anything on the floor, throw it on your bed!"

But even that wasn't going to be enough to save most of our belongings.

"Get to cover!" a man shouted from outside. A moment later the door flew open, a gust of wind, rain, and palm fronds flying inside as several soldiers gestured for us to get out. "Let's go! Let's go!"

"Char! Leave it!" I yelled, seeing my friend trying to shove some of her precious dresses into a knapsack as a large cracking sound filled the air. "Go! Go! Go!" I said, shoving her toward the front of the tent at the same moment a tree fell through the roof onto hers and my beds.

"Shit!" she screamed as we ran outside with everyone else, shielding our heads and faces as sand pelted our skin. Trees bowed low, branches cracking and falling, and supplies of all kinds tumbled across the base. Beyond us, the narrow river that usually ambled calmly, bucked and thrashed, its waters rising.

"Where are we going?" Paulette yelled, her voice nearly swallowed by the rain.

But nobody answered. Nobody knew. We just kept our eyes on the ground and followed the feet in front of us.

"In here!"

I didn't look to see who said it or where "here" was, I just went, hurrying inside a building with actual walls and gathering with my roommates and several dozen soldiers at the center of what turned out to be the mess hall.

The tables and chairs had been pushed to the perimeter of the room, and the men moved when they saw us, making room in the middle and then shifting so they surrounded us, providing cover should the storm find its way past these walls too.

Someone tapped my arm and I turned to see a familiar face as we sat on the floor.

"Hi, Joe," I said.

"Hiya, Kate. Fancy meeting you here."

Joe Dunning was one of the first people I'd met when I landed on the island. He was also one of the happiest people I'd ever known, despite having what my uncle called a "hound dog face" and being in the middle of a war. When he wasn't being sent off to fight on the front lines, he could often be found with his back to a tree and a book in his hands.

"Any idea how they're faring at the hospital?" I asked.

"Nah. But they tend to have protocols in place for these kinds of situations and the injured."

I nodded and shifted on the hard floor, cringing as the wind whistled through the rafters and shook the doors and windows. There was a loud crack as something hit the building, sending a shudder through the beams and floorboards. Several of us ducked our heads in response.

Char moved closer to me, one of her hands wrapping around my arm as she buried her head in my shoulder. I leaned into her, taking measured breaths in an attempt to keep calm, and almost laughed. We'd all been in far scarier situations.

As if reading my mind, Paulette on the other side of me

muttered, "If I survived being shot at just to be killed by a little wind…"

But one could still die in a storm like this.

"How can such a pretty place be so terrifying?" I heard a voice whimper. My mind instantly went to another pretty place I'd once lived. A place others thought looked like a fairy tale, but they had no idea of the nightmares that were incurred there.

The door flew open, causing several people to shout out in surprise as a gust of wind and rain whipped through before the door banged closed again on its own. In response, three of the men carried several collapsed folding tables over and set them in front of it.

It lasted for hours, many of us growing weary and curling up on the floor, our bodies, covered in a film of sweat from the humidity, pressed together nonetheless, the closeness providing comfort.

It was nearly three in the afternoon when I woke from a fitful nap to several voices in discussion. They sounded strange until I realized the noise outside had stopped.

"Is it over?" someone asked.

"Seems to be," someone else said before a small group of men hurried to the door, moved the tables, and pushed it open, a beam of sunlight stretching past them.

"Holy sh—" one of them said, his voice cutting off as though the surprise was too great to be able to finish the sentiment. The rest of us scrambled to our feet.

There was debris everywhere. A jeep overturned, canvas ripped and hanging from trees, clothes, dishes, tires, weapons. Anything and everything was scattered across the base.

"Our stuff," one of the women said. A smattering of expletives from the rest of us followed as we hurried in the direction of our barracks. But when we got there, there wasn't much left. The tent we'd called home the past few months was gone, its wood base cracked and splintered in several places. The bunks that were left were on their sides or in pieces, mattresses scattered or gone, and most of the footlockers were either overturned or missing.

I held my breath as I ran to where my bunk had stood only hours before, but was now a pile of metal, scattered on the floor.

"Do you see my duffel?" I asked, but no one answered and I scanned the mess around me, searching for my bag.

"Look!" a woman named Winnie shouted, pointing toward the river, which had risen at least two feet since the storm started.

On the bank were a few of the footlockers, shoes, and a bunch of other items. Other things could be seen floating away. Several of the women hurried across the bank, gathering everything they could find and placing it all on a piece of torn canvas in the center of the spot where our home had been.

"What are you looking for?" Char asked, her knapsack with the few precious dresses she'd shoved inside clutched to her chest.

"My duffel," I said, lifting the edge of a wet mattress. "I thought I threw it on my bed."

"It was in your locker," she said.

"You're sure?" I asked, scanning my surroundings.

"Yeah. I saw you take your wallet out of it and then put it in there."

I patted my pajama pants pocket, feeling the small billfold my aunt had bought me before I left the States. I'd forgotten I'd grabbed it in the chaos.

I looked around me again, searching for my footlocker. There were palm fronds, blankets, sheets, and clothing strewn everywhere. I knelt, shifting the debris around me while Char helped.

"There," she said, pointing to something at the edge of the wooden platform our tent had stood on.

The locker had been knocked over and swept along the floor where it had fallen to the dirt below. I jumped down and flipped it over, exhaling at the sight of the blue duffel still shoved inside its little cubby.

"Thank you," I said to Char, who grinned and then immediately cried out as she bent down to pick up a red scrap of fabric coated in mud.

"Oh no," she said, holding it up. "Just look at my dress!"

"At least you have clothes," a woman standing nearby said. Her bunk had been at the opposite end from us and everything she'd owned was gone.

"We can share," another woman said and the rest of us nodded. "Until you can buy some new stuff."

As the two wandered off and Char went in search of more of her dresses, I sat on the edge of the wood platform and unzipped my duffel, feeling around for the small, hidden pocket inside and the photograph tucked in its folds. Making sure no one was watching, I carefully pulled it free and stared down first at the young girl looking back at me, then at the name written on the back.

Catrin.

"Kate?"

I inhaled and tucked the picture back inside.

"Yeah?" I asked, turning to see Paulette and Tilly standing nearby.

"You okay?" Tilly asked, a wisp of blond hair stuck to her cheek.

I jumped back onto the platform and joined them.

"I'm good. Shall we help gather what's left?" I asked, leaning down to pick up someone's wet nightgown and a shoe.

We ate dinner as we always did, side by side with the men, each of us experiencing a new kind of weariness in addition to what we normally felt. I smiled at Tilly, who'd fallen asleep where she sat across the table from me, her head propped on her hand.

Afterward, with extra bedding supplies brought in from the

men, we made ourselves as comfortable as we could on one side of the mess hall, our belongings in a dirty pile in the corner.

"Sweet dreams, ladies," Paulette said, her head resting on a balled-up jacket.

"Don't let the bedbugs bite," someone called out in the dark.

The rest of us laughed, and then one by one the exhaustion of the day caught up with us, our breathing slowing until we were fast asleep.

We woke the following morning to the smell of coffee being brewed and breakfast cooking.

"I could get used to this," Char said from beside me. "Think they'll let me bunk in here permanently?"

I grinned, my eyes still closed. It had been months since I'd woken to the scent of brewing coffee and food being prepared. My aunt and uncle had started every morning with a large, leisurely breakfast.

"There's no better way to start a day," my aunt Victoria had said to me the first morning I'd woken in their home with them.

I'd grown used to their ways quickly, and missed them when I'd left, my new routine stark in comparison.

"Mornin', ladies," a male voice said, leading to several squeals of embarrassment at the state we were probably all in, and irritation at being bothered at all after a night on the hard floor.

I opened an eye to see Mac, hands on hips, looking quite satisfied with his position standing before us in all his clean-clothed glory.

"What do you want?" I asked, not in the mood for his overbearing charm after barely getting any sleep.

"I am happy to inform you all that a new barracks is being erected at this very moment, and bunks are being assembled."

"Oh, thank god," Paulette mumbled.

"Are there mattresses for those bunks?"

"What about clothes? I lost everything."

"I don't have any shoes!"

"Hey!" Mac said, backing away, raising his hands as if by doing so he could ward off the questions being thrown his way. "I just came with news of lodging. I don't know about the rest of it. Except the mattresses. Everyone will have a mattress."

"What about mosquito netting?"

"And netting," he said and then turned and hurried from the mess hall.

We were a ragtag group in all states of dress as we made a line to use the facilities outside the mess hall before returning to get some breakfast. Most of us were in our pajamas, though some had managed to change into day clothes before we'd had to run for shelter.

After breakfast, we gathered what was left of our things and made our way across the base, still strewn with odds and ends, to our new home that stood where the old one had only twenty-four hours before.

"How'd they get a new one so fast?" someone asked.

"They keep spares in the supply facility," Paulette answered. "In case they need to expand the base."

"Or if there's a storm," Tilly said.

The footlockers that had survived had been cleaned off, but were now littered with scrapes and dents along their metal bodies. New lockers had also been brought in from the supply building to replace the ones that had gone missing, and dispersed so that every woman had one.

"If only I had anything to put in it," a woman named Joan said. She stood in a pair of too-big borrowed shoes, staring at her new locker. In the rush to leave the day before, she'd forgotten to put on shoes and every pair she'd owned had washed away.

"Whoever's in need of clothing and shoes should head to the exchange now," a soldier called Bucky said. "Get what you can and then we'll put in an order for anything still needed. Until then, borrow what you can from your bunkmates."

As several of the women hurried in the direction of the exchange building, I looked to Tilly, Paulette, and Char. Our hair and clothes were streaked with mud and our state of dress was ridiculous. But most of our things, though dirty, had survived, and we would have a roof over our heads again and beds to sleep in tonight.

"We sure were lucky," I said.

"Apparently there's some benefit to being last to arrive," Paulette said, referring to the day we'd shown up on base. We'd been the last to make it, and thus relegated to the last two bunks, situated at the stuffiest and darkest end of the tent. Which meant during the storm, our belongings had been furthest from the river.

I grinned, grabbed the clean bedding off my new mattress, and began to make my bed.

5

WE SETTLED BACK into our regular routines, our days long, a blur of minutes, hours, and meals as we passed one another, hurrying off to catch flights, take showers, assist in the hospital, and return to our barracks after dinner, dead on our feet and scarred from the things we'd seen but didn't talk about.

Winter turned to spring, the weather getting even warmer as the holiday season back home showed up on the island in the form of candies and cards and small gifts to remind us what we were missing, and that we weren't forgotten.

Thanksgiving was celebrated with a turkey dinner in the mess hall, complete with all the fixings. There was wine, mashed potatoes, pumpkin pie, and some autumn inspired decorations that looked out of place among the palm trees and white sand beaches of Espiritu Santo. But the efforts were appreciated. Even if they made us long for home and our families.

Christmas came, and with it boxes from abroad sent by our loved ones.

"What am I going to do with this?" Paulette said, pulling a knitted scarf from the box in front of her.

We'd gathered in the mess hall for Christmas Eve dinner, some of us bringing our care packages with us, others leaving them to open Christmas morning. All depending on when we had to work—and our impatience levels. Paulette was due for an early shift the next day, thus her opening what she'd received while we ate.

"Ugh," Char said. "Didn't you tell them it's hot? All the time?"

"Of course. But every year my mother knits everyone in the family a new scarf."

"I think that's sweet," I said, reaching over to touch the soft red yarn. "And it's very festive."

She threw it around her neck where it stayed for less than a minute before she clawed it from her skin and dumped it unceremoniously back in the box it had come from.

"What else is in there?" Tilly asked as Paulette reached back in for another gift.

The four of us were sitting together at the far end of one of the many tables covered in red tablecloths with faux pine garlands in their centers. Tilly had brought the package she'd been sent too, despite the fact that she had the next day off.

"I'm impatient," she'd said with a shrug.

"To thine own self be true," Char had said with an impish grin.

Char and I had also received packages, but we liked the idea of having something to open on Christmas morning.

"What can I say," Char said, pulling Paulette's scarf from the box and wrapping it around her neck. "I'm a kid at heart. I have to wait until morning to see what old Saint Nick brought."

We sat in the dimly lit room that had been decorated with hand-cut snowflakes, string lights, and a huge wreath made of palm fronds. In one corner was a small palm tree some of the men had dug up and put in a pot before decorating it with lights and ornaments someone's mother had sent. It was cozy. Happy. We sang carols, shared treats that had been sent from abroad, and for a little while, we were almost able to forget we were at war and that there were patients a few doors down fighting for their lives.

Dinner brought memories of Christmas Eve meals with my aunt and uncle. And while there was ham instead of a roasted chicken, rice in place of potatoes, taro and yams instead of green beans and glazed carrots, dry dinner rolls, and watery Jell-O salad, it was being with family, blood related or not, that made it special. We had pie for dessert and there were rumors of pancakes for the morning. The pie wasn't like the one my aunt Victoria ordered special every year, packed with fresh berries and surrounded by a flaky crust, delivered to the Upper East Side townhome I'd moved into when I was sixteen. And there wouldn't be the babka ordered from Orwashers Bakery the following day. But it would be lovely nonetheless.

Our bellies full, spirits high, we returned to our barracks just after midnight, calling out Merry Christmas to one another, as drunken soldiers sang carols off-key, their voices fading as we parted ways, each of us finding respite within our small tented homes.

As I drifted off to sleep, I remembered another Christmas Eve. The last one I'd celebrated in my parents' home. The elegant white-and-forest-green decorations reflecting in the windows and the crystals of the chandeliers above. The warmth of the fireplace in strict opposition to my mother's tight smile and father's watchful gaze. The relief of being dismissed so I could change out of my stuffy dress into my favorite nightgown with its soft fabric and unfussy neckline. The small hand of my baby sister in mine…

I woke with a start hours later to the sound of crying. Anabel, the youngest nurse in our midst, missing her family and fiancé.

"I wanna go home," she sniffled quietly into her pillow as her bunkmate stood on the frame of the lower bunk and rubbed her back.

We cheered her by convincing her to open the packages she'd been sent. One box from Missouri where she was from, another from Paris where her fiancé was stationed. We exclaimed over a new blouse, a pretty silk scarf for her long, light brown hair, some cream with a fancy French name for her skin, a locket with a picture of her fiancé, and a box of chocolates that had partially melted in the heat.

She was in much better spirits when she was done, and hurried to try on the new blouse before her bunkmate took her to the mess hall for breakfast.

"You gonna open that before I have to go?" Paulette asked, pointing to the box sitting on top of my footlocker before pulling on her uniform.

"You just want to see what treats are inside," I said. Paulette had a bit of a sweet tooth, and often claimed it was the only sweet thing about her. But we all knew better. Under her oftentimes gruff demeanor, she had a heart of gold.

"Damn right, I do," she said. "I'm working Christmas Day! I need something to look forward to."

"Fine," I said, grabbing the package and taking a seat next to Tilly on her bunk. "Char? You gonna open yours?"

"I don't know. I'm thinking I wait until after Paulette's taken half your loot with her so she won't take mine."

But she grinned and sat on Paulette's bunk, setting her own package on the bed beside her.

Char's package came from her sister in San Diego, but it held gifts from her parents, brother, grandma, and best friend, Jo. Each present was individually wrapped and she made us laugh by telling us who they were from by the quality of the wrapping.

"Definitely my brother," she said, holding up a small box with horribly wrinkled paper. "My mom." A slender gift wrapped with pristine edges. "Granny." Tissue paper with a ribbon.

There were candies, a makeup compact, socks, a coveted pair of nylons she squealed over, a diary, and a pair of men's pajamas, size small.

She grinned at me and I laughed. Finally, someone else would know the comfort I'd found in the men's sleepwear section.

When she was done, all eyes turned to me.

My aunt gave gifts that made you feel known. Seen. And appreciated for exactly who you were, not what she thought you should be, like my mother used to do. The change from living with my parents to living with my aunt and uncle was felt in many ways, but the most important one was, I was accepted just as I was, for who I was.

"Look at that paper," Paulette whispered, an oddity for her as she was always so brusque and loud.

"Our own little machine gun," Tilly had once said. "Shooting words instead of bullets."

The paper they all gasped over was pristine white with barely a wrinkle, despite the traveling the package had done. Bright red ribbons were tied around some of the gifts. Green around others.

"It's like something from an advertisement," Char said. "Or a fancy shop window."

I grinned, thinking of my aunt and how she was raised. Some things just never left a person.

Inside the box were the kinds of things one would find in my room in their home. A set of journals, a fountain pen, and thin satin camisoles that Char gaped over. There were scarves for my hair in sensible dark colors, a copy of my favorite book, *Cold Comfort Farm* by Stella Gibbons, and a new one, *A Tree Grows in Brooklyn* by Betty Smith. Hard candies, little boxes of chocolates, a handwritten card with a photo of their dog, Harley, and a necklace with a small bird charm, the note attached reading "Fly safe, my love," in my aunt's beautiful penmanship.

"She's so elegant," Tilly said, reading the card.

"She is," I said. "But also smart as a whip and has a wicked sense of humor."

I handed Paulette one of the small boxes of chocolates and a few hard candies, then placed the rest of the items carefully back in the box.

"Be safe," I said to Paulette, who was shoving the sweets I'd given her into her duffel.

"Steady hands," Tilly said.

"Bring me back a cute one," Char yelled as Paulette waved on her way out the door. "Preferable single too!"

New Year's came and went, nineteen forty-four blowing in with another storm that rocked our tented home but did less damage than the one that had whisked our last one away.

Injured men came and went, and we worked tirelessly to keep them alive as we flew them out of war-battered islands back to our own tiny island in the Pacific, praying daily we made the trip back and forth safely.

But war took as it pleased, and more often than not one of us returned having lost someone along the way.

"You did all you could do," we'd tell one another.

Or "There was nothing more you could do."

"He did his duty. It was just his time."

"It's the nature of war..."

The words that tumbled from our mouths didn't make any of us feel better. The cruelty of war had left its mark on us. It had stripped us of an innocence. A belief that at their core, all men were good. We knew better now. We'd seen firsthand the atrocities one human could inflict on another, and we were changed forever. While we were proud of our countrymen for standing up for what was right, for sacrificing their lives for the survival of a community, we couldn't help but wonder—wasn't there another way? But as Germany marched on, we knew in our hearts there was not.

"How was it?" Tilly asked one evening as I came in from a flight.

I sighed and shook my head, my shoulders hunched from exhaustion.

"They all made it," I said. "But it was terrifying for a while up there."

My hands were stained red, even though I'd spent a long time in the restroom scrubbing at them with soap and a rough rag. A patient had woken midflight, delirious from pain, from medication, from whatever images haunted him, and thrashed, ripping stitches from a head wound and bloodying not only me, but the soldier in the bunk below him and another to his side. By the time we landed, it looked like someone had gone on a rampage.

"Holy shit. What happened back here?" the pilot, a wiry man called AJ, had asked.

I could only look at him. Through him. My body weary from the fight I'd just fought and barely won.

I didn't bother with dinner that night. I stripped out of my bloody clothes, shoved them in my laundry bag to be dealt with tomorrow, put on my pajamas, and went to sleep, the sound of the young soldier's screams following me into slumber.

6

"WE MIGHT RUN into a little trouble today," Mac said as I approached him and the plane that would fly us out today.

"What kind of trouble?" I asked, glancing at the sky.

"The front's been pushed back."

"How far back?"

"We might need to make a run for it as soon as we land."

I sucked in a breath, held it, let it out.

"Thanks for the warning," I said, and climbed aboard the transport.

"You secure back there?" Mac shouted a few minutes later over the sound of the engines starting up.

I gave my straps a last tightening and glanced around the body of the plane, making sure one last time that everything was in its place and tied down.

"All secure!"

I watched out the window beside me as he swung the plane around and we bumped slowly toward the runway, kicking up dust as we went, palm trees swaying in the distance. After a moment's hesitation and a little back-and-forth with the tower, we were off. As this was probably the only moment I'd have time to rest today, I tried to put Mac's warning out of my head, crossed my arms over my chest, tipped my head back, and fell asleep.

"Kate!"

I startled awake and braced my feet on the metal floor beneath my boots as the plane shuddered around me.

"Yeah?"

"Hold on!" he shouted. "We're headed into it."

Outside the window smoke billowed, obscuring the blue sky beyond.

I grasped the straps holding me to my seat as we tilted right, rocked back and forth, then tilted left, the sound of gunfire closer than I liked.

"We need to get out of the air," Mac said. "I'm gonna get us down fast. Gonna be a rough landing. Hang on!"

I yelped and squeezed my eyes shut as a loud bang erupted outside the aircraft, the metal beds clanging loudly, the sound echoing through the cavernous fuselage. Mac let loose a string of expletives as he maneuvered the plane, my ears popping at the sudden change in pressure. A couple minutes later we hit the ground hard, my body pressing into the straps holding me in my seat, and we came to an abrupt stop.

"Come on!" Mac shouted, as the ping-ping-ping of bullets sent a shudder through the plane. "We have to go!"

I unfastened the straps and grabbed my bag as he ran past and threw open the door. I squinted, blinded momentarily by the sunlight, and jumped down behind him into water. It took me a second to realize we'd landed on a beach, white sand stretching out before us, gunfire ringing out from our right.

A handful of soldiers appeared, running toward the trees. "Go!" Mac pushed me to follow. "Keep your head down!" he shouted as a bullet went whizzing by. I ran faster, my heart galloping in my chest, breath coming hard.

Ahead of us, the soldiers were hurrying into a trench, dropping to their knees and sliding out of sight. I heard someone cry out behind us and slowed, but Mac grabbed my elbow and kept me going.

"Nope," he said.

A moment later we were at the trench. He jumped and I followed, landing hard as more men clambered in after us and Mac looked around frantically.

"We need to get out of here," Mac said, looking up and down the trench as if trying to determine which way would be best.

"Now?" I asked incredulously, pressing myself into the dirt wall behind me as a nearby explosion sent a spray of dirt and rocks over us.

"As soon as there's a break in the fighting."

"Down!" someone yelled and I was pushed to the floor of the trench, a body laid out on top of me as the ground around us shook.

Hands over my head, ears ringing, I breathed into the dirt pressed against my lips, tears, smoke, and sand stinging my eyes.

"Kate?" I heard someone yell. "Kate!"

I was pulled roughly to my knees and stared into Mac's eyes.

"You okay?" he asked.

I nodded, swiping at the tears running down my face with shaking hands. I wasn't. I was terrified. Dying while saving men I was prepared to do. Dying trapped in a trench or pulled out and made a prisoner was not something I was ready for.

"We need to go," he said and pointed to a man. "He's going to get us out. Are you armed?"

With trembling fingers I grabbed my duffel and pulled a pistol from a pocket inside.

"Good," Mac said. "Few minutes. Be ready."

I watched as he ducked and weaved through the men to the

soldier he'd pointed out to me as bullets flew overhead. The two men had a quick discussion and then Mac looked back at me and waved me over.

"We're going to follow the trench down," Mac said, pointing. "And then climb out under the cover of those trees. Base camp isn't far and the men will provide cover fire if needed, but keep your safety off just in case."

I took in a shaky breath and nodded.

"Let's go."

Mac stood aside so that I could walk in front of him, sandwiching me in between him and the man leading us out. We kept low as bullets whizzed around us and I jumped at the sound of our own men firing back in response, the sound deafening. I had never been this close to the fighting before and I wondered with both respect and bewilderment how these men did it. How day after day they put their lives on the line, risking what was most certainly a painful and terrible death. It was terrifying.

We reached the end of the trench and I was relieved to look up and see that we were indeed now under the cover of trees.

"What are we waiting for?" I whispered to Mac as we stood, crouched down, no longer moving.

He placed a finger to his lips and watched the other man who was staring back the way we'd just come. Looking over Mac's shoulder, I saw three soldiers peeking out of the trench, two with binoculars, all with rifles. One had his hand out in a "stop" signal. He started to move it into a thumbs-up and then all three moved, taking aim, three shots ringing out as one.

"Go!"

I didn't see who said it, I just reacted, scrambling out of the trench with Mac and the other man and hurrying into the trees, my gun clutched in my sweaty hand, my heart racing as I tried to keep up.

I looked back only once. I could see our plane parked haphazardly in the water, where it would most likely remain abandoned for days if not weeks, the surf lapping at its wheels, and bodies. So many bodies. They littered the sand between the enemy and the trench they'd so desperately run to, their luck running out as bullets pierced their skin and stopped their hearts. I'd never seen a battlefield, I'd only seen the aftermath as the men who'd fought were loaded onto a plane for me to keep watch over. I ached for those slain on this beach, their blood staining the white sand where they'd fallen. I wondered if I'd had the chance, could I have saved any of them?

"Eyes front," Mac said from behind me and I turned my eyes from the dead and hurried on.

Every so often we'd stop and listen, my heart pounding so hard in my chest I was sure the men could hear it. After a moment or two of silence, we'd press on until we came into a clearing and I saw the familiar buildings.

"You okay?" Mac asked as I stood rooted to the ground, my body reverberating from the sounds of gunshots inches away.

I nodded. "I think so."

"I'm gonna see about transport out of here. We'll likely have to wait until one of the other planes flies in and hitch a ride back with them. Where you gonna be?"

I pointed to the hospital.

Mac chuckled. "Of course. It was a silly question. Get yourself some food first though."

"Yessir," I said, stowing my pistol and heading for the mess hall as he loped toward the airfield.

The smell of coffee hit me as soon as I walked in the door and I smiled wearily at a few familiar faces as I grabbed a cup and a tray and made my way through the food options before taking a seat at one of the tables and taking a bite of oatmeal, my eyes drifting closed. I was still sitting there, my food half-eaten and cold, when Mac came to find me.

"Kate?"

I opened my eyes and stared up at him.

"Yeah?" I said, covering my mouth as I yawned.

"Our ride should be here in a couple hours. I'm gonna grab a bunk somewhere and get some shut-eye. Meet you at the airfield?"

"See you there."

I got to my feet and grabbed my tray, placing the dishes in the dirty bin and stacking the tray before heading to the hospital and offering to lend a hand. I met some of the soldiers I was supposed to have flown out, plus a few others who would recover here and return to the front.

"Heard you had a harrowing flight in."

I looked up and smiled wearily at the familiar face of Dr. Haddan, the head doctor on base.

"The flight wasn't so bad," I said. "But the landing could've been better. Sorry we weren't able to get the patients out."

"Not your fault. Just glad you're okay and not another body on my roster."

I gave him a grim smile and then went back to helping with the patients.

Two hours later I'd assisted in a surgery, packed three wounds, had been bled out on, and had drained an infected injury. By the time our ride out had landed, I'd showered and was dressed in a fresh set of scrubs a size too big for me.

"Well, aren't you a sight for sore eyes."

I glanced up from the chart I was scanning into the cheerful face of Char. I gave her a weary smile and then bent to reroll my pant leg.

"Heard you had a rough flight in," she said.

"That's putting it mildly."

"What happened to your clothes?"

"The ones I was wearing were no match for the patient who bled out, despite being covered by a surgical gown. So..." I held my arms out to show off my too-big attire. "Here we are."

She winced. "Sorry. You okay otherwise? I saw Mac. He looked a little shaken."

I shrugged. "It was terrifying. I've never been that close to…"

The word was *dying*. But I didn't want to say it and she nodded, understanding.

"Well," she said. "I'm glad you're okay."

"You have any trouble?" I asked, and she shook her head.

"Nah. Looks like you guys cleared the way for us."

"You're welcome," I said and then pointed down a line of beds. "These are our guys."

"How do they look?"

"We lost one in the past hour. The rest should make it okay. Especially with two of us onboard."

At her silence, I looked over at her. I sighed at the empathetic look on her face.

"I'm fine," I said. "Really. It was awful but… I've recovered. Mostly."

She reached out and squeezed my hand.

When Char, Paulette, Tilly, and I had first met and agreed that the four of us were going to be friends, Tilly had asked in her quiet way what we all needed when times were tough. We'd been sitting on Paulette and Tilly's lower bunks, Char and Paulette on one, me and Tilly on the other, playing cards on an overturned box, laughing, and sharing bits about ourselves when the question arose.

"At the last hospital I worked at," she'd said, shuffling the cards like a pro, "the lead nurse had a policy that we could come to her if the job was ever too much. She asked us each what we needed to feel safe and comforted. I thought we could do the same here. For each other."

We'd all looked at one another and shrugged. Seemed like a good idea to us.

Char liked to be hugged when she had a bad day.

"A good long one," she'd said.

"Not me," Paulette had said. "Just leave me be. No touching. No sad smiles. Ignore me. I'll come around when I'm ready."

"Tilly?" I'd asked.

"Just sit beside me for a while," she'd said. "Don't say anything. Just be there."

"What about you, Kate?" Paulette had asked.

I'd thought about it for a moment. I wasn't much for physical touch, thanks to cold parents whose only forms of affection were the tight, satisfied smiles they gave when I brought home good grades or displayed excellent manners in front of their friends during one of their stuffy dinners. It wasn't until I was living with my aunt and uncle that I saw genuine joy and love between a couple. It had initially made me uncomfortable. And embarrassed. But after a while I'd begun to crave the feel of a simple hug. A hand run over my hair. The squeeze of my hand in a moment of joy. I grew comfortable enough receiving that kind of affection from my aunt and uncle, but I was still wary of it with others. I'd steered away from having a boyfriend in my late teens and early twenties because of it, but in the three years before shipping out for the New Hebrides, I'd had two. Neither of whom had fulfilled any sort of desire in me. I wasn't even sure I had desires like other women, seeing as I hadn't felt much for either man, and had told them as much in the end. But it had felt like something I should try. The normal course of action for a woman my age. Most of the women I knew were keen at the idea of being attached to a man. I'd never really understood the draw. I was most happy by myself.

"You're so frigid," Calvin, the most recent, had said as he'd dropped me off in front of my aunt and uncle's house.

I'd considered the word and then nodded.

"Perhaps I am," I'd said. "Or perhaps you just do nothing for me."

The look on his face, a bewildered sort of disbelief, amused me to this day.

"I'm not sure," I'd said to Paulette, looking from one friend to the next over my hand of cards. "I'm not one for a lot of physical affection. Maybe just a squeeze of the hand?"

I looked at Char now as her hand began to slip from mine, and held it tighter. Her eyes, full of questions, met mine. And then she nodded, understanding. I was not fine.

At half past two we began loading the patients into the plane. I grinned at the familiar figure doing a thorough check of the aircraft.

"Hey, Gus," I said, happy to know he'd be the one flying us back.

"You doing okay, kid?" he asked, moving out of the way for two soldiers carrying a large metal trunk toward the plane. "Heard you had a bit of excitement this morning."

I shrugged, and he patted my shoulder before hurrying off to the mess hall to get a quick bite before we took off.

"It's nice to have company!" Char yelled over the engines an hour later, looking first to me, then to Mac who was sitting up front beside Gus, then to the full bunks running to the back of the plane. "And extra hands!"

It had taken us a while to get all the patients onboard. One blew the stitches on his chest and had to be taken back inside to be tended to. Another, a young man with a head injury, ran off when the male nurse escorting him stopped to help another soldier who was struggling with his crutches. By the time everyone was finally in their bunks, I was exhausted.

I smiled wanly at Char and she patted my leg.

"We'll be home in no time," she said and then closed her eyes as the plane began to move.

The flight was mostly uneventful. Char and I moved through the bunks checking wounds, administering oxygen, and chatting quietly with our patients.

"You got a fella?" a soldier with a head wound asked.

We were asked that a lot on these flights.

I shook my head at the soldier and patted his arm before moving on to the next.

"Why not?" he asked. I sighed. I hated when they were persistent with this particular line of questioning, but also knew it provided a distraction.

"I like keeping my wits about me," I said. "Having a man to worry about would just distract me."

"Well, you wouldn't have to worry about me," he said. "I'm goin' home."

"She don't want no brain damaged man, Davey," the soldier below him said, thumping the bottom of the bunk.

My eyes widened and I prepared to defend one patient against the other, until Davey laughed.

"Hush, man! She don't need to know how bad it is until I get her home."

Now several of them were laughing and I turned to Char, who was shaking her head.

"I think maybe we've given them too much oxygen," I said with a grin.

"That's it, fellas," Char announced. "No more breathing for you lot."

My ears popped then and I glanced toward the front of the plane where Mac was just turning to shout at us.

"Starting our descent!" he said, and I nodded and picked up the pace, checking my half of the patients and stowing the oxygen.

I was buckling myself into my seat when I felt the rumble of the landing gear. But a moment later the plane tipped into a right turn and I glanced at Char, who frowned. We knew the route home like the back of our hands. We didn't usually make a turn to get there. It was a straight shot.

"Where's he takin' us?" she asked before turning her head and shouting toward the cockpit. "Where you taking us, Gus?"

But there was no answer as we stayed in the turn, evened out, then dipped into another turn.

I felt the landing gear again.

"Gus?" I shouted.

"Hang on!" Mac yelled.

The landing gear rumbled again.

"Gus?" This time when Char yelled his name, the timbre of her voice rose an octave. When he didn't answer, she looked to me. "What do you think it is?"

I closed my eyes as I answered.

"It's not coming down."

"What?"

"The landing gear isn't coming down. Didn't you feel it? He's tried three times now."

"What does that mean?" Her voice went up in pitch again.

"It's going to be a rough landing."

She said a string of words and then wiped her eyes with the back of her hand, trying to get ahold of herself.

"What about them?" she asked, nodding toward our patients.

But I didn't answer. There was nothing to say.

Mac appeared then, his face covered in a sheen of sweat, forcing a smile so as not to alert the men in back in case they were watching us.

"Landing gear is stuck," he said. "We're gonna bypass the airfield and go for the beach just past it." He looked to me with an almost apologetic smile.

"Twice in one day?" I said.

"At least we won't be landing under fire."

"Not sure which is better, landing gear and bullets buzzing my head, or no landing gear at all."

"It'll be fine," he said. "Just a little rough. And then we'll have to hike a little ways, get some of the men to come help unload the patients."

I felt Char's body rise and fall beside me as she sighed.

“I’m never flying with you again,” I said with a smile that was anything but amused.

“We’re just trying to keep it exciting for you ladies.”

“I like my flights boring,” Char said.

“I’ll keep that in mind for next time, doll.”

I grabbed Char’s hand.

“Ready when you are,” I said to Mac, who gave us a salute and then rejoined Gus up front.

“Shit,” Char whispered. “Shit shit shit.”

We came in low and fast, the plane shuddering as we hit trees on our way down before the belly of the fuselage finally touched ground and we skimmed the surface and then bounced twice before crashing down hard and sliding for what seemed like forever.

The men in their beds shouted in fear and pain as Char and I grasped the straps of our buckles, our eyes squeezed shut. Which was why when the large metal trunk came loose of its bindings, neither of us saw it careening toward us.

7

William

Seattle, 2003

"DAD?"

I turned and saw Lizzie, a look of concern creasing the space between her brows. She glanced at the woman standing on the porch and gave her a hesitant smile.

"Everything okay?" she asked, looking back at me.

I nodded, my heart racing in my chest. So many years I'd longed to know. To hear something. To have answers. After enough time had passed with no word, I'd assumed I had that answer. It was the nature of the time. Of our jobs. Of war. So many of us didn't make it back. When the letters had stopped… When she didn't show up like she'd promised… I knew her future and mine were no longer intertwined. And slowly… painfully…I'd moved on.

"Do you want to come in?" I asked Selene, my voice suddenly hoarse. "I have a nice spot out on the back deck where we could talk?"

Her chest rose in a small sigh and she nodded and stepped inside.

"Can I get you anything?" I asked as I led her through the house, hoping she didn't notice the tremor in my voice. The tremor radiating through the entirety of my body. "Tea? Lemonade? Soda? Perhaps a beer?"

"A glass of water would be lovely, thank you," she said in her accented voice.

I nodded and stopped in the kitchen, pulling two glasses from a cupboard while she stood, one delicate hand resting on the countertop while her eyes took in the many boxes stacked against the wall.

"Are you moving?" she asked.

"No. My wife died a year ago. We're just finally going through her things."

"I'm so sorry. Loss is difficult. But...*en face de la mort, on comprend mieux la vie.*" She gave me a small, sad smile. "It means, in the face of death, we understand life better."

I nodded. "That is the truth of it, I've found."

"It is a lovely home," she said. "Have you lived here a long time?"

I looked around, trying to see it as she did. The beautiful furnishings Olivia had chosen over the years, the paint colors, the rugs, the items we'd brought back from trips around the world, and photos. Of me, of her, of Lizzie and Emma.

"Decades," I said. "There have been lots of memories made here."

She smiled and then stepped toward a shelf, looking to me as if seeking permission before walking hesitantly to a black-and-white photograph. It was of me, dressed in my uniform, taken by a comrade a few hours after we'd arrived in France. Before I was injured.

Before I met Kate.

"You were very handsome," Selene said and then looked bashful. "You still are."

I grinned. "You flatter an old man. I appreciate your kindness, but I've seen this face in the mirror and my days of being handsome are far behind me."

"Not at all."

I gestured to the back deck and she nodded and stepped outside while I followed with our glasses of water.

She headed for the far corner to the black iron bistro table with its happy mosaic tile top that Olivia and Lizzie had made one sunny summer afternoon. She took a seat and I set the glasses down and sat across from her.

I took a sip of my water and stared out at the view for a moment before turning back to Selene, waiting for whatever she'd come here to tell me, my heart racing in my chest.

"I've been going through some boxes myself lately," she said. "Sifting through the remnants of people's pasts. It is how I came across these."

She reached into her bag and pulled out a small stack of yellowed envelopes. I recognized the writing on them as my own.

I exhaled and reached for them, staring down at Kate's name. How painstakingly I'd written it. How excited I'd been to send them off, anticipating the words I'd receive in return.

"You've read them?" I asked.

"I have." She smiled. "You seemed very in love."

"Oh, I was. She was…magnificent. Funny. Smart. No-nonsense at first. Wasn't having any of my sh— Excuse me. My flirting. But I got her to come around." I grinned and she laughed.

"May I ask how you two met?"

I nodded, thinking back.

"I was injured. Shot three times. Once in the arm, once in the leg, and one life-threatening shot through my back to my abdomen." I met her eyes across the table. "She was the nurse on the plane taking me from France to a hospital in England. I thought she looked like an angel. Partially from the blood loss, but mostly because she looked like an angel. She had these beautiful pale blue eyes and soft-looking long blond hair that was pulled back into a bun. But a lock had come loose and I was mesmerized by her slender fingers and the way she kept tucking the strand of hair behind her ear, the look on her face so serious as she checked my wounds. So I asked her to marry me."

Selene's eyes widened. "While she tended to your injuries?"

"Is there a better time?" I laughed. "She apologized and said she'd already promised herself to a guy with a head injury the day before. She said it with such a straight face—I laughed so hard my stomach wound started to bleed. She was mortified." I shrugged. "The pain was worth it just to have her attention on me that much longer. In fact, she ended up saving my life. Because of the nature of the wound and being in the air..." I waved a hand and laughed. "I'll spare you the gory details."

"What happened after that?"

I turned back to the view and smiled.

8

Kate

January 1944

"KATE?"

I groaned and then screamed out in pain as I opened my eyes and reached wildly for something…someone…anything.

"You're okay." Char's face came into view and she grabbed my hands as they flailed and held them tightly to her as she leaned in closer. "You broke your leg during the landing. I've splinted it, but it's gonna hurt like hell until we get you back to base."

I let out a stream of expletives and she nodded.

"I know," she said and then turned to look at Gus, who'd just come into view.

"How you doin', kid?" he asked.

I swore and he laughed. "Sounds about right," he said and glanced behind him at the patients.

"They okay?" I whispered.

"A few bumps," Char said. "A lot of whining. But no worse for wear amazingly."

"You ladies had them strapped in nice and tight," Gus said.

"And Mac?"

"He's fine. He took off for base about twenty minutes ago. You were out like a light. I imagine the pain hit you over the head."

I didn't remember anything.

"What happened?" I asked.

"That damn utility box they packed came loose," Char said, wincing and shaking her head as though reliving the moment. "I saw it just in time to move my legs, but apparently you didn't. It narrowly missed your left leg, but it wedged in pretty damn good against the right one. The guys pulled it away and I splinted it as fast as I could while you were still unconscious."

"I don't know how you gals do it," Gus said. "I nearly lost my lunch at the sight of bone. Mac did lose his. But Char wasn't fazed in the least."

She grinned and gave my hand a squeeze.

"That's the job, right Kate?"

I nodded. "Thanks, Char." I gestured with my head toward the soldiers still in their bunks. "They really okay?"

"Incredibly," she said. "Worst injury was that one." She pointed to my leg and I ventured a look down. My pant leg had been cut away midthigh. Just below my knee it was wrapped, splinted, and bloodstained. There was a sticky pool of red beneath my blood-soaked sock and boot.

"Shit," I said.

"I think it's a clean break," Char said.

It was good news for my healing. But a break was still a break, and that meant I wouldn't be able to do my job for a long while. Panic filled me as I wondered if I'd be sent home. The thought of leaving depressed me and I tried to push it from my mind as I watched Char move to check on our patients. Correction: her patients. Of which I was now one.

Mac returned not much later with every able-bodied man he'd been able to find on base.

I waved them off as they tried to help me, pointing toward the men in bunks instead.

"Not true," Mac said when I argued that they were more important. "We need you with two good legs so you can continue to help guys like that."

"But we need them to fight the war," I said.

He rolled his eyes, grabbed my bag in one hand, and pulled me to my good leg with the other.

"Let's go, Campbell," he said, holding out his arms.

But I shook my head. "No way. I can limp my way back."

But when I tried to put even the smallest bit of pressure on my broken leg, my eyes filled with tears and I nearly passed out.

"Whoa," Mac said, reaching out to steady me. "Kate?"

I concentrated on taking in several long breaths before meeting his eyes.

"That offer still open?"

He grinned and held out his arms.

"Stop smiling," I said as he lifted me.

"Oh hell no. I'm going to enjoy every bit of this. I might even parade you around the base."

I smacked the back of his head and his laughter filled the air around us.

"Well, don't you two look cozy," Char said with a grin when we entered the hospital about thirty minutes later.

"Shut up," we both said, Mac with a bit of a growl, me tearfully.

"Get her on the table over there," Doctor Fischer said, pointing to an empty spot. Mac nodded and delivered me carefully to where he'd been directed.

"You're gonna be fine," he said.

I grabbed his hand and squeezed. "Thanks, Mac."

"Anytime, kid."

Char held my hand while the doctor examined my leg, a dose of anesthetic now flowing through my veins and making everything a little bit fuzzy, the pain of my injury nothing more than a bit of irritation and pressure.

"How bad is it?" I asked, watching as the wound was inspected and cleaned.

"As far as breaks go, it's a good one," Doctor Fischer said, scribbling something in a brand-new chart with my name on it.

"Good?"

He set the chart down and met my eyes. The look on his face spoke volumes.

"Good as in bad," he said. "You're going to need to stay off it for quite a while, I'm afraid. It's going to require surgery and, while we could do a decent job here, you'll be far better off and have a better prognosis if you have it done stateside with some therapy after to get you strong and back on your feet again."

"Stateside?"

While I processed this information, he stood, gave my hand a squeeze, and then signaled to Char, who handed me two pills and a cup of water before grabbing some clean gauze and bandages. I felt her eyes on me, but was unable to look at her for fear I'd start crying.

"It's going to be okay," she whispered. "They'll fix you up and you'll be back in no time."

But we both knew that might not be the case. My absence would leave a space for someone else to come in. In all likelihood, I'd be sent elsewhere once I was well enough to work again. The thought of leaving my friends, the hospital staff I interacted with daily, this strange and too-hot island with its crazy weather, damn bugs, and creatures making up camp in our beds…

I threw the pills in my mouth, drank the water down, and handed the cup to Char.

"I'll be here when you wake," she said.

I nodded, closed my eyes, and drifted off.

I slept fitfully, waking with a cry on my lips as I came to every so often, having shifted my leg unintentionally and sending a fresh wave of pain through it.

Each time I woke I saw Char sitting beside me as promised, a book in her hands, a look of concern on her face as she sat up, prepared to help, and then sat back again as the pain medicine pulled me mercifully under once more.

When I woke fully a few hours later, she was still there. She looked tired, her hair a mess, her clothes wrinkled, but a smile on her face as her eyes met mine.

"Good evening," she said.

"Whatcha reading?" I asked, my words slurred.

She held her book so I could see the title. *Evil Under the Sun* by Agatha Christie.

"Is that your diary?" I asked and she threw her head back and laughed, earning her several hushes from the medical staff.

"Sorry," she whispered and then smacked the side of my bed with the book. "I see the pain medication didn't dull your humor."

She stood then and stretched.

"You hungry?" she asked.

"I'm not sure."

"Well, I am. Why don't I go grab us both some chow."

She returned a little while later with Paulette, Tilly, and a tray of food. Tilly helped me sit up while Paulette readjusted my blankets, and then Char placed the tray before me.

"I can't believe this," Tilly said, sitting at the foot of my bed.

None of us could. It was even more unbelievable when two days later I was being loaded onto a plane for the US, a telegram having been sent to my aunt and uncle ahead of my arrival so they knew I was coming.

"You'll write?" Char asked as she secured me to my bunk for the ride. I had never once expected to be leaving the island this way, as a patient like the ones I'd cared for over the past many months.

"I will."

"And send chocolate?" she asked.

I laughed and then winced, gripping the rails and nodding. "I'll send what I can."

"I can't believe you're really going. Who's going to listen to me in the middle of the night? Who will I drag out to get a drink?"

"Paulette?" I whispered and she glared.

"Never. Again," she said and I grinned.

Paulette and Tilly squeezed in then, trying not to get in the way as soldiers were loaded onto the plane.

"Take care of yourself," Paulette said.

"Don't forget about us," Tilly said. "Write often. I want to hear what it's like back home. What kind of news they're getting."

"I will," I said. "Promise."

I'd said goodbye to the rest of the women in our barracks that morning, but most came by anyways. As did Gus and Mac.

"One of the toughest I've worked with," Gus said. "Get better soon and then get your ass back to work. We need you."

"Will do, Gus."

He ruffled my hair, gave me one of his gruff goodbyes, and then moved out of the way so Mac could step in.

"Take care, kid," he said. "Won't be the same here without you."

"Thanks, Mac. Keep an eye on Char for me, will you?"

"I don't think that'll be a problem," he said, a blush reddening his cheeks.

"And stay safe."

"You too, kid. Hope we cross paths again soon."

With last looks, one by one they all took their leave until it was just me and a dozen injured men the medical staff on base had taken care of until it became clear they would not be returning to war. These were the men who would pray to lead a somewhat normal life again without the limbs, and eyes, and mental capacity they were now missing.

The blue sky was as clear as ever, a breeze rustling across the tarmac and through the open door of the plane. It felt like an omen. A sweet send-off from the island where'd I'd made friends, learned a thing or two about my own resilience, and saved more than one life. As much as I wanted the war to end, I crossed my fingers I'd soon be back. That my time serving wouldn't end like this.

The nurse, a young woman who looked to be around my age, gave me an empathetic smile as she checked my bandages and made sure I was as comfortable as I could be. Behind her, a young man I'd been told was called a medical technician, reviewed the charts of some of the other patients.

"How long were you here?" the nurse asked me.

"Nearly a year. Where did you fly in from?"

"Australia." She gave me a nervous smile. "This is only my fourth trip."

"It gets easier," I said.

"Really?"

"Well, you'll learn to handle it better as time goes by."

She leaned toward me, lowering her voice.

"Did you ever throw up?"

"From nerves or an injury?"

"Both?"

I grinned and patted her hand.

"You're going to be fine."

The engines started then and she hurried to her seat, fumbling a little as she buckled herself in and then double- and triple-checking she was secure.

I smiled, closed my eyes, and drifted off to sleep as we sped down the runway and then lifted off.

9

New York
February

I WOKE, as I had the past three mornings, confused and disoriented by my surroundings. Gone was the netting above me, gathered at the center and stretched and tucked around a mattress too thin to hide the three bars that ran perpendicular to my body. Gone was the soft snore of Tilly below me, the sight of Char beside me, her arm thrown above her head as if she were on vacation, and not in the stuffy, humid, too-hot canvas barracks. And Paulette below her, talking in her sleep.

Instead, the ceiling above was a pale blue, the walls sturdy and covered in white wallpaper with tiny blue flowers. The bed was white-painted wood with a curved headboard and footboard, the joints quiet instead of creaking with every move I made, the mattress plush, my body sinking into it.

The air was cold. Too cold.

And it was quiet.

No buzzing of bugs, feet tripping over someone's bag that didn't get tucked away properly, people mumbling in their sleep, quiet breathing, loud breathing, the gritty steps of a soldier walking by, someone shouting in the distance, a plane flying overhead…

I sighed and pulled the comforter to my chin, trying to get warm, my body not yet acclimated to the cooler climate, and tried to turn over and pull my legs in, forgetting in my sleepy haze that I was injured.

I shouted as pain ripped through my leg and heard the thunder of footsteps before the door flew open.

"Kate?"

I pried open my eyes and a single tear trickled to my pillow, staring across the room to my aunt's and uncle's worried faces.

"Did you try and move it again?" Aunt Victoria asked, entering the room and filling the space with the soft, comforting scent of her perfume. I nodded.

"I keep forgetting," I said.

She gave me a pained smile and lifted the stack of newspapers I'd scoured the day before, placing them on her lap as she sat carefully on the edge of my bed, her pale blue eyes, a shade darker than mine, taking in every inch of my face.

"Can I get you anything, kiddo?" Uncle Frank asked from where he still stood in the doorway, his tall, well-built frame nearly overwhelming the space, every strand of his dark hair in place, his suit impeccable.

They were something to behold, my aunt and uncle. Something to aspire to. Good-looking, intelligent, informed, kind… and warm. They'd spent their lives sacrificing for others, and it had only made them more empathetic, more understanding, and infinitely wise. They'd opened their home to me, giving me a safe haven to grow and explore in. A place I was accepted in, just for being me. For them, I didn't need to change. It was something of a revelation when I'd moved in so many years before.

I shook my head and gave him a smile. There was nothing anyone could do. For now, all I could do was wait for time and biology to heal me.

The two of them lingered though, like overprotective parents, and I chuckled.

"I'm fine," I insisted, just as I had a few days ago when I'd landed at La Guardia Field and saw the two of them watching me as I first got lifted, then wheeled from the plane across the chilly tarmac. "You two are such mother hens," I'd said.

Aunt Victoria had laughed and bent to kiss the top of my head while Uncle Frank gave my shoulder a squeeze. It had been our ongoing joke since I'd moved in nearly a decade before. She and Uncle Frank had no children, and raising a teenager had been something of a shock to their system, no matter that they'd set the whole thing up and had been expecting me for years.

And yet, no one could be completely prepared when going from no child to a nearly grown child. As thrilled as they were to have me and had planned for me, I was a disruption in their lives. Lucky for them, I was used to my mere existence being a disruption. At least here I was wanted. In my parents' home, I was a chess piece, brought out and moved around the board as their cunning plans saw fit.

"Well, I won't ask how you're feeling," Aunt Victoria said now. "Clearly, it could be better. Can I get you some food to go with your pain medicine? And perhaps the day's newspaper?"

She patted the stack on her lap and gave me a rueful smile.

"Yes, please," I said as she got to her feet, the skirt of her periwinkle blue dress swinging gracefully around her calves.

My aunt, like my mother, was a stunning woman. They had the kind of fragile beauty that made people stop and stare. Though, where my mother's looks had begun to take on a hardened demeanor as she aged, my aunt's had only become more charming. Five-eight and five-seven respectively, their pale blond hair and sky-blue eyes, creamy skin and slender figures made them the most sought-after girls when they'd been in school. A year apart, my aunt the oldest by thirteen months, they couldn't have been more different than night and day. Where my mother loved to enhance her looks and use them to lure people in and gain favors, my aunt barely seemed to notice hers, and always seemed surprised when people were shocked that behind that angelic face was a brain not to be toyed with. Something I'd always admired about her.

We'd had a connection for as long as I could remember. When she'd come for holidays or one of the parties my parents threw, I'd run to her, finding refuge in her arms, my small body seeking solace against her warm one.

"Stop coddling her," my mother would say, to which my aunt would scoff.

"Children need coddling," she'd say. "It's how they learn things like empathy and love."

But my mother thought those things would make me weak.

"Why does she hate me?" I'd once cried to my aunt in a back corner of our garden.

"She doesn't hate you, little love," she'd told me, running a gentle hand over the perfect ringlets my nanny had been directed to put in my hair that morning. "She's always been this way. I've never understood it. Our parents, your grandparents, were kind, loving people. But your mother...she was born different. Angry. Fierce. Always on the hunt for better and more, as if it were owed her. And she's never cared who she hurt to get it. Some people are just born—" She'd stopped herself, letting out a long sigh and shaking her head.

"Born what?" I'd asked.

She'd given me a sad smile and wrapped her fingers around mine.

"Ugly."

Unfortunately, people like my mother tend to marry a puppet whose strings they can pull, or they find a mirror image of themselves. Someone with the same harsh outlook on life. The same selfish goals. The same cruel nature.

My mother met Gerhard Holländer her last year of high school in Dresden. They married after he graduated college four years later. According to my aunt, they were a perfect match in all the worst ways.

"They fed into each other's worst qualities. Two people who seemed bent on destroying the happiness of others for their own wicked desires."

"But…how can you stand to be around them?" I'd asked.

"I don't come here for them. I come here for you and Cat."

The arguments between my mother and aunt happened nearly every time she came to visit.

"Gisela needs to learn to be strong and not rely on others," my mother shouted one afternoon as I listened from the upstairs landing. "She needs to learn how to sacrifice for the greater good. And whom to form alliances with."

"She's ten, Gabriela," my aunt had said.

"Exactly."

It was then that my visits with my aunt began to shift. Rather than tea parties in the garden or in the playroom with my baby sister nearby, we went for long walks that took us away from the house so that she could ask me about school, my friends, and inquire carefully about what I was hearing—within my school, but also at home.

"Father doesn't like our butcher anymore and insisted we change," I'd told her one day. I was upset about this because sometimes I got to go along with our cook to pick up the week's meat and I was always given a treat by the kindly old man who showed off the selection he'd chosen.

Not long after we changed butchers, we changed florists too.

And then I wasn't allowed to go in my favorite bookshop any longer. Or go to my friend Ruthie's house.

"Why can't you go to Ruthie's house?" my aunt asked as I cried on a park bench.

"Father says she's the wrong kind of friend. But…she's nice to me and we like the same games. How can that make her wrong?"

Eventually, I began to understand that to have the friends I wanted, or frequent the shops I liked, I'd have to become two versions of myself. One my parents found acceptable, and one I did. But only for a while.

Only until the plan hatched with my aunt in the back corner of my parents' garden became my reality.

"You ready?"

I looked up from the article I was reading and glanced at my aunt, flawless in a pair of wide-legged gray slacks and a white blouse with a high lace collar, and then stared down at my dress and the cast below. After weeks spent inside, my leg resting on pillows, my every want and need tended to by my aunt Victoria, Uncle Frank, or Angeline the cook, today was the first day I was being allowed outside the house for something other than injury checkups.

"I suppose," I said, setting the newspaper aside.

"I thought you'd be more excited," she said, her smile disappearing.

She was taking me to Delmonico's for lunch, and then shopping. She'd taken the day off from her volunteer work at one of the area's two hospitals after the doctor gave me the go-ahead to start being more active.

"I am excited," I said. "But getting around with this thing is going to be difficult."

"That's why we have the wheelchair."

I nodded and she frowned, coming to sit beside me on the bed.

"Would you rather not?" she asked. "Is it too much?"

"No. I just..."

As nice as it had been being home...the comfortable bed, the food, the hot water whenever I needed it, the availability of books and clothes... I was restless. And shopping and eating out at a fancy restaurant wasn't going to feed the need in my soul.

I glanced at my bedside table where a small radio and a framed photo of Aunt Victoria, Uncle Frank, and me sat amid a collection of letters. Four from Char, two from Tilly, and one from Paulette. In my absence I'd missed another squall. "It ripped the roof and sides off the showers and there were naked men running for cover!" Char wrote. Paulette had had a near crash, Tilly had lost two men on one plane ride, and Mac had gone missing for a day, only to be found drunk and hiding in a ditch, having lost his way on his walk home from Luganville.

But it wasn't just the drama of living on base, it was the lives I guarded thousands of feet in the air.

"You miss the work. And your friends," Aunt Victoria said. "Your purpose."

My eyes filled and I closed them, tears running down the sides of my face.

I'd known at the age of seventeen, when I'd followed her into Lenox Hill Hospital on the Upper East Side of Manhattan where we lived, and donned a candy-striper apron, that helping others was what I wanted to do with my life. Tending to the sick, holding a hand, helping the injured... I was good at it. And the sense of worth it gave me, after the verbal and sometimes physical abuse I'd endured for years, was priceless.

I remembered following my aunt around those first couple of weeks, watching as she chatted with patients, taking their mind off needles and injuries and sickness, bringing smiles to their faces and oftentimes even a laugh. She was graceful and respectful and most importantly, kind. And I wanted to be her. I wanted to emulate how surely her hands moved and how comforting her words were...the soothing tone of her voice.

I'd stood in my bathroom for hours, staring at my reflection, practicing how to speak like she did. Slowly, I began to shed the old me, coaxing my mannerisms into new ones, quieting my accent until it had all but disappeared and no one ever asked again where I was from.

And then the war began. I found myself reading the paper and listening to the radio constantly, sick with the news being reported, worried and angry and determined to do something. When Pearl Harbor was bombed, I began to think I might have found a new purpose for my acquired skills, guilt driving my need to get overseas and help wounded soldiers. Wounded Allied soldiers. To be in the thick of it and sacrifice myself should I have to. It was the least I could do in my determination to right a dark, incomprehensible, and infuriating wrong.

But it was more than that.

There was also shame. Shame for where I'd come from. Shame for what I'd left behind.

I opened my eyes and stared at the woman I'd revered since the first moment we'd met.

"I want to go back," I said. "If the war is still going, my skills are still needed."

"I know." She took my hand and smiled. "I've sensed it since you landed. Your entire body screams, 'take me back!'" she said and we laughed.

"That obvious, huh?"

"Oh, Kate...you are selfless and brave, and have been since the day you split yourself in two to be who they wanted, but also who you wanted. Who you *needed* to be." This time her eyes filled, her delicate nose reddening. "I'm so proud of you—and furious you're not my child."

I squeezed her hand. "But I *am* your child. You have always been the mother I wanted and needed."

She sucked in a breath and looked away for a moment, nodding, a single tear making its way down her cheek. She wiped it away, her chin quivering as she met my gaze once more.

"I've failed you," she said.

"You haven't. You and Uncle Frank went above and beyond. What's done is done."

"Do you ever think about—"

"I always think about them," I said, my voice soft. "What's done is done," I repeated.

She sighed and nodded. "We don't have to go out if you don't want to."

"I actually think I could do with lunch and a little shopping. Maybe we could pick up some things for my friends? I'll never hear the end of it if I don't send chocolate."

"That sounds like a perfect day out," she said. "And then next week, why don't we see about getting you back to work where you belong."

10

IT FELT WONDERFUL to get out in the city, although strange. I'd grown so accustomed to living in the jungle, I'd forgotten how loud and full of life Manhattan was. Even the frigid temps didn't keep people from hurrying down the sidewalks to meet with friends, walk in the many parks, or run to catch a bus, a train, or a taxi. The honks of horns from impatient drivers, the rumble of trucks, music and laughter and chatter—it almost felt as though there wasn't a war going on—until I saw a group of men in uniform, clearly boys who'd never been to the big city and walked with their eyes staring upward at all the towering buildings. And yet, lovely as it was to see the familiar sights and hear the familiar sounds, I felt guilty being in the land of excess and ease, where things were accessible and many of these people had no idea about the hardships of war.

"That's not true though, is it?" Aunt Victoria said, perusing the menu as we sat at a corner table with a view outside. "They may not be experiencing war like you have, or like soldiers on the front line, but they most likely have loved ones overseas and are frightened every day when a letter they're waiting on lingers a bit too long. How they act out in the world does not necessarily reflect the fear and sorrow they feel inside. As you well know."

Full from lunch, we wandered in and out of shops, her holding up items and asking if they'd survive the island we'd be sending them to. I nodded at some, shook my head at others, and nearly fell out of my wheelchair laughing when she held up a racy nightgown, thinking of Char as I did.

"That definitely wouldn't survive," I said and we moved on.

My cast came off a week later, a removable splint put on in its place. The pain was bearable, but then I had to begin the task of strengthening my leg once more, my aunt hiring someone to come in daily to work with me and my calf, which had diminished in size, the muscle weak and inflexible.

"Not to worry," my therapist Alexander said when he took in my pale, skinny lower leg. "We'll have it back in shape in no time."

It didn't take as long as I'd feared, my determination to get back on a plane and to the soldiers in need driving me to work harder and longer, pushing myself to my limits until Alexander had to stop me every day, for fear I'd injure myself again.

"What's the rush?" he asked at our seventh appointment as I blew past the number of repetitions he'd set for me.

"I have to get back to work."

He gave me a placating grin and patted the knee of my good leg as if I were merely missing shifts as a shopgirl. "I'm sure whatever job you were doing can spare you a little longer."

"I'm a flight nurse," I said. "For the military."

His smile faltered, his hand sliding from my knee.

"You were overseas?" he said, his eyebrows raised in surprise. "I'm sorry. I hadn't realized."

"Obviously."

He sat back, considering me.

"That's pretty dangerous work for a girl."

"It's dangerous work for anyone."

"Right. Of course. Well..." His eyes narrowed, taking me in as if really seeing me now, and my injured leg. "I can work you harder. But you have to promise to listen to me. If you don't, you could set yourself back, understood?"

"Understood."

And so we worked harder.

In between appointments, I finally gave in to requests from friends and neighbors who had called asking to see me, and sending flowers and gifts when I said no. I was in too much pain, I'd had my aunt tell them, not wanting to admit that I just didn't have it in me to act interested in their simple lives of keeping house and attending luncheons, even when they were in support of the war effort.

"You're sure?" Aunt Victoria asked, still dressed in her uniform for volunteering at the hospital. "I can keep them all at bay longer."

"I should see Janie and Claire at the very least," I said.

Janie and Claire had been my best friends in high school when no one else wanted to get to know the strange girl who'd arrived midyear of eleventh grade and barely said a word for fear someone would hear something not American in her pronunciations, despite practicing for months before entering the private school her aunt had registered her in.

Both were married now, Janie a mother of one, Claire biding her time.

"I'm not sure I'm ready to raise a child yet when I still throw tantrums myself," she'd said once while watching Janie bounce her crying infant in her arms.

Of course, now with her husband in the war, she was worried she might not get the chance to have a child with the man she loved. It was something she had spoken of often in the letters she'd sent me.

"It will be my biggest regret," she'd said. "To never see my husband reflected back in our child's face."

I'd tried to reassure her, but when you'd seen so much death, it was hard to be positive. Thinking of that now, I was anxious to see both women and felt terrible for having put them off.

"Shall I ring them and set up a lunch here?" Aunt Victoria asked.

"Yes, please," I said. "For as soon as it's convenient for them."

The following day, the three of us cried when we saw one another, the two of them hurrying across the sitting room, shedding purses as they went, to hug me.

"You're very thin," Janie said with a hint of envy, looking me over from where she sat in one of two matching armchairs after we had settled in for the afternoon.

"Janie!" Claire said, leaning over and smacking her hand. "What a thing to say. She's been in a war. They probably didn't even have good food to eat."

"Sorry," Janie said, her cheeks flushing pink.

Janie had always been shorter and rounder than Claire and me, something she'd bemoaned at least once a day every day during our time in high school. She'd slimmed some since I'd seen her last, which wasn't a surprise since she'd been on and off some crazy diet since the day we'd met. Her mother, a glimmer of what mine was, was always bringing her articles she'd clipped to encourage anything from only eating grapefruit to taking Bile Beans, a pill she found advertised in a magazine while getting her hair done at the salon.

Claire, the tallest of us, looked the same as she always had, her raven hair rolled but a little messy, her clothes expensive but partially wrinkled, her makeup an afterthought, blush not all the way blended, lipstick on her front tooth, a smear of mascara beneath her eye. She hated all of it, but did it to make her mother, who was a well-known stage actress and purchased it all despite Claire's protests, happy.

I looked down at my thin arms that only two months ago had been lean, strong, and browned from the sun. Now they were just thin. And pale.

"Food definitely wasn't what it is here," I said with a laugh. "And I haven't had much of an appetite since returning stateside, thanks to the pain."

"Well, you look beautiful," Claire said. "And your hair has gotten so long!"

I ran a hand over it and then twirled a blond lock around my finger. For years I'd kept it just below shoulder length and perfectly styled, but on the island there was no time for that. I'd always had it pulled back, barely giving notice to how long it had gotten. It wasn't until I got home and my aunt mentioned calling in a hairdresser to give it a trim that I gave it any thought.

"Hair care has been the last thing on my mind," I said.

"Well, it suits you," Claire said. "You look like a princess."

"Secret princess," Janie whispered and we all laughed.

It was first thing she'd said to me when we'd met nearly ten years ago. Apparently, she and Claire had been watching me for days, wondering who I was and where I'd come from, finally making up a story that I was really a princess in hiding. It was only when we tentatively became friends and they came to my house and met my aunt and uncle that they decided I was just a regular girl like them. I just sometimes pronounced words in a slightly funny way.

"What was that word she always used to say?" Claire asked, peering first at Janie, then at me. "It was as if you had an accent. I loved it."

I pasted a smile on my face, the old worry I'd thought I could finally bury resurfacing in an instant.

"Oh yeah!" Janie said. "What was it again?"

"Measure," I said, in a perfect American accent.

"Oh right," Claire said, and then repeated the word how I'd done years before, giving it, unbeknownst to her, a slight German accent.

"Yes, well," I said, sitting straighter and lifting my chin just so. "That's what you get when you grow up with a mother who loved vacationing in Switzerland and got it in her head that one sounds more elegant and refined if you pronounce certain words in a particular way."

They had no idea how true the statement was. How many hours I'd stood beside her vanity, straight-backed, head held high, while pronouncing words just so as she applied her makeup and had her hair done, smacking the backs of my hands with her glass emery board if I said something wrong or slouched.

"She sounds like she was a riot," Janie said. "You must miss her so much."

It was certainly the lie I told. My poor parents, dead in a car crash, leading me to move in with my aunt and uncle, the only family I had left.

In reality, I'd escaped a monster.

We ate in the dining room, a meal dreamed up by Angeline, our cook, who felt the occasion deserved "a bit of style," the idea sending her and Aunt Victoria hurrying to the kitchen to plan a menu the day before. Creamy potato soup, sandwiches with the crusts cut off, a bowl of fresh fruit, and for dessert, tea and individual cakes.

"Your aunt sure went all out," Janie said.

In truth, it was a simple meal, rationing taking a toll on some of the finer ingredients that might have been chosen. But fresh herbs from the greenhouse we kept out back helped any meal taste better.

As we ate and talked, I found myself quieter than I might've normally been, listening, watching, comparing. Even though I'd been home for nearly two months now, I still felt out of place. The problems here were not the problems overseas. True, my friends worried for the lives of their husbands who were fighting in the war, and for good reason. But their own lives had barely changed. They talked about shopping and shows they'd seen, friends they'd lunched with, and the best way to get a pureed pea stain out of the carpet.

They had no idea what it was to bathe using water shared out of a helmet, find creatures in their beds, sweat through their clothing but keep wearing them because your supply of clean clothes was limited. They didn't know how our hearts got ripped out every time we flew, the cries of the soldiers staying with us, echoing in our dreams at night long after we'd delivered them safely to the hospital.

And they definitely didn't know what it was to be at that precarious preteen age and lose your best friend to an unspeakable evil. To turn up to school one morning and find her not in her seat. To rush from class and search the halls, the library, and every bathroom, and not find her. To hurry to the nurse's office and claim sickness, because the nausea was building as worry coursed through your body. And then to lie so they'd let you get home on your own, but really you went by that friend's house to find her and her mother packing their things in a hurry, fear and dread reflected in their eyes.

Ruthie.

I'd had no one to talk to. No one I could turn to or cry to. My aunt had left by then, my only other friends the ones approved by my parents, and thus not people I could trust with the truth of my ongoing friendship with sweet, funny, Jewish Ruthie.

She was the only reason I almost faltered when it was time to go. What if she returned and I wasn't there? But the truth I knew even then was, she probably never would.

As Janie regaled us with tales of her son's new ability to crawl, I lifted my hand and grasped the charm hanging from a simple gold chain around my neck. It was the letter G. A gift from a disappeared friend to a girl who no longer existed. Whenever anyone asked, I told them the necklace had been my mother's.

As the weather warmed, the city glistening with heat, I began to take walks, working on my strength and gait, pushing my endurance until I could walk two miles and return home with only a whisper of an ache.

"It looks good," my doctor said as he put me through a number of tests, making notes in my chart.

"Does that mean I can return to work?" I asked.

"You'll still need to be a little gentle with yourself for the next few weeks. Put it up at the end of the day, ice if it swells. But you're cleared by me," he said. "Obviously you'll need to contact someone over on the base to get clearance on the military's end, but as far as I'm concerned, it's a yes."

I grinned at my aunt, who smiled back.

"Guess we'd better make a call," she said.

An hour later I had an appointment scheduled.

"Next Wednesday," I told my aunt as I entered the elegant navy-and-gray office she shared with Uncle Frank on the main floor. "June seventh."

She sighed. "I hate to see you go. It's been so lovely having you home. But I know your heart is there. And I certainly know why." She grinned and held out a hand to me, which I took in my own and squeezed. "I'm so proud of you, Kate."

"You've taught me well."

After dinner that night I pulled out the standard issue bag I'd been given and set it on the floor beside my closet. It was funny to think about what I'd packed the first time I'd gone overseas. Blouses that had gotten ruined, a pair of heels that dug into the dirt on one of the nights I'd gone out with Char, the strap on one breaking as I pulled my foot free. This time I'd know better.

For the next week I prepared for my trip, sure I'd pass any tests the military physician put me through with flying colors.

I sent a letter to Char, Tilly, and Paulette, telling them I was nearly on my way, and on June fifth I met Janie and Claire for dinner to let them know I'd be shipping out soon.

"You're so brave," Janie said, her nose pink as she sipped her second glass of wine.

"I'm not," I said. "I just want to help where I can."

"But why not get a job working at one of the hospitals here?" Janie asked. "There must be lots of soldiers here that need help. Single ones too." She winked.

It was an argument I'd heard from the two women before, their concern for my safety appreciated, but my deeper reasons for going weren't something I could explain to them. Only my aunt and uncle really knew why I had to go.

"It's okay to let the guilt you feel drive you to help others," my aunt had told me when I'd made the initial decision to go overseas the year before. "But don't let it make you stupid. Don't let it make you blind to the very dangerous risks you are taking."

I smiled at my friends and took a sip of my own wine.

"You just want me to babysit," I told Janie, who laughed and shrugged.

"Maybe," she said and then pointed at Claire. "Because this one never will."

"I've seen what comes out of the back end of that child," Claire said, wrinkling her nose.

Much to my relief, the subject matter moved to Janie's son and after a while we said our goodbyes, me promising to let them know what the doctor said, and the two of them threatening to never talk to me again if I didn't let them take me out one last time before I left.

"How was your night?" Uncle Frank asked when I returned home.

He was sitting in his usual spot on the sofa in the sitting room, a glass of bourbon in one hand, a book in the other, the shades and curtains drawn as they always were now once the sun had gone down.

I grinned and collapsed beside him.

"It's so good to see them," I said. "But they talk about such silly things."

"I remember a time when you spoke of silly things."

"I have never spoken of silly things," I said, pretending to be shocked.

"I seem to remember a particular hat you went on and on about and just had to have because you saw Greta Garbo wear one in a film."

I laughed. "And I looked terrible in it."

He chuckled and then reached for my hand.

"You have to remember, your friends haven't seen what you have. They haven't had the same kinds of experiences in their lives. Not in the war, and not before it either. And what they are dealing with now, their husbands away in some far-off land, fighting in ways they can't even imagine, is terrifying for them. This isn't how anyone expects their life to go. And so they talk about silly things. To distract. To keep their minds busy. It may seem like they don't care or aren't paying attention, but I imagine they're doing exactly what you are behind closed doors. Reading every newspaper article they can find and listening to the radio late into the night. I can't imagine you didn't notice the dark smudges beneath their eyes?"

I sighed. I had noticed.

"You're right," I said.

"Let them have their distractions. Because there may come a time when they can't think of one silly thing to bring a smile to their faces, and that will be a terrible, terrible day."

"Why are you and Aunt Vic so smart?" I asked.

"Life has a way of doing that to you. If you're paying attention."

I stood then, landed a kiss on his head, and went up to bed.

As I slid between the covers, I made sure to take in the feel of the soft cotton sheets, the quiet and calm around me, and the very breath that echoed in my ears as I drifted off to sleep. Despite my past…the moments weathered, the stories weaved, and the pain endured, I knew I was one of the lucky ones. And I couldn't take one second of life for granted.

As usual though, life didn't let me dwell in peace. When I woke, it seemed all hell had broken loose.

"Kate."

I blinked, my eyes adjusting to the dim light to see my uncle standing beside my bed as he leaned down to turn on the radio that sat on my bedside table.

"What's going on?" I asked, panic racing through my body as I sat up, my leg giving a slight twinge as it always seemed to now when I woke.

I rubbed my eyes, watching him fiddle with the dial.

"Uncle Frank?" I said, and then quieted as a man's voice came through the speaker.

"It's just after four," Uncle Frank said and pressed a finger to his lips. "Listen."

I sat quietly for a moment, trying to register what the man on the radio was saying, my eyes widening as I slowly began to understand.

"We've invaded?" I asked.

"We have. Troops landed in Normandy, France. That's all we know for now. Your aunt is in the sitting room with the radio on there if you'd like to join us."

I swung my legs over the side of the bed, grabbed my robe, and hurried after him.

We spent the day inside, listening to the radio, scouring the newspaper when it finally arrived—though there was nothing yet of the invasion, and grazing on food put out by Angeline. I nearly missed my doctor's appointment the following day as the three of us, like I assumed most of the world, sat glued to the radio, taking in every account we could find that was being broadcasted.

"It looks good, Lieutenant Campbell," Dr. Armstrong said, watching me walk, crouch, and stand on tiptoe.

He checked my reflexes, asked me to touch my toes, shuffle back and forth, jump in place, and walk like a duck.

"I'm marking you as cleared for work," he said, making a note in my chart. "I'll have an official letter typed up and you can give it to whomever you need to. Sounds like your services are definitely going to be needed." He pointed to the radio in the room, its volume on low.

"I don't know if I'll be seeing any of that action," I said. "I was stationed in the Pacific."

"You might not be anymore. Regardless, stay safe out there."

I exited, letter in hand, a frown on my face.

"Did he not clear you?" Aunt Victoria asked.

"He did," I said, handing her the letter.

"Then what's wrong? I thought that's what you wanted."

"It is. I just always assumed I'd go back to the island. But… what if I'm sent somewhere else?"

She stopped walking, her blue eyes searching mine.

"Would that change your mind?"

"Of course not. I just…"

A shiver of trepidation ran through my body. A large part of me wanted never to return to that part of the world. I had mostly only ever experienced pain there. But there was another part of me that yearned for something left behind. And even though it no longer existed in reality, the memory of it created a longing in me. To walk where I had as a girl. To remember the slivers of joy I'd been granted. A smile. The little sister I'd doted on.

"I assume you'll be stationed in England if they don't send you back to the Pacific," Aunt Victoria said. "There are dozens of bases and hospitals there. Of course, I can't be sure, but it seems the likely scenario as it's away from the fighting."

I breathed a tiny sigh of relief, but was still sad at the thought of not returning to my friends and previous base.

Aunt Victoria reached out and squeezed my hand. "You'll make new friends," she said.

"Mind reader," I said and she shrugged with an impish smile.

"Are we headed home or…" She raised her eyebrows.

I shook my head.

"Lead the way then."

Within the hour I was across the desk of one of the supervisors for the nursing division while she read the letter I'd handed her. When she was done, she gave a little nod, held up a finger, and left the room, leaving me to shift nervously in my seat, drumming my fingers on the wooden arm of my chair while my aunt calmly perused a magazine.

"Okay, Lieutenant," the supervisor said, returning with a piece of paper in hand. "You have three days to get your affairs in order and then you are to report back here at oh-eight hundred hours Sunday morning. Understood?"

"Yes, ma'am," I said, getting to my feet. "What about the Atabrine? Don't I need to start taking it?"

"Not for where you're going."

Silence became a thick wall between us as I looked down at the paper in my hand, my eyes flying over the words, looking for Espiritu Santo as the location I'd be assigned to once more. But it wasn't there.

"Fulbeck, England?" I asked.

"Give my best to the king," she said.

11

US Army base, Fulbeck, England
June 1944

"FIRST TIME?" the man next to me shouted over the sound of the plane's engines.

I turned away from the window, where I'd been staring out at a sea of green land below, and looked at the soldier buckled in beside me. He was young and had a scar across his cheek that looked fresh, the skin still pink and healing. Gunshot? Knife wound? It was hard to tell.

"To England?" I yelled back. "Yes."

"You a nurse or something?"

I nodded.

"You ain't never seen what you're gonna see over here. Hope you have a strong stomach."

I didn't bother to tell him that while it was my first time in England, it wasn't my first time experiencing this war.

"I'm prepared," was all I said.

"If you want, I can show you around. There are some nice little towns not too far away. If I can get a truck we could—"

I wanted to laugh, and wished I had Char, Tilly, and Paulette to turn to and roll my eyes. Instead, I just smiled and shook my head.

"I'm tired," I said. "But thank you anyways."

"You sure?" he asked, his eyes wandering down my blue uniform.

"Positive."

A few minutes later the wheels touched down and I got out of the way as the supplies onboard were hurriedly removed.

"Office?" I asked another one of the men who'd been on the flight.

"I'm happy to show you," he said, giving me a dashing smile.

I sighed. It would be like this until they got to know me and realized I had no interest. After which, it would still be like this, but then I could at least tease them about how silly they were.

"Fine," I said. "Thank you."

He talked while we walked, and I nodded and murmured, feigning interest as I took in the lay of the land.

The base here was much different than where I'd been in the New Hebrides. Instead of palm trees and jungle we were surrounded by low, sweeping green hills dotted with sheep. The flat plot of land the base was spread out on was scattered with wooden buildings rather than tents. There were hangars for planes, buildings with actual walls and roofs, and pavement instead of dirt and sand. As much as I missed my friends and the island I'd spent months on, I had a feeling I'd be comfortable here. A feeling that came with a tiny bit of guilt.

"Here we are," the soldier leading me said, waving toward the one-story building in front of us. "I'm Jim, by the way. If you're not busy later—"

"Thanks for your help, Jim. See you around," I said and hurried in the door.

There was no one at the front desk when I entered, though I could hear the murmur of voices coming from elsewhere in the building. I looked for a bell to ring or a sign-in sheet, but there was nothing so I headed toward one of the chairs in the lobby to sit and wait.

"Oh!" a voice said. "I didn't know anyone was here. Can I help you?"

I turned back around and saw a woman who looked to be around my age coming out of a nearby office, a stack of papers in her arms. Her light brown hair was neat as a pin, her uniform of button-down shirt, jacket, and trousers a familiar one. I had several just like it, though mine were normally wrinkled and covered in dust or blood.

"I'm Lieutenant Kate Campbell," I said. "I've just flown in from La Guardia Field. I'm MAETS. Medical Air Evacuation—"

"Transport Squadron," the woman finished for me. "Of course." Her warm brown eyes crinkled in the corners as she smiled. "I was told to expect you. Follow me, please."

I did as I was told and found myself trying to keep up as she strode through the building, delivering papers here and there before pushing out a side door into the rain that had started coming down.

"Has anyone shown you around?" she asked over her shoulder as she led me around the building to where several bicycles were lined up.

"No. I've only just arrived."

"I'll get one of the other nurses to give you a tour of the base later. But that's the mess hall," she said, pointing to a one-story white building. "And the hospital is over there." She pointed to another one-story white building that looked identical to the first. "I'm Luella, by the way."

"Nice to meet you. You're a nurse too then?"

"I am. I was injured a couple weeks ago though and have been relegated to shuffling paperwork until I heal." She held up a hand wrapped in a bandage. "Bullet ripped through the fuselage…and part of my hand."

"How long you out for?"

"Not much longer. Thankfully it only took a chunk off the outside edge. But I could barely grip anything until a few days ago. Hopefully, I'll be back at it next week. Until then, if you have a paper you need pushing, I'm your gal."

She rolled her eyes and I laughed.

"I'll keep that in mind," I said.

"So," she said, pointing to the bicycles. "I think you're going to like your living accommodations. I'm not sure what your situation was at your last post, but I've heard some real horror stories. One of the other gals came here after working in India. Apparently, she once woke to a cow in her tent. It was licking her face. Because they're sacred, she had to shoo it out with a scarf. The next day she woke to find two in the tent."

I laughed. "There were no cows in my tent. Just twenty women, a few rats, and a snake or two every so often. Oh, and mosquitos."

"You'll definitely prefer what we have here." She gave me a little grin, pulled a bike free, and pointed to the one next to it. "The only bad part is it's about a mile away. I actually don't mind. The ride is beautiful. But after a day of work in the field, it can be exhausting having to pedal home. Especially in the dark. Some of the girls walk their bikes, or don't even bother with them if they've had a particularly grueling day." She frowned then. "You can ride, right?"

"Of course," I said, pulling a bicycle free and setting my bag in the basket on the front of it. I held it in place with one hand as I looked to Luella, who nodded and took off pedaling.

She wasn't lying. The countryside was stunning. Green and

lush with small stone cottages nestled into the countryside, their gardens flowering, and views of the valley below sweeping. I grinned into the wind, the warm summer air embracing me as we rode.

As we came around a bend in the road I gasped. Ahead of us, standing majestically against the green countryside, was a stunning mansion made of cream-colored stone. The courtyard in front boasted a fountain that didn't seem to be running, and impeccably kept gardens. It reminded me of another country home I'd known.

Luella turned into the driveway of the house, and my mouth fell open as I followed.

"Are you serious?" I asked when I pulled up next to her at the foot of the front porch.

"Welcome to Fulbeck Manor," she said, and then led me to the side of the house where several bicycles were parked.

"We take turns cleaning," she said as she led me into the grand entryway. "There's a sign-up sheet here." She tapped a clipboard on the foyer table. "Of course, if you end up called out on the day you're signed up for, someone will move your name down the list."

"How many women live here?"

"We had twenty-four. Then twenty-three. You make us twenty-four again."

Luella spoke in a way I appreciated—straight to the point, informative, and efficient. My father would've attributed it to being around men. I'd often been told I spoke in a similar manner. I attributed it to having parents who didn't have time for what they referred to as the "flowery details of life" that no one needed.

She led me through the downstairs, showing me the kitchen, the dining room, three sitting rooms, two bedrooms, and the bathrooms before leading me up one of the two staircases.

"There are twelve rooms so we all share," she said. "Some

of the nicer furniture was moved for safekeeping and cots brought in. You're sharing a room with Hazel. She's swell. A hard worker."

She stopped at a closed door where a piece of paper announced "Hazel and…" I peered at the name beneath that had been scratched out.

"Who's Deidre?" I asked.

"She left. Cracked up."

I nodded. It happened. Not just to the soldiers who saw and took part in the atrocities, but to those who cared for them after.

She knocked then opened the door and I followed her into my new bedroom and looked around. It was clear which side of the room was mine, as my new roommate's things were strewn all over hers.

"Hazel is a bit unkempt," Luella said with a laugh as I set my bag down beside my cot. "I believe she's off, which means she's probably at the mess hall since she's not here. It's sort of the social hub on base. If you'd like, I could take you there and introduce you to whoever's around. I have to get back to shuffling papers, but one of the other girls could show you around base more thoroughly."

"Sounds good," I said and followed her back out to our bikes.

The mess hall was no different than any other I'd been in. Busy and loud. Luella led me to the buffet where we took what little was left and sat at the far end of a table full of women.

"Ladies!" Luella called, waiting until all heads had turned our way. "This is Kate."

I smiled and was instantly barraged with questions.

"They send you straight from Bowman?" a woman asked, her eyes narrowed as she took in my clean uniform, washed hair, and clean nails.

Everyone here looked tired. Ragged from little sleep and long shifts. I realized how I must look to them with my clean, shining hair, pressed suit, and many nights of restful sleep.

New. Inexperienced. And like a liability.

"No," I said, taking a seat. "I'm just coming back after an injury. I was in Espiritu Santo before that."

I got several blank looks in response.

"It's in the Pacific," I said. "Near Australia."

"Damn. I've heard it's rough out there," another woman said, earning me glances of admiration now.

I shrugged. "It was definitely no picnic. Nothing like what you've got here. I doubt you get many snakes or rats in your beds."

There was a squeal of disgust and I laughed.

"What kind of injury?" someone else asked.

"Fractured leg."

There were a few nods and then they began to introduce themselves. There were seven of them, the rest out on missions, and I tried to remember their names, noting my new bunkmate Hazel didn't appear to be among them.

They peppered me with more questions and we swapped stories. Worst injury we'd seen so far. Funniest moment. Saddest. After a while, Luella had to get back to the main office and the rest of us wandered outside to our bicycles. We rode back to our fancy barracks and I unpacked while the others popped in to talk and busied themselves tidying, writing letters, reading, or talking quietly among themselves.

When Luella returned after her shift, she found me in one of the sitting rooms.

"They aren't wasting any time," she said. "You're on at oh-five hundred hours tomorrow."

I grinned, adrenaline racing through my veins.

"Can't wait."

12

WE LANDED IN a field, the sound of machine gun fire not far off, men rushing around caked in mud, sweat running down their faces, bloodstained and red-eyed.

"This way!" said the medical technician I'd been assigned, pulling my sleeve to get my attention as I took in the scene.

I'd never had a med tech, as he called himself, and certainly had never worked with a man I had rank over. But Theodore didn't seem to mind it. He'd been on a dozen or so trips to Normandy already and had filled me in on the ride over with how it would go once we landed.

There were tents set up everywhere, men reloading weapons, checking gear, moving supplies here and there as the sun beat down on us, the urgency in the air fraught and trembling around us.

The patients we were bringing back with us were gathered off to the side of a makeshift runway that had been marked off with flags. I made my way through the litters, kneeling beside each man with a gentle smile as I read the piece of paper attached to his uniform or blanket.

They were in bad shape. The wounds fresh and caked with dried blood. Sand and mud dripped from their pockets and was smeared across their faces. It was unsanitary and ripe for infection. We needed to move them. Now.

Keeping out of the way of the men unloading the supplies we'd brought, I boarded the plane again and began attaching the brackets used to hold the litters. It was going to be a full flight and I was glad to have Theodore onboard to help.

"Campbell?"

I turned to see the med tech standing with a worried look on his face.

"Yeah?" I asked, turning back to the brackets.

"We have three prisoners coming back with us."

"Okay," I said, not registering what that meant.

"Our boys won't like that."

It struck me then what he'd said and I sucked in a breath and turned to look at him with wide eyes.

"Have you flown with prisoners before?" I asked.

"Yes. It can be…" He shrugged. "Our boys don't like it, as you can probably imagine."

I blew out a breath. "Will they give us trouble?"

"Which ones?"

"Any of them."

"They'll all certainly try."

"Great." I turned back to the brackets. "Any ideas on what to do?"

"We remind our boys that they have to keep calm or they could make their injuries worse. As for the prisoners, they don't always speak English so…"

"Understood," I said and continued the task at hand.

He left then and a moment later the patients were being loaded onboard.

Theodore and I helped strap them in and make them as comfortable as we could, which wasn't easy for the couple of men who'd managed to have casts put on their broken bones to immobilize them for the trip. And then there was the soldier with his jaw sewn shut, wicked black stitches laced from mouth to ear.

"What are the scissors for?" I asked Theodore. There was a pair pinned and hanging by a string from the patient's uniform. Something I'd never seen before.

"If he vomits you use them to cut the stitches. Otherwise he could choke."

"Oh."

Most of the men had been given morphine for the trip and I hoped they would sleep, including the Germans, who were the last to be loaded and thus at the far end of the aircraft. My heart raced at the thought of having to tend to the enemy. But as Theodore had explained quietly, we were to treat them just as we would our own so that they would heal and could be bargained for or interrogated.

But it wasn't just that they were the enemy. It was that they were German. German soldiers fighting for a cause that made me feel sick, angry, and not sorry for their pain. As far as I was concerned, they didn't deserve my help. They had betrayed their country. And their countrymen.

I barely looked at them as I made sure they were strapped in securely, my eyes glancing over their injuries. The two younger ones had lost limbs, the oldest of the three had a head injury. They'd all been given morphine, which I hoped would sedate them and keep them from starting any trouble, but the younger two, who were situated across from one another, spoke in German to one another about what they would do to the "Ami", their slang for Americans, once they had healed.

"De Mund halten!" the third one said from his upper bunk, nearly making me grin. He had probably been listening to them talk like this for hours now, thus his exasperated "shut up."

"Ready?" the pilot shouted.

I gave each litter one more look as I hurried up the aisle and strapped in beside Theodore.

"Ready!" I shouted.

As soon as we were at altitude, I unbuckled.

"I'm going to make the rounds," I told Theodore, who nodded and moved to a little desk beside us that had been fastened to the wall.

"Shout if you need me," he said.

Most of the men were asleep, a few drowsily staring at me as I checked for fever, swelling, or bleeding. I moved down the aisle, kneeling to look over the men in the lower bunks, then standing on tiptoe to check the upper bunks, making my way slowly toward the back, dread filling my body the closer I got to the prisoners, who I hoped were sleeping.

As I reached the last of the American soldiers, I noticed a pair of eyes, a blue the color of faded denim, watching me.

My gaze skimmed the paper attached to his shirt and I reached for the blanket covering him, but he placed his hands over it.

"Don't you think you should ask first?"

His grin was teasing, his dark hair tousled and streaked with mud. I chuckled and shook my head, looking again at the paper for his name.

"My apologies," I said. "May I check your wound please, Sergeant Mitchell?"

"This is how they get you," he said, his voice a quiet drawl. "They pretend they're interested in your wound, and the next thing you know, you're married."

I pressed my lips together, trying not to laugh and failing.

"I promise I won't trick you into marrying me. I just want to check your injury."

"Okay, but don't say I didn't warn you. This time tomorrow, we'll be betrothed. A wounded man is hard to resist."

"I'm sorry to tell you, but I've resisted more than a few wounded men in my time."

"Your loss."

"The thing is," I said, working hard to ignore his determined gaze and dazzling smile. "I'd be tempted…if I hadn't already promised myself to a lovely man with a head injury just yesterday."

"Oh yeah?" he asked.

"Mmm-hmm. He probably doesn't remember asking. But a promise is a promise."

He was handsome, even with dirt covering half his face, a split lip, and a bloodstained T-shirt. But it was his laugh that really drew me in. A deep, husky sound that had an intimate quality to it, laced with a bit of naughtiness.

"Oh," he said suddenly, the laughter gone as quickly as it had started, his good arm clutching his stomach.

"Let me see," I said, and lifted the blanket and looked at the bandage covering the left side of his abdomen.

"Shit," I said, frowning when I saw blood seeping through the white gauze. "I'm going to need to undress this."

"You work quick. Already undressing me?" he said. But the teasing tone in his voice was fading and I realized now he didn't have a drawl at all, he was losing blood and woozy.

"Theodore?" I called, gesturing for him to join me. "I need stitching, a needle, and fresh bandages. More morphine too."

I lifted the blanket for him to see.

"Hey," the sergeant said. "This ain't a free show. He has to pay."

One of the young Germans muttered something and I ignored it as I looked to Theodore who nodded and strode up the aisle to get what I'd asked for.

"William," I said, using the soldier's first name now in an attempt to sound familiar. Comforting. But his eyes were starting to flutter. "Your stitches tore and I'm going to need to put in some new ones, okay?"

"You're nice," he murmured, reaching up with a bloodstained hand to touch a lock of my hair that had come loose from its bun.

"You think that now, but it's probably going to hurt. We're going to get you more morphine though, okay?"

He nodded and his eyes closed, his head slumping to the side.

"Shit," I whispered just as Theodore arrived with the items I'd asked for.

I pulled back the blanket and carefully removed the bandages that were soaked with blood and had begun dripping down William's torso and the side of the litter to the floor and my boots.

"I'll clean that up," Theodore said.

"Later," I said. "I'm going to need you to help hold the wound closed while I sew." I pulled a bottle of morphine from my pocket and handed it to him. "Be ready if he wakes."

"Er word stern," one of the Germans said and I sucked in a breath. William was not going to die. Not on my plane.

I got to work sewing, my fingers slipping on the needle as blood continued to spill from the wound, Theodore trying to hold the torn skin together where a bullet had ripped into the soldier and then had been hastily removed by the field doc before being sewn closed.

"Sorry," Theodore whispered as his hand slipped again. But I was almost there. Just a few more stitches and I could tie it off.

There was a grunt followed by a sudden scream and William lurched upward, smacking my hand away as he hit his head on the litter above him.

"Hold him down!" I shouted as one of the Germans began laughing and taunting us.

"Ich sagte der dummen Schlampe dass er sterben würde!" he yelled.

I exhaled, steadying my hands as William writhed in agony.

And then it was done. I tied off the string, covered the wound with a fresh bandage, and grabbed the morphine from Theodore's pocket, hurriedly administering it and counting silently in my head until the thrashing began to abate.

Theodore let out a breath and stepped back, his eyes still on William.

"It's okay," I said, placing my hand on his arm and then looking at our patient. "You okay, William?"

"Are you done?" he murmured.

"All done."

"Sorry for the screaming."

I smiled. "I think you earned some screaming."

"Will you still marry me?" he asked.

Theodore chuckled as he gathered the bloodied bandages I'd removed and took them up front to dispose of them.

"I don't believe I ever agreed to marry you," I said, watching the soldier fade into the haze of the morphine, his blue eyes disappearing behind increasingly slowed blinks.

"You want to say yes though. I can tell."

My eyes traced his straight nose, chapped lips, and square jaw darkened by a shadow of whiskers. An ache I'd never felt before, low in my belly, made me want to run my fingers along his cheekbone.

"Die Sau," I heard the young German say. It was a childhood insult to be called a swine. I'd been called worse. But I was on edge.

Losing my composure I turned and whispered, *"Leck mich am Arsch!"* watching his eyes widen in surprise at me telling him to screw off in his own language before I turned back to William and covered him again with his blanket.

"You speak German," he said before turning his head away from me, the morphine finally taking full effect.

Shaking, I stepped back from him, horrified at what I'd done. I glanced around, seeing if anyone else had heard, and found myself staring into the eyes of the older German soldier in the top bunk who had managed to turn onto his side in the cramped quarters and was watching me quietly.

"You do good work," he said, his English thickly accented. "My apologies for my comrades. They are young. Brainwashed. They have not seen the world like I have. They have no friends beyond the youth they have been forced into training with. They know nothing now beyond what they are fed, through their mouths, and through their ears."

I inhaled.

"Then they should ask questions," I said.

He shrugged. "Young men don't ask questions. They think they know it all at that age. They think they understand the truth of it, don't you, boys?" He glanced down at the men lying below him. *"Du weibt alles, nicht wahr?"* he said, asking in a cruel, teasing tone if they knew it all.

One of the soldiers snapped a curse at the older man, who chuckled in response.

"But if you know the truth," I said, "why are you wearing that uniform?"

He sighed and held my gaze. Accepting of his part or defiant, I couldn't tell. After a moment of silence, he waved away my question, turned onto his back, and closed his eyes.

I rested my hand on the edge of William's bunk and took a breath.

"You okay?"

Startled, I looked up to find him watching me.

"I thought you were asleep," I said, averting my eyes and pretending to be very busy tucking in his blanket.

"Not yet." He was quiet for a moment and then: "You didn't answer me."

I sighed and met his eyes, my shoulders sagging as I nodded. "I'm fine. Thank you."

He gave me a sleepy smile. "Fine is not okay. But I suppose it gets us by, doesn't it?"

"It does the job. Or at least, it keeps *us* doing the job."

"Yeah," he murmured and reached out a hand, briefly squeezing my wrist before letting go again. "Thanks for saving my life."

He wasn't joking with me now. The teasing from earlier had left his voice and demeanor altogether.

"Just doing my job."

"Still…thank you."

"Well, I can't marry you if you're dead, William."

He chuckled and then winced, pressing his hand gently to his wound. "What about the head injury guy?"

I shrugged. "He probably won't remember asking me anyways."

"I have a feeling I'll one day regret a lot of things I've done and said in this war," he said. "But asking you to marry me while high on blood loss and morphine won't be one of them."

And with that, he stopped fighting the medicine, closed his eyes, and went to sleep.

13

AFTER DELIVERING SERGEANT Mitchell and the other men aboard that first flight to my base in England, I was immediately put on another plane, returning to the same field to bring back another group of wounded. This time there were no prisoners and Theodore and I gave one another a look of relief.

There were several men in casts, the plaster still wet, and I marveled at the quickness at getting them immobilized, a move crucial to their survival, but hard to manage under such dire circumstances.

I took in one man covered from neck to toe in plaster, his face bloodied, head wrapped in bandages stained with blood, mud, and something else I couldn't identify but didn't bode well for the young soldier. If I were a religious woman I'd have prayed for the man. Instead, I gripped the bottle of morphine in my pocket.

"Ready?" the pilot shouted from the cockpit.

I looked to Theodore beside me, who nodded.

"Ready!" I yelled over the roar of the engines, and we were off.

As soon as we landed back in Fulbeck and the men were unloaded, I grabbed my bag and strode wearily across the tarmac to where my bicycle was parked.

It was evening, the sun just making its way down for the night, the air thicker than usual and warm. I breathed in, smiling at the green hills beyond and a lamb following behind its mother as I pedaled home, hoping in the dimming light that I didn't miss my turn.

"How was your first day?" asked a woman sitting at the kitchen table when I entered in search of a snack before heading upstairs.

I couldn't remember her name. Olivia? Olive? Ellen? I'd met so many the day before, first at lunch, then in the evening as they returned from missions and began filtering in, exhausted and bleary-eyed.

"Busy," I said. "But good. Didn't lose anyone."

"That's the goal," she said and went back to the letter she was writing.

I grabbed an apple and smiled at the others I passed on my way to my room. A few were playing cards, a couple reading, and several others were sprawled about chatting quietly.

My bunkmate, Hazel, was fast asleep in the cot across from mine, her dark hair splayed across her pillow, a stuffed dog nestled in her arm. She'd gotten in this morning as I was heading out, having been sent to another base nearby to unload injured before catching a ride back before the sun came up. We'd had a brief introduction and then I'd hurried out as she'd fallen fully clothed into bed where she still lay, taking full advantage of a day off.

Grabbing my towel, toiletries, and a fresh set of clothes, I padded to my assigned bathroom where someone had just left, the mirror still covered in condensation and the air steamy and warm. With a sigh, I peeled off my clothes and stepped into the pristine tiled shower, luxuriating in my surroundings, and for the first time truly thrilled I'd been sent to England instead of the New Hebrides.

While I stood under the warm water, letting it wash away the grime of the day, my mind drifted to the soldier I'd had to stitch up and his woozy marriage proposal. I grinned under the spray, remembering how handsome he'd been, though pale and barely conscious. Char would've stood by his side the entire plane ride, and by the end of it, would've had a date. Sometimes I wished I was a different sort of girl.

But thoughts of him reminded me of the other passengers we'd had onboard that same flight. The German prisoners. My heart sank as I remembered letting them get the best of me.

"Stupid," I whispered, my eyes filling with tears. I couldn't let that happen again. It was too dangerous.

"What time is it?" Hazel asked when I returned to the darkened bedroom.

"Twenty-three hundred hours," I said, turning on the small lamp on the crate serving as a makeshift bedside table. "Have you been asleep all day?"

"No," she said, sitting up, turning on her lamp, and rubbing her eyes. "I got up around noon and ate and took a walk around the gardens."

"That sounds lovely."

"It was. It's such a great spot. I heard you were in the Pacific before. What was that like? Beaches and palm trees?"

"And rats," I said with a laugh. "Sometimes snakes. A storm that carried away the tent we lived in. And had to take Atabrine so we wouldn't get malaria, which turned our skin a not very attractive shade of yellow."

She wrinkled her nose, and I nodded and got into bed.

"You going to sleep already?" she asked. "I'm usually wired after a shift. Except for yesterday. That was too long."

"I want to get up early. There's a patient I want to check in on before I fly out for the day."

"Uh-oh," she said, a smile in her voice.

I grinned and shook my head. "It's not like that."

"It never is, hon."

She swung her legs over the side of her bed and stood.

Hazel and I were about the same height, but opposites in every other physical way. Her long hair was raven black, skin olive, eyes a reflection of her name. Where my figure was slender, hers curved. Where my skin was free and clear of what my mother had deemed imperfections, hers was beautifully marked with the freckles my childhood self had read about in books and dreamed of having.

"So," she said. "Who is he?"

I shook my head. "He's just a patient who had a rough flight. Nothing untoward."

"Well then, that's a damn shame. We could all use a little untoward. Unless you're married, of course." She glanced down at my left hand.

"I'm not."

"Me neither!" she said and clapped her hands, reminding me of Char. "Maybe I should come with you. Is he cute? Or do you think he maybe has a cute injured friend for me, in case you change your mind? Preferably one on his way home so we can write letters and he'll wait for me, but won't get in the way while I check out other options."

She was definitely like Char.

"Hazel," a woman walking by our open door said. "For goodness' sake. Give it a rest already."

"That's the problem, Beez," Hazel said to the woman I now remembered was named Beatrice. "I've been at rest for far too long."

I laughed as Beatrice walked away.

"I'm gonna shower," Hazel said, giving her armpit a sniff and grabbing some clothes off the floor. "You really off to bed?"

“I am.”

“Alright. Guess I’ll see you in the morning? Unless you’ve left to see your love before I wake.”

“He’s not—”

“Nighty-night!” she called, disappearing down the hallway.

The house was silent when I woke the next morning, no one wanting to wake before they had to.

I crept quietly from my bed to the bathroom where I got dressed in a hurry and pulled my hair back into a bun. Staring at my face in the mirror, for once I wished I owned a bit of rouge or lipstick, my pale skin like a blank sheet of paper compared to Hazel’s sultry looks.

I rode through the quiet of the early-morning hours to base, listening to leaves rustle softly in the breeze and the metallic scent of rain in the air. As I parked my bicycle, a drop landed on my cheek and I hurried inside the hospital.

A gentleman sitting at a desk in the entryway glanced at the insignia on my shirt and gave me a tired smile.

“How can I help you, Lieutenant?” he asked.

I’d never checked in on one of the soldiers I’d brought in before, but this man didn’t know that. For all he knew, I always followed up with my patients the day after flying them in.

“I’m looking for a First Sergeant William Mitchell. I flew him in yesterday. It was a rough trip. I just wanted to check on him.”

He nodded and grabbed a clipboard, scanning the list of names.

“Two rows over and five beds down,” he said, pointing me in the direction.

“Thanks.”

I made my way past nurses and doctors, taking in the wounded, many of them in casts, their heads and appendages bandaged, the floor bloodstained and scrubbed to no avail.

William was right where I'd been told, his eyes closed as I bent to look at the clipboard attached to his bed.

"Am I gonna make it?"

I grinned, my eyes still on the paperwork.

"Do you want the good news or the bad news?" I asked, glancing around before finally meeting his gaze.

"Give it to me straight, doc," he said.

"The good news," I whispered, "is that you are going to make it. The bad? They didn't remove your terrible sense of humor."

"It's my secret weapon," he said. "It's why they sent me to fight. Thought I'd annoy the Jerries into giving up."

"How'd that go over?"

"Turns out they don't understand American humor."

I pursed my lips together, trying not to laugh, and set the clipboard back down.

"How are you feeling?" I asked.

"Like I got shot in the arm, leg, and stomach."

"I have news for you, Sergeant."

He smiled and something low in my belly lit on fire. I'd thought him handsome on the plane, even with his chapped lips and his face half-covered in dirt. But cleaned up he was a bit dazzling with his dark hair and light eyes. He had a smile that could make a girl's knees weak, something I'd only read about, scoffed at, secretly hoped to experience, and doubted existed.

"Can you sit for a while?" he asked.

I looked around, worried I'd get in trouble for fraternizing. It was discouraged because of the distraction it could cause. Distractions caused accidents, and I was not a rule breaker. But the way he was looking at me…

"For a few minutes," I said, tucking a lock of hair that had come loose behind my ear and pulling up a chair that had been left at the foot of his cot. "I just wanted to check on you after that harrowing stitch job I had to do in the air. I have to fly out again soon though."

"I appreciate that," he said. "Any chance I get to know your name? I think it's only proper. Since we're to be married and all."

I laughed softly. "I'm surprised you remember that. You lost a lot of blood. And were on a lot of morphine."

"I never forget my proposals."

"Have there been many?" I asked, feeling absurdly jealous.

"Just the one. Which is why it's so memorable."

His eyes held mine and I nodded.

"I'm Kate," I said.

"Kate," he repeated. "I've always liked that name."

"No, you haven't."

His eyes widened as if he were appalled I'd question this. "I have. It's a sensible name. But also feminine and strong. It suits you."

I looked away, unsettled by this man and the feelings he was stirring in me. I knew I should leave, but for some reason I found I couldn't move.

"Where are you from, William Mitchell?" I asked, attempting to make innocent conversation.

"Seattle, Washington. And you?"

"Manhattan."

"I was based there before I flew out. Fun city, although a little too big for me."

"Is Seattle not big?"

"It is. But it's also not."

He rested a hand on his abdomen, winced, and laid it on the bed beside him instead.

"Are you okay?" I asked. "Do you need more pain medicine?" I looked around for the nearby doctor or nurse in charge of his care.

"Not yet," he said, his voice quiet as he took in a couple slow breaths. "Tell me what you like to do when you're not taking care of patients. When you're not in the English countryside, flying back and forth to France to save lives like a heroine in some novel."

I shrugged, ignoring his heroine comment. "I like to walk. Take in the city. Sit in cafés and read. Meet my friends for lunch. Sit in parks and feel the sun on my face."

"I didn't hear mention of a boyfriend or husband."

"Of course not. I'm to marry you, remember?"

"Right," he whispered, his smile faint.

"William?" I moved to the edge of my seat, slipping my hand into his as I did so. He squeezed. Hard. "You're in pain, damn you. You should've said."

"But then I'd have fallen asleep and you'd have left."

I huffed and he smiled faintly.

"I'm mad at you," I said, turning to wave down a nearby nurse.

"Is the wedding off?" he asked.

But I ignored his joke as the nurse hurried over.

"Yes?" she asked, glancing from me to William.

"He needs something for the pain," I said.

She glanced down, noticed the sheen of sweat that had arisen on his brow, checked his chart, and nodded.

"I'll be right back," she said and hurried away.

"Don't go," William whispered to me, his hand still in mine.

I squeezed his fingers. "I'll stay until you're asleep."

He nodded, his brow creasing from the pain. A moment later the nurse reappeared and administered morphine.

He fell asleep quickly, his eyes on me until he could no longer keep them open and his hand went slack. With a sigh, I removed my hand from his and laid his arm beside him, put the chair back where I'd found it, and stood at the foot of his bed, watching this soldier who, while in the throes of extreme amounts of pain the day before, had seen me. Had been selfless enough to notice I was dealing with my own internal pain.

Sure, my curiosity in him was helped by the fact that he was handsome. But there was more to him than looks. Something deeper in those faded denim-blue eyes of his. A knowledge. A wisdom. And a warmth that had permeated and enveloped me on that plane, cementing in me a need to see him today. To know he was okay. Beyond that, I couldn't pinpoint what the feelings running through me were. But I wasn't stupid enough to get myself wrapped up in a situation that would most likely end in heartache. War, as I'd seen time and time again, was cruel. It didn't care who it took.

"Goodbye, William," I whispered, and then hurried out into the burgeoning morning to await my flight out.

I was up the following day at four thirty, on a plane less than an hour later, and before I knew it was landing in the same field I'd seen twice in the two days before.

Theodore and I made the rounds on the men waiting to be loaded onboard, checking the papers pinned to their shirts, pants, and blankets, depending on where they were injured. There were at least two men who most likely wouldn't make it home, but I'd do my best to at least keep them alive so they'd have a fighting chance back at base.

Not long after we'd landed in Fulbeck I was informed we would be heading back out.

"Already?" I asked Theodore, who merely shrugged and headed back toward the plane we'd disembarked only an hour before. It was rare to have two shifts in a day, but if they needed us, we weren't about to claim our exhaustion. Not when there were men out there fighting for the rights and freedom of others.

By the time I fell into my bed it was midnight.

"You on again tomorrow?" Hazel asked from her cot across the room.

"Oh five hundred," I said, covering my mouth as I yawned.

"See you and the sun in a few hours then," she said and turned over.

The pang of sadness I'd been keeping at bay all day crept

in as sleep pulled me toward it. I wondered how William was doing. I'd wanted to stop by the hospital, but I'd made myself resist. He was lovely. Funny. And had a mischievous glint in his eyes, when his bullet wounds weren't making him wince. And while many of the women I knew would've jumped at the chance to spend time with the charmer, I had to keep my wits about me. Being distracted while flying into war zones and trying to save lives wasn't an option.

But as I left the waking world for the unconscious one, a vision of those pale blue eyes filled my mind and I heard his voice in my head ask, "Are you okay?"

14

"THERE'S A WOUNDED man with a spectacular pair of blue eyes asking about you."

I looked up from the bandages I was counting in the medical supply building situated next to the hospital and into the face of Edith, one of my housemates at the mansion.

We crossed paths nearly every morning, but had barely said more than two words to one another since I hadn't had time to socialize much yet. I hoped to get to know everyone a bit better when I finally had a day off. It felt strange to only have conversed with Hazel and Luella. And barely at that. I had to remind myself that I'd had plenty of time to get to know my last squadron because we'd gone through training together. It had been quite the experience learning how to use gas masks together, swimming underwater, the surface lit on fire, and sitting through classes in geography before moving on to properly tend to a burn, a gunshot wound, or a head injury. And then there were the three days we had to make camp in the nearby woods and learn to survive should we ever be stranded. That experience alone had made Paulette, Tilly, Char, and me close as sisters.

"Did he charm you into coming to find me?" I asked, turning back to the bandages.

"I'd have done it without any charming," she said. "He's a looker, that one. Sweet too."

I tried to ignore the twinge of jealousy. Had he teased her too? She was nice-looking with her golden waves and warm brown eyes. There was something comfortable about her. Friendly and open. Maybe William found her more appealing than me. Perhaps he found my looks cold and off-putting. My slender figure boyish instead of enticing.

"Kate?" Edith said and I blinked.

"Sorry," I said and gestured at the mountain of supplies stacked nearby. "I'm a little distracted. Did he say what he needed?"

"I think he just needs you, love." She winked and then waved as she hurried out the door, leaving it to slam after her.

I felt my cheeks warm as I stared at the closed door, chewing my lip as I considered popping in for just a minute to see how he was doing.

The door swung open again and I jumped.

"Short delay," Theodore said.

"What for?"

"Weather."

I looked past him at the sky. It was cloudy, as it had been the two days previously, but nothing to write home about.

"Not here," he said. "There. A call just came in. Windy as all heck. Last plane in had a hard time landing."

"But what about the men?"

He shrugged. "They'll keep them as comfortable as they can until we can get to them."

"I don't like that."

"No one likes it, Kate," he said, his voice soft, and then closed the door gently as he left.

With a sigh, I noted the number of bandages I'd just counted on the supply list I'd been going through, hung the clipboard back on the wall where I'd found it, picked up my bag and slung it over my shoulder. I couldn't go back to the mansion in case the weather changed again and we were called to leave immediately. And I'd already eaten, so going to the mess hall was a waste of time.

I opened the door and stared at the hospital only a dozen or so feet away.

"Dammit," I whispered, and started walking.

It was busy, nurses and doctors rushing about, soldiers awake and in pain, calling out for help. The clatter of trays rolling across the floor, instruments hopping on top, the smell of rubbing alcohol, and hush of voices trying to calm those in distress, and in the middle of it was William, watching me from the moment I stepped inside.

"You didn't come yesterday," he said, watching me carefully as I approached his bed.

I glanced at the men on cots on either side of him. One was asleep, one leg and arm each in traction, the other bleary-eyed and staring at the rafters above.

I grabbed a nearby chair and sat, setting my bag in my lap and fidgeting with the shoulder strap as I met his blue gaze.

"It was a busy day," I said.

He nodded, still watching me, taking in my restless fingers.

"Are you okay?" he asked and then looked around the room as best he could, taking in the men around him. "I imagine your job can get a bit rough."

"Not as rough as yours."

"Neither is ideal," he said, meeting my eyes once more, a small smile on his face. "You didn't answer my question though."

"I'm okay," I said.

"You don't seem to get your feathers ruffled much by all this." He waved a hand at the room. "But something has you bothered."

"What do you mean?"

He pointed at my fidgeting fingers and I stopped playing with the strap, slid the bag to the floor, and folded my hands in my lap.

"My flight got delayed for weather," I said. "I hate the thought of the wounded having to wait."

He stared at me quietly for a moment and then nodded.

"How did yesterday go?" he asked and I shrugged.

"Fine."

"There's that word again."

"Sorry. I just don't usually talk about my day. It's..." My eyes clouded as images crowded my mind. "It's hard to talk about. I prefer to leave it in the air."

"I get that. Must be tough though. Do you at least talk about it with your comrades?"

I shook my head.

"One of the many unspoken rules of war, right?" he said.

"Yeah," I said, my voice soft.

"Well then, let's talk about something else. What did you do before this? Before the war."

"I was a nurse."

He laughed and the sound made my entire body light up.

"So, you're either a glutton for punishment or a real-life heroine."

I grinned, my shoulders relaxing as I sank back into the chair.

"I would say neither."

"I would say that's a nice story you tell yourself."

Our eyes held, and after a moment I sucked in a breath and averted mine. It was like he could see into me. It was like I'd revealed a secret without saying a word, and I wondered then if he remembered hearing me speak to the German prisoner. If he'd somehow put together the puzzle pieces. But he couldn't have. He'd have no way of figuring it out. For all he knew, I took a class to learn German or had picked up a few choice phrases thanks to my line of work.

"What are you thinking about so hard over there in that chair?" he asked, pulling me from my thoughts.

"Your marriage proposal," I said, lying.

"We have so much planning to do."

I could tell he knew I was lying, but was going to let it go, not wanting to press me. William Mitchell was a gentleman regardless of what situation he was in, bleeding out on a plane, or lying among dozens of other wounded men in a hospital. Shoot, he'd probably introduce himself and shake my hand while bleeding on the battlefield.

I grinned at the thought and he caught me.

"And what are you thinking about now?"

"Your manners."

His eyes widened and he grinned. "My mama taught me well."

"Well, she'll be pleased to know what a fine man her son is, regardless of whatever terrible situation he's in."

"Lieutenant?" I turned at the sound of a man's voice behind me and saw that it was Theodore. He glanced curiously at William, glanced at the paperwork attached to his bed, and saluted. "Sir," he said before turning back to me. "Weather's cleared enough to fly. We're heading out in ten."

"I'm right behind you," I said, getting to my feet and reaching for my bag as I looked at William. "Get rest."

"Seems I have no choice," he said, pointing to each of his three wounds. "You be safe out there."

"I will," I said and started to turn away.

"And Kate?"

I stopped and met his eyes, a current of something passing

between us and landing square in my chest, my heart racing in response.

"Yes?" I said.

"Come see me again?"

I wanted to put him off. To shrug. To not commit one way or the other. But there was something about him. A magnetism that drew me to him, shoving aside my resolutions not to get attached to or involved with a soldier. I was here to work. To do my part of righting a wrong. I didn't have time to get distracted by charming smiles or eyes that reminded me of days lying on my back in the grass, staring at cloudless skies, a little voice singing silly songs as small feet danced around me. And I certainly didn't have time to fall in love. I knew others had, and more would, but I'd always thought myself immune.

Perhaps I was wrong.

"I'll see you soon," I said, and hurried off after Theodore.

"So?" Hazel said later that night as we parked our bicycles out front of the house and made our way inside, our feet dragging after the long day.

"So what?" I asked, opening the ornate front door and waving her in in front of me.

We'd ridden home side by side, our planes flying in one after the other, and she'd told me her entire life story along the way, barely taking time to take a breath.

"I'm from Florida," she'd said as soon as we were seated on our bikes. She'd pulled her long dark hair from its tie and let it tumble down her back, ignoring the whistles that came from the tarmac as we rode away. "Miami. You'd love it there. Well, maybe not, you're kinda pale. Do you burn in the sun? I don't burn. I love the heat. The music. The food. I was born in Puerto Rico but we moved to Miami when I was three..."

By the time we reached the mansion, I knew the names of her five siblings, her dog, Mischief, her nana and papa, her first, second, and last boyfriend, her favorite breakfast made by her *tía* Issa, and which friend stole her best blue sweater in the tenth grade. My mind was reeling by the time we pulled up to the house. So when she finally took a breath and turned the conversation to me, I was at a loss.

"So, tell me about the guy," she said, slightly exasperated, as if I should've known exactly where she was going.

"I don't know what you're talking about," I said, closing the door and trying to think back to if I'd mentioned one of the wounded soldiers I'd seen that day. But she hadn't given me a chance to speak until just now so I had no idea who she was referring to.

"You are a terrible liar, Lieutenant Campbell."

If she only knew. But still I was confused.

"Edith told me about your handsome first sergeant," she said, slipping off her blood-splattered shoes and nudging them to the side of the front door with everyone else's. "How he was asking about you this morning."

"Oh!" I said, finally putting two and two together. I shook my head, feeling a blush warm my face. "He's not *my* first sergeant. Just a patient who nearly bled out on me the other day."

"Mmm-hmm...and the one you went to check on, right?"

I shrugged and kicked off my own shoes, then sifted through the mail on the entryway table, finding a letter with my name on it in my aunt's familiar penmanship. Tucking it into my pocket, I turned back to Hazel.

"I was worried about him," I said.

"I worry about a lot of them," she said. "But I've never gone to check in on one after I've delivered him."

She stood with her hands on her hips, waiting for me to say something. She was more like Char than I'd given her credit for, and I wasn't sure whether I should feel amused or annoyed. But the way she looked at me, eyes wide like an eager puppy desperate for information, interaction, or just plain attention, made me laugh. She was kind, funny, and sassy, holding tight to the person she was and reminding me of something my aunt Victoria had told me several times over the past decade—that I could not allow other people or circumstance to take my humanness from me.

"There's no point in doing the job," Aunt Vic had said when I first brought up the idea of going overseas, "if you cease living as a result."

I stared at Hazel, weighing my options. If I told her, I knew I'd never hear the end of it. There would be endless questions so long as he was on base. If I didn't tell her, I risked putting a wedge between me and my new friend. She'd feel I was keeping her at arm's length, which was no way to build trust and encourage camaraderie.

"Fine," I said, giving in. "I'll tell you about him. But upstairs. In our room. I don't need everyone knowing my business."

"Ooh!" she said, hurrying up the stairs. "There's business to know! I can't wait. And who's the letter from? Did I ever tell you that only one of my siblings ever writes?"

As she prattled on, I shook my head, following her up the stairs at a much slower pace, already regretting giving her any information about First Sergeant Mitchell, but also loving the idea of having a friend to talk to once more.

I woke the next morning at four thirty when the alarm went off, Hazel, across the room from me, letting out a loud groan before stumbling from her bed and turning it off.

"Sure you don't want to take my shift today?" she asked, turning on her bedside lamp. Her hair was in its usual morning disarray around her shoulders.

"No thanks," I said, and turned over, placing my pillow over my head as she loudly opened and shut dresser drawers.

The great house shook with the activity of those scheduled to work and, try as I might, with the front door slamming over and over again as the women hurried out into the day, I wasn't able to get back to sleep.

With a sigh, I threw off my comforter, swung my legs over the side of the cot, and padded barefoot to the shared bureau where I pulled out a pair of denim trousers with button detailing on the pockets, a short-sleeve white blouse, yellow cardigan, and my favorite pair of brown-and-white oxfords from the closet.

"What are you doing up?"

I jumped, staring through the dim light of the kitchen in the direction of the voice and finding Darla, another of my coworkers I'd barely been able to exchange a hello and goodbye with as we passed one another coming and going. She was sitting at the kitchen table, tucked into the corner, her head resting against the wall behind her.

"Good morning," I said, yawning into one hand as I took a mug from the cupboard with the other. "I couldn't get back to sleep with all the noise. You?"

"Couldn't get to sleep after my last shift." She slid a plate across the table toward me and I peered down to find a bunch of grapes. "I've been up all night."

"That's awful," I said taking two grapes and popping one in my mouth. "Where'd these come from?" It gave a satisfying burst of flavor as I bit down.

It hadn't been that long since I'd eaten a grape, my aunt always keeping fresh fruit on hand, but here it was a delicacy and I savored the cold, bright flavor on my tongue before eating the other one and moving back to the counter to pour some coffee.

"Fresh load of fruits and vegetables came in last night," she said. "I happened to be standing by when they unloaded these. I may have snagged this bunch without asking."

"Well, I won't tell," I said, taking one more. "Thanks."

"You headed out or staying in?"

"Thought I'd take a ride, check out a bit of the countryside."

She glanced out the window, the sky a dusty blue, the sun about to make its debut.

"Good day for it," she said. "Take a raincoat just in case though. The weather here is not to be trusted."

Twenty minutes later, coffee mug emptied, washed, and put back in the cupboard, a slightly bruised apple in hand, I left the house, placed the apple in the basket on the front of my borrowed bicycle, and was off.

I bumped down the long driveway, the cool morning air whipping my hair around my shoulders, the quiet disrupted by the crunch of the tires over dirt and rocks. At the end of the drive, I turned right, heading in the opposite direction of base, smiling at green hills dotted with sheep, the scent of grass and flowers in the air. From here, one could almost forget a war was going on.

At the top of a small hill I stopped, leaned the bicycle against a short stone wall, grabbed my apple and rested my arms on the cool, damp stones. Before me the land sank and sloped for miles, soft and green, mist hanging in the glen, the sky turning from a dark, dusty periwinkle to a crisp blue.

As the sun finally made its appearance, I heard the faint sound of reveille and stood, turning toward the sound. When it finished, I ate my apple, tossed the core in the field, climbed back on my bicycle, and pedaled to base to see how William was doing.

15

"YOU'RE SITTING UP!" I said when I saw William.

I'd seen him spot me as soon as I'd entered and he watched me walk from the door to his bed, making me feel a bit self-conscious as I went.

"Not quite," he said. "But I'm getting there."

He was propped up on two pillows, instead of just the one, and his color looked better than it had when he'd arrived, and certainly better than the greenish color he'd been when I'd sewn him up on the plane.

"How do you feel?" I asked.

"Like the luckiest man alive." His eyes swept over me. "You look like a ray of sunshine."

I glanced down at my yellow sweater and fidgeted with the cuff.

"It's my day off," I said.

"And what will you do with your coveted day?"

I shrugged. I didn't want to rub in the fact that I could get out and about while he was stuck inside. It seemed cruel. But he somehow saw the internal struggle I was having.

"Come on," he said. "Don't feel sorry for me. I'll get out there soon enough. Tell me what you have planned."

I sighed and sat in the chair beside his bed, wondering if it had been left from the day before, or if he'd maybe requested it be put there in case I came to see him.

"Well," I said. "I already went for a bike ride to watch the sunrise."

"That sounds magnificent."

"It was. The countryside here is gorgeous. The land is so gentle. Not like Manhattan with all its cement and hard structures. And then the trees and sheep… It reminds me of—" I stopped, shocked at what I'd nearly said.

"It reminds you of what?"

I searched my mind for something to say, twisting one of the buttons on my cardigan.

"When I was a kid," I said, my voice taking on a sudden nonchalance. "My family would go out to the countryside every summer. We had a house there."

I didn't tell him our country house was a mansion. Bigger than the one I was staying in now. I didn't mention how lonely I was when we went. How there were no other kids nearby, just me and my little sister and our nanny. How my mother insisted on quiet during the day so we were forced to find daily activities outside, which was fine for the most part because the weather was usually lovely. But sometimes we got bored walking the same length of fence, riding bikes to the same pond, stopping in the same shops in the village, and picking bouquets of wildflowers we'd bring back for our mother and find thrown out with the trash the next day.

"That sounds idyllic," William said. "We used to go camping every summer. Me, my parents, and my little brother, George. Fishing, campfires, a couple of tents…"

"Where's your brother now?" I asked.

"He's a pilot in the Army. He's probably flying somewhere over France right now. Little brothers...always have to outdo their big brothers." He chuckled. "Do you have siblings?"

I hesitated. I always dreaded this question, and it always came. The natural course of a conversation when families were spoken about. Aunt Vic, Uncle Frank, and I had long since made our peace with the lie we told, but it still pained me. Not because our version of what happened was false to keep our pasts secret, but because I had to say it at all. Because my sister was gone.

I shook my head, a sad smile on my face.

"I did," I said. "A little sister. Her name was Catrin. Cat. Kitty Cat." I whispered the last part, picturing her impish grin and wispy blond hair. "She got sick. It was years ago now. And she died. I don't like to talk about it."

William's hand reached for mine, the warmth of his fingers bringing a calm to my soul I'd never felt before. He was a salve. A balm. And I wondered what it would be like to be held by him.

"I'm so sorry," he said, his voice low. "I can't imagine how hard that was, and still is."

I nodded, unable to meet his eyes for a moment. I hated that I'd lied to him about how she'd passed. But some things, I knew, were better kept secret.

I cleared my throat and sat up a little straighter, finally looking over at him again.

"Maybe when you feel better," I said, changing the subject, "you can borrow a bicycle and take a ride around the area. I hear the nearby towns look like they came straight out of a fairy tale. I can't wait to explore them."

"Is that what you're doing today?"

"I think so."

"You'll have to come back and tell me about it if you do."

I nodded, not committing to the idea, but not saying no.

“May I ask you something?” he said and I looked around, wondering what he might say and hoping it wasn’t more about my sister. “I promise it’s nothing untoward.”

I laughed softly. “Okay then.”

“Were you injured?” He gestured toward my leg, which I’d crossed over the other and was running a hand over, gently rubbing the muscle. “You seem like you’re maybe in a bit of pain.”

My hand stopped.

“Not pain,” I said. “Just some tightness every now and again. I was stationed in the Pacific before I came here. Espiritu Santo in the New Hebrides. Our plane crashed and a large metal chest came loose and slammed into my leg. Thankfully, it hit just so, only fracturing the fibula. If it had broken my tibia too I’d still be at home.”

“That must’ve hurt something awful.”

I laughed. “It did. But it’s minor compared to what happened to you.”

He nodded and looked away, sadness washing over his features for a moment before he turned his attention back to me, a small smile masking the emotion I’d just seen a hint of.

“I had called my men back,” he said, his voice soft. “But one guy…a kid really…barely eighteen…he just wouldn’t listen. Wouldn’t back down. Wanted to be a hero. I had to go after him. Dragged him by his shirt as he kept shooting until we both got shot. He didn’t make it, and his body falling on mine kept me from getting hurt worse.”

“I’m so sorry,” I whispered.

“The price of freedom.” His voice sounded light, but I could hear the pain behind it as he looked away from me again.

“Doesn’t make it hurt any less,” I said and he nodded, blinking, his eyes red.

“It’s not easy. We go in knowing not all of us will make it back out. But seeing it…seeing your men and friends fall…it’s terrifying. You want to turn and run. You want to hide. You want—" He stopped, looking around at the men in the beds beside him. The one to his left was reading a book. The one to his right was asleep, a fresh bandage wrapped around his head. Willaim's eyes met mine again and I reached out my hand and took his, as if to tell him, without saying a word, that I understood.

We sat quietly for a time, and after a while I removed my hand from his and set it back in my lap.

"I should leave you," I said. "You need your rest, and probably some breakfast soon."

"Stay," he said. "Please? At least for a while longer?"

And so I did.

Unlike my days in the Pacific, where the hot sun and humid air made me feel as though I were moving in slow motion, things seemed to move faster in this part of the world.

Thanks to our proximity to France, we often had multiple flights back and forth each day, unlike in the Pacific where it was rare for any one woman to go out more than once. The whole operation here ran like a well-oiled machine as we loaded up with supplies in England, unloaded them on the other side, picked up our patients, and flew back. Only to do it all over again as soon as the plane was cleared and restocked.

Sometimes we took men with us who were returning to the front, their injuries healed, their spirits restored. Other times it was medical supplies, food and kitchen supplies, weaponry, and ammunition. But today, for the first time in my career, our cargo was neither medical nor human. Today we had livestock. Chickens, rabbits, and ducks.

"Don't make friends with them," the navigator warned. "It'll only make you feel terrible later."

I wrinkled my nose and then glanced beside me at Theodore and tried not to laugh as he swiped irritatingly at the air, brushing away the feathers and hair circulating through the cabin.

At least once a day I made a point to see William. He was healing slowly, the leg wound having gotten infected and needing to be reopened and cleaned out, a round of penicillin administered to clear anything trying to hold on inside his body. His arm looked good though, and his stomach wound was healing nicely, as I'd seen one day the week before when I'd arrived just as the doctor was finishing up looking it over, the nurse standing by to redress it.

"How does it look?" William had asked me.

"Swell," I'd said. "You're nearly ready to go out dancing."

"Really?" He'd looked down at the wound then and cringed. "Oh. Yuck." Closing his eyes, he'd rested his head back on the pillow until he was rebandaged.

"You can open your eyes now," I'd said when the nurse left.

He opened one. "I don't know how you stand it."

I shrugged. "I don't think about the wound so much as the life the wound is hurting. It makes it easier." I grinned then. "But I also find the human body fascinating."

"Yuck," he'd said again, making me laugh.

It was mid-July when he finally was able to step outside without being pushed in a wheelchair.

"Where are you off to?" I asked, having hurried in to see him in-between flights and catching him as he hobbled on a pair of crutches toward the front door, a nurse following close behind.

"I've been cleared to get some fresh air," he said. "I heard there was sun and asked if I could see it."

"It's a gorgeous day," I said, moving to fall into step beside him. "I wish I could stay and enjoy it with you."

"Maybe on your next day off?"

"It's a date," I said, and then felt myself blush. "Or—"

"Can't take it back," he teased. "Besides, if we're to be betrothed, we should probably have a date or two."

I glanced back at the nurse and she looked from him to me, a crestfallen look on her face. I'd seen her several times over the past weeks, always sitting with a soldier, hooking up an IV, or any number of the dozens of tasks needed to take care of the wounded. She was quiet, efficient, and looked to have a crush on William.

"He proposed in the midst of major blood loss," I told her.

"Oh," she said, grinning, her shoulders sagging a little in relief.

"I never propose if I don't mean it," William said and I met the nurse's eyes again with a smirk and a shake of my head.

"Looks like I have to go," I said, noticing Theodore walking our way, his steps quick. "Enjoy your sunshine! And Claire?" I said to the nurse hurrying to take my spot next to William.

"Yes?" she said.

"Watch out for him. He likes to throw around promises of marriage."

I boarded the plane and said hello to the copilot and radio operator who were putting their gear away, but neither met my eyes, keeping them averted as they gave half-hearted greetings in response. Frowning, I stashed my helmet and gas mask. As I placed a bottle of morphine in my pocket, I watched Theodore climb aboard and glance toward the ceiling, then at me, his eyebrows raised.

"What?" I asked, and then looked up. "Oh."

I pursed my lips, my face warming, but amused nonetheless. Sometimes it was hard to keep the wounded who were awake for longer flights entertained. They got bored and restless. For those able to hold them, we'd hand out decks of cards or books we kept tucked in a small box near the radio operator. But at some point, whoever had been on this plane previously had decided the men might like something a little different to keep their minds off their injuries, which was why the ceiling had been plastered with nude pictures of women from the pages of magazines. What was more amusing was that clearly one of the other nurses had tried to make the scene a little less obnoxious by applying Band-Aids to some of the women's naked bits.

"Well," I said, moving around the crates that had been loaded. "At least I won't have to worry about them staring at me."

The men laughed, slightly relieved by my response, but still looking embarrassed, and then the door was shut and we were off.

Summer in the English countryside during a war was strange. It was peaceful, the green sloping hills giving way to sprawling valleys sprinkled with quaint towns we often visited on our days off.

Food was scarce once we were away from base, but sometimes it was worth it to forgo the mess hall for a small meal in a pub, listening to the locals chat. It almost felt like one was on vacation. At least until you heard the sound of planes rumbling overhead.

As August approached, William was able to get up and about more, leading us to finally go for a bicycle ride together on one of my days off.

I dressed in a light blue dress and my oxfords, packed sandwiches and apples, filled my canteen, and met him inside the hospital where he was getting stern instruction from his doctor.

"Take it easy," Doctor Haddan warned. "The infection may be gone, but if you rip those stitches, I'm not going to let you leave your bed for two weeks."

"Yessir," William said, and then limped out the door beside me.

"You sure you're up to this?" I asked. "We could just walk for a while."

"I promise. I want nothing more than to see a bit of the countryside that lights up your face whenever you talk about it."

"Then let's go."

We rode side by side, keeping our speed low and sometimes

dismounting to walk our bikes when a hill was too much for William. His strength was returning with the daily exercises he did, but not enough that he could ride uphill easily, and we had to be careful he didn't disturb the stitches on the newly re-sewn wound.

After thirty minutes or so we pulled off to the side of the road, slipped through a section of stone wall, and sat on the blanket I'd brought and placed over the grass.

"You weren't kidding," he said, staring out at the view.

It was early in the day still and a cloud hung low over the valley before us, sheep grazing here and there, the sun just beginning to warm the earth.

"Did you explore much when you arrived? Before the invasion in France?" I asked, pulling out the food I'd brought and handing him my canteen.

He took a long sip and then shook his head.

"Not really. I was stationed near London and went a few times to pass the time while I waited to ship out, but mostly I stayed in. Kept myself amused on base. Read books, played cards with the fellas, stuff like that." He handed the canteen back and our fingers brushed, sending a shot of electricity up my arm.

"Do you get scared?"

He looked back out at the view, his chest rising and falling as if in slow motion before he turned to me again.

"Absolutely."

We were quiet then, each of us with our own thoughts as we stared out over the countryside.

"What about you?" he asked as I unwrapped the sandwiches. "Do you get scared flying into war zones?"

"Of course," I said. "But I'm more scared of someone losing their life because I'm not paying attention. My focus is on my patients. My job. I imagine it's the same for you in a way?"

He nodded. "It is. My focus is on my men. Strategizing the best I can to keep them alive. Those are my friends. They're someone's son or brother or husband. It's a lot of pressure and it doesn't matter how many you lose, each one hurts. Each one is a terrible notch on a terrible belt I will wear for the rest of my life."

His eyes welled and he looked away. I reached my hand out and slid it into his, inhaling as his fingers, warm and strong, wrapped around my own. We sat in silence once more while he gathered himself, his thumb gently rubbing against my fingers, the sensation bringing me the first real comfort I'd felt since returning to duty.

"How stupid do you reckon it is for a soldier to fall for a flight nurse during a war?" he asked softly.

I considered the question for a moment.

"No stupider than a flight nurse falling for a soldier when she swore to herself she wouldn't let herself get distracted by such things."

"So...monumentally then?"

There was a look in his eye, and an all-consuming swell of feeling and emotion sweeping over me, that I knew only death would make me one day forget. And maybe not even then.

"Monumentally," I said with a grin.

16

William

Seattle
2003

"THAT MUST'VE BEEN HARD," Selene said. "Being in love while in a war."

"It was terrifying is what it was," I said, meeting her gaze and taking a sip of my water. "And stupid. But worth every second."

She grinned and something in my chest hitched. It was somehow a familiar grin and I wondered, as I had the moment I'd seen her standing at my front door, how she knew my Kate. There was the whisper of something in her face I recognized but couldn't put my finger on. Were they related somehow? A distant cousin?

"William?" Selene said.

"Sorry." I ran a hand over the stack of letters again, a memory filling my mind. "The Army provided us with bicycles," I said. "When I was able but still healing, on Kate's days off we'd get up early and take long rides through the countryside. She'd pack a picnic and we'd stop at some point and sit and stare at the view. She loved all the sheep. Said they reminded her of summers at her parents' country home. I used to tease her, telling her I'd steal a couple and bring them back to where she was staying so she could have them as pets."

Selene laughed.

"Other days we'd ride into one of the neighboring towns, have a watered-down pint and some chips, and listen to the locals gossip. It was idyllic. Summertime in the English countryside." I smiled, remembering the smell of the air, the sound of the wind brushing against the blades of grass in the fields, the ever-present buzz of airplanes in the distance.

"She lived in a mansion," I continued. "Did you know that? That's where her living quarters were."

Selene shook her head, her eyes widening.

"I always imagined her in one of those low-roofed, one-story buildings," she said.

"Like you see in pictures?"

She nodded.

"I mean, that was the typical living situation. Something that could be built fast and then torn down when the war was over. But depending on where you were stationed, there were homes that had been vacated and taken over by soldiers. Sometimes for good, sometimes for bad, if you happened to live in an area occupied by the enemy. But the squadron she was with got lucky. About a mile away from base was a beautiful mansion they got to live in while they served, riding their bicycles to and from base for work. In fact, she snuck me in a couple of times when no one was around."

"She did?" Selene asked and I felt my face warm as I was once again lost in a memory of twenty-seven-year-old me waiting outside for the last woman to leave before Kate appeared and waved me inside, taking my hand and pulling me up the staircase to her room where she shut the door and let her nightgown fall to the floor.

I cleared my throat and took another sip of beer.

"She knew having access to a long, hot shower was basically a fantasy on base and offered to let me use one of theirs. It was incredible. Best showers of my life." I didn't mention that Kate had joined me, or how I could still remember, all these years later, the way her hair had looked, wet and streaming down her back, her long, lean body strong from the physical work she did every day.

"Were you two able to go anywhere else? Did you ever go to London?"

"We talked about it. Catching a train, spending a weekend..." I shook my head. "But we never did. We liked our quiet bike rides, visiting towns...becoming familiar faces to the locals. We had a small group of friends back on base who we spent time with some evenings. And there was a favorite spot we'd go to, a tree we sat beneath, talking about the future. Our hopes and dreams." I chuckled. "The usual stuff the young and in love talk about. Sometimes we'd read a book we'd found in one of the town's bookshops. There was a book of poetry I picked up one day. I was never much for poems, but there was something about the poet's words that struck me. They were full of hope and promise. They reminded me of Kate."

Selene quietly reached for her bag, pulling it onto her lap. A moment later she placed a navy blue leather-bound book between us on the table.

The smile left my face and a lump formed in my throat. I didn't ask for permission. I picked it up, the feel of the cover beneath my fingertips bringing back a cascade of memories. As if pulled by an invisible force, I held the book vertical between my palms and then moved them apart, letting it fall open as I'd done so long ago. The pages parted and when I looked down, my eyes filled with tears. Stuck between the pages was a braided chain made of long blades of grass.

Kate.

17

Kate

England
August 1944

"READ IT AGAIN," I said, my eyes closed against the hot afternoon sun, the skirt of my yellow flowered dress hitched up midthigh as I worked on my tan.

William tugged a lock of my hair.

"Bossy," he said, and I laughed and shielded my eyes from the light as I looked up at him.

"Please?"

"As if I could resist you." His eyes swept down my body and something inside me squeezed sweet and low.

I rolled over onto my stomach, propping my chin on my hands, and he sighed, setting down the book of poetry he'd found earlier that morning when we'd poked around a bookshop that had become one of our favorite stops in a nearby town.

"How can I read when you're looking at me like that?" he

asked, stretching out beside me and tucking a strand of hair behind my ear.

I leaned forward, closing my eyes as his warm hand cupped my face, his lips finding mine. He rolled me gently onto my back, his injured leg, nearly completely healed now, intertwining with mine as my free hand made its way slowly up his arm, pausing to brush my fingers over where a bullet had pierced his skin, and then to his shoulder before digging into his hair and pulling him closer.

He swore softly against my lips, pulling away and staring down at me.

"Shall we go back?" he asked.

He'd rented a room in a small hotel in the neighboring town. We'd gone a half-dozen times, the woman at the front desk giving us empathetic smiles whenever we checked in and then out the next morning, always at an ungodly hour because of my work schedule.

I leaned down and pulled my dress up an inch, looking at my tan line.

"Not yet," I said, and he laughed and rolled onto his back.

I could care less about my tan, what I really wanted was this moment. How many more of them would we get? I couldn't bear the thought. I wasn't sure what spell William Mitchell had put over me, but for once in my life I didn't want to overthink it. I just wanted to be in it. Fully. Immersed in him and us. Never wanting to come up for air.

"Shall I read more then?"

"Yes, please," I said, plucking three blades of grass and carefully knotting one end before proceeding to braid them.

His voice was low and husky as he read again a poem about a rekindled love, found the first time by chance, the second by happy accident.

"And I shall love you," he read. "Forever. For always. Forevermore."

There was silence as the words floated around us.

"Forevermore," he said again, his voice a whisper.

I stared across the blanket into his denim-blue eyes. I had never had a sense of home before. The one I was born into I'd been made to feel unwelcome in. The one I'd shared with my aunt and uncle, while cozy and warm and accepting, had never felt quite like mine. Despite their efforts…their love and encouragement to make the space mine as well, I'd always felt a bit like a guest. And then there were the barracks I'd found myself in. Fun in ways, but certainly not home.

But William…he had no roof to shelter me. No four walls to ward off the elements. No floor, no door, no window. Yet being with him felt like home. He was home. My home. The only place I'd ever felt I'd belonged.

I smiled at him.

"Forevermore," I whispered, and then handed him the braided strands of grass, which he plucked from my fingertips, put it in the book to mark where he'd left off, and jumped to his feet.

"I can wait no longer," he said, holding out a hand, his other on his heart. "I must make you mine, milady."

I rolled my eyes and shook my head.

"The poetry is going to your head," I said, letting him pull me to my feet.

"Hush thy lips, sweet maiden," he said before laughter got the best of him.

"I'm burning that book."

But it was a joke. I would never burn it. I would keep it with me every day, tucked in my medical bag after he was sent back to the front. It was a romantic promise I'd made to him after the first day we'd read from it, but it was one I planned to keep. No matter how sappy the poems could sometimes be, the memory of reading them…of laughing and sighing and staring at one another as a phrase or verse hit just so…was special. And I planned to hang on to the memory of that while I waited for him to return to me.

The following morning we rode back to base before the sun was up, the air promising another warm day, the sheep in the fields to the left and right of us nestled in small groups, a few raising their heads, watching as we pedaled by.

"Be careful," William whispered in my ear as we shared a last embrace behind one of the buildings. "I need you in one piece. Promise?"

"Promise," I said, lifting my face to kiss him again. "And you don't overdo it today."

"I can't promise that," he said.

"I wish you weren't so determined to leave me."

I was joking, I knew he was just anxious to get back to the job he'd signed on for. To fight for not only our freedom, but the freedom of millions of others. To do his part to right this unbearable wrong that was happening. And yet I still felt a sense of sadness at his resolve to be well enough to go back to battle. I wanted him safe and here with me. But if he didn't get well enough to fight, then he'd be sent home and be even farther away, with absolutely no chance of us seeing one another until after the war ended. It was hard to know what to wish for, so I wished for nothing but both of our safety and an end to this war that had taken so many lives and ruined so many more.

An hour later I'd stowed my bag, gas mask, and canteen, and had a bottle of morphine tucked safely in my pocket should the need for it arise.

"How was your day off?" Theodore asked, buckling in beside me.

I felt my face warm and he chuckled.

"That good, huh?" he asked.

It was no secret First Sergeant William Mitchell and I were a couple. I'd initially tried to keep it quiet, preferring to keep my private life private. But he was too much of a flirt, and my constant visits to see how he was, despite my excuses of just checking on him after so much blood loss, were smirked at. There was no point in trying to hide it. We'd fallen for one another, and while there were several female broken hearts, everyone on base seemed genuinely happy for us.

"It was lovely," I said. "The weather was nice so we rode our bikes into town, read some books we picked up, and had a picnic with some sheep." He shuddered. Theodore hated what he called the "British wildlife." Anytime we had to fly livestock over he tucked himself into his seat, put a blanket over his face, and pretended to sleep the entire flight to France.

We landed and Theodore and I stood aside as troops hurried in to unload the supplies we'd brought over with us. Blankets, bandages, rubbing alcohol, IV bags…

While the plane was emptied, I made rounds, checking in with the nurses tending to the patients waiting to be loaded and reading the tags attached to their clothing, blankets, or litters.

A young man sat off to the side, rocking himself on top of the litter, his ankles bound so he couldn't easily run off. He didn't look to have any physical injuries, but sometimes the wound went deeper than that. Sometimes what was damaged was the mind. The heart. The soul.

"Cracked up," one of the nurses said, seeing me watching the young man who couldn't have been more than eighteen.

He was mumbling to himself, staring blindly at the commotion around him, his hands twitching.

"Dangerous?" I asked.

"Not so far," she said. "But we'll sedate him before he gets onboard just in case."

I nodded. "Any moments of clarity or…?"

"No. Not that I've seen."

It broke my heart to see these young men so damaged by war. By the realities of how brutal humanity could be. It was cruel to pull them from lives where they'd dreamed of a future—

working any number of jobs, educating themselves at universities, striving for an exciting future, marrying their sweetheart, perhaps having children—and plunging them into training to kill. Training to save their own lives, as well as the lives of the men around them. Men who had become brothers as they worked side by side maneuvering, shooting, building, and discharging weapons of destruction. Destruction of towns. Destruction of lives. Not a one of them would leave unscathed. Some would wear their battle wounds on their body. Some deeply within. And others would take them to their grave.

So many graves.

I smiled at the young soldier, his baby face caked on one side with the dirt he'd been pulled from before he'd been led to safety.

"Hey there," I said, kneeling beside him, my voice soft as I looked at the paper pinned to his torn jacket. "Your name is Joel?"

He stared blankly at me.

"Well, I'm Kate and I'm going to hang out with you today on that airplane over there." I pointed. "Do you think that would be okay?"

He was silent, his big dark eyes looking through me.

I wondered where his people were. If he had a mom and dad still. Siblings who would rally around him when he got home, a place he may or may not recognize, a place he may never see should he be deemed too dangerous, whether to others or just to himself, to be anywhere but a hospital for the rest of his life.

I squeezed his hand and stood, and then moved on to the next patient, my heart heavy but my smile light as I went from injured to injured.

We didn't land back at base until the sun had gone down, having to take a load of wounded to a base in Scotland first before flying back to England.

"Hello there," William said, when I wandered wearily into

the mess hall after looking for him in his bed. "I came over figuring you'd be hungry when you got in and head here first."

"You're sweet," I said, kissing him and waving off the whistles from the soldiers nearby. "But I always go to the hospital to see you first."

"Well then, you're the one who's sweet," he said, leaning forward to kiss me again. There was another round of whistles and we laughed as he pulled away and pushed his tray toward me. "Also, I knew these animals would eat all the good stuff if I didn't save you some. I've been here for nearly two hours."

"William!" I said. "You didn't have to do that."

"If I had to, it wouldn't be as much fun. Now, eat up."

The food was still warm, thanks to him asking one of the cooks to set a plate off to the side under one of the warmers for me and keeping guard over it until ten minutes before I arrived when the kitchen was shutting down.

I tried not to wolf it down, but I was starving, having not had time to stop for lunch or even a snack due to the hectic schedule.

"How did it go?" William asked.

I shrugged. Most days I didn't mind talking about it, but sometimes I had a hard time finding the words, the images of the men etching themselves into my mind and heart. My interactions with the young soldier named Joel had sat heavy with me for the remainder of my missions. He was so young. Too young to have had to experience what he had. I thought of all the others. The hundreds I'd heard about being marched from their homes, down the streets they'd known all their lives, and loaded onto trucks and trains, only to be taken far away, put to work, and never seen or heard from again.

An image of my childhood friend Ruthie rose in my mind and I sucked in a breath. It was indescribable still, the feelings of guilt I had surrounding her. Regardless of the fact that I'd been too young to do anything to help. When her father was arrested on suspicious charges the year before I'd left home, I knew that somehow my own father had had something to do with it. My mother had always relished telling her friends that he knew everyone and there wasn't anything that happened in our city that he didn't know about.

"He knows everyone, that man," she'd say with the grin that always caused a chill to run up my spine. "And has his finger in every pot."

Two weeks after Ruthie's father was imprisoned, he was moved to another facility farther away. Then another. Then came the day Ruthie hadn't shown up for school, when I'd run the many blocks to my friend's house to find her and her mother packing.

"Where are you going?" I'd asked, looking around desperately, wanting to tell them to stop, tears hovering on my lower lids.

Ruthie had looked at her mother who hesitated before nodding.

"My aunt's," she said. "We've told everyone we're just going for the weekend but..." Her big brown eyes had said it all and the tears that had hovered now streamed down my face as I nodded and stumbled to her, wrapping my arms around her.

"Can we write?" I'd asked when we'd parted, looking to her mother.

"Not at first," she'd said. "To be on the safe side. For all of us."

I'd nodded, understanding the things she didn't say. They didn't want to be found. And I could get in trouble for keeping their secret.

"I will write though," Ruthie had said.

"Under a different name," her mother had said.

I never knew if a letter came. I left home having never heard a thing, without knowing what had become of my friend, and wondering for all the years after if they'd escaped.

William squeezed my hand and I leaned into him, reveling in the warmth of his body against mine.

"Where'd you go?" he asked.

I stared into his eyes and then leaned my head on his shoulder. I never answered. He didn't push. It was one of my favorite things about him. His silent acceptance of my sometime need to quietly wade through whatever feelings I was having until I was ready to talk about them.

Or not.

18

I KNEW IT was coming. He was doing so well. The wounds on his arm and stomach had healed and faded to a dark pink, and his limp was nearly gone, the infection in his leg having healed, his strength and mobility returning.

"A week?" I said, sinking to the blanket he'd just laid out.

It was my day off and we were enjoying another picnic under our favorite tree.

"At least I'll be close," he said.

But we both knew his proximity to where I was stationed or where I flew in to pick up the wounded didn't matter. It was the fact that he was reentering the war that was the very terrifying problem.

"William," I whispered, reaching for him.

He pulled me close.

In the end, we didn't stay long under our tree. I was too distracted to listen to the new poems he read, the grass I pulled from the earth wilting beneath my fingertips as I forgot to braid it, my mind on the fact that by this time next week he'd be running toward the enemy as bullets flew toward him.

"Kate," he said, taking the blades carefully from my fingers. "Let's go."

"Where?"

He smiled softly and held out a hand, pulling me to my feet.

We spent the remainder of the day in the room we always rented, his body curled around mine, my body curled around his, as we talked, made love, and dozed in the sunlight streaming through the crack in the curtains.

At dinnertime we wandered downstairs and made our way to one of our favorite pubs, smiling and nodding to the familiar faces as we took a seat at a corner table and ordered from the meager menu.

We returned to our room afterward, William sitting on the edge of the bed and wrapping his arms around my waist, resting his forehead on my stomach as I ran my fingers through his hair.

"I don't want to leave you," he said as tears ran down my face and fell, landing on the back of my hand.

"I don't want you to go," I whispered.

When we made love again, we did so quietly, slowly, our eyes drinking each other in as we moved together. I felt as though my every nerve ending was alight, his hands on my skin making me feel more alive and more aware than I'd ever been before. His breaths echoed in my ears, the beating of his heart reverberated against me…through me.

Afterward we lay together, our bodies intertwined, our gazes fixed on one another. I was unable to say a word. All I could do was watch him, drink him in, as I tried to absorb every second I had with him until he fell asleep, and then I did.

"Kate."

I woke to William whispering my name, his lips trailing a path over my shoulder to my neck.

It was still dark out and I groaned and shook my head. I didn't want the night to be over. I wasn't ready.

"Come with me," he said.

"It's time to go already?" I asked.

"Not yet. But I need you to wake up a little early today. Please?"

I blinked in the dark, confused, tired, and then smiled at his face above mine. I could not and would not ever resist him.

"Okay," I said.

We left a half hour earlier than we normally did, the sun still a couple hours away from appearing, making the ride on our bicycles a little more difficult, the air a touch too cool.

I didn't ask questions. I knew if William had asked me to get up earlier than we normally did, he had a good reason, and I would follow him anywhere.

As we coasted down a slight hill, he looked over his shoulder and smiled at me in the dark. I grinned back, my chest swelling with love for this man I hadn't expected to meet. Hadn't wanted to meet. And yet succumbed to his charms regardless, because that was how love worked. No matter how determined one was to not find it. How difficult and frightening it was to feel it. Love didn't care. Circumstances be damned. It wanted to be known, felt, and returned.

As we came to an intersection, William took a right and I smiled. I knew exactly where he was taking me.

In the dark, our tree stood black and elegant against the navy sky. William slowed and then stopped, pushing down the kickstand of his bicycle and then waiting patiently as I did the same.

The grass was damp and I worried for a moment how it would look if I turned up on base, my backside wet with dew, but William didn't sit, he merely leaned against the tree's trunk and pulled me to him.

"I remember the first moment I saw you," he said and I chuckled.

"No, you don't," I said. "You were too woozy from pain and blood loss."

He grinned and pinched my backside playfully.

"That came later," he said. "You weren't paying attention to me, you were too busy doing your job. And boy, were you beautiful as you looked so seriously down at the tag attached to my shirt before giving me a brief smile and moving on to the next guy."

My mouth opened but I had no words. I was embarrassed to admit he was right. I barely had recollection of him outside the plane, just his name and injuries. The first time I remember really noticing him was when I checked on him midflight, and then of course when I realized he was bleeding and I had to stitch him up.

"It's okay," he said, tucking a strand of hair behind my ear. "I loved watching you without you knowing. I'd never seen a woman so focused on her job. So efficient and caring and knowledgeable. You were like an angel in that field, and then on the plane, moving from patient to patient, administering medications and bandages, making conversation, squeezing a hand, feeling foreheads. And the way you weren't bothered by those Jerries..."

I shrugged. "I'm no different than any of the other women out here doing the same."

But he shook his head. "But you are. You care so deeply. I can see it in your eyes when you're tending to your patients. I can see it in the way you look after your friends when they come in from a shift. You're kind and strong. You make me laugh. You listen when I'm frustrated about not being out there, fighting beside my brothers. And even though you didn't want to love me. Even though it scared you. You did it anyways. In a way I've never been loved before. And I promise you now, I will never love anyone the way I love you."

We were both silent, his words hanging between us.

"I was only a little bit serious on that plane," he said. "But I'm very serious now."

He stood upright then, causing me to take a step or two back as he pulled something from his pocket and held it out to me.

"I swore to myself I wouldn't get involved while I was over here fighting. Not even a fling. It wasn't worth it to me to feel or cause heartache like that. But the moment I saw you I knew the universe had sent me a challenge. And when you came to check on me in the base hospital, well…that sealed the deal. I was smitten. But now… Now I'm in love. And so I have to ask, my wounds healed, no blood leaving my body, Kate Campbell, will you marry me?"

Marriage was not something I'd ever considered in my short life. I'd grown up listening to my parents scheme and shame and feed off one another's ugliness, causing me to decide my life would have a purpose larger than finding "the one." And no matter that I'd later had a wonderful example of what marriage could be from my aunt and uncle and then watched my high school friends fall in love and proclaim how lovely and wonderful it was to find "the one," I'd decided it wasn't in the cards for me. I'd find a different path.

And so when boys asked me out, I pointed them to Janie or Claire, offering them up as an alternative. When I was approached in pubs or the library or the hall of the hospital where I volunteered, I politely shook my head and returned my gaze to whatever chart I'd been poring over.

But then I met William. And suddenly all the reasons I'd had for not falling for someone fell away, and left in their place was a stark and beautiful truth.

I loved him.

Where before I might have dissected the how and why of it, I found I didn't care to now. I just wanted to feel it. To allow it. To revel in it and him and us. I wasn't curious. I didn't need to study it. It just was. An absolute. And I wanted more of it.

"Yes," I whispered, and then grinned as his face lit up, my heart feeling like it might burst out of my chest as he opened the box he'd held out to me and slipped a ring on my finger.

"I'll come by the field hospital whenever I'm near to see if you're around," William said, wiping a tear from my cheek. "And I'll write."

We were standing around the corner from the airfield, savoring every second we had left before he had to go.

I nodded. "And I'll see about getting a few days off."

Our plans were tentative. Getting letters to one another would be simple enough, but spending time together would prove more difficult. He had no idea when he'd be eligible for leave, but when he was, he would fly back to England and we'd stay in our usual room at the little hotel we'd found and made ours in town.

I could feel the time ticking down, each second a beat of my heart, the sound filling my ears as I stared up at him and he looked down at me, his eyes moving over my face as I tried to memorize every detail of his.

I ran my fingers through his soft brown hair, taking in his lightly tanned skin, faded-blue-jean eyes, and the lips I'd already kissed at least a couple hundred times. Smoothing my palm across his jaw, I breathed in the scent of him, filling my lungs, holding him there, before breathing him out and melting into him.

He wrapped his arms around me and I wished that somehow I could merge my body with his. To be part of him. To never have to leave him.

"If only there was some kind of magic," I said and he held me tighter, his chest rising and falling against mine.

"I think perhaps there is," he said, and I looked up. "Because there's no other explanation for you saying you'll marry me."

I grinned up at him and he smiled.

"I can't wait to marry you," I said.

"But you will, right?"

I laughed. "I will. I'll wait forever if I have to."

"Good. But let's not wait that long. Deal?"

"Deal."

He kissed me then, my fiancé, long and hard until I was breathless and tears filled my eyes, blurring his face when we parted. And when we did he pressed something into my hand. I looked down and my eyes welled once more. It was the picture he'd taken of us beneath our tree.

"I should've taken more," he said. "So I have one too. Keep it safe?"

"I will."

He hugged me to him again and then pulled away.

"Stay safe up there," he said, pointing to the sky.

"Stay safe over there," I said, pointing east.

"I love you, Kate. Forevermore."

"Forevermore, William. I love you."

And then, with a last kiss, he flung his bag over his shoulder and strode across the tarmac to the plane waiting to take him to France. Before disappearing inside he waved once more and then he was gone.

I stood alone at the edge of the runway, watching as the aircraft taxied, paused, and then began rolling, picking up speed before its wheels lifted and the plane was airborne, a gust of wind chasing behind it and swallowing my last whispered "goodbye."

19

IN THE DAYS after William left I felt hollowed. Bereft. And more than a little distracted, my mind constantly wandering as I wondered where he was and what he was doing. Who he was with and if they were watching out for him.

"Lieutenant?"

I looked over at Theodore, who was pointing to a soldier struggling against the straps securing him to his litter.

"Oh," I said, getting to my feet to find the wounded man had vomited and was having trouble ejecting it from his mouth due to the stitches keeping one side of his lips and cheek together.

"I need a bin," I said to Theodore while carefully removing the scissors pinned to the soldier's shirt and beginning to snip, making room for him to expel the vomit.

"You okay?" he asked from where he was seated at his desk after I'd finished cleaning up my patient and giving him morphine for the pain.

"Yes," I said, crossing my arms in defense against the cold.

"First Sergeant Mitchell returned to the front, did he not?"

"He did."

I glanced at him, and he gave me a sympathetic smile and patted my leg.

I was grateful that he didn't say William would be okay, because we both knew that wasn't guaranteed. Those words only worked on those back home. For those of us with a front row seat, we knew better.

We flew in with the last planeload around eight that night. I bid Theodore good-night and stared longingly at the hospital, missing being able to pop in quickly to see William before heading home for the night. Swinging a tired leg over my bicycle, I pushed off and rode home, listening to the sound of nature falling asleep and coming awake around me.

I could hear music playing in someone's room when I came in the front door, voices talking, footsteps thudding up above on the second floor, laughter, and the clanging of dishes in the kitchen. The sounds were comforting. It felt like home.

I set my bag at the base of the stairs, checked the tidy entryway table for mail, smiling when I saw my aunt's handwriting on one of the envelopes, and headed for the kitchen, tucking the letter in my pocket, my stomach grumbling as the smell of someone's dinner wafted throughout the house.

"Kate!"

I smiled wearily at Luella, who was standing at the stove, one hand on her hip, a wooden spoon in the other, stirring something in a pot.

"The mess hall was gonna throw out a huge box of tomatoes," she said. "There were still plenty of good ones in it so I took 'em. I'm making spaghetti. You want some?"

"You have enough?"

"I think I've made enough to feed the entire base," she said with a laugh.

"Well then, I'd love some. I'm starving."

The smell was delicious and brought several of the other women in from wherever they'd been enjoying the evening.

With so many of us eating, we gathered in the grand dining room, giggling as we sat around the massive table, more than half of the women in pajamas, the rest of us still in uniform, or at least parts of it. Hazel had removed her shirt and was wearing just a camisole. I'd peeled off my button-down and was in a T-shirt, sitting with one leg folded beneath me, something that would've earned me a stern look from my mother could she see.

I ate while listening to the others talk, sharing details from their day and telling of their plans for their next day off. Summer was ending and everyone was trying to take advantage of the nice weather while they could.

"I am not looking forward to the rain," someone at the far end of the table said.

Not that we hadn't had a few rainy days in the two months since I'd arrived, but from what we'd been told, fall and winter could be quite miserable. Gray, windy, wet, and seemingly never-ending.

"And how's our newly engaged member doing?" I heard someone ask and didn't realize they meant me until Hazel nudged me with her foot under the table.

"Oh!" I said, my thumb rubbing against the band around my ring finger. There was a smattering of laughter. "I'm…okay?"

"Any word since he's been gone?" Beatrice asked, twirling a strand of strawberry blond hair around her finger.

Beatrice, I'd learned, was always twirling her hair. A nervous habit, she'd told me one evening while we drank beers with the small group we'd become part of by accident.

The group had formed one night after William and I had hurried into a pub to escape the rain and found Beatrice and Shirley, another nurse from the mansion, already bellied up to the bar. I'd introduced William to the two women just as the door opened and two soldiers from the base came in. When someone suggested we pull two tables together, the rest of us agreed it was a good idea, and the group was born.

There were others who had joined us on occasion. Hazel, Luella, Theodore, and a surgeon named John, who once nearly fell asleep in his meal. But usually it was just the six of us meeting up whenever we were all on base at the same time and not too tired.

I smiled at Beatrice now.

"He left a letter for me at the airfield," I told her. "Had one of the guys give it to me the day after he left. There was another the second day. And the third. But none today."

"It's sweet that he thought to do that," Edith said. "My fiancé remembers to write so infrequently, I've started to tell myself he's dead. That way if a letter never comes, I've prepared myself. And when one does, it's a wonderful surprise."

"Edith," Hazel said. "That's awful."

"Maybe," Edith said. "But it's easier than panicking every day, like I was doing."

There were several nods around the room as everyone understood the plight of a woman whose man had gone off to war.

The talk turned to other things then. Someone hadn't followed the chore schedule and the trash in the kitchen hadn't been emptied. Someone else had tracked mud on the main staircase.

"And there are beer bottles and cigarette butts outside the back door off the kitchen," Marlene, the head nurse said, her golden blond hair pulled back in its usual unyielding bun. "We have to keep the house clean, ladies. They could do an inspection at any time."

"I mean, what are they gonna do to us?" Betty was from Alabama and as usual, her easy-sounding drawl made at least one of the women around the table giggle. She had a way of saying things that made even the most important information sound un-rushed and not important.

"Can you imagine her in an emergency situation in the air?"

Hazel had said to me once, making me purse my lips so as not to burst out laughing. "She talks slow as molasses. By the time she asks her tech for help, the patient will be dead."

I didn't mention that Hazel spoke so fast it was sometimes hard to understand what she'd said. Which could also result in a dangerous outcome. So far, thankfully, neither woman seemed to have any trouble with their patients. And neither of them would be here if the instructors at Bowman hadn't found them fully capable.

Marlene gave a small huff in response to Betty's question and pasted a smile on her face.

"They could fine us," she said. "Or take away shifts. Or add shifts. And most certainly write us up."

"Seems like a lot of trouble over some cigarette butts and beer bottles," Betty said. "Good thing I don't smoke or drink."

There was a smattering of laughter around the table as she took a swig from the bottle in her hand and adjusted the cigarette behind her ear. Marlene sighed.

"I'm going. I'm going," Betty said, pushing back from the table to go clean up her mess.

"Truly, ladies," Marlene said, her eyes taking in each of us. "I don't want to mother you, but it's on me if this house isn't kept in tip-top shape."

There were several nods and murmurs of understanding, and then one by one we got up from the table and began to clean before making our way to our bedrooms for the night.

"You okay?"

I turned to see Beatrice behind me on the stairs.

"Yeah," I said, my voice quiet.

"You miss him."

It was a statement, not a question, and I nodded. I missed him in ways I couldn't put to words. It felt as though I'd lost a limb, the thought reminding me of what I'd learned about people who'd actually been through it, and the ghost limb phenomenon many experienced after. The itching of a leg that no longer existed. The ache of an invisible arm. William had become that for me. But instead of a limb, I felt as though I'd lost my heart, the beating inside merely an echo of the organ that had once resided inside me.

It was shocking to me how fast it had happened. One day he was just another face in a sea of so many others. The next, I couldn't stop thinking about him. Imagining a life with him. Aching to be with him again.

"You on tomorrow?" Beatrice asked.

I shook my head.

"Me neither. Wanna go into town?"

I wanted to say no. But my plans to lie in bed all day wallowing in grief and wasting our dwindling sunny summer days would only put me in a worse mood.

"Sure," I said, and waved good-night as she passed me to go to her own room two doors down.

Hazel was already asleep when I opened the door and I grinned and shook my head. I didn't know how she did it. The girl could talk right up to the very second she passed out.

"It's a gift," she'd told me when I'd mentioned it a few weeks ago. We'd been having a conversation and, as usual, she was prattling on, my brain trying to keep up with her mouth. When it was my turn to talk, my own words were met with silence and when I glanced her way, I saw that she'd fallen asleep, mouth open as if she'd been waiting to respond but sleep had moved even faster and stolen her away.

I pulled my aunt's letter from my pocket, set it on my bedside table, and changed quietly into my pajamas. Slipping into the hallway, I waited my turn in line for the bathroom, then padded back down the hall when I was done, and climbed into bed to read Aunt Vic's letter.

Usually the pages were filled with the normalcy of life in Manhattan, just like I'd asked of her.

"Won't it make you feel bad?" she'd asked.

"No," I'd said. "It will remind me of what I get to come home to."

And so, in previous letters, she'd regaled me with the latest ailments of the neighbor's dog, Mr. Bones. Mr. Bones was always having something treated. A sore on his paw, a scratch on his nose, a sniffle…

I was told of new shops coming to the neighborhood, and old ones going out. Who'd gotten married, whose daughter or aunt or cousin had had a baby. And who had received telegrams, telling them their loved one wasn't coming home. As always, Aunt Vic's letters, with small scrawled notes and drawings in the margins from Uncle Frank, were filled with details I could practically see and smell.

But this letter was different. In place of the usual jovial greeting was a more serious one. No notes from my uncle in the margins. No terribly drawn pictures of Mr. Bones. And instead of flowing thoughts and funny tidbits, there were halting and unsure sentences that made my blood run cold.

My Dearest Kate,

I am at a loss and unsure how to write this letter. The news I must convey is not happy, but there is some good to share as well. Please bear with me.

An old associate of your uncle's, thought to be dead these past many years, resurfaced. Apparently his work made it impossible for him to come forward sooner. He made contact and passed on some news. I wish I were there to tell you myself. It seems cruel to put it all in a letter, but I can't bear to keep you in the dark.

Your father has been killed. The circumstances at this time are unknown. Your mother is alive, but has apparently been ill for some time and the prognosis is not good. She is not expected to live another year. Possibly not even through the next six months.

I imagine you must feel some sense of loss, and yet maybe all you felt for them was buried when you stepped foot on that ship so many years ago. Regardless, I wish I were there in person to deliver this news. Most especially because the next bit might be harder to bear.

Catrin is alive.

I stopped reading, my mind and body growing cold and numb.

Catrin. Kitty Cat. Little sister.

Alive.

Images flashed through my mind. Her small hand in mine. Her long pale hair across my arm as she slept beside me, having once again escaped her bed for mine in the middle of the night. Her giggle when I teased her as we ran around the back garden. The sound of her cry when our mother once again smacked her, merely for laughing too loud. For being filled with joy. A child, yearning to play and sing like other children got to.

But not us. There were rules. We were to be barely seen, rarely heard. And if we needed to speak, then we must do so quietly.

I stared back down at the letter, my eyes taking in the rest of the words, but my brain unable to comprehend them, the previous words still swirling in my head.

My father was dead. My mother was ill and dying. After all the grief, abuse, and neglect we'd suffered because of them, did I care?

I waited for a stirring inside me. A sadness. Something that let me know I still cared, even just a little. But all I felt was anger. Fury that I even had to think about them. I'd have been fine to never know what fate befell them, wishing since the day I left that I'd never have to see them again.

But Catrin…

The plan had been to get her out too. Two years after me so that it wouldn't seem so suspicious and she'd be twelve and better able to keep a secret and remember the information that would keep her from falling under suspicion. But when the time came, the plan fell apart. Contacts were compromised. And then there was the explosion.

Those able to escape watched the family for days…weeks. But all the reports were the same. Catrin Holländer had been killed in the blast that had also claimed the lives of four other children and two adults at a small gathering for one of the children's birthdays. There were arguments about who planted the bomb, and fingers pointed. My father at that time had been the target of several attacks. This was the first time his only known living child had been targeted. And as far as the attackers, and the country knew, it had been a successful mission.

I had been shown an image of the funeral cut out of a newspaper, my sister's name in stark letters below, a gleaming casket at the center with my parents beside it, their heads bowed.

I'd been inconsolable for months, and never spoke her name aloud again. I'd failed her. I never should've left without her.

My mind went back to that day. I'd been on edge for weeks, and my hands shook that morning as I picked at my breakfast, trying to breathe normally, my eyes flitting from my plate to my sister, taking in her features, the way her hair had been tied back that morning by our nanny, the collar of her blouse, the way she chewed her lip in-between bites of her food as she concentrated on getting an appropriate amount on her fork.

She'd sat in my room with me, playing with one of my old dolls, while Nanny Paulina finished packing my bags.

"What do you think you'll do there?" she'd asked. "In California."

She'd practically whispered the last part, in awe that I was going to a place so far away it almost didn't seem real.

I'd forced a smile. "We'll go to the beach, shop..." I'd trailed off with a shrug, trying to downplay the lie that had been advertised to my parents as a fun, sun-filled time with my American pen pal. For them it was a chance to spread their ideologies through their child. For Catrin, it meant losing her sister and best friend for a few weeks. Something that had never happened before. Little did she know she'd be losing me for much longer.

As soon as I was all packed, Nanny Paulina, Catrin, and I stepped one by one down the grand staircase of my parents' Hamburg apartment to the main floor where they waited with my mother's good friend, Alina, who would be my escort for the trip.

"You're going to have such a wonderful time," Alina had said, embracing me. "I love California." She'd looked to Catrin then. "Next time we'll take you too."

"Perhaps next time," my mother had said. "We'll all go."

I'd swallowed hard, pasting a smile on my face and trying to seem as carefree and excited as Alina. I didn't know how she so effortlessly acted as though we weren't doing something bad. As if she weren't essentially kidnapping me—and wouldn't be killed on sight were we to be found out.

At Nanny Paulina's urging, I hugged each of my parents and then turned to Catrin, whose eyes were glossed over with tears as she reached for me.

"You'll be back soon?" she asked.

"I'll see you again," I told her, pulling her closer and breathing in her fresh, soapy scent.

"Promise?" Her wide blue eyes implored me.

"I promise, Kitty Cat," I whispered.

20

I WROTE MY aunt the following morning before Beatrice woke for our ride into town. My words were stilted. Guilt-ridden. But in the end, determined. I included a list of items I'd need. A few clothing items for the colder weather that was coming, money, the appropriate paperwork, and a list of contacts I might be able to check in with should I find myself in trouble.

"You're quiet today," Beatrice said when we arrived in town a couple hours later.

"I got a letter from home," I said, keeping my voice light. "There was some news. A family member died." I held up two envelopes in my hand. "Mind if we swing by the post office?"

"Not at all," she said. "I'm so sorry for your loss. Someone you were close to?"

"Not at all," I said.

As we moved from shop to shop, I was distracted by both thoughts of my sister, and of William. He was everywhere here, trying on hats, flipping through pages of books, smelling different cheeses, and picking out bouquets of flowers for me. Every so often one of the memories would be replaced with one of Catrin, jolting me from a place of wistfulness and making me feel as though I'd swallowed a stone, stealing the breath from my lungs, the weight of the news she was alive and I hadn't known heavy in my belly.

I caught Beatrice watching me with concern and pasted a smile on my face, making a concerted effort to bring my mind back to the man I loved, rather than the pain that threatened to swallow me whole.

I remembered watching him as we rode through town. I had adored peeking at him as we walked, or staring down at our intertwined fingers between us. He'd always caught me looking and the delight on his face was like the sun on a cloudy day.

It was overwhelming when I found him doing the same to me. Studying me as I chose this apple over that one at the market, or watching me as I woke, and smiling in a way that was at once shy and sexy, leading me to slide my body toward his, my hands pulling him close.

After I'd written to my aunt this morning, I'd pulled out another piece of paper and written to William as well. I said nothing of the letter I'd received, the loss of my father, my mother's illness, or the sister I'd long thought deceased. Instead, I told him about work, the girls at the house, and my upcoming trip into town with Beez.

"I'm sad to go without you," I'd written. "To ride past our tree and see the many things we laughed at together. To glance up at the windows of our rented room..."

At the post office I dropped both letters in the mailbox, and then Beatrice and I rode around the corner and parked our bicycles next to a café to grab some breakfast before we wandered.

"You sure you're okay?" Beatrice asked as I stirred my weak coffee and stared blindly out the window.

I put on a bright smile. "Never better."

★ ★ ★

Two weeks later I received William's and my aunt's next letters within days of one another. His was full of news from the front. Most of it grim.

"Lost five men today," he wrote. "One pushing me out of the way and taking a bullet meant for me. I'm not sure how any of us will come out of this okay."

But there were bright spots mixed in among the harder musings.

"The guys in my unit are a bunch of cards. Playing pranks to keep morale up. There's nothing like putting your boot on, only to find it filled with rocks. I thought for a minute I'd broken a toe."

He asked how our tree looked, if the town felt different without him, and said he expected me to visit our favorite bookstore. "Pick me out a truly atrocious book of poetry."

I grinned as I folded the letter and tucked it back into its envelope, pressing it to my chest before setting it aside and opening the one from my aunt.

I hadn't paid attention to the writing on the envelope until I went to slice it open. There was no return address. No stamp. Just my name written across the front in her beautiful penmanship.

"That's odd," I murmured and got up from the window seat I'd been perched in.

I entered the kitchen with the letters in my hand and a frown.

"Does anyone know anything about this letter?" I asked.

I held it up and looked around the room where five of my roommates were making late-night snacks.

"I think Luella received it," Edith said. "She said a man dropped it off."

"A man? The postman?"

She shrugged. "She just said a man. You can ask her. She went upstairs a few minutes ago."

"Thanks," I said and hurried from the room.

Grabbing my duffel bag from where I'd left it when I'd come in, I hurried up the stairs to Luella's room and knocked.

"Yes?" she called and I opened the door. "Oh. Hi, Kate. Did you get your letter?"

"I did," I said, holding it up. "Edith said a man dropped it off? What man?"

She shrugged. "He didn't leave his name. He said he was a friend of your uncle's and that he had a small care package from your aunt to give you. But he didn't want to leave it with me." She shrugged and then her eyes went wide. "Oh! And he left an address." She stood and patted her hips, and then remembered she was in a nightgown and grabbed her uniform trousers and pulled a slip of paper free.

"Here it is," she said, handing it to me. "This is where he's staying. He said you can get in contact with him there. He'll be in town for the week."

I stared down at the paper. Lee Baker, it read, along with an address of a hotel in the next town over, and the dates confirming what Luella had just said. A memory pushed its way to the front of my mind. I knew his name somehow; I just couldn't recall why.

"Thanks," I said, staring at the paper as I backed out of the room and shut the door.

"Whatcha got there?" Hazel asked as I entered our room, William and my aunt's letters in one hand, the slip of paper Luella had handed me in the other.

"A friend of my uncle's is in town. This is the address to where he's staying."

"Ooh. Is he handsome? Young? Does he maybe want a tour of the nearby towns from a local?"

I peeled my gaze from the slip of paper, the name Lee Baker nagging at me, and stared at my roommate who had struck an alluring pose.

"You're not a local," I said.

"He doesn't know that," she said, putting on a terrible version of a British accent.

I laughed.

"Well, if he's in the market, I'll be sure to tell him about your offer."

"Perfect. Because the boys around here are getting dull. All they talk about are the Jerries and their itchy feet."

I snorted, set the letters down on my bed, grabbed my pajamas, and went to stand in line for the bathroom.

A half hour later I was midshampoo when it hit me. Lee Baker was the name of a man my uncle worked with. A fuzzy memory tried to make its way in. A tall man with sandy colored hair and a nice but forgettable face. It wasn't until I was safely moved into their home in Manhattan that I learned more of my aunt and uncle's many secrets. The work they'd continued to do from the States, the lives they'd saved, including my own, and the things I'd need to store away, either physically or in my mind, for what my aunt liked to call "Just in case moments." One of which was, "Should we ever need to get information to you, we'll send it by way of Lee Baker. That's how you'll know it's from us and it's to be believed."

My heart gave a little lurch.

Lee Baker wouldn't have come if it wasn't important. He must have the items I'd requested from my aunt.

I hurriedly rinsed my hair, dried off, put on my clothes, and ran past the others waiting for the bathroom to my bedroom and my aunt's waiting letter.

"That was fast," Hazel said when I returned to the room.

"There's quite a line tonight," I said, sitting on my bed and ripping open the envelope. "I felt bad making them wait too long."

"You're too nice. I take my damn time. After what we go through? We deserve a relaxing shower."

I shook my head and unfolded the single page I'd been sent, my eyes flying over the words.

"My Sweet Niece," the letter began.

Her words were careful. She'd received my letter, was glad to hear I was well and hoped William was safe. A tidbit of life in New York, and a casual mention of "a dear old friend of your uncle's and mine will be in the area. We told him to look you up. I've entrusted him with a small package from home for you. I hope it finds you well."

Her sign-off was warm, if not formal, and that was it. One page instead of her usual three or four. It was unlike her, but I had a feeling there was a good reason she was being so cautious.

Tucking the letter back in its envelope, my heart racing in my chest, I slid beneath the covers and prayed for morning to hurry up and arrive.

"You're quiet today," Theodore shouted over the noise of the engines as we flew toward France, puffy white clouds like wisps of cotton floating past the window nearest us.

I shrugged and gave him a smile. "Just tired."

"Late night?"

I suddenly wanted to tell the truth. A truth I hadn't even told William, the weight of which made me feel sick to my stomach. What would he think of me if he knew where I'd come from and the kind of people I'd been born to? Would he understand? Would he stick around to hear how I'd been against them and their ideals, as had my aunt, who'd been working against them right under their noses for years? Or would he find me disgusting and no better than them, merely for being their daughter?

And what would he think when I told him I'd left my little sister behind, and had assumed, in a strange twist of fate, that she had been killed just as my parents had been made to believe I'd been killed.

I couldn't tell William. And I most certainly couldn't tell Theodore.

I shook my head. "No. Just another early morning."

He yawned then and I laughed and pointed to the deck of cards poking out of his chest pocket. He nodded, pulled them from their box, and started shuffling.

21

THE NEXT DAY I stood outside the Hare and Hound Hotel. It was one William and I had nearly stayed at the first time we'd decided to spend a night together. But then we'd seen the Rose Cottage, with its sprawling garden and picturesque countryside views and we'd chosen that one instead.

"Excuse me," I said to the gentleman at the counter. "I'd like to leave a message for someone staying with you."

"Of course, miss," he said and shifted some things on his side of the counter before proffering a piece of paper and an envelope. "Feel free to have a seat in the lobby if you need."

"Thank you," I said, taking the items and turning toward the lobby where a single man in a hat sat in a chair near the fireplace, a book open in his lap, a cup of tea on the table beside him.

He looked up and smiled as I sat in a nearby chair.

"Miss Campbell?" he asked, narrowing his eyes.

"Yes?" I said, my own gaze taking in his plain face…the sandy-colored hair beneath his hat. "Oh. You're—"

"Lee Baker," he said. "You can call me Lee."

"How—" I looked to the gentleman at the counter, but he was busying himself dusting the shelves behind him. "How did you know it was me?"

"I've seen your picture. Also, you look a lot like Victoria. It would be hard not to figure it out."

I smiled. He wasn't wrong. We were often mistaken for mother and daughter.

"My aunt said you have a package for me?" I said, getting up and moving to the chair nearest him.

"Indeed I do. Can I interest you in some lunch? We can discuss the contents of the package I've brought while we eat if you have time."

"Of course."

"I found a lovely restaurant just down the street a ways that does a half-decent sandwich. Will that do?"

"Lead the way."

As we walked, he talked, reminding me a lot of my uncle. He was informed on a variety of subjects, deftly moving from one to the next. He asked questions and listened intently to the answers. And there was a warmness to him that contradicted what I could only describe as a wall. My uncle Frank had the same wall. I'd mentioned it once to Aunt Vic and she'd laughed and nodded.

"It's part of what drew me to your uncle," she'd said. "He was so mysterious. And handsome, of course. Friendly, kind, attentive, intelligent…but there was a space between us I could never quite get past. Eventually, I stopped trying. I knew he loved me and assumed it was only because of his job that he was the way he was."

I'd often wondered if that was the truth, but had never asked. I stopped in the middle of the sidewalk now, my head tilted as I looked up at Lee with curiosity.

"Is it because of your job that, while you are friendly and talkative, you also seem far away?"

He chuckled. "You're observant like your aunt, I see," he said and nodded. "And to answer your question, yes. We are trained well in a variety of things and encouraged to keep up on events of the world, no matter how big or small. We're well-read, are good cooks, great drivers, enjoy a good whiskey or bottle of wine, and can ride horses with the best of them… All so that we always have something to discuss and never succumb to awkward silences that might get us questioned. But at the same time, we have to observe. The expression on someone's face, their body language, the telltale signs of a weapon hidden beneath clothing…"

"Well, that explains how my uncle knew I was hiding an extra cookie in my pajamas when I was eighteen, and how he knows how to make such a great mutton chop and lemon chiffon pie."

Lee laughed. "Exactly."

At the restaurant we were led to a table in the center of the room.

"Is it alright if we take that one?" Lee asked the hostess, pointing to a table in the far corner.

"Of course," she said brightly. "Right this way."

We were seated, tea ordered, when Lee reached into his briefcase and handed me a slender box and an envelope.

"From your aunt," he said.

I saw her neat penmanship and smiled. This envelope was thicker than the last. But the box I was confused by. There were definitely none of the winter clothes I'd requested in there. As I moved to open it, Lee stopped me.

"Best save it all for later. In the privacy of your room. What's in them is for no one else's eyes."

"Is it…" I trailed off, glancing around the room.

"The documents you requested." His voice was quiet as he

perused the menu. I set the box and letter in my handbag and picked up my own menu, my hands shaking a little as I tried to read the few options offered.

"But the other things I asked for?" I asked.

His eyes moved over the food items listed and I got the distinct impression he wasn't reading at all.

"I believe there is money included to get what you need." He lowered his menu. "Your aunt did not come by the decision to send that—" his eyes slid toward my handbag then back to me "—lightly. But apparently your request came with quite the plea. One that she didn't feel it was her place to dispel. I've not read the contents of her letter, but she did express to me what it entailed."

While his demeanor and face didn't change, his dark blue eyes bore into mine from across the table.

"What you are wanting to do is near impossible for anyone not in the upper echelons of German society. One has to be a high-ranking official, an important prisoner being moved, a movie star, or a very wealthy member of German society to move like we'll have to through the country."

"We?" I asked.

"I'm no military man. Nor am I a prisoner. And as you can probably imagine, I wouldn't make much of a movie star."

I felt my cheeks warm, not wanting to insult him. He definitely wasn't leading man material.

I frowned, trying to make sense of what he was getting at. "So you're…"

"A man of great means in a country that reveres such things," he said before snapping his menu shut and smiling up at the waiter who'd come to take our order.

A weak soup was brought out first, and as we sipped the heavily salted liquid, the chef's attempt to hide the lack of ingredients, I attempted to form questions and found myself at a loss. Who was this man? And who exactly was my uncle? I realized in this moment I knew very little about who and what he was. What organization he worked for. And how he'd been able to pull off my disappearance ten years before. My aunt had only ever given the vaguest of details, and being young and scared, I'd accepted that. But now I had questions. And I knew it wasn't likely I'd get answers. If I wanted to do this, I was going to have to trust that they knew what they were doing, and this was the man who could help me.

"I can see the questions forming in your mind," he said, resting his soup spoon on the plate beneath the bowl. "Best leave most of them for when we don't have an audience. What I can tell you is, read the letter your aunt sent. Consider her thoughts and worries. And then we'll talk again. Perhaps it will be a short conversation. Perhaps not. But read the letter first. There are things you should know about where you are wanting to go."

I nodded, setting my own spoon down, my bowl still half-full, my appetite having left me.

"If I should choose the longer conversation," I said, "you would be accompanying me?"

"There's no other way. You'd never get in on your own and not many others are available or willing to take a young woman behind enemy lines for reasons not ordered by their superiors."

I took him in then. Really took him in. From his tousled sandy blond hair, and sharp navy blue eyes, to his affable demeanor, kind face, and broad shoulders. He could easily pass for the friendly American I believed him to be. But smarten up the hair and demeanor, sharpen the clothes, and he'd look just as at home in my father's austere office in downtown Hamburg, a distinctive armband wrapped around his suit jacket.

Our sandwiches were brought out then and he changed the subject deftly, asking about my time in the Pacific, noting where I'd been stationed as if we'd spoken previously on many occasions. From there he asked me about my missions to France, told a couple amusing anecdotes about my aunt and uncle, and by the time our simple dessert was served, he'd all but disarmed me of my concerns.

"You are good at your job," I said, dabbing the corner of my mouth with my napkin before taking a last sip of tea.

"You should taste my meat loaf and apple pie."

I grinned and then stared down at the letter in my handbag, wondering what it might say about this man. Wondering if my aunt's words, that had comforted me more times than I could count, would serve to do the same now when I was contemplating something I never had since the day I stepped foot on the ship that had taken me far from my motherland. The idea that I was now thinking of returning, in the midst of our world's greatest war, was not only probably my stupidest idea, but certainly my most terrifying. And yet I had to go. I had to at least try to keep the promise I'd made so long ago to a little girl who'd trusted me with her entire little being, even if the journey itself killed me.

I touched the ring on my finger. I just hoped William would one day understand when I finally told him the truth of who I was and where I came from.

22

I DIDN'T HEAD straight home after my meeting with Lee. Instead, I rode my bike to William's and my tree, smiling at an ewe and her lamb sleeping nearby, and calling softly to them as I sat in the grass, resting my back against the trunk.

With a sigh, I pulled the letter and box from my handbag, setting both on my lap and running my hand over the lid before lifting it and taking in what lay inside.

Nestled between sheets of delicate tissue paper was a large sum of money, in both francs and reichsmarks, and the documents I'd need to return to my home country. Another new name, Lena Klein, a forged signature I'd need to practice to perfect, and a recent picture of me, stamped with what were most likely stolen but official stamps and another forged signature or two.

Blowing a breath out, I put the lid back and picked up the envelope.

The first page was filled with Aunt Vic's humor. An anecdote about Uncle Frank, a story from the corner grocer, something silly she saw in the newspaper. The second and third pages were a plea, as well as information.

> I understand why you want to go. For her. To save her like we were unable to do eight years ago. But it wasn't your fault. It was no one's fault, my dear girl. It is war. And there are hard truths to be told in war. Such as, the sister you seek may not be the same sister you knew. We don't know what she has seen, nor what she has been told. Perhaps what didn't work on you did on her. It is something worth considering, because what you are thinking is not only dangerous, but mad. And yet.
>
> I know you carry in you a deep-seated and justified anger for the treatment you and she were subjected to. I know there are things you wish to say. I bear the same need, and have for even longer than you. But I also know of the guilt you've carried for years. A guilt that needn't exist. You had no choice in the matter, my love. No choice. No means. It was not your fault, it was your uncle's and my failure. And for that, I will never forgive myself.
>
> Should you choose to go, I cannot stop you. And so I will do what I can to help keep you, my most precious treasure, as safe as I can.
>
> As you've always closely followed the news of the war, I'm sure you're aware of a great many things. But per our sources, here's what you should know in case you don't already. Hamburg is not the same city you once knew. Not just because of the Nazi forces keeping guard over it, but because of Operation Gomorrah, an air strike by the Allies that left the city in ruins. We now know that your

parents' home is still standing and your mother returned there before the strike with her loyal servant, Paulina.

We do not know where Catrin currently resides. After she was reported dead, we think she was hidden away under a different name with a family who has since moved. She does not seem to be living with them, and we are uncertain if she has contact with them. The name we discovered she'd been using while in their care has led to dead ends, making us think they, or she…or even your mother, changed it again at some point.

It is through our diminished network that she has been spotted making visits to your parents' home. They are positive it's her, despite the fact she wears a wig and doesn't stay long. When they asked around, they learned she visits every couple of months. Our people have not tried to follow her when she leaves your mother's house, as she is not their mission.

Kate, I do not know what you will encounter. Please, take to heart, she could be just as dangerous as your parents were. Keep your guard up.

Now, getting into the country could prove tricky, and that's why we've asked Lee to assist. He knows a great many people and has the resources to keep you safe and get you where you are going. Trust him. If he says something, it is to be believed. If he asks you to do something, do it. No questions asked.

I turned to the last page.

I can't send this letter without imploring you. The thought of you there, in that country being run by a lunatic, is the worst thing I can imagine. I am terrified and want to plead with you. But should you decide to go, know that we love you beyond all else, and will keep you in our thoughts every day and every night, and pray for your safe return to us.

I read the rest through eyes blurred with tears, sniffling quietly as I pulled my knees up and rested my chin on them while staring out at the valley below, tracing the distant hills with my eyes. So many hours I'd sat here with William, dreaming of our future in Seattle.

"Or maybe somewhere else?" he'd asked once. "Is there anywhere you've always dreamed of living?"

An image of blue-green waters and sunny seaside homes had flashed in my mind.

"The South of France," I'd said, and his eyes had widened, a curious grin on his handsome face.

"I've never been," he'd said. "But I think I'd quite like it. With you."

I'd told him the things I loved about the area, and he spoke in a terrible French accent that made us both laugh, staring into one another's eyes until I was breathless, my heart pounding in my chest as he pulled me to him.

I wondered what he would think of the decision I was making now. If he'd try to stop me. Or if he would understand why I had to go. She was my sister. I had to save her. There was no other choice. She was alive and I had to get her out of there.

Except, William didn't know my real story. I had told him the lies so many others had been told. The lie that kept me safe. The lie that caused me incredible amounts of guilt, because I'd gotten out.

"Tell me about your family," he'd asked the first morning we found this tree. "You didn't say much back at the hospital. Just that your sister passed away."

I'd told him my parents died when I was younger and I had

lived with my aunt and uncle in Manhattan until being sent overseas the year before. I'd glossed over the details, turning the conversation back to him and the exploits he and his younger brother had engaged in as kids, which he'd enjoyed telling me about at length as we laughed quietly.

But on this day, his attention was entirely on me and he wasn't easily dissuaded from getting information, my tactics of changing the subject not working quite as well.

"There's not much to tell," I'd said.

"Tell me how your parents died," he'd said quietly. Carefully.

I'd hesitated, staring out at the valley spread below us as I'd contemplated being honest. But in this time and place, there was danger in coming from where I did, born to the kind of people I had been born to. People whose circles had been the upper echelons of German society. People who had hosted the enemy himself in their home. I could be mistaken for something I wasn't. Even by the one I loved. And so.

"They died in a car accident," I'd said. "I was sixteen at the time."

"That must've been so hard."

I nodded, unable to meet his eyes for fear he'd see the lies within mine.

"Thankfully, I was already staying with my aunt and uncle at the time. They had a room for me for whenever I visited. They didn't hesitate to take me in permanently."

It was only then that I met his eyes, the lie now told. Mostly. What came after me moving in with my aunt and uncle was all truth.

He'd smiled sadly, squeezing my hand and, probably assuming it was hard for me to talk about, let it go, moving on to other happier subjects like me and him and our future together.

I twisted the ring around my finger now and stared at the pretty, modest stone, twinkling in the daylight.

"Please forgive me," I whispered.

I tucked the box and my aunt's letter back in my bag and then stood, stretching my back and breathing in the warm, late summer air. I wondered, once I'd left, if I'd ever come back here. Or if I'd go straight to the States and never return to this place. Maybe I'd meet William there. Maybe we'd make plans to meet somewhere else.

I looked toward the base as an airplane flew in. For as long as I could remember, this had been my purpose. To help. To try and alleviate the guilt I felt for my country's failings. I trained for it. I was proud of the lives I'd saved, the hands I'd held, and the teams I'd been part of. I hoped this wasn't the end, just a pause in my service to the country I'd adopted. And I hoped my country, its men, and my chosen sisters would understand one day when I finally stopped telling the lies and told my whole truth.

A soft breeze ruffled the leaves of the tree and I rested my hand against its beautiful old trunk, smiling as I thought of William, what a romantic he was, and our time here.

"We'll be back," I whispered, and then slipped through the stone wall and rode my bike home.

Hazel sat staring up at me from her bed, a blue scarf holding her dark hair back, brow furrowed, lips parted silently as if waiting for her brain to absorb what I'd just told her and deliver a response.

"But..." she said, her frown deepening. "For how long? Are you coming back?"

I'd told her what I'd told Marlene, the head nurse, only moments before. There'd been a death in the family and I had to go home. It wasn't a complete lie. My father had died. They didn't need to know who or that he'd passed a year ago.

"I'm planning on it," I said. "I'm not sure how long I'll be gone, but hopefully I'll be back soon."

"I'll throw a fit if you're not!" she said. "Will you leave your things here then?"

I looked around. I hadn't thought about that. But since I was planning on returning eventually…

"If that's okay with you?" I said. "I can box them up so they're out of your way though."

Or in case I didn't come back and they replaced me. But I didn't say that.

I didn't leave for a week, which left me plenty of time to work, pack, determine what I should box up and store beneath my cot for my return, shop for clothing I'd need, and write letters, both to Aunt Vic, and to William.

I'd told Lee of my decision the day after I'd made it, hurrying into town after my shift to leave a message with the front desk of his hotel. A response was waiting for me at home when I returned the following evening, tired and sad after learning I'd missed William by an hour the day before, him turning up after I'd already left.

"He was here?" I'd asked the young doctor who'd told me.

"He was," he said, a sympathetic smile on his face. "He left a letter for you. It's at the front desk."

"Was he okay then?" I asked. "He wasn't here because he was injured, was he?"

"Nah. He flew in with a plane full of injured and took a dozen or so recovered soldiers back with him. Was hoping to catch you, that's all."

I sighed. We had hoped our paths would cross often, especially as the Allies pushed their way through France, taking back what Germany had taken previously. But though my stops moved along with the border the soldiers created, we'd yet to see one another since he'd left.

I'd run to grab the letter he'd left, then hurried back to check my new crop of patients and help get them loaded for England.

My letter to Aunt Vic was full of gratefulness for her help, and apologies for not heeding her pleas and warnings.

"It's something I feel I must do," I wrote.

> I have to at least try. I know you understand. I promise not to be stupid. To not take more chances than I already am. And to do everything in my power to stay safe and alive. But should the worst happen…please know how grateful I am to you both. For your sacrifices, your bravery, and your unconditional love.

My letter to William was harder and I propped the photo of us beside me as I wrote.

"My Love," I wrote, and then sat for a long while staring at the blank page.

Rather than try and go into too much detail, I brushed past the details of who had died and why I was going home. I didn't explain the home I was referring to was not where he thought it was. I didn't give a definitive date of return, just that I would. And I promised I would write as often as I could, leaving him my address in New York, knowing that if it were possible, my aunt would find a way to get any letters he wrote to me. And as for my letters to him, I'd been told the postal system in Germany was a mess, if it existed at all, so I would just pray that they'd get to him eventually.

I hated that we'd be cut off from one another. But the pull of my past…and the little sister I'd left behind, were too strong. I had to go, but I would return as soon as I could. To him, and to the life we'd promised one another.

Making light of the trip I was about to embark on, so it would seem less than what it was, I turned my letter to other subjects, reminding him of silly moments we'd had together, hours spent in bed beneath the covers, sitting across from one another in our favorite pub, our knees scraping beneath the table, and how very much I loved him.

I will return to England, and to you, as soon as I can. I cannot wait to start the rest of our lives together.

I love you, William.

Forevermore.

Kate

23
William

Seattle
2003

I SET THE leather-bound book of poems down, the braided grass bookmark smooth and pale and fragile between my fingertips.

"I was heading to battle when I got the letter," I said.

"The letter?" Selene said.

I nodded, remembering the young soldier who had delivered it to me. We were in a makeshift barracks on our way across the country to take up arms in place of the men that had fallen. The city of Metz in France and her many fortresses had proven one of the hardest cities to take back, the Germans in underground bunkers and a central fort with a fifteen-foot reinforced concrete roof, and dozens of tunnels leading to and from it like the unwieldy legs of an octopus.

I was tired. Weary from travel and from keeping up the morale of my men. So when the letter was handed to me, wrinkled and dirty from its own travels, a weight I'd been carrying on my shoulders lifted. Until I read the contents.

"Yeah," I said. "She sent me a letter. Someone in her family had died. She didn't say who and I remember being curious. The only people she ever talked about were her aunt and uncle, whom she lived with in New York. She didn't say if it was one of them. And I knew her parents had died years before. I had no idea who this person was who was so important to her she'd leave her post and go back home. Lots of people lost loved ones while they were overseas fighting or helping, and they didn't go home. I thought maybe an old boyfriend…? Anyways, I got the letter and of course wrote her back immediately, telling her how sorry I was for her loss and if there was anything I could do, to please tell me. Not that I could do much from the mud in the middle of France."

I looked out at the water then, remembering that next month. How depleting the battle at Metz had been. The numbers we'd lost. The fear when communication and equipment failed. The desperation as we waited for more men, more weapons, and more food, our rations barely getting us through.

So many nights I'd wake from hunger, only to hear those around me suffering the same fate and shivering in the cold and damp, rain gear, like everything at that time, in short supply.

"War is strange, you know?" I said aloud. I turned to look at Selene, my eyes lingering on her features, looking for something I didn't want to name, but not finding it regardless. And yet there was something. Not now, but when she smiled. And those eyes…

"Strange how?" she asked.

"Oh." I waved a hand, laughing at myself a little. She hadn't come here to listen to an old man wax poetic about the tolls of war.

"Tell me," she said and my heart hitched inside my chest.

There it was. Something in her voice. A timbre I knew I'd heard before.

I shook my head, trying to shake it loose from me. I was imagining it. Wanting to believe something wouldn't make it so.

"You're kind to listen to an old man's ramblings," I said.

"I love history. Love what it can teach us, if only we pay attention. Which so many of my generation do not." She smiled and I peered at the way her lips lifted on either side before returning to the conversation.

"I was just thinking of that battle. Something I haven't done in ages. Like most people who fought in the war, or any war for that matter, whether it be with weapons or some other kind of trauma, we don't like to talk about it. Reminiscing is painful. Internal scars threatening to tear and break open..." I laughed then. "Can you tell I was married to a writer for years?"

She tapped the stack of letters on the table.

"I think you have always been something of a writer yourself, William. Credit where credit is due?"

"Perhaps." I shrugged and went on. "Metz. I'd fought before then. And I fought after. But the letter from Kate sat strange with me. It was too bright. Not that she wasn't often bright in her messages to me. But it felt forced. She listed so many memories we'd made together. And that worried me. It was as if she expected something bad to happen."

"To you?"

"That's what I assumed at the time. But then..."

I took a long drink of my beer, rubbing the braid of grass between my fingers once more, my gaze resting on the book of poetry.

"But then what?" she asked.

"But then one after another, my letters to her went unanswered." I met her eyes across the table, my own burning with emotion at the memory. "I never heard from her again."

Her breath was soft, her chest rising and falling as she watched me. After a moment, she gave me a small smile and nodded.

"I think I may know why," she said, and pulled out another book.

24

Kate

France
October 1944

"READY?" LEE ASKED.

I took in a long breath, looking around the small but elegant hotel room I'd been in for the past three days.

The last time I was in Paris I'd been thirteen. As usual, my parents had sent Catrin and me off daily with our nanny while my father met with friends and investors, and my mother shopped and met friends for tea. In the evenings, the two of them went out to expensive dinners before attending a myriad of shows they raved about the following morning over breakfast.

On the rare occasion, they hosted a dinner in our penthouse apartment. I'd find a dress and accompanying accessories in my room with explicit instructions.

"At your mother's nod, you are to curtsy," Nanny Paulina would tell me. Or, "You are to kiss each of your parents' cheeks upon entering the room, circulate for thirty minutes, and then return to your room."

Circulating with a room full of adults was a most excruciating request. I both didn't know how and didn't want to start a conversation with any one of them. But I dared not complain. To complain was to be punished later, after the guests had gone, when no one but my sister and Nanny Paulina could bear witness.

When Catrin and I weren't being put on display, little dollies to be dressed in designer clothes to be shown off, twirled, and pinched, we got to explore the city with Nanny Paulina whom, out of eyesight and earshot of my parents, became my conspirator. My confidante. And many times, my only friend in the world, besides Kitty Cat.

It was strange to return to the city as an adult after so much had happened. But with Paris now back in the hands of the Allies, it was the best starting point to what Lee had planned. Thanks to his connections and work within the government, we were able to fly straight into the city and take two rooms at a hotel he'd chosen "because I am familiar with the staff," he'd told me.

I knew from a conversation we had before embarking on our mission that he would need to tread carefully in France. While he didn't expect to run into any of his former German colleagues, "One can never be too careful," he'd said. And thus, we were staying somewhere discretion could be counted on. As could the information he was given about the comings and goings of other guests.

While he conducted business during the day, about which I asked no questions, having learned early on from my aunt and uncle that sometimes being in possession of information was more dangerous than not, I explored the city, staring up at windows still blackened with paper, empty shop fronts, and piles of trash collected and waiting to be taken away.

Everywhere there were vacancy signs. Homes of those who had left or were taken up for grabs by desperate landlords trying to make a buck. But what if they came back, I wondered? It angered and saddened me to learn what some had done to survive. Something Lee had warned me not to speak of.

"The French, as you probably know, are a proud people. They are not proud that their government chose not to fight. There is a lot of shame. Tread carefully, and if you speak to anyone, I recommend only speaking of the weather."

But he needn't have worried. The only words I exchanged were with the young woman waiting tables in the café on the corner when I'd ordered food, which was scarce, rations still in place as the war raged on in other parts of the world. Restaurants where Nazis had frequented, ensuring food was brought in for their own consumption, were still benefitting from the business they'd created. American, British, and French soldiers and high-ranking officers took the enemy's place at the bars and tables, their uniforms hard to get used to, a reminder of the men who had occupied those spaces for the past four years, but the company admittedly much friendlier. They reminded me of William, and when I'd first seen the American insignia my heart had leaped, thinking maybe he'd be here. But unfortunately I never saw those faded, denim-blue eyes among the many that swung my way.

Even though I was used to being surrounded by soldiers, it felt strange to sit among them in this place, sipping my weak coffee and trying to enjoy the pastry before me when so many in the city were still hungry. And I knew I looked out of place, a young, blonde woman on her own with her clean, pressed clothes, styled hair, and money to buy fresh baked goods. I could see the questions in their eyes, but kept my body language uninviting, my eyes turned toward the window to discourage their approach.

While I'd spent the daylight hours walking the city, giving

shops what little business I could to help support them without increasing my load by too much, by nightfall I was back in my room where I waited for Lee to knock on my door at seven with an offer to join him in the restaurant downstairs. I was introduced as his niece and doted on by the staff while he told me a false account of his day in case anyone were listening.

I had no idea what business he'd been tending to when he was gone all day, but I assumed now some of it had to do with the car I'd seen him drive up in only a few minutes before, leaving it at the curb, the doorman keeping watch while he came up to get me. It was time to make our next move.

I grabbed my handbag, gave the room a last look, picked up my valise, and closed the door behind me.

Three weeks, he'd estimated, to get me from Paris, through northern France, to Germany and Hamburg. His plan was to follow in the footsteps of the Allied troops gaining back ground ahead of us. We were to head east first to Nancy, then up through Metz into Germany where we'd cross the border and head to Luxembourg, which was also now controlled by the Allies.

"From there it will possibly get trickier," he'd warned me the night before over a small berry cobbler I couldn't believe existed. "My contacts in Luxembourg will direct us on the safest route. But even they won't be able to be absolutely certain what we'll come up against in some of the smaller towns. Frankfurt has yet to be taken by our men. We should be okay with our papers and my contacts there, but we'll need to be alert. It certainly wouldn't do if we were to hand over the wrong set of papers to the wrong set of hands."

"And after Frankfurt?" I'd asked.

"Everything north of Frankfurt is still under German control." He leaned forward then and spoke softly. *"Wie ist dein Deutsch?"*

How was my German.

I grinned. I knew we would not have left England if he hadn't been assured by my aunt and uncle that my German was perfect. What no one knew was that the three of us still spoke it at home when no one else was around.

"Gut," I answered now, receiving a nod in return.

I set my fork on the plate and slid it away from me, resting my elbows on the table.

"Do you have people in Hamburg as well?" I asked.

"I do. It could get precarious though if the Allies are moving in."

"But won't that be good for us? For me?"

"It depends. You will be posing as...well...you. Should the Allies come, if you present as a German citizen, you could be jailed or worse. Sent to a work camp...or hurt." He didn't expand on that last part before changing the subject. "If you present as an American and they find your German papers, you could be brought in for questioning."

"For what?"

"For being a German spy."

I nodded, sweat dampening beneath my arms, my heart racing.

"And should the Germans somehow find you out," he said. "They will deem you a traitor." His eyes turned steely, sending a shiver down my spine. "They are not kind to traitors, Kate."

I took in a shuddering breath.

"So, we will do this as thoughtfully as we can," Lee said. "I have done my best to think of every situation and outcome, and I will give you names and addresses should you find you need to hide and I'm not around."

I'd spent much of the night awake after that. And when I woke in the morning after only a couple hours' sleep, I ran to the bathroom to be sick.

I'd never spent much time in the French countryside, my parents preferring the glamour of Paris or the sea views in Monaco or Nice instead every summer of my childhood. We stayed for a month at a time in beautiful hotel rooms that took up entire floors, our parents out nearly every hour of the day and night, Catrin and me racing ahead of Nanny Paulina as she took us for long walks near the Seine or by the sea.

But it was in the South of France that I got to experience childhood in a way I imagined other kids did. It was there I had freedom to play and explore, sing and dance, and run… as fast as my coltish legs could carry me, Catrin on my heels, Nanny Paulina urging us on from behind. It was there that our parents didn't force us to join them, their days too busy with their friends to bother with us. And so we flourished, building memories cocooned in laughter, and whispering promises to the setting sun every time we left that one day we'd be back.

I stared out the window of the car Lee drove, remembering those sunny summer days as I took in the barren fields stretched out around us. We drove through towns like La Ferté-Gaucher, Sézanne, where we stayed a night in a small hotel with hardly any staff, and what was left of Vitry-le-François, which, from the looks of it, had suffered a terrible fire. Huts had been erected near the rubble that had once been homes and shops, small faces peering out from windows as we drove slowly by, the American insignia on the car on full display, letting them know they had nothing to fear from the people inside.

Every new town we entered we were stopped and asked to show our identification, questioned about our whereabouts, and the car was checked.

He parked in the newest town we'd be staying the night in, and we retrieved our bags from the trunk, my shoulders sagging a little as we walked into the entrance of the hotel. It was much like the ones before it. Small, quaint, with hardwood floors, flowery wallpaper, a gleaming if slightly shabby front desk, and the person standing behind it looking slightly shocked to see someone not in uniform approaching him.

"Do you have two rooms for the night?" Lee asked.

It wasn't always guaranteed there'd be openings. Many times soldiers took up the rooms. But we'd only had trouble once so far, when there was a single room available and nothing else. Lee had given me the bed and had made himself a space on the floor. I'd felt a bit uncomfortable, lying in the dark with this man I hardly knew, despite our long hours in a car together. I'd wondered if he did too. But his breath slowed quickly as he fell to sleep, and so I'd turned over and done the same.

"We do," the gentleman at the desk said. "And a dinner service at six in the dining room. Shall I make you a reservation?"

"Please."

While Lee gave the man his information, I moved to the large front window and stared at the scene out front. Not that there was much of one. A woman and her young child, bundled against the cold, hurried into a shop across the street, while a handful of soldiers meandered, chatting as they went, their eyes taking in everything.

"Is there a post office?" I asked, turning back to the concierge.

His lips settled into a straight line.

"There is," he said. "But it's been closed the past three years. The man who ran it was..." He took in a breath and looked away, composing himself before turning back to me. "Well, he's no longer here. I'm not sure if it will ever reopen. We've been driving two towns over to send mail, but no one's received much. The Germans made communication nearly impossible in these parts. If you have something you need to send though, I can see about getting it out for you."

"Thank you," I said, resting my hand on my purse, where a letter I'd written to William four days ago sat safe inside. "Perhaps I'll just wait and check the next town we stop in."

I wondered if he'd written to me. If so, I hoped my aunt would find a way to forward his letters to me. But with the postal system not even existing in some cities, I was starting to have my doubts. What would he think if I wasn't able to get a letter to him? If he wrote to me and his letters went unanswered?

My eyes filled at the thought.

"You alright?"

I jumped, not realizing Lee had finished checking us in and was standing before me, holding out the key to my room.

I sniffed and took the key. "Just tired," I said, and followed him up the stairs to our second-floor rooms.

25

WE WERE TWO weeks into the trip, staying in rooms at the house of one of Lee's contacts, when I came down for breakfast and found the two men talking quietly. They stopped as I entered, and I pointed to the coffeepot.

"Help yourself," our host, a tall, all-American-looking gentleman said. "There are pancakes in the oven."

I raised my eyebrows and opened the oven door, hardly believing what he said was true. But there they were. Real American pancakes. There wasn't any syrup, but I made do with a sprinkling of sugar.

"Shall I..." I pointed to the door that led to the dining room.

"No," Lee said. "Please. Join us. You're going to find out anyways. Might as well hear it from the source."

My stomach turned over. Something it was doing a lot these days, lack of sleep and fear making me feel sick almost daily.

"Hear what?" I asked, sinking into one of the four kitchen chairs.

It was then that I noticed my surroundings.

We'd gotten in late the night before, Lee pushing to get us to this checkpoint to keep us on the schedule he'd created.

"What happens if we don't get there today?" I'd asked when we were still hours away.

"We might miss our contact," he said. "Like me, he moves around a lot. Even now as the Allies are taking back territory, we still have jobs to do, information to gather and share. I'm not just getting you to Germany. My presence here serves a great number of purposes. We'll have to press on into the night and hope we make it by curfew so no one shoots us."

He'd winked and I'd given a faint smile in return.

We arrived at our destination within minutes of curfew, the sky a steel gray that was darkening by the minute. Our host, a man called Mr. Jones, answered the door with a candle in hand and motioned for us to hurry inside. There were introductions, a small meal by candlelight, and then I was shown to my room where I hadn't been able to make out much, just that there was a bed, an attached bathroom, and a glass of water on the bedside table for me. But now...

In the hutch behind Mr. Jones was a menorah. Beside it was a saying, framed, the words on it in Hebrew, which I recognized from seeing a similar item in Ruthie's home so long ago.

Lee tapped my hand with his forefinger and I jumped. The two men exchanged a look, and Mr. Jones turned to see what I was looking at.

"Ah," he said, his voice soft. "Yes. This home apparently belonged to a Jewish family. Something I didn't realize at first, but figured out when I moved in and did a little investigating. One never knows if the home belonged to someone who escaped the war, or was taken from their home against their will. Of course, the family could have escaped and have plans to come back. As such, when I found the box of items hidden in the basement, I brought them up here where they belong."

I nodded, but my throat was tight, my stomach threatening again. It was all a bit too much. I'd seen a lot of things. Injuries that were enough to make one hate their own race for the destruction they were capable of, but sitting at the table of a Jewish family that may never return reminded me of Ruthie, and a wave of grief washed over me.

"Are you alright?" Lee asked.

I took in a long breath and nodded.

"Yes, thank you. What were you two discussing before I interrupted?"

"Right," Mr. Jones said. "Well, we've hit a bit of a snag in the plan. The car I was to provide for you got waylaid, the driver delivering it detained for official reasons he can't immediately untangle himself from. This is not necessarily a bad thing though. The roads north of Luxembourg, where the car was to be, are a bit treacherous at the moment. The Allies are still working to push forward farther into Germany. So, I've come up with a bit of a workaround."

As he explained the plan, dread crept up my spine like icy fingers slowly stepping one vertebra at a time. The plan was to drive north and then ditch the car we'd been using in Luxembourg. From there we'd take a rowboat in the dead of night up the Moselle River to a location farther north.

"Is the river not patrolled?" I asked.

"It has been," Mr. Jones said. "But the guards along the path have lessened considerably. So long as the boat is kept near the riverbank, you should go undetected."

I looked to Lee. "I've never rowed a boat before."

"We'll have a guide," he said. "He's done the trip several times and knows the different areas and what to listen and look for."

"There's no other way?" I asked.

"Not for this part of the trip."

I nodded, my heart racing in my chest as I considered what

I'd just been told. I didn't like the idea of being on a river in the middle of the night. Not being able to see, in temperatures that were nearly unbearable. On the water they'd be worse. What if we capsized? What if we were seen and shot? There'd be nowhere to swim or run. We'd most likely drown.

"Kate?" Lee said. "Are you okay with this?"

I pictured Catrin, her blond curls and wide blue eyes the same shades as mine. Her small fingers constantly reaching for me, in the garden, at the beach, in my bed that she'd snuck into once again, her voice seeking me out at all hours of the day.

Our mother had just begun to scrutinize her the way she'd been doing to me for years. And then I'd left her, barely able to tell her, warn her, or comfort her, because in doing so, I might risk the plan.

I remembered when it had begun for me. My mother's impersonal demeanor as she asked probing questions and inspected my body. I'd been young. Younger than Catrin. But also less agreeable. I recalled being sixteen and taking a bath, enjoying the solitude after a particularly uncomfortable dinner with my parents, Catrin in her own bathroom being tended to by Nanny Paulina. My mother had barged in and demanded I stand so she could inspect me, pinching the skin at my waist and inner thighs before making me turn so she could see my backside.

"Your father mentioned you look heavier. I see he's right. Have you been snacking between meals?"

"Of course not, *Mutter,*" I'd said, turning to face her once more.

The crack of her hand meeting my cheek echoed throughout the bathroom, the sound circling back and settling in my head, the force causing me to slip. I grabbed the side of the bathtub as she stood glaring down at me.

"I don't believe you," she'd said. "Until you stop. Until I see some change in your appearance, you will not be allowed breakfast and your dinner will be cut in half."

I hadn't said a word. It wouldn't matter if I did. I'd merely nodded and waited until she'd left the room to let the tears fall.

I looked back at Lee, fury burning in my veins. I'd left Catrin with that monster. I had to make it right.

"Yes," I said. "I'm more than okay."

26

THE CROSSING OF the border from France to Germany was daunting, my entire body on alert as we left one country for a much more dangerous one.

"You okay?" Lee asked, his voice soft.

It was the first time since we started out on this mission that he'd been quiet. Up until now, he'd kept conversations flowing in our hours in the car and during our many meals together. Like my uncle, he was a skilled conversationalist. His silence stoked the fire of my fears.

I glanced at him, watching him watch the road, his eyes seeming to take in every inch of the small town we were driving toward and the short line of cars idling at a checkpoint littered with armed guards.

I glanced at Lee, considering his question, my hands gripping my purse as I prepared to present my identification at the checkpoint.

"Yeah," I said.

He nodded, pulling to a stop behind two other cars. When it was our turn, a guard stepped up to the driver's side window and held out a hand for our papers as a tank rumbled by on the passenger side, shaking the car…and my nerves.

The guard handed back our IDs and paperwork and waved us through. As we drove through a small town that looked like so many of the previous towns we'd passed, Lee pulled out a small square of paper from his pocket and handed it to me.

"Commit this to memory and then give it back," he said.

"What is it?" I asked, unfolding the small square and reading the name and address written on it.

"If for some reason we get separated before Hamburg, that's my contact there. She can hide you if need be, provide information, or help you escape."

"How will she know to trust me?"

"You'll give her my name."

"Lee Baker?" I asked and he shook his head.

"Maximillian Brunner," he said, giving me a sidelong look. "Or just Max."

"Is that…"

"That's my name here. That's the name that will let her know you mean her no harm and are in need of assistance. It will also mean she'll do whatever she can to help you. Even risk her own life."

"But—" I stared at him, but his eyes were once again on the road.

I hated the idea that yet another person might have to risk their life for me. What I was doing was dangerous, selfish, and downright stupid. The only reason I was okay with Lee taking me was that he was apparently going this way anyways. Though I of course realized the addition of someone with no experience at moving through countries at war was a terrible imposition.

As the car rolled quietly through the streets, I looked out the window silently, staring up at buildings hollowed by fire, ash catching the sunlight and swirling, resting on the surface of the vehicle as we pressed on to a destination I hadn't been told about.

At a tall, stark building we stopped. But as I reached for the handle, Lee stopped me.

"Stay here. I'll be but a moment."

I nodded and sank back into the seat, making sure both doors were locked after he exited. Despite the fact that we were in friendly territory, and had been for days, I couldn't shake the feeling that we weren't safe at all. Maybe because of the forged documents hiding in the lining of my valise. Maybe because I was terrified someone would take one look at my pale hair and eyes and assume I was the enemy.

Maybe it was just because we were in Germany, the root of the evil that had spawned dangerous arms and a viselike grip on so many, causing me to question almost daily if they were so weak-minded that they were easily convinced.

Or had they always been that way? Evil, waiting for the okay.

I jumped at the sound of Lee trying to get in the car. Seeing him through the window, I reached over and unlocked his door.

"I'm told there's a post office with a staff not far from here," he said, getting into the car. "Shall we?"

"Yes, please," I said, hugging my purse to me.

I'd taken to writing William every day. Sometimes twice a day. Some were long and meandering letters, others short bursts of thought, opinions, and ideas. I missed him. Missed hearing his thoughtful responses. His laughter. The feel of his skin on mine. I hated that I hadn't been able to send him my words. He must be so worried. And not knowing how he was drove me mad.

The post office was indeed close by and I smiled a little, my chest lifting with a breath of happiness as we pulled in and parked.

"I'll only be a minute," I said, opening the door.

It felt strange. Almost normal. To be walking up the steps to the post office, my purse strap over my shoulder, a hopeful spring in my step. Just a young woman mailing letters to her love. I smiled and glanced at my reflection in the window as I strode toward the front door, grimacing a little as I noticed the wrinkled state of my blouse and trousers. Hours in a car in clothes that had been hand-washed, wrung out, and hung to dry over a radiator time and time again these past several days hadn't been kind to my clothing. But as I stood in line behind several others, I saw I had nothing to worry about. I didn't stand out. We all looked worn and wrinkled.

"How can I help you?" a friendly young woman who looked to be my age asked in heavily accented German.

I placed the stack of letters I'd written before her.

"I'd like to mail these, please."

She nodded, checking the address on each, then gave me a price. As I dug the money from my wallet I asked, "Do you know how long until they'll arrive at their destination?" To which she laughed.

"Could be next week. Could be next year. One never knows these days with the train system an absolute mess."

My heart sank as I handed over the correct change.

"Well, thanks," I said, staring longingly after the letters as she turned and dropped them in a bin. Part of me wanted to tell her to stop. To please give them back. I'd send them from another location. But in an instant they were out of sight and she was looking past me, her voiced raised a little as she said, "Next!"

I ate dinner alone that night, Lee having plans to dine elsewhere.

"I won't be too late," he'd said from the doorway of my room where he'd stood after his usual abrupt knocking that nearly always sent my heart racing in fear. "I'll have the front desk ring you when I return."

I'd nodded. It was usual for him to have me rung by the

concierge after he'd returned from one of his briefings, knowing it made me feel safer to have him nearby. Despite being in friendly territory, there was still cause to be on alert, he'd informed me time and time again.

"The Germans could regain footing and push back," he'd told me.

I was always on alert.

As usual, when left to my own devices for a meal, I headed to the hotel restaurant and asked to be sat in a far corner away from the rest of the diners, then pulled out a book in hopes of warding off any single men who might consider the sight of a young woman eating alone to be an invitation for company. The book was to show I was perfectly content in my aloneness. It often worked, but sometimes…

"Excuse me."

Steeling myself, I looked up.

The soldier standing across from me, his hand on the back of the chair I'd forgotten to ask the waiter to take away, reminded me a bit of William with his blue eyes and dark hair. But the look in his eyes was one that concerned me. One I was very familiar with. I'd seen it hundreds of times as I'd transferred injured men from the front. It was the look of a man in distress.

The invisible armor I'd encased myself in melted away and I set down my book and leaned forward.

"How can I help you?" I asked, my voice low and soft. It was my "nurse" voice. The one I reserved for those in pain.

"Are you using this chair?" he asked.

I smiled and shook my head, watching him carefully, taking in the wear on his face and the haunted look in his eyes.

"I'm not," I said. "You can take it."

"Thank you, miss," he said, ducking his head and sliding the chair from the table.

"Are you—" I stopped as his eyes met mine again. I slid my hand across the table toward him. "Are you okay?"

His eyes moved across my face as if unsure where a safe space to land was, my own gaze too knowing for him to meet it again. He shifted his gaze to the table and nodded, then tightened his grip on the chair, mumbled "thank you" again, and went back to the group he was with, a boisterous lot of young men in American uniforms.

A couple glanced my way as their comrade returned to them, clapping him on the back as if he'd accomplished something grand. Perhaps they'd sent him over. Maybe they'd been trying to bolster his spirits by having him talk to the pretty girl in the corner. Maybe they saw it too. That look of loss in his eyes. The sign of having seen too much, the heart and soul and mind churning through images of human life being taken over and over again while plastering on a fake smile in the aftermath and downing a beer in hopes of drowning out the screams, the sights, and eventually, maybe even his own life?

Or maybe they didn't see it at all, and he'd be just one more eventual casualty to this war, the toll of all he'd been through too much to bear, the nightmares claiming his mind for their own.

I turned my book back over and stared down at the pages. But the words blurred as my thoughts turned to William.

"How do you do it?" I'd asked him one night as we'd lain curled around one another in the bed of our rented room.

"How do I do what, my love?" he'd asked, nuzzling my neck.

When I didn't immediately answer, he'd pulled back and met my gaze.

"Ah," he'd said. "That. How do I kill another human being?"

I'd closed my eyes for a moment. That wasn't exactly the question.

"Not how do you do it," I'd said. "Just...are you affected by it?"

He'd kissed my head then and rolled onto his back, staring at the ceiling.

"Of course I'm affected. It's a terrible feeling to take a life, even as I know I'm not only saving my own, but my men's lives, those of the country we're fighting in, and everyone back home. And yet, there is never a part of me that feels like it's right. I always wish there were another way. And as time goes on, it sickens me how numb I become to it. It makes me mad. No one should become numb to taking a life. But I think it must be the way the brain protects itself. Which unfortunately, as we've both seen, isn't the case for everyone."

His voice had caught at the end and when I'd looked up, I'd seen a tear tracing a path down the side of his face to the pillow beneath his head.

"I'm sorry," I'd whispered, and then slid my body on top of his and tried to help him forget.

The waiter brought the check and I paid for my dinner, gathered my book and purse and got to my feet. As I moved through the restaurant toward the front door, something pulled at me and I found myself walking toward the group of men and the young soldier who had asked for the chair.

He turned at the touch of my hand on his arm and again I was reminded of William, though a little less so now as I saw his gaze was now swimming in the effects of alcohol, shoving some of the earlier pain I'd seen aside.

"Take care of yourself," I said.

For a moment he sobered, taking in my words and nodding. But a second later he turned back to his comrades, the noise of the table luring him back under its spell.

I moved toward the exit, smiling at the concierge as I stepped out of the restaurant and into the hotel.

"Good night," I said, heading for the staircase.

"Miss?" the concierge said.

"Yes?"

"Mr. Baker is waiting for you in the bar."

"Oh," I said, frowning. I hadn't expected him back so soon. "Thank you."

"How was your meal?" Lee asked after I'd reentered the restaurant and took a seat at the bar beside him, eyeing his half-empty drink. He'd been here at least a little while and I wasn't sure if it should worry me that his meeting had ended quickly or not.

"It was fine," I said, waiting for him to tell me why we were meeting. "Is… Are we…" I wasn't sure what my question was.

"We leave tonight," he said and then reached across the table and tapped a finger on my engagement ring. "Hide this."

Now I had several questions, but I knew asking them was useless. I nodded and got to my feet.

"I'll go pack."

27

WITH CURFEW STILL in place, we didn't have much time. Thankfully, I hadn't unpacked much, just my toiletries, the picture of William and I, and my pajamas, all of which I gathered and placed back in my valise before staring down at my ring. But I didn't have time to reminisce. Pulling it from my finger, I searched the lining of my little suitcase for a loose stitch, finding one and giving it a hard yank. Managing to make a small hole, I slid the ring in and zipped the case closed. After giving the room a quick last look to make sure I hadn't missed anything, I opened the door and hurried downstairs.

The drive was relatively quick, Lee watching our surroundings as usual while I sat in my seat, my hands clasped between my thighs, palms damp with sweat.

We pulled off the road and he parked behind a building and then turned off the ignition and turned to me.

"Should we be caught, there will be questions," he said. "Why we're here. Where we're headed. Who I am to you. None of that worries me. We've practiced all that. What does worry me is time. We have a window to get where we're going and retrieve the vehicle that will get us up through the country."

"I understand," I said.

He nodded and glanced out the windshield before turning to me once more.

"We'll be meeting an old friend of mine. Klaus. He will help get us up the river to where we need to go. Your job will be to sit in the middle of the boat with your head down while we row. Understood?"

"Yes."

"You'll need to have your identification readily available."

"Which one?"

"Both," he said. "Stow one in your pocket and one in your bag. It is crucial you remember which one is in which place."

"Okay," I said, and pulled both sets of identification from my bag.

"Should we get caught, they will likely question you first."

"Why?" I asked, and immediately wanted to bite my tongue for asking questions.

"Protocol. Ask the youngest one. Ask the female. They assume if you're a child or a woman you will be more easily intimidated and more likely to tell the truth, rather than the story you were told to tell. They will be harsh. Rude even. And desperate. Looking for a last chance to make their mark before the Allies inevitably push them back yet again. This makes them more dangerous than ever. So be smart."

"Okay," I said, a tremor in my voice.

"What's my name?"

"Maximillian Brunner."

"Spell it."

I did as he asked, he nodded, and then opened his door while I followed suit on my side.

The boat was a small walk from the car. Down a path, through some trees, and then I could hear it, the clunk of the oars being jostled by the water below.

The silhouette of a man appeared and I sucked in a silent breath. Klaus, our contact. A moment later my valise was taken from me and a hand, calloused and cold, took mine and helped me into the rowboat that would take us north, farther into Germany, and closer to the place I'd once called home.

It was colder on the water and my teeth chattered as the men got situated, each grabbing a set of oars while I shifted the pile of what seemed to be blankets beneath me.

"Unter," Klaus said, his voice gruff.

Under?

I turned and looked to Lee, now Max, on the seat behind me.

"Lie down," he said quietly. "Beneath the blankets. Out of sight."

Carefully, so as not to rock the boat too much, I did what I was told, grateful to have so many layers around me, insulating me, but not liking being blind to where we were going.

I felt the boat tilt as we pushed off from the bank, and then we were gliding along through the pitch-black, the only sounds the muffled slap of water against the sides of the boat, and every so often an oar scraping gently along the edge. I prayed we wouldn't get caught, but more than that, I hoped we wouldn't capsize. The water would be too frigid to fight against, and death would be slow and much too cruel.

I wasn't sure how long we'd been on the water, but my body began to ache from being curled in one position on the hard, cold boat floor. I shifted carefully, repositioning my legs and hips, arms and shoulders. Above me I thought I heard the sound of voices whispering, but when I stilled, there was nothing.

The rocking of the boat as it glided across the water began to lull me and I started to drift, my eyelids closing, my breath slowing, until I was asleep.

"Scheisse."

I woke to the word, whispered with intensity, and waited, listening.

A bark in the distance and shouting. The shifting of feet on the floor of the boat.

"Lena."

For a moment, I forgot my new name.

The blankets covering me were pulled back and I was staring up into the face of Max. "We've been spotted," he whispered. *"Vorbereiten."*

Prepare.

I pulled in a shaky breath as I sat up, my body aching with the effort, and glanced over my shoulder to where the commotion was coming from, terrified by the half-dozen flashlights cutting through the darkness in our direction, voices calling out for us to *stoppen. Kommen.* Footsteps hurrying toward us. The sound of bodies pushing through the brush as Max and his friend maneuvered the boat toward the riverbank, calling back our compliance.

As soon as the boat touched ground, a light was shone in my face and I was hauled by my arms by two men and pulled up the steep slope of the embankment until I was standing alone at the top, my accomplices having been left in the boat, four soldiers pointing guns at them.

"Identification," one of the men barked at me.

I nodded and pointed to the boat.

"Meine tasche," I said, my native tongue rolling off my tongue as though I'd never stopped speaking it.

He shouted to the others to get my bag. A moment later it was shoved at me.

Hands shaking, I reached in, finding the little zipper inside and grasping on with numb fingers, pulling it with some effort until it released. I handed the man my ID and waited for the questions I knew would come next.

"Lena Klein," he said, reading my name and looking at the photo and then me.

I nodded.

"And what, Miss Klein, are you and these two gentlemen doing out on the river at this late hour?"

The words were cordial, the tone was not, and though I was quaking inside, Max had prepared me for this, taking me in the car two days before to a spot where no one could see or hear as he shouted in my face over and over until I could answer without fail each of his questions.

"I am going home," I said simply. For it was the truth.

My innocent answer seemed to stump him for a moment and so I continued.

"We got trapped behind enemy lines when the Allies came in. We've been in hiding. Biding our time. We'd hoped they'd get pushed back and were waiting it out. Unfortunately, they didn't and we waited too long."

He glared at me, shining his too-bright light in my eyes, trying to shake me. I feared my knees might give. I could assess an open stomach wound without so much as a tremor, but this... At any moment I knew this man, just for the fun of it...just because no one would stop him, could shoot me if he thought my answer not good enough.

"And who are they?" He sneered and turned his light on the men in the boat.

"Klaus, our guide," I said, gesturing to one man and then the other. "And Max, my uncle."

Again, he glared at me and then motioned to the men watching the boat. There was a splash as one of the oars fell overboard, and the two men were hauled from the boat and shoved by rifle barrel up the hill.

"Papiere!" the soldier shouted and both men pulled their identification papers from deep within their layers of clothing.

Klaus's were inspected and then passed to one of the other

soldiers who gave it a long look before handing it roughly back to its owner. But it was upon the inspection of Max's papers that the soldier examining it took a small step back, his entire demeanor changing.

"You are Maximillian Brunner," he said, eyes wide as he held out the papers. *"Entschuldigen sie, herr."*

Max's demeanor too had changed now, his shoulders pulled back, his facial expression haughty as he took his time collecting his papers, gaze flicking over the young man before him that had stood so tall before, but now shrunk a bit in size, worry prevalent in his eyes.

"Apologies are not necessary," Max said, smiling coldly as he tucked his papers away inside his jacket. I watched in fascination as he smoothed back his hair, his chin raised. It was not just that he seemed like a different person, he looked like one too, all by the mere act of changing his body language. "You were only doing your job, isn't that right, soldier?"

The way he said "soldier" made it sound like an insult and the younger man flinched.

"Yessir," he said.

"But now that you have interrupted our little journey and scared my niece, perhaps you would like to provide us a place to sleep for the night and a vehicle in the morning to resume our journey?"

My blood turned cold. How badly I wanted to turn and stare at him. To grab his sleeve and beg no. Not here. Not with these people. But I couldn't. To do so would turn their eyes back on us, and perhaps they'd demand to search us more thoroughly, finding our hidden IDs in the process.

"Absolut!" the soldier said, and then shouted to his men to gather our things and bring the boat ashore. "You will stay with me, of course. I have plenty of room. I am Hauptmann Keller, at your service."

"Wonderful," Max said and fell in step beside him, the two

men suddenly acting like old chums as I glanced worriedly at Klaus, who merely gave me a grim smile and held his hand out for me to follow along.

Two of the soldiers, who'd only minutes ago been aiming guns at us, carried our bags. I kept an eye on them, making sure neither got curious and slid a hand inside our things.

The accommodations of the young captain weren't grand, but the house had two stories, a large downstairs, a fire in the fireplace…and it smelled of food.

"You are hungry?" he asked.

I didn't want to say yes, but my stomach grumbled quietly and along with the others, I nodded.

"Come. Sit. I'll have the cook bring you some food."

I tried not to look at my surroundings. Tried to ignore the furnishings that had clearly belonged to a family and not this single man. But it was impossible to miss the small chair built for a child at one end of the table.

"How long were you in France?" Hauptmann Keller asked Max, taking a bottle of wine out of a cabinet and holding it up for him to see. Max nodded and the bottle was uncorked, the dark red liquid poured into four glasses and set before each of us. "It was rumored you'd gone to Switzerland."

Max laughed. "Switzerland, Spain, America… I heard the rumors too. But I've been in France. Found a nice penthouse in Paris and another in Nice. Was stupid of us to stay as long as we did. Didn't believe we had anything to worry about. Alas…" He shook his head, putting on a grim face as our host nodded in sympathy.

"Alas, indeed," Hauptmann Keller said and then turned and raised his glass. "To staying in the fight. Heil Hitler."

He watched us carefully as we each raised our glasses in answer, and repeated the filthy words, bile rising in my throat as I mouthed them, unable to let myself put sound behind the salute.

While the others dug into their food, I pushed mine around my plate, exhaustion and fear quelling the hunger I'd felt before.

"It is not to your liking, fräulein?" the captain asked.

"It's delicious," I said. "But I'm afraid I'm more tired than hungry."

"Of course! It was a tiresome ride on that tiny boat, I am sure. Please." He scooted his chair back. "Allow me to show you to your room."

I glanced at Max, but he was chatting with Klaus and so I smiled and nodded, letting him slide my chair back and then daintily placing my hand in the one he held out.

"I shall rejoin you soon," he told the two men.

"Good night," I said. This time, Max looked up. For a moment I thought he was going to ignore what was happening. But just as I was about to turn away, he nodded and scratched his jaw.

"Good night, sweet niece," he said. "Sleep well."

I nodded, relief spreading throughout my limbs. The scratch of his jaw was the first and only signal he'd taught me early on. To ward me off if I entered a room and I was to act as though I didn't see or know him. To tell me something was awry. Or to let me know he was paying attention, and if more time went by than seemed necessary, he would be up the stairs and in my room to remove the German soldier if need be.

But thankfully there was no need for heroics. Hauptmann Keller showed me to my room as promised, lit the candle on the bedside table, and bid me good-night, turning on his heel before the latch on the door clicked into place. With a heavy sigh, I sat on the neatly made bed, gasping a little as a puff of dust arose around me. I looked around, noticing a thick layer covering every surface. This room had been left devoid of its owner for a long time. It sickened me once more to know what these people had done not just to other countries, but to their own people. I wanted to leave. To march down the stairs and demand we go. But to do so would put our lives at risk, and it was one thing to be so foolish in regards to my own life, but another to endanger others. And so, I pulled back the quilt, flipped over the pillow, and curled my body into a ball in an attempt to keep warm through the night.

28

I WOKE EARLY, having had a hard time sleeping in the dust-covered bedroom that had once belonged to another. When I found myself lying awake, my watch ticking the seconds away, my body aching and weary from all the different beds it had slept in recently, I gave in, swinging my legs over the side of the bed and hurrying into my clothes for the day.

Minutes later, dressed in a rumpled pair of blue trousers and a dark blue blouse, a tan sweater over top, I slipped on my favorite pair of oxfords, which were slightly damp from the night before, and stepped quietly from my room.

I had been hungry the night before, but scared to eat or drink any of the food and wine the captain had told us to help ourselves to. Thankfully, the cook, an older woman with a wide face, her pale hair scraped back into a tidy bun, arrived a few moments later and put the kettle on for tea before meeting my hesitant gaze.

"What can I offer you?" she asked, her tone dull but not unpleasant.

I shrugged and smiled. "Whatever's easiest."

"The master of the house will want you to be impressed with what he has to offer. Don't be shy."

But I didn't want her to go to the trouble of cooking something just for me. Didn't want to wait alone in the dining room or partake of more food than one should at times like these. A time when so many didn't have the same access and were starving.

"I'm not much of a breakfast person," I said. "Do you have porridge?"

She looked torn at my response, twisting the fingers of one hand with the other. I sighed, understanding. If she didn't serve me a proper meal, Keller would be angry with her.

"Whatever you feel like making," I said. "Will be fine with me."

I watched her broad chest rise and fall as she gave me a tight smile and a little nod before turning to the stove and getting to work.

Pfannkuchen, the German equivalent of the American pancake, eggs, bacon, and fresh-squeezed orange juice. I had no idea where one got oranges this time of year, but I hadn't seen one since before I'd enlisted. I marveled at the smell, the tart and sweet tang on my tongue as I sipped it slowly, savoring every drop, unsure when I'd get to taste it again.

"It is good?" she asked as I dragged a piece of bacon through egg yolk.

"It is miraculous," I answered, meeting her gaze. *"Danke."*

She nodded and then turned her back to me, pouring more batter in the pan, her cheeks flushing pink from the heat.

"May I ask your name?" I said quietly. She froze for a moment before turning her face toward me without meeting my gaze.

"Why?" she asked, turning back to the stovetop and flipping a flapjack.

"To be friendly."

She made a neat stack of three and delivered them to the oven before pouring more batter and then facing me.

"Magda," she said.

"It's nice to meet you, Magda."

She nodded stiffly, seeming to not know where to look, her eyes darting here and there around the room.

"You are Lena?" she said.

"I am," I said, shifting in my seat, uncomfortable still at the strange name.

"It is a good name," she said, turning back to the stove. "Strong."

"I'm not sure it suits me then," I said and she looked over her shoulder at me, her eyes taking me in.

"Ja," she said with a nod. "It suits you quite perfectly." She poured more batter and continued talking. "My daughter is Ediline. She is more flower than strength."

Her eyes met mine again and she grinned.

"It's a beautiful name," I said. "Where is she now?" I was afraid to hear the answer, but wanted to ask, in case she had no one else to talk to.

"With her younger brothers. With my sister. I sent them away when..." She swung her arm in a wide arc and I nodded, understanding her meaning.

"Did you live in this town before the war?"

Her smile was back. But now it wasn't tight, nor was it soft. It was twisted, ugly, and mad.

"I did," she said. "This was my home."

The food I'd consumed churned in my belly, my limbs going cold. I thought of the small child–sized chair in the dining room. My lips parted, a question on the tip of my tongue, but the sudden sound of footsteps on the staircase in the other room stopped me, and I stared down at the remains of my breakfast as the kitchen door swung open.

"Guten morgen," Hauptmann Keller said, a jovial smile on

his face as his eyes took in what felt like every strand of hair on my head, the exact color of my eyes, and the food on my plate.

"Guten morgen," I said quietly as Magda put the kettle back on the stovetop.

"That looks like it was a fantastic meal."

"It was, thank you. Your cook is wonderfully skilled."

"Agreed. Though for some reason she didn't think it proper to serve you in the dining room?"

His tone was light, though I could feel the threat he laced it with. By the stiffening of Magda's shoulders, I could tell she had too.

"That's my fault," I said. "She did insist, but since I was the only one up, I asked to sit in here so I wouldn't be eating alone."

"Hm. Well, I suppose you ladies are more prone to needing others, aren't you."

"Indeed, we are a social species."

"I quite like dining alone," he said. "Gives me time to assess the day, organize my thoughts, plan ahead..." His eyes flicked over me. "Women don't have need for such things. You should be grateful there are men to take care of the more serious things in life."

I saw Magda's hand tighten on the handle of the searing hot frying pan and for a moment feared...hoped?...that she'd use it, swinging around with all her might and slamming it against his head. But a moment later she relaxed her grip, delivered the last of the flapjacks to the oven, and turned to her boss with a smile.

"Would you care for orange juice with your meal, sir?" she asked.

Klaus and Max arrived to the dining room a few minutes later and while the men dined, I went back to the bedroom I'd slept in to pack my things and tidy up. But as I looked around the room in the daylight, I couldn't help but feel sickened. This had clearly been the room of a young woman. Ediline. The furnishings were feminine, but not childlike. Elegant. A teenager coming into her own. My room in Hamburg, though three times the size and filled with much more expensive furnishings, had had the same feel. The feel of coming into one's own.

I quietly opened the door and tiptoed down the hall to the built-in cupboard in the hall, smiling when I saw I'd guessed right, the shelves inside filled with linens and bath towels. Grabbing a washcloth, I hurried back to the bedroom and shut the door. Opening the window, I gasped as a gust of frigid air blew in, and then hurriedly began wiping down all the surfaces, clearing away the dust that had gathered in its owner's absence. When I was done, I removed the quilt and, holding on tight, gave it a hard shake near the open window before putting it back on the bed and fluffing the pillows.

I hoped the young woman who had lived in this room got to come home soon.

After the men had finished their meal and washed up, Max, Klaus, and I followed the captain out to his car and were driven to a small military base where Max was given a set of keys and a pat on the shoulder.

"It was an honor to have you in my home, sir," Hauptmann Keller said. "I wish you all a safe journey."

"Thank you for your hospitality," Max said.

"And my boat?" Klaus asked.

"You are going back?" Keller asked.

"There are others who are trapped. I must do what I can to help."

"You are a true patriot. We'll be sure to be on the lookout for you now." He waved down a nearby soldier. "I'll have one of my men drive you to it."

"That would be lovely, thank you."

"You're sure?" Max asked. "I'm happy to drop you off myself."

The two men's eyes met and held, as if asking silent questions back and forth.

"Please," Keller said. "We held you up last night. Let me at least save you some time now by giving him a ride."

Klaus gave Max a nod. "You should get on the road. Make up the lost time."

Max sighed and then he clapped the man on his shoulder. "Klaus… Thank you. May your travels back be swift and safe."

"It was my pleasure to assist you both."

The two men shook hands, and then Klaus turned and shook mine as well.

"Thank you, Klaus," I said. "Be safe."

"You too, miss."

We got in the car then and sat for a moment, watching as Klaus drove off with the soldier.

"You think he'll be okay?" I asked.

"I think he will leave here okay. But now he has to survive his return."

As the car started to roll away from the base, I stared out the window, hoping I survived my return as well.

29

William

Seattle
2003

THE BOOK LAY on the table between us. It was brown leather. Worn. No title across the front or along the binding, just some floral markings etched along the border, the edges of the pages yellowed with age.

I looked to Selene and she stared back, an expectant look in her clear blue eyes.

"What is it?" I asked, leaning forward and resting my forearm on the table. I'd never seen it before, but for some reason my fingers itched to touch it. To feel the soft leather. To open the cover and reveal what was inside.

"It's a journal."

"Whose journal?"

But I knew before she said—

"Kate's."

Silence stretched between us, the sounds in the house, the footsteps and muffled voices of my daughter and granddaughter, the traffic out front, the noise of the world…stopped. A rushing sound filled my ears as I stared down at the book again.

"From when?" I whispered.

"The first entry is early November," she said. "Nineteen forty-four."

I pulled in a breath and sat back in my seat, my gaze moving to the view. A seagull gliding across the sky. The water beyond. A ferry coming in to dock.

The fall of 1944 was when a different kind of silence fell over me. My platoon fought mercilessly, pushing the Germans back, our guns discharging as we ran forward, shouting, grunting, crying out as they fired back, their bullets whizzing by, clipping our jackets, our helmets, our hands. Taking pieces of us with them if they didn't bury inside our bodies completely. But as I ran, ducked, jumped, and skidded to the dirt, taking cover, rolling into ditches and diving behind trees, rocks, and overturned and burned-out vehicles, I heard none of it, my mind on Kate and the response that still hadn't come.

I was worried. Sick with dread. My brain told me she was gone. Dead. Her plane home had maybe crashed. Or if she'd taken a boat, maybe it had capsized. All my inquiries to comrades who might've heard something about those things happening though brought no information. And so, while my head still urged me to get on with it, my heart told me to hang on another day.

I placed my hand on the journal. The cover was soft, pliable, and I could imagine what her hands had looked like as they'd pulled this particular book from the shelf, admiring the tiny flowers, flipping the pages, her head dipping as she took in the scent of them.

My breath caught as I opened the cover and saw her name,

written in her handwriting, on the front page. Eyes blurred, I looked away, afraid a tear might fall and mar the paper.

"Are you okay?" Selene asked.

I nodded and sniffed.

"Please excuse me," I said. "It's just that, at the time she wrote this, I thought she must have died. I'm not sure… I guess I don't know what to feel. I'm glad she was alive, but I want to know why she never wrote. And yet, I'm afraid to. Even this many years later, after living a happy and satisfying life, I've always wondered. I searched…" I shook my head as the memories bubbled to the surface. "I continued to send letters to the address she'd given me. I even sent one to her aunt. But there was never a response. Even after decades had passed I searched, using the internet every few years or so to see if there was an obituary or an article. Something—anything to tell me what had happened to her. But there was nothing."

I looked down at the journal again and ran my fingers over her name.

"And now, here she is. And I'm afraid." I met Selene's eyes again. "Are the answers in this book?"

"There are answers, yes. But it may create more questions at first. And she only wrote in it for a short time. I think, if you read it, you'll understand why."

I flipped the pages then, feeling the soft edges of the paper beneath my thumb, watching words go by until there were no more. She'd only filled about a third of the journal and I wondered why she'd stopped writing. Was it too hard? Was she too sad? Maybe she met someone else and no longer needed to write about whatever was in this book?

I sighed and went back to the beginning, running my finger once more over her name.

"Would you like me to give you some space?" Selene asked.

"Maybe?" I said, not quite knowing what I needed in this moment.

She smiled and scooted her chair back, getting to her feet.

"May I?" she asked, pointing to the sprawling yard below.

"Of course."

As she passed me on her way to the stairs, she placed a gentle hand on my shoulder and gave it a squeeze.

I watched her as she descended the staircase, slipping off her sandals and stepping barefoot into the grass, a smile on her face as she wandered my late wife's blooming garden filled with yellows, pinks, and lavenders. For the briefest of moments she reminded me of Emma, but then I blinked and the resemblance I thought I'd seen was gone.

I looked back down at the journal and turned the page.

"November 1, 1944," the first entry began.

It has been a long time since I kept a journal, the last one filled with the silly hopes and dreams of a twelve-year-old me, hidden, of course, from my mother's ever-prying eyes. But as I saw the bags of letters, dozens of them waiting to be burned behind the post office like the many still smoldering in the corner, I realized I should be documenting what I have seen during my time witnessing this terrible war. It is my duty to accurately describe the horrors and injustices. If not for others to know, then for myself to never forget what I will hopefully overcome.

The letters… My heart was heavy at the sight of them. Bags upon bags, stuffed with letters that were either never sent, or received and not delivered. Yet another tactic to separate, confuse, and extinguish hope. Which was what I felt when I saw them, my mind immediately going to William and the many letters I'd written and sent. Or thought I'd sent. But had they suffered the same fate as these?

My chest rose with a long inhale. She *had* written me. I was confused though. Why would a post office in Manhattan not deliver letters?

I glanced down to the yard. Selene was sitting on one of the stone benches, her eyes closed, head tipped back, the sun on her face.

Getting to my feet, I stood at the rail.

"Why would a post office in Manhattan burn letters?" I shouted.

She turned and raised a hand to shield her eyes from the sun.

"Is that all you've read?" she shouted back.

"So far."

"Did you not turn the page?"

"You said it might create more questions. I…have a question. It makes no sense that a New York post office would burn letters. It's against the law to tamper with mail. I don't—"

"William."

"Yes?"

"Turn the page!"

I looked down at the book and turned the page. What I read next nearly made my heart stop.

"November 2, 1944—Hamburg, Germany."

I looked back to Selene.

"What the hell was she doing in Germany?"

30

Kate/Lena

Hamburg

I CLASPED MY hands tightly in my lap, my palms damp, as we rolled into the city of my childhood.

So many of the beautiful buildings, homes, and apartments had been hollowed, blackened, or were now piles of rubble from the Allied attack the year before.

Streets I had run down and shopped on, bakeries and sweet shops I'd frequented, parks I'd played in…all gone.

There was barely anyone on the crumbling sidewalks, save for the soldiers who watched us as we drove slowly by. Tanks and other military vehicles sat around every corner. Here and there an old lady limped by, or a woman with her young child hurried along, their heads bowed, their eyes on the ground in front of them.

A line of people waited for food, their ration tickets in their hands, their faces drawn and pale. An older man was handcuffed and being shoved roughly into the street. I turned my eyes away.

"You're sure my parents' home still stands?" I asked.

Max nodded.

"It is my understanding that there was some damage, but most of the house is still in livable condition."

"Of course they would be so lucky," I said bitterly. "And I'm sure they offered to take in those displaced with all the spare room they still have."

My voice dripped with sarcasm, and he glanced at me.

"You're sure you don't want to come with me?" he asked. "At least for a couple of nights? Get yourself acclimated to the city a little before going home?"

He had plans to stay in one of the few hotels still standing and had offered to let me sleep on the sofa the day before, after seeing my face when we'd both returned to the car during a quick stop in Luneburg. He'd had an errand to run there and I'd noted a small bookshop nearby.

While he'd hurried off across the street, I'd walked to the bookshop in hopes of finding a book to distract me when I was alone in my room, and maybe even a journal. I wanted to start documenting what I was seeing. Without friends to talk to and confide in, to entrust my fears to, I was lonely. I hoped that by keeping a journal I'd feel less so somehow. At least I'd have my words to keep me company.

The man at the front desk of the tiny shop had looked surprised to see someone entering his store, and not a little bit nervous. I'd given him a small smile in hopes of letting him know I wasn't a threat and asked, *"Zeitschriften?"*

He'd nodded and pointed. "The journals are over there."

"Danke."

There were several to choose from. Most of them masculine looking, with sharp edges and serious-looking covers. Several had the Nazi insignia on them and I shoved those back in place hard, feeling my skin heat at the mere sight of the symbol.

And then I found it. Near the end of the shelf. It was slender, the leather soft. And on the front, tiny flowers were etched into the cover. I'd smiled and pulled it free, flipping the pages with my thumb and ducking my head as I'd breathed in, smelling the scent of the unmarked pages.

I moved along a wall of books, taking in titles, my heart sinking with each step. Nazi propaganda on every shelf.

"Fräulein?" the shopkeeper said.

When I turned, he pointed to the back corner of the store where a small selection of novels had been shoved and mostly obscured by books on Germany's geography.

I smiled at the sight of *Cold Comfort Farm* by Stella Gibbons and pulled it from the shelf.

"I'll take these," I'd said to the clerk, who nodded and rang me up promptly.

As I walked back toward the car, I noticed a small, stately post office, several people coming and going out the front door. But as I passed the narrow alleyway behind it, I paused at the sight of several cloth bags stuffed and piled on top of one another, paper littering the ground around them. A gust of wind sent one of the pieces toward me and I knelt to see what it was, frowning when I saw it was a letter, addressed to someone in France.

Assuming the bags were waiting for someone to take them inside and sort them, I walked quickly behind the building and carefully slid the envelope inside the nearest bag. But the scent of something burning caught my attention and, curious, I squeezed past the stacks of bags until I found the source. In the far corner was a metal barrel, the flames inside it licking upward. At first I thought perhaps a homeless person had lit it and was living back here, the piles of bags providing protection from the elements, but then a bit of charred paper drifted up out of the barrel and landed on the ground beside it. An ugly feeling twisted inside my stomach. Glancing at a nearby back door, I hurried to the scrap and picked it up, finding exactly what I'd feared. Handwriting and a partial address. Beside the barrel, I now saw, were more bags. But these ones were empty. They weren't sending or delivering the letters, they were burning them, collecting their citizens' money and hope and playing a terrible trick on them.

A thump on the other side of the door made me drop the scrap of paper and hurry from the alley and around the corner.

It was then that I remembered the handful of letters I'd sent William. Or at least thought I had. Were they too now a pile of ash at the bottom of a barrel? Saddened and angry at the thought, I hurried back to the car to where Max was waiting to drive us onward.

"Not too much farther now," he said.

I inhaled and nodded, a tremor shaking my body at its core.

Despite my running from Hamburg years ago, I had loved my city. Not the house I'd lived in with my family, with the expensive furnishings I was barely allowed to touch, or the fussy bedroom decorated by my mother that had felt more like a prison than a sanctuary. But the city I'd roamed as a girl had been beautiful. The parks and gardens, shops and cafés, the many street corners I'd hung out on with my friends, the alleyways Ruthie and I had run down, laughing, our footsteps echoing off the walls, our hair streaming behind us.

As we drove from the outskirts farther in, we were stopped every so often, our papers checked, eyebrows raised as they saw his credentials, and then offered me a smile. We were home, their grins said. We were welcome.

I'd never felt more scared.

"Where you headed?" a soldier asked, handing back our paperwork to Max.

He gave him the street name of my parents' home. The man frowned and nodded.

"I believe that's right on the border of the worst of the destruction. You may have to park and walk the last couple of streets. There are a lot of roads closed off due to rubble and the fear of buildings toppling."

"Understood," Max said. "Thank you. We'll be careful."

The closer we got to our destination, the more barren the city became.

Thanks to his intel, we knew the government had relocated many of the survivors of the attack the year before farther out or to other cities. It felt like a ghost town, and I wondered if the information both he and Uncle Frank had received about my mother still living at home was correct. But when I'd asked Max again as we'd crossed over the border into Hamburg, he'd told me simply that per all reports he'd received, she was still residing in our family home.

"And Catrin?" I'd asked. "Has she been seen?"

"She was spotted two weeks ago. I have no information past that."

I tried to picture my younger sister. When we were children, people had said we looked alike, but any similarities were mostly due to our coloring. The pale hair and eyes, the slender build. We were our parents' children through and through, though she'd favored our father's classic good looks, while my features were a combination of my mother and aunt's more lush attributes.

It was hard to imagine Catrin as a young woman. She'd been so spirited as a girl. Always giggling and getting admonished by our parents. Creative, bright… What had life been like for her? What had life been like living with another family? Had she been kept away from the worst of the war? I had so many questions and ached to see her, hear her, and learn everything that had happened in my absence.

We'd always been so close. I was frightened she'd be angry

with me. That she wouldn't believe our aunt and uncle had tried to get her out too. That I hadn't left her behind on purpose.

Would she forgive me for leaving? Would she forgive me for the lie that was my death and for taking so long to come back?

The plan, per Max, was that while he tended to some business nearby, I would go to my parents' home in hopes of seeing Catrin and convincing her to leave with me. If she was there and agreed, both of us would then go to a safe house. The woman who lived there would get word to Max.

"The safe house is there," he said, pointing discreetly as we turned down another street. "Three doors down. Number four. The blue door."

I nodded.

He reached forward and knocked three times on the dashboard, paused, and knocked once more.

"That's the knock," he said. "Do anything other than that and she won't answer the door and you'll be out in the cold, exposed."

The house was at least twelve blocks from where my parents' home was, the streets between becoming more and more treacherous as we drove farther into the city.

I stared in quiet awe as we bumped over potholes and stones, looking at buildings and shops and parks that had once been filled with families, friends out for an afternoon, and businessmen hurrying to and from meetings. They now stood empty, devoid of life, doors closed, windows dark or boarded over, sprawling lawns unmarked by the footfall of children running across them.

The car slowed and stopped and the two of us leaned forward, frowning at the sight ahead of us. The road was blocked by wooden partitions. Beyond them a tank sat off to one side, its metal body charred and covered in ash. Behind that was a scene I couldn't quite comprehend.

"What is that?" I asked, looking past Max out his window.

"I believe that was a building," he said of the cascade of rubble covering most of the street.

He turned then and looked out the passenger-side window where a large hole obstructed anything or anyone from getting through. My parents' home was still several blocks away, but to get to it…

"I can try and go around," he said. "Otherwise, you'll have to go on foot."

An older woman appeared to the right of us and hurried across the street, her body bundled against the cold, her face worn, eyes wary as she watched us. She didn't look familiar to me. I wondered if there was anyone still in town I'd recognize—and who might recognize me.

"I can walk from here," I said, my voice low.

"You're sure?"

"Yes. It's not far."

He was quiet for a long moment.

"You remember where the safe house is?"

"I do."

"The knock?"

"I remember."

"Go there as soon as you're done," he said and I nodded. "With or without her. If you don't see her, we'll talk tonight about next steps."

"Okay," I said.

"And don't take longer than necessary," he said.

I reached for the door handle, but he stopped me, his hand on my arm.

"She may not be the same person you remember. And to her, you might be a traitor. You need to be careful. Aware at all times. A lot has happened since you left. You shouldn't trust anyone. Not even the baby sister who loved you and looked up to you."

But he was wrong. I knew he was wrong. And I would prove

it when I met him later at the safe house, Catrin by my side, or at least information on where I could find her.

I grabbed my bag from the floor of the car and opened the door.

"I'll see you soon," I said.

"Please. Remember what I said. And keep your papers hidden. I'll wait here until I can't see you anymore."

I opened the door and got out, slinging the shoulder strap of my bag over my shoulder and looking back inside the car at my traveling companion. I wouldn't say we'd grown closer as the days had gone by, but we'd developed a relationship. A fondness for one another. A sense of respect. And for me, a feeling of safety in his presence. I was nervous to be without him, but this next part had to be done alone.

I looked up the street, so different than it had been ten years before, then back at him.

"Lebewohl," I said.

"Farewell," he said, and I shut the door.

It was strange walking down the old streets. The quiet disconcerting. Even the soldiers, so prominent several blocks away, didn't bother to monitor this area, the lack of inhabitants making it not worth their time or efforts.

As I drew closer to the building I'd once called home, I was shocked at what I saw just around it. Homes, shops, and businesses that had once stood strong and beautiful, were now shells of themselves, reduced to their bare bones by the fires that had ripped through the city, burning history, art, and lives. The city center was a shell of itself, the asphalt in some areas melted in large patches. There were mountains of brick piled everywhere, and the dust I kicked up as I walked settled on my coat and in my throat, making me cough.

Some of it I was glad to see in ruins. Government buildings, the homes of those I'd known supported the tyrant who had brought this disgrace down on our country. But other places, like my favorite bookstore, the sweet shop Ruthie and I spent our allowance in nearly every week, and the bench that had been our meeting place before we wandered off on some silly adventure, were harder to take, their absence tearing small holes into my heart.

The few trees that still stood were scorched, others bent and disfigured, their bark charred, ash dusting their exposed roots below. It felt otherworldly. But no world I wanted to be a part of.

My heart raced as I approached my old home, stepping carefully around the mounds of rubble, and noting that while the windows in the building across from it were blown out, somehow the windows in ours were all intact.

It wasn't until I reached for the handle of the large front door that I realized the longtime doorman, Jürgen, wasn't there to greet me. When I stepped inside, there was no concierge at the desk, and none of the other tenants milled about talking quietly in the lobby. There was just the echo of my footsteps skittering across the marble floor as I made my way to the elevator, taking in my dusty surroundings and the eerie emptiness around me.

I pressed the button for the elevator, but it didn't light up. I noticed the large crystal chandelier hanging in the entryway was dark. The little lamps on either side of the concierge's desk weren't on either. No electricity. I'd have to take the stairs.

Grasping the handle, I pushed the door open and looked up, memories flooding back as I remembered Catrin and I begging Nanny Paulina to let us take the stairs whenever she took us out. Looking up the stairwell now, I couldn't remember what was so magical about them, except perhaps that my parents never deigned to take them, and it had felt like going against their rules and lifestyle to not take the elevator like "civilized people." I was pretty sure the only reason Nanny Paulina agreed was because she knew it would help wear us out.

I began climbing the fourteen flights to our top-floor apartment, stopping periodically whenever I reached a landing and heard a noise on the other side of the door. I was tempted to peek. To see who might still be residing in this building on the edge of the disaster that had ravaged buildings only a few doors down, but I pushed on. Contact with anyone but my family was a dangerous game I knew not to play.

At the top floor I paused, catching my breath and steadying myself before entering the narrow hall that led to the small, elegant lobby outside my family's home.

Two identical benches still flanked the ornate double doors to the apartment. How many times had I peeked out here during one of my parents' many parties to find guests had drifted out and perched, drinks in their hands, in this very space?

I looked at the doors that led inside, my eyes tracing the wood-carved pattern as they had so many times before. My breath trembled as I inhaled. I suddenly felt small. Scared. Once more that child, that young girl, that woman—on the verge—who wanted to run. Far and fast. Away from here.

And now I'd come back.

A flash of worry spread through me, Max's words coming back as I reached my hand out to knock. I paused. *What if he was right? What if too much had changed?*

I glanced out the window to my right, taking in the sight of a city covered in ash. It wasn't too late. I could leave now. Hurry to the house with the woman who would contact Max. It would take minutes and I'd be safe and soon on my way back. To France. To England.

To William.

But my hand moved on its own, rapping softly on the thick wood door, the sound echoing throughout the lobby. A minute passed. Two. Had I knocked too quietly? Maybe the reports were wrong and no one was here. I grasped the strap of my bag still hanging from my shoulder…waiting, listening. But there was no sound. No movement felt. It was strange to hear nothing. There had always been something, even from out here. The steps of our trusted butler, August. The hushed voices of my mother's personal secretary or maid. The clank of pots and pans from meals being prepared by the cook. Perhaps it was a bad time. Perhaps there was never going to be a good time to return.

Perhaps my mother was already dead.

My heart sank as my mind immediately went to my sister. Had I come all this way only to receive no answers at all?

I took a step back, still listening, still hoping. But as the seconds ticked away, I began to fear the worst.

I turned to go—and then I heard it. Footsteps. A pause. And then the locks being released and the doorknob turning.

Suddenly, I was looking into the familiar green eyes of my former nanny. She looked scared, but like the clouds parting to reveal the sun, recognition began to dawn and the fear turned to something else.

"Fräulein?" she said in a whisper.

"*Hallo*, Paulina," I said, taking in the woman who had cared for me and my sister lovingly for years.

She was thinner, her round face showing the signs of scant food at the ready, her clothes hanging on her frame more than hugging it. There was gray in her light brown hair, and wrinkles around her eyes. But the gentle smile on her face was one I knew well.

"Hallo, kleiner Hase," she said.

I couldn't help it. I smiled back. *Little bunny* was what she had called Catrin and me. But a moment later the terror of the situation came back to me and my smile disappeared.

"I am here to see my sister," I said.

She looked over her shoulder, hesitating, and then back at me, clearly trying to decide the right thing to do. Letting me in after being gone so long, having clearly duped them all, would be a transgression my mother might not forgive her. I was a traitor.

"Your mother is not well," she said, avoiding my mention of Catrin.

"I know. That's partly why I've come." It was a lie. I didn't care if I never saw my mother again, but whatever it took to find out where Catrin was, I would do.

She nodded and her shoulders sagged, and then she pressed a finger to her lips, took a step back, and opened the door wider.

Despite finding my way here, I wasn't prepared for the emotions that filled my entire being as I stepped inside my childhood home. The furnishings, though still opulent, had faded with age, the brass and silver losing much of their shine, the windows covered in dust on the outside, clouding the view of the city, which was probably for the best.

I stepped lightly, as was habit in this household, the only one allowed to make a sound being my father, his foot strikes marking his place in our home. I had tried often to steer clear of those footsteps.

I touched a vase, trailed my fingers along a tabletop, glanced at the chandeliers, recalled a peaceful moment in a corner chair after my parents had left for a night of dining and drinking, and then stood at the foot of the curved staircase and looked up, gasping at the sight that greeted me.

"Thankfully there were still men around at the time to help patch it," Paulina said, her voice barely more than a whisper as she came to stand beside me.

At the top of the stairs where the landing led off to different hallways and bedrooms, the ceiling had caved in, leaving a large gaping hole that had been covered with several long boards.

"Was it a bomb?" I asked.

"It hit two buildings over, but the blast pushed through the one next to us and into our roof. There's more damage farther down the hallway."

Farther down the hallway was where Catrin's and my rooms had been.

"It's still there," Paulina said. "Exactly as you left it."

I blew out a breath and gripped the handrail. I didn't want to see the remnants of the childhood I'd run from. It wasn't why I was here.

"I've only come to see Catrin. And to say goodbye to my mother."

She touched my sleeve, her eyes meeting mine, and I wondered why she was still here. As far as I knew, my sister hadn't lived here in years, and even if she had, a nanny wouldn't still be needed now when Catrin was a woman of twenty. Why had Paulina stayed on? And where was the rest of the staff? Obviously not all were needed with only one woman to tend to, but my mother had always had a small entourage to accommodate her every need and whim.

"Where's the rest of the staff, Paulina?" I asked. "August? Ingrid?" I looked around, expecting my mother's secretary to appear in the doorway of the study my mother had conducted her meetings in.

But Paulina shook her head and then motioned for me to follow her to the kitchen where she shut the door so we couldn't be heard.

"They are all gone," she said, moving to the kitchen table and taking a seat. "Ingrid fled early on. The maid soon after. August stayed to look after the house when we left to stay in the country estate. When we returned last year, he was gone, having left a note to say he was going to stay with his daughter and her family. And Freya, the cook, was killed when the ceiling caved in. She had just delivered food to your mother when the blast took her."

I bowed my head. I had always liked Freya. A stern woman, she hadn't been averse to spoiling Cat and me with little treats every now and then.

"I'm sorry," I said. "That must've been hard for you to lose so many people. But…how did you end up staying with both Catrin and me gone?"

She shrugged.

"I think at first your parents didn't realize I was still here. They never saw me much in the first place. And then when Catrin was quietly brought around for visits, it was handy to have me around to tend to her needs. But then Ingrid left. And the maid and…suddenly I was needed by your mother as well." She looked at me, guilt filling her eyes, pleading with me to understand her plight.

"I know she was a terrible mother to you," she said. "They were both…so horrible. So many of us in the household felt such pity. How could one be so cruel to their own children? You were perfect girls. Kind, funny, smart, and so beautiful. But they saw none of it."

I sat across from her and her eyes met mine again, this time filled with a fierceness that startled me.

"She has not changed, fräulein. Evil runs through her blood. She will not be happy to see you. You can still change your mind. You can still go."

"No. I can't," I said. "Not until I've seen Cat. Where is she?"

Paulina's eyes searched mine.

"You did not hear she died?" Her voice was faint. She knew I knew the truth.

"I did hear that. But I know it was a lie."

The older woman sighed.

"She does not live here."

"I know. But I also know she visits. When will you expect her next?"

Paulina shook her head.

"I never know. She comes when she can. She was here two weeks ago. It could be a month, even two, before she's back again."

My heart sank, but this wasn't unexpected.

"Do you know where she is? Can you contact her?"

She clasped her hands in front of her. "I... No. Your mother wouldn't like it."

"Why not?"

"She has kept your sister's existence carefully hidden. If she came more often, your mother worries someone would take notice. Maybe the same people who tried to kill her years ago. And then there's the matter of the young soldier who checks in every other day or so."

"What do you mean?"

"It is disgusting," she said, sitting back and crossing her arms over her chest. "It is clear the way he eyes your mother's belongings that he is counting the minutes until she dies. He has asked many times my plans for after, making sure I aim to leave. He thinks there is no one else to claim all this." She waved a hand at the room. "If he knew your sister was alive...that there was an heir to collect...who knows what he might do."

I nodded, understanding.

"And now you are here," she said.

"She won't care about keeping me safe," I said. "And I don't want anything from her—or this house. I've only come for Cat. Can you help me? Please, Paulina." I reached for her hand. "I don't have much time. Can you tell me where to find her?"

She pulled her hand from mine and pressed her fingertips to her lips, her gaze drifting past me. A moment later she took in a long breath and got to her feet. As she passed me on the way to the door she squeezed my shoulder, and then she was gone.

I sat quietly, waiting, my eyes on the clock on the far wall. A minute passed. Two. Just as I began to fret that she wasn't coming back, the door swung open and she stood before me, holding out a small square of paper. I reached for it, but she pulled it away, her gaze holding mine.

"I must warn you," she said. "She is not the same girl you knew."

My smile was grim.

"Are any of us the same people we once were, Paulina?"

She sighed, shook her head, and pressed the slip of paper into my palm.

31

PAULINA WALKED ME to the door, but as I reached for the handle, she wrapped a hand around my wrist.

"Wherever you're going next," she said, "hurry. Keep out of sight as much as you can, and if stopped, be careful what lies you tell. They'll ask you to prove them and won't give you much chance to do so. And don't forget, your surname means something in these parts."

"Not for me it doesn't," I said. "I'm dead, remember?"

Her lips parted as she gasped.

"How stupid I am," she said.

"Not stupid. Brave and kind." I looked toward the stairs. "She does not deserve to have you stay with her."

"Had I any better offer, I'd have gone. But I was safe here, so long as I was taking care of her."

Safe. A word I never would've associated with my mother.

I reached out then to hug her. She held on to me for but a moment, and then I was gone, hurrying to the stairwell, my feet light and fast on the steps down.

At the front door to the building, I stopped, peeking out the windows and looking up and down the street. A woman holding on to the arm of an older gentleman walked down the crumbling sidewalk across from me. I watched them for a moment, waiting to see if anyone stopped them. When no one did, I pushed out the door.

The safe house was only a few blocks away. I kept my head down, trying not to walk too fast in case it raised suspicions should a soldier see me. The woman and man were half a block ahead of me, their presence bringing me comfort that I wasn't the only one out and about. But then they turned down another street and a feeling of dread filled my body. Without them, I was a target.

I moved closer to the buildings at my side, added a limp to my gait, and slowed even more, hoping my appearance and hindered walk would make me look too pathetic to bother with.

The minutes ticked by painfully, my slowness frustrating. I wanted to run. Hurry. Get out of sight. But to do so would only draw attention to anyone watching, and so I took a deep breath and kept going, navigating carefully around holes blown into pavement melted from the blasts that had sent fires up and down the streets a year ago.

My shoulders straightened when I looked up and saw I was nearly there.

"Number four. Blue door," I whispered into the scarf wrapped around my neck.

At the corner I stopped and peeked around the building, checking to see that it was all clear. But the sight of several military vehicles, a dozen or so soldiers, a door I'd memorized only a couple hours before, and a woman being pulled from the home I'd been heading for stopped me.

She was slight. Blonde. Wearing only a long-sleeved navy dress and socks in the freezing air. She moved calmly, seemingly unfazed by being pulled from her house and made to stand in the unbearable cold. I watched her, terrified for her. Watched how her lips never moved as she allowed them to push and pull, hit, and run their hands over her as if looking for weapons but violating her as they worked.

One of the men stepped forward, barking questions at her. What was her name? Was this her home? Was anyone else inside? Who did she work for? Had she seen this person or that? Had she let them stay with her now or at any time?

She shook her head again and again, allowing him to question then berate her over and over, never flinching from his shouts and acts of brutality. Never once looking over her shoulder as men filed in and out of the house behind her.

One of the soldiers came out carrying a small box. The officer before her took it, rifled through it, held it up to her face. Her simple shrug seemed to infuriate him. I sucked in a breath as he pulled a pistol from his belt and held it to her forehead. Still she said nothing. He pushed the barrel of the gun to her head, making her take a step backward. He held the box up again, demanding an explanation. Again, she shrugged.

He turned away for a moment, lowering his gun and saying something I couldn't hear to one of the men behind him. I exhaled my breath. They were going to let her go.

But when he turned back my stomach did a slow roll as his arm raised again and the air was filled with the crack of the gun firing, her body jerking back before falling lifeless to the ground.

I gasped and moved out of sight, pressing my back to the wall, eyes scanning my surroundings. A few people had gathered not far away and were staring down the street where the woman had just been shot. None of them looked surprised. No one even looked sad. They turned away, chatting to one another, and then moved on down the street and out of sight.

But my heart was pounding. I'd seen many people die in this

war, from injuries they'd sustained in battle. Not point-blank while standing on the sidewalk of their own country.

And now I was trapped. I had no idea where Max was having his meetings, or where he and I were staying for the remainder of our time here. The woman was to have been my contact. A way to get word to him. My way out. I had no way of letting him know I hadn't seen Catrin. That my journey to find her wasn't yet over.

I peeked back around the corner, watching as the men got back in their vehicles, leaving the woman's body where it lay, her blond hair splayed across the pavement, her blood splattered on the wall behind her and pooled beneath her head. As the engines roared to life, I ducked back and tucked myself into a nearby doorway, waiting as they passed, my body trembling from fear.

When the trucks were out of sight, I turned and stared back at number four and the blue door, wondering if I should still go. If I should hide inside and wait. Maybe Max would come looking for me when he didn't receive word. Or maybe I could leave a note inside and go back to my mother's home.

But as my gaze moved up, I saw faces looking out from behind curtains in several windows, their view of the blue door unobstructed. If I went inside, they'd see. And who was to say one of them wasn't behind giving the woman up. It was too risky. I'd have to hope and pray that when Max didn't hear from her, he'd come looking for me.

With a shuddering sigh, I turned my back on the dead woman and began making my way back toward the building I'd once called home.

"Fräulein," Paulina whispered when she opened the door to me, her brow creased with worry. Fright. I imagined any knock on the door was terrifying these days and felt bad for having startled her not once but twice.

"My contact…" I said and felt my eyes fill with tears.

She nodded silently and stepped back so I could enter.

"I didn't know where else to go," I said. "The man who brought me here… I have no way of getting word to him without the contact at the safe house. I don't know where he is."

Paulina clasped her hands in front of her, twisting her fingers, her eyes seeming to search the air around me for answers. She shook her head and crossed her arms over her chest.

"If you stay here, I'll have to tell her. I can't hide you. The soldier that comes, he is thorough. A right greedy bastard of a man just biding his time for your mother to pass. I'm positive he counts the silverware each time he comes to make sure I haven't hidden any away. He will find you. And when he does…"

"We'll all be in danger," I said.

But who was to say my mother wouldn't throw me out? Or tell the soldier about me herself. Her traitor daughter who had faked her death and hid for the past ten years. Her eldest daughter, who would both threaten his claim to the estate's belongings—and Catrin's.

But what was my other option? To sleep on the street? To find a closet somewhere in the lobby to hide in? What if a resident found me? They would surely turn me in. And what if Catrin came back unexpectedly in the next two days?

I decided it was worth the risk.

"Tell her," I said.

32

I SAT AT the kitchen table, my hands wrapped around a warm cup of tea Paulina had made me, my stomach queasy from the anticipation of what she would come to tell me after speaking with my mother.

The door swung open and I jumped, spilling tea on my fingers and the table. But I barely noticed, my eyes glued to Paulina's.

"She will see you," she said, the crease between her brows deep with concern.

"Was she…surprised?" I asked. "That I'm alive? That I'm here?"

"If she was, she didn't show it."

I nodded. My mother had always been a master at keeping emotion from her face. There were times I'd found it impressive, like when I knew she was disgusted by someone, or angry. The way she smoothed away any expression, her features taking on a serene, if not scarily calm demeanor, was remarkable. I imagined the shock of my appearance was taken in with barely the blink of a pale blue eye.

I wiped the spilled tea with a napkin and got to my feet.

"She's in her room?" I asked.

"She never leaves it."

As I passed her, Paulina squeezed my hand.

"Don't let her appearance fool you," she said. "She is unchanged, fräulein. And possibly worse."

The banister was smooth beneath my palm and I remembered my hand, much smaller, running over its gleaming wood in what seemed a lifetime ago.

I trod lightly, each step closer filling me more and more with dread. What had I been thinking coming here? And would it be worth it?

But an image of Catrin the day I left filled my mind and I knew there was only one answer.

Yes.

At the top of the stairs I stopped, staring up at the patched hole in the ceiling as I steeled myself for whatever was about to happen next.

Down the long hall I'd avoided as much as possible when I was a child, I stared at the paintings hanging on the walls, the expensive rug beneath my feet, and the vases and lamps and sculptures collected from my parents' travels around the world.

At the threshold of my mother's bedroom, I stopped. The door was open, the room beyond dark. The heavy curtains that were usually tied back during the day, offering the same sprawling view of the city that one got from the main sitting room, were closed, the only light coming from a small gap that barely illuminated the space.

For a moment I thought she must be in the adjoining bathroom, her body barely registering beneath the blankets covering her. And once I saw she was there, I couldn't tell if she was awake or asleep, looking at me, or eyes closed.

I took a step closer, taking in what I could of the room in the dim light. None of it seemed to have changed in my absence. There were the same elegant his-and-hers bureaus, the table and armchairs in the corner, the chaise lounge, and her collection of magazines filled with fashion advice.

The only thing different was the smell. The faint hint of his cologne mixing with her fragrance had long since faded, a sour, sickly smell replacing it.

The scent of a dying woman. The perfume of decay.

I felt more than saw the shift of her body in the bed and froze, feeling her eyes taking in what she could see of me in the dark. Assessing me as she always had. Scrutinizing with her critical eyes.

And then a voice from my past, weakened but unchanged, the high-pitched timbre curling around my birth name and sending a shiver of fear down my spine.

"Welcome home, Gisela."

33

Gisela

"TELL ME," she said, struggling to sit up, the knit hat on her head too big, her dressing gown gaping open to reveal jutting collarbones and sunken skin flushed pink from either fever, the fire lit in the fireplace in her bedroom, or both. "Did my traitor of a sister help you?"

Every instinct told me to help. The sick and wounded were my responsibility. I'd taken an oath. I'd sung a song with my chosen sisters.

But I resisted.

"I don't know what you mean," I said, moving across the room to stand beside my father's bureau, my eyes never leaving her. She, like my father, had always slept with a gun in arm's reach. I could imagine her small silver pistol resting beneath her pillows, waiting for the moment to use it.

"When we got the news you were dead, two years after she and that husband of hers disappeared, there was a part of me that wondered," she said. "Something about it. I couldn't put my finger on it, but..." She shrugged. "The two of you were so close. So alike. If you wanted to be dead, I decided so be it. Your escort returned with a certificate of death and your ashes. I didn't question it. Your father had one of his contacts investigate, but he came back with the same information. We had a funeral, a gravestone was placed, and it was done."

It had been an elaborate plan with more moving pieces than I'd known about until it was all said and done. I remembered my terror. That my parents would find out. That they'd come for me—or at least send someone to collect me. But my aunt and uncle had every possible angle covered—from my fake pen pal and her family in California, the car crash that supposedly killed me and left my body burned beyond recognition, and the news reports in the papers. The escort that had come with me was one of my uncle's people. The man sent by my father to investigate, also one of my uncle's men.

The truth was, there had been no body in the car that went careening off a particularly windy coastal road at night. And the people I was supposedly with, friends of the fake family my parents thought I was staying with, didn't exist. It had been a network of people and lies, feeding my parents information that made them feel as though not only was I in safe hands, but through me, they would be making a wealthy connection in America—one they might be able to use to their advantage in the future. My death didn't sadden them so much as disappoint them because of the contact they'd lost because of me, their eldest, who in their eyes had always failed them.

"And did you grieve?" I asked my mother now.

"I wore black for as long as I could stand it. I never did look good in dark colors. Our friends were of course devastated for us. We received a number of lovely gifts. The Seidels offered us their summer home in Spain for a month."

"Did you go?"

"Of course. It was very therapeutic. I found a gorgeous little desk for the guest room en suite."

I inhaled, letting her words wash over me. Her eldest child had died, or so she had been told, and she'd gone to Spain to soak up the sun and shop. I hadn't expected anything different from her, but it was shocking nonetheless. And of course there was no mention of Cat. How she'd coped. How the loss of her sister had affected her. Our parents probably hadn't even noticed. That would've been Nanny Paulina's job.

"Light some candles," Mother said. "I want to see you."

I knew she would want to see what had become of me without her to guide me, keep me painfully thin, groom me into the same kind of monster she was.

I felt around on the bureau and found a candle and a box of matches. I lit one, then noticed several more placed around the room and lit them as well before standing at the foot of her bed and taking her in as she did the same of me.

For someone who had never left her bedroom without a full face of makeup and every hair in place, wearing a beautiful outfit made especially for her, to see her now was shocking. Her blond hair was white, her face sallow and sunken, pale blue eyes cloudy, body emaciated to such a degree it was hard to look at.

"You've gotten fat," she said and I nearly laughed.

I was not what anyone would call fat. Unless, of course, you were my mother.

"What have you done with your life?" she asked. "Where did you go? What ridiculous things did my idiot sister get you into? You were with her, were you not? Tell me now."

"I'm not here to talk about me. I merely came to see you."

"Because I'm dying?" She waved a bony hand. "You were always too sentimental for your own good. Too teary and pleading and tenderhearted. Always wanting to save something or someone that wasn't worth our time or money. Like your little friend. What was her name?"

I stiffened, sound rushing into my ears, my hands balling into fists at my side.

Ruthie.

When I didn't speak she continued.

"You should've thanked me when I recommended her father be brought in for questioning. Who knows what he was doing to the Germans stupid enough to see a Jewish doctor."

My blood ran cold, my chest burning with hatred, tears welling in my eyes. Part of me had always wondered if she'd had something to do with Mr. Friedman's arrest, but I hadn't wanted to believe my own mother would do such a thing to my best friend's father.

She waved her hand again, impatient with my emotions.

"What did I always tell you about those feelings of yours?"

"Bury them," I murmured, wiping away the tear running down my cheek. "They have no place on one's face."

"Good girl. Now, tell me the real reason you're here."

"You know why."

"You've come for Catrin." As she said it, her eyes flicked over me again, a sneer lifting one side of her dry, thin lips.

"I have."

"Well, you've just missed her and I'm afraid she won't be back for some time. She can only come when her work allows."

I wanted to ask what kind of work my sister did, but didn't want to give my mother the satisfaction of having information I didn't. Even though we both knew she did.

"I might be here a while," I said. "Perhaps I'll see her when she's next in town."

"Perhaps, though I wouldn't expect a happy reunion."

"And why is that?"

My mother's eyes flashed.

"You left her. You deserted her. And when she finds out it was on purpose…"

"She was meant to come too. We had a plan."

"She'd never have gone."

"Of course she would have. To be with me."

"I always knew you were foolish, Gisela, but I didn't know you were downright stupid. Catrin is not you. She is made from something different. Something stronger. She is a Holländer. Unlike you."

I didn't want to believe what she was telling me. Couldn't even fathom what she was hinting at, and so I turned my gaze elsewhere, refusing to let her pull me in and rile me.

"Tell me what you've done with your life in America," my mother said, her voice taking on the familiar tone of disinterest. "I'm assuming that's where you've been all these years?"

"I'm a nurse," I said, ignoring her question.

Her cackle filled the room and I felt acute satisfaction when she began to cough and choke, Paulina running in to help her sit up and holding a glass of water to her mouth when the fit had finally begun to subside.

"Some nurse," my mother gasped, spittle from her sip of water spraying the air in front of her. "Clearly, you're no good at it, the way you just stood there as the dying woman before you choked."

"You're no woman," I whispered. "You're a monster."

I watched her for a moment more, her frail frame seizing with another coughing fit, Paulina standing by with the water glass, waiting patiently. When the coughing stopped again, Paulina pulled a handkerchief from her pocket and dabbed my mother's thin, dry lips and helped her back onto her pillows, tucking the blankets around her as she mercifully fell asleep. When Paulina pocketed the handkerchief once more, I noticed the blood on it.

"She'll sleep for a few hours," she said. "The talking and coughing will have worn her out."

I nodded, gave the woman that had given birth to me a last look, and turned on my heel.

By habit, I walked down the hall and took a right, hurrying down another corridor, anxious to put as much distance as I could between me and my mother. I was halfway to the door at the end of the hallway when I stopped, realizing where I was heading. My childhood bedroom.

The door was closed, and I paused as I reached for the knob, bracing myself for what was on the other side.

Taking a breath, I opened the door and stood on the threshold, staring in wonder.

It was like a time capsule. Everything in its place, as if I'd never left. As if I were coming back at any moment to pick up the book lying open on my vanity, or snuggle up to the white teddy bear nestled beside my pillow. Mila, I'd called it. A gift from my aunt when I'd turned four.

The air was musty, but the layer of dust I expected wasn't there.

"She makes me dust the entire house."

I turned at the sound of Paulina's voice.

"How would she know?" I asked. "It doesn't look like she gets around much anymore."

"She doesn't," she said, running a hand down her uniform, which sagged on a body that had once been rounder, but was now thin from the scarcity of food. "But the truth is, I need to do something to fill the hours. She sleeps a lot, which, as I'm sure you can imagine, is a relief. When she's awake she's..."

"A tyrant?"

"Unpleasant."

I smirked at the polite word and she shrugged.

"As I said, I'd have left," she said, wandering my old room, her fingers trailing over ballerina figurines and tiny glass flowers in a tiny glass vase. "But I was willing to look the other way because of the protection it afforded me. And of course, in the beginning there was the matter of caring for your sister. And getting word to your aunt."

"My aunt," I said, frowning. "What do you mean?"

"Someone had to get information to her when you couldn't. Let her know you were on your way. Had made it onto the boat safely."

My mouth opened, but no sound came out.

"Do you know how your mother found me?" Paulina asked. "The year before you were born, she was asking around about nannies. Her good friend Alina recommended me. We'd met years before. At a meeting."

Alina was the woman who had gone with me to America when I was sixteen.

"You knew," I whispered.

"I knew," she said.

"That's why you didn't seem shocked to see me at the door."

"Oh. I was shocked. I knew you didn't die ten years ago, but I never thought you'd return here."

I sat on the bed that had once been my sanctuary.

"Once I learned Cat was alive… I had to. No matter what kind of danger it put me in. To know she'd been here all this time, waiting for me to make good on the promise I'd made to her the day I left… I couldn't stay away." I looked around the room again and then back at Paulina. "If you knew I was alive and with my aunt, how come you never let her know Catrin was alive?"

She sighed and sat in the armchair I used to curl up in with one of the many books I'd spent my allowance on.

"When the plan to get your sister out failed and the network fell apart, I took it upon myself to care for Cat the best I could, mostly from afar. I tried, Gisela. Oh, how I tried. Whenever your parents weren't around, I told her stories I'd memorized and tried to feed her little brain the same things yours had been fed by your aunt. Kindness and empathy. Right and wrong. But Cat was—*is*—not you."

"What does that mean, Paulina?"

"Did you look at the address I gave you? For where you could find her?"

I shook my head as I reached into my pocket for the piece of paper. For a moment I just held it, but then, as Paulina watched, I unfolded it and stared down at the hastily written address.

"Berlin," I whispered.

"She is one of them," she said. "Indoctrinated with their ideologies. A child of the Hitler Youth."

My stomach turned over as the shock washed over me.

"No," I whispered, tears welling in my eyes. "No no no..."

I covered my face with my hands, images of Catrin as a little girl filling my mind. Sweet, sunny Catrin, her rosebud lips burbling with laughter, big blue eyes filled with mirth, tiny fingers intertwined with mine.

"I'm sorry," Paulina said, rubbing my back softly. "I failed you. I failed both of you."

I shook my head.

It wasn't her fault. It was my parents'.

"That's why she was smirking at me," I said.

"Who?"

"My mother. She is giddy at the thought of me finding out Catrin is no longer mine, but hers."

Paulina nodded.

"She has always been cruel, your mother. And the only person she has ever served was herself. The only *thing* she served was a lifestyle. When your father died she insisted on a funeral, no expense spared. It was winter. The ground was frozen. But she made them dig. Requested flowers. Had me hire whoever I could find to help clean the house for guests to come and mourn. Some stayed for weeks. I was expected to cook grand meals for them all. We had more than most, of course. The Holländers were above the rest. And I'll admit, I welcomed the food, knowing how so many others were suffering. But the way they wasted… The way they mocked those with less than them… Of course she is finding joy in your pain. In your ignorance. If you allow her, she'll rub your nose in it. Don't let her. Now that you know about Catrin, ignore her barbs."

There was a warning in her voice.

"Why?"

"Because I fear if you rile her, she won't be able to help herself. She'll tell that nosy little soldier that comes by exactly who you are."

A shiver ran down my spine.

"Keep your distance while you're here. I'll lie as much as I can if she asks for you, but if you are in this house, she will want to see you. She will expect it if you are under her roof and the protection of her name."

"I don't want you to lie," I said. "Not for me. Not anymore. If she wants to see me…if she wants to torture me…I will let her. I will do whatever it takes to see Catrin again. And that means not getting sent to jail or killed."

I stood then and wandered the room, touching my old things. A dollhouse, complete with a family of four, a lamp, a jewelry box, a silver-handled mirror.

"Your bureau is still filled with clothes," Paulina said. "But I doubt any of them fit you anymore. I'll bring you one of your mother's nightgowns."

"Thank you."

"Is there anything else you need?"

I stared at her and she gave me a sad smile, understanding that there was only one thing I needed.

Catrin.

"I know, *kleiner Hase*," she said, reaching out and pressing her palm to my cheek.

As she turned toward the door, I reached for her hand.

"Thank you, Paulina."

"For what, Gisela?"

I met her gaze and held it.

"You're welcome," she said.

34

I WOKE THE following morning confused at where I was at first, which happened a lot these days after all the traveling I'd done. It was surreal to look around and find I was in my childhood bedroom. It felt like a dream and a nightmare all rolled into one.

Grabbing the heavy robe from the foot of the bed that Paulina had brought me the night before, I stood and pulled it on, tying it tight as I shivered from the cold.

Quietly, I opened the bedroom door, waiting…listening. But other than the wind whistling through the boards that had been nailed to the ceiling, there was no sound.

I hurried on tiptoe down the hallway to the staircase, my socked feet a whisper on the stairs.

"Guten morgen," Paulina said when I entered the kitchen. The smell of eggs cooking made my stomach turn.

"Good morning," I said, glancing into the pan. "Have they gone bad?"

"The eggs?" she asked, frowning and leaning forward to give them a sniff. "I was told they were laid two days ago. Do they smell bad?"

"I think I may have a touch of the flu," I said. "My stomach has been turning all morning. Is there bread?"

She pointed to the bread box on one of the counters. "Freshly baked yesterday."

My mouth fell open. I hadn't had bread that fresh since I'd last been in New York.

"How?" I asked.

She pointed in the direction of my mother's room and I nodded. It paid to be one of the wealthiest families in Germany. The thought sickened me further. While others got small chunks of old bread to share with their families, we, because of my parents' wealth and stature, got fresh-baked bread. There was even real coffee, not the diluted stuff so many others drank. The icebox had meat. There were fresh vegetables. And though there wasn't a lot of it, it was plenty for three, especially since my mother barely had an appetite.

I picked small pieces of the bread, placing it gingerly in my mouth as I watched her cook, and feeling relieved when my stomach calmed some.

"Do you have a plan for today?" Paulina asked, scraping the eggs onto a plate.

"I thought I'd go back to the street where the safe house is," I said. "I imagine my contact heard what happened and will be watching for me."

"And then? If you find him? You will head to Berlin?"

"Yes. Maybe? I don't know. If he won't take me there, I will have to find my own way."

The thought terrified me. At least with Max there were contacts, safe houses, and options. On my own… I didn't trust that someone wouldn't get hold of my belongings and find the documents that would reveal me as a traitor.

"You must be careful," Paulina said. "If anyone is watching that house and saw you yesterday…and then again today…"

I nodded.

"Maybe we disguise you a little?" she asked. "A scarf over your hair…some padding around your middle? A different coat and bag?"

And so that is what we did. While my mother slept, Paulina removed several items from her closet and then met me back in my room.

I slipped the nightgown over my head and reached for the items she'd brought one by one. A thick pair of stockings, another pair to go over the first, a pale pink camisole, a long-sleeve top in my mother's signature blue that she'd probably worn in the Alps during a ski vacation, and a cashmere dress in a beautiful beige color.

"Cashmere?" I asked, raising my eyebrows at Paulina, who merely shrugged.

"It's the warmest thing she owns," she said. "I'd give you one of my wool dresses, but you'd drown in it."

"What if someone sees it? Realizes it's expensive?"

"You'll be wearing that over the top," she said, pointing to a black coat. "It was your father's."

We swapped my bag for a cloth one that had seen better days, and then she handed me a small pillow that I shoved beneath the dress, using the waistbands of the stockings to keep it in place.

"I hate letting you go out there alone," Paulina said, eyeing my padded stomach and reaching to adjust it.

"Then come with me," I said.

For a moment, she looked wistful. But then she gave her head a little shake and handed me the coat.

"Paulina?"

"I am too old. Too slow. Too fearful to take such risks," she said. "And your mother… Just promise me you won't do anything stupid. You won't try to be a hero if you see something bad happening to someone on the street. You go, take a look around, and if you don't see your friend, you come right back, understand? I imagine they still have people watching the house you went to and if someone sees you and thinks you look suspicious because they don't recognize you..."

"I understand."

"Good."

We walked swiftly past my mother's room where her soft snores could be heard, and down the stairs.

Paulina led the way to the kitchen and reached a hand out for my bag. I gave it to her and then watched as she placed an apple and a sandwich wrapped in wax paper inside.

"In case you find yourself having to hide somewhere for a long period of time," she said.

At the front door, she pulled me close.

"I know it is awful for me to wish that you'll need to come back," she said. "But despite the circumstances, it's been so lovely to see you again, Gisela."

"And you, Paulina," I said, holding her tight. "If I don't see you again, take care of yourself."

"I will. And you remember what I said. Don't linger. Don't be a hero. And come back immediately if you don't see your friend."

I nodded, gave her a last squeeze, and hurried out the door.

The cold was biting as I walked slowly so as not to garner attention, my head down, the scarf covering my hair feeling as though it might blow away.

There were even fewer people out today than there had been yesterday, and I kept close to the walls of buildings as I made my way to my destination, hoping no one took notice of me or, if they did, would dismiss me as someone not worth bothering with.

At the street where I'd seen the woman get shot, I crossed to the other side so as not to be standing in the same spot where

I'd been when she was killed. From the opposite corner I had a better view of the front of the house. Her body had been moved, but a bloodstain on the pavement could be clearly seen. Not wanting to linger in one place too long, I began to walk down the street, ducking my head, my eyes searching my surroundings for signs of Max as I passed an older man walking his dog, a young woman pushing a pram with a crying baby inside, and a flustered-looking woman with two young boys trailing behind her. But neither Max, nor the car we'd arrived in, were anywhere in sight.

At the end of the street I stopped and looked back. The quiet was eerie. Unnatural. I had imagined a different sort of scenario here. A hostility in the faces of the people I'd pass. But then I remembered. Not all of them had chosen this, and they were paying a price for the monsters who had. Monsters like my parents.

My stomach turned uncomfortably and I pressed a hand to my lips as I paused beneath the barren branches of a tree, leaning against the trunk and trying to look as inconspicuous as possible as I ducked my head and glanced around.

It was a risk to stop. I was a stranger here and should anyone be watching, I would stand out. This would be good if someone Max knew was keeping a lookout for me, but bad if a nervous neighbor noticed and called the police on the suspicious-seeming woman loitering about.

I pretended to be searching for something in my bag while discreetly scanning the area. Should anyone stop and ask, I could say I'd lost my key. Since there wasn't one in my bag, it was the perfect lie.

But as the minutes ticked by with no contact from anyone claiming to know Max, I began to falter, defeat weighing me down, disappointment and fear welling in my eyes. It had been a risk to come here. An unknown woman stood out. Especially on a street where a safe house had been found. I wouldn't be able to come again.

I gave the street one last look before pushing off the tree and slowly beginning my journey back to my mother's house.

There was a box of food on the kitchen counter when I returned. After changing out of the borrowed clothing and back into my own, I returned to the kitchen to see how I could help Paulina.

"Stir," she said, pointing to a pot on the stove where the scent of an aromatic broth filled the air. "Your mother will be up any minute and will be hungry."

"She sleeps a lot these days?" I asked, remembering a time when she always seemed to be awake, watching, scrutinizing my every move.

"Most of the day," Paulina said, removing a cloth bag of vegetables from the box. "And the night."

I nodded and picked up the ladle to give the soup a stir.

"The groceries were delivered by the store's owner today," she said.

There was something in her voice that made me turn around.

"Is that odd?" I asked, worry filling my limbs. Had someone seen me and grown suspicious? Was the house being watched?

"Not really," she said, and slipped something into the pocket of my cardigan sweater before taking the ladle from me and grabbing a bowl.

I watched as she placed the bowl and a spoon on a tray, followed by a small, blue ceramic teapot, a matching cup and saucer, and a thin slice of bread. She picked up the tray, glanced down at my pocket, and then disappeared out the kitchen door.

Taking a breath, I sank into one of the kitchen chairs and reached inside my pocket, pulling out a folded scrap of paper.

4 compromised, it read. *Exit tomorrow. 2pm sharp. Same place as drop.*

I exhaled. The grocer had delivered a note from Max. I only

had to survive one more night here and then I could leave. But what would Max say about me going to Berlin? Would he help me? Or would he insist I give up my plan and take me back to England?

While I contemplated an argument for taking me to see my sister, the kitchen door swung back open, causing me to jump.

"She wants to see you," Paulina said, the look on her face apologetic.

"Why?" I asked.

Paulina shook her head. "She didn't say and..."

"You couldn't ask," I said, nodding. "I know. It's okay."

I got up from the table and handed her the paper. "I have to leave tomorrow or I may be stuck here with no way out."

A few minutes later I was standing outside my mother's darkened room, the sour scent of dying seeping into the hall, while my stomach threatened to give and my knees buckle.

"Gisela," my mother said.

Her voice was a ragged whisper that made my body go cold beneath the layers of clothes.

"Yes?" I said.

"Come."

When I was a girl I was never allowed in my parents' room. It was a grown-up room, I was told time and time again. Not a room for little girls with sticky fingers and dirty shoes. I'd been confused by this, as I was never sticky and my shoes checked constantly. God forbid I track in a speck of dirt. I remember watching guests enter for a party once and watching as Paulina and our other servants allowed them in without checking the bottoms of their shoes for grit. Did only a child's shoes attract such things? Regardless, my parents' bedroom remained a mystery to me much of my life. I got glimpses now and again as I passed by and one or the other of them came in or out, but I wasn't to knock if I wanted to talk to them. I was to ask my nanny and she would relay any messages or inquiries I might have. What I did see in those brief moments though made me think, at least when I was very small, that my mother was a princess, making my father, of course, a prince.

Gleaming wallpaper, a four-poster bed with decadent covers that changed for each season, luminous curtains, and a clean, almost effervescent scent. Like fresh air with champagne bubbles floating through.

I stepped inside the room and gagged as the smell intensified. Urine, sharp and putrid. Sweat. And something else that nearly made me gag. I assumed it was the festering lesion Paulina had told me about.

"Do you need Paulina?" I asked, standing in the doorway, unable to take a step closer, the smell like a wall.

"No. You're the nurse. You can help me."

"What do you need?" I asked, praying it was merely a glass of water. Perhaps a cold cloth on her forehead.

"I've soiled myself. I need you to clean it up. Me, and the bed."

"I think Paulina is more suited—"

"Help me, or when that sniveling soldier boy with the greedy eyes comes, I'll tell him you're an American spy."

I sucked in a breath. My mother was horrible in a great many ways, but I'd never once considered she'd willingly put my life at risk.

Steeling myself, I moved toward the bed, the stench growing with every step, my stomach threatening to give.

"Ma'am?" Paulina said from the doorway. "What's going on? What can I do?"

"Nothing," my mother said, waving her away. "Gisela will take care of it."

She watched my every move as I peeled her many layers off until I reached the soiled nightgown and removed it from her emaciated body. Wetting a cloth to clean her, I returned to the bathroom at least a dozen times to rinse it or get a new one when the other became too dirty to continue using. When she was clean, I pulled a fresh nightgown, socks, and several other items from her large walk-in closet and dressed her as she pretended not to be bothered by the indignity of the situation. But the goose bumps covering her pale skin, the shivering, and the little mewls of pain gave her away.

Once she was clean, I helped her to one of the armchairs and covered her with a blanket before beginning the task of removing the linens from the bed.

"You look..." Her voice trailed off and I glanced over at her, wondering if she'd fallen asleep midsentence. But she was peering at me, her pale eyes scrutinizing as they always had.

"I look what?" I asked.

"Come here."

It was the oft-snapped command of my childhood. *Come here. Stand still. Don't make a face. Be strong. Don't make a fool of me.* The list went on.

Sighing, I set the pillow in my hands on the bed and went to stand before her, watching as she reached out with her curled, boney fingers, running them over my stomach.

I flinched. I'd hated being touched by her for as long as I could remember. She'd never had a kind word for me after her scrutiny and physical examination of my hips, stomach, thighs, and ass. No doubt I would hear something demeaning now too.

Her hand rose, cupping one of my breasts, and I took a step back.

"No," I said.

"It's heavy," she said. "And your belly is soft."

"I'm hardly fat, Mother," I said, wanting badly to roll my eyes, but stepping away from her instead and going back to work on the bed.

I was the thinnest I'd ever been. Though she was right about my breasts. They had felt strangely heavy for the past few days. And they ached.

But she still peered at me, suspicious, her lip suddenly curling in a way that reminded me of getting caught being naughty as a girl.

"Have you done something even more stupid than leaving here ten years ago, girl? Have you gone and gotten your traitorous self pregnant by the enemy?"

"Of course not," I said, unfurling the clean top sheet.

"I hope not. Your father would roll over in his grave if you tarnished his family name."

"He already did that himself," I said, tucking the sheet in and then grabbing a fresh blanket.

"Don't speak ill of your father."

I bit my tongue to keep from arguing. This conversation was pointless and I knew it. Instead, I kept working, placing a second blanket on top of the first before hauling a clean quilt from the closet and placing it on the bed as well.

But her words circled my mind. Pregnant?

"Ready?" I asked her, and then leaned down to help her to her feet, across the room and back into bed.

I tucked the covers in around her and then turned my back on her and headed for the door.

"Come back here!" she yelled after me. "I need things!"

"I'll send Paulina," I said as I hurried out the door and practically ran to my room.

I heard her shout my name, but I ignored her, closing the door and slowly moving toward the full-length mirror.

One by one I pulled off my layers until I stood only in my underwear, staring at my reflection. I'd ignored it for weeks now, but I could feel it. The shift in my body. My breasts were larger, my stomach softer, there was more weight in my face, and a fullness inside me. Not to mention the morning sickness I'd tried to convince myself was exhaustion mixed with a stomach bug. But I could no longer hide the truth from myself.

I was pregnant. I was going to have William's baby.

35

THE FOLLOWING DAY I kept busy cleaning, my eyes constantly drifting to the clock in whatever room I was in, the minutes ticking by at a snail's pace.

My mother woke around noon and I waited to be summoned, discriminated against, and verbally abused. But mercifully, she seemed too tired today to bother with me. I watched as Paulina readied her tray and then cleaned up after she went to serve the lady of the house.

At one forty on the dot I gave Paulina a tentative smile and a brief hug, and then grabbed my bag and hurried to meet Max.

I was early, but so was he. I slid into the passenger seat and his eyes did a quick assessment of me as he spoke.

"I'm sorry about the safe house," he said.

"It's not your fault."

"Still, that must've been terrifying. And not knowing how to get in touch with me..."

"I knew you'd get a message to me."

He nodded and then asked. "Your sister?"

"Berlin."

He nodded again and we sat quietly for a moment before the words burst out of me.

"I want to go there."

"No."

There was no hesitation.

"Why not?"

"It is unsafe for you here," he said. "But Berlin is downright dangerous. Do you know what she's doing there?"

"She works at an office. She's a secretary." My voice was low. Sad. Max peered at me.

"For them?" he asked and I nodded.

"Right. Well then, what you're thinking is basically akin to suicide and I cannot, in good conscience, take you there. I would advise you not to try to go on your own either."

"I thought you might say that. The only other option I can see then is… I stay."

"What? No. I cannot allow—"

"It's not up to you, Max."

"It's too dangerous. The Allies are getting closer. They could bomb the area, take you prisoner…"

He was right, of course. And now I knew I was risking so much more than just myself. There was the life growing inside me. And there was the life I wanted to build with William to take into account. By choosing Catrin, I would be putting it all in jeopardy. But how did one choose one life over another? And would I be able to live with myself if I abandoned her again? True, she was an adult making her own decisions. But only because I'd left her behind when she was too young to fend off our parents' and the government's teachings. I should've fought harder for her to leave when I did. I should've refused to go without her. And now that I was back here, I couldn't just go.

I had to at least try to help her see the error of her ways and get her far, far away from here.

"She's worth the risk," I whispered.

"Kate. Lena." He frowned as he uncharacteristically stumbled over the names. Names that weren't really mine.

"My name is Gisela," I said, my eyes filling with tears. "And I can't go. Not until I've seen Catrin. Not until I've talked to her. I know she is not the same girl I left, but we are sisters and I have loved her since the day she was born. I will not leave her again."

He stared at me and I stared back, resolute in my decision.

"Your aunt and uncle will never forgive me," he said.

"They will. They'll know you would've tried to make me see reason."

"If anything happens to you—"

"Then that's my fault, not yours."

He looked away from me and sighed. A moment later he pulled a pen and small pad of paper from this coat pocket.

"This is my last contact in the city," he said, scribbling something on the paper. "I was just with them and they know about you. I have no idea how long they plan to stay. Could be until tomorrow, could be until the war's end. But here is the address and the name you're to give them should you need a way out."

He tore the paper from the pad and handed it to me. I read the address, then the name.

Raphael Dubois.

"Is that…"

"That is my name. My real name."

"Tu es Français?" I asked.

"Born and raised in Burgundy."

"It's nice to meet you, Raphael."

"And you, Gisela."

He touched the tip of his finger to the paper. "If you go and they are not there, you have two pieces of identification to help get you out. Just be sure you give the right one to the right person."

I nodded, giving him a small, sad smile.

"You're sure about this?" he asked.

I took in a long breath and then let it out.

"No," I said. "But I have to see my sister. I *have* to."

He watched me for a long moment and then reached out his hand. I placed mine in it and for a minute we just sat there.

"Thank you," I said, breaking the silence.

"I'll bet you're a great nurse," he said and I gave him a quizzical smile.

"Why do you say that?"

"Because you'd have made a good spy. Calm in any situation."

"I much prefer working on a life-threatening gun wound to having a gun in my face," I said and he chuckled.

"A good point." He shifted in his seat, his eyes growing serious once more. "You are sure?"

"I am sure."

"Okay then. Be safe, Gisela. And come home soon."

"I'll do my best. Please give my love to my aunt and uncle. And tell them I'm sorry. When I can, I'll send word."

I didn't wave as he drove away. I didn't even watch. I merely listened to the sound of tires crunching on the broken cement as I turned and walked toward home.

"Fräulein," Paulina whispered as she opened the front door and pressed a finger to her lips. She pulled me inside and we stood staring at one another, listening. Somewhere in the house I could hear movement. The sharp clip of footsteps echoing through the hallways.

"Who's here?" I asked quietly.

"The soldier."

My body went cold with fear. The soldier. The one I'd heard

came every few days or so under the guise of making sure my mother was safe, but with a clear interest in what he would take once the lady of the house passed away. I hoped that calm I supposedly had would make itself known.

"Remember the story?" Paulina asked. We'd spent time that first evening after the woman was shot at the safe house coming up with a story for why I was there, in case the soldier came before I could get away.

I nodded.

"Good. Let's get this over with."

She led me to the kitchen and reached for my bag, but I grasped it tightly and held on, shaking my head.

Her eyes told me she understood and she pointed to the pantry.

"He's already checked there so he won't check again," she said. Reluctantly, I let her have it and watched as she stashed it behind a box of sprouting potatoes.

She pointed to the cutting board where a small pile of vegetables waited to be cut, and then to the pan on the stove. I moved quickly, picking up the knife and beginning to chop, my fingers trembling.

His boots were on the staircase now, each strike of the man's boot heel making me flinch. A moment later the kitchen door swung open.

"Who are you?"

His voice was like gunfire. Sharp. Quick. And came at me with a speed so fast I nearly took off my own fingertip

I was shocked at how young he was. Younger than me. Twenty at the most. His face was bland, void of any interesting characteristics, the bit of his hair I could see a dark blond, eyes blue. He was the perfect German soldier, and the ugly look in his eyes made my blood run cold.

"I—"

"This is Lena," Paulina said, putting on a casual if not slightly irritated voice. "Her mother was a nurse and she's learned some tricks of the trade so I've hired her to help with Mrs. Holländer."

I gave him a quick smile before lowering my eyes again.

"Lena," Paulina continued. "This is Lieutenant Schmeiden." She said it in a way that made him sound important.

"She stays here?" he asked, moving closer to me.

"She does," Paulina said. "As of two days ago."

"Where do you normally live?" he asked me, his eyes taking my clothing, my battered shoes. "I've never seen you before."

"I'm from Wismar, sir."

"How did you find a girl from Wismar to help you?" he asked Paulina.

"One of the neighbor women told me about her."

"Hm," he said, circling the kitchen island where I was concentrating on not cutting myself as I kept chopping vegetables. "And where were you when I arrived?"

"She was running an errand for me," Paulina said, moving to the pantry.

He stopped beside me, his uniform brushing against my elbow.

"You have identification, I assume?" he asked, his breath brushing against my neck.

"Of course," I said, setting down the knife and moving to the sink to wash my hands.

"I don't have all day."

I wiped my hands on my skirt and hurried to the pantry for my bag where I pulled my German identification from the small purse inside.

Silently, I handed it over and watched as he opened it, took a long look, stared up at me, and then snapped it closed.

"Lena Klein," he said and I nodded. He gazed at me a moment more and then handed the ID back. "Your assessment of Mrs. Holländer?"

I glanced at Paulina, who had busied herself at the stove as if unworried about my interaction with the young solider. Remembering what she'd said about his visits, his obvious interest in the estate's many expensive items, I gave him an answer I knew he would like.

"She is gravely ill," I said. "I don't expect her to last more than a month."

I commended him for trying to keep the smile off his face. It was a valiant effort.

"Well," he said, clearing his throat as he strode to the other side of the room. "I am sorry to hear that. It is good of you both to take such care in her comfort these last days of her life."

"It is our honor," Paulina said.

"I shall return in a couple of days," he said and then gave us a curt nod and disappeared out the kitchen door. A moment later, the front door shut.

"Is he gone?" I mouthed.

Paulina held up a finger and hurried from the room. When she returned, her face was filled with relief. I picked up the knife and resumed chopping while she set a pot of stock on to boil.

36

BY DECEMBER, Paulina and I had fallen into an easy routine. We met in the mornings, bundled against the cold, in the kitchen. She'd put the kettle on while I lit fires in the two downstairs fireplaces to begin warming the house. After that, the two of us would begin preparations for breakfast.

We ate together at the kitchen table, sometimes talking, sometimes saying nothing at all, the long day ahead stretching before us and our minds preparing to find ways to pass the time until we could sleep again.

My mother was barely conscious most of the day, making my interactions with her few and far between, though that didn't lessen the ferocity of her words to me when she was awake. If anything, it made them worse.

Clothing began to be an issue for me, my own meager belongings, as well as what Paulina had pulled from my mother's extensive closet becoming too tight around my chest and waist. The only things I could fit in well were nightgowns, dressing gowns, and a few billowy dresses my mother used to wear in warmer weather, which meant the fabric was thin and did nothing to fight against the cold of winter.

The time had come to tell Paulina.

"You're sure?" she asked, her eyes worriedly sweeping over me.

"I'm sick nearly every morning now," I said, and then pressed a hand to my breasts. "They hurt and feel heavy. Swollen. And the waistbands of my pants and skirts are tight. I'm sure."

"Well," she said, clasping her hands in front of her. "Okay. We will just…figure it out, yes? You are a nurse. You are trained for such things?"

"Not babies. Gunshots and severed limbs. But…yes. We'll figure it out."

I smiled gratefully and she pulled me to her and kissed my forehead.

"Do not fret, fräulein."

The next morning before I came down for breakfast, she knocked on my bedroom door.

"Here," she said, a pile of clothes in her arms. "These were your father's. You can belt the pants and I can hem them so they are not too long. Everything else will be big, but you will grow into them."

I nodded, trying not to balk at the familiar smell of his cologne still clinging to the fabrics.

"If you want something a bit more feminine to wear," Paulina said. "I can alter some of it."

"I'm not particularly worried about looking feminine," I said, running my hand over a gray wool sweater. "But thank you. I'm sure these will be just fine as they are."

"Should you see a doctor?" she asked. "There's one I can call to the house. He used to treat your mother, but when it became clear there was nothing to be done, we agreed there was no point in him coming anymore and he armed me with pain medication to keep her comfortable."

"I don't think so," I said. "After I see Catrin, I will try to get us out of here as quickly as possible. It's been three weeks now. She should come again soon, right?"

"If she keeps to the schedule she's been on, then yes. But with the way the war is going, who knows. It could be longer. You need to think not just of her now, but of the baby growing inside you."

The baby. *My* baby. Mine and William's.

I looked at Paulina with desperation in my eyes. "I can't give up. Not yet."

"We'll give it two more weeks," she said. "If Catrin hasn't come, you must reach out to your contact. For the sake of *your* child, Gisela, not the one you feel guilty about leaving behind so many years ago."

I was about to say more, but then my mother screeched my name from her bedroom, startling us both. She didn't often wake this early and it made me wonder if this was it. By the look on Paulina's face, I could see she was thinking the same thing.

"I'll go," she said, starting for the door.

But I placed my hand on her arm to stop her. "She'll just insist you get me. You know how she is. It's fine. You start breakfast, I'll call if I need you."

The room stank of the bile I found spewed across the bedside table, her glass of water, and the lamp that was rarely turned on.

"Mutter?" I said, my voice low. Her back was to me, her spine protruding grotesquely through her layers of clothes. It seemed impossible that she'd lost even more weight since I'd arrived, but where she used to be able to walk across the room with help, she now had to be carried, her body a mere skeleton, her skin stretched so thin it looked like it might break.

When she didn't respond, I walked to the other side of the bed and checked the pulse at her wrist, staring down at the veins and tendons running up the inside of her arm, and realizing for the first time that she wore no jewelry.

Her pulse was weak but there, and I noticed that despite her many layers and the fire burning in the fireplace across from her, she was shivering. I wanted to walk away. Pretend I hadn't noticed. She had never lifted so much as a finger to help me as a child, instead leaving me for the nanny to deal with. She had humiliated me, abused me both verbally and physically. Neglected me. And never, not for one day, had she made me feel loved or accepted.

And yet, I could almost forgive that if those were her only sins. But they were not. She and my father had donated millions to the Nazi Party. It was that which they gave their time and attention to, throwing parties, fundraising, and attending function after function. The destruction of a community was what they'd chosen to focus on—not their own flesh and blood.

But would I be no better if I stood here, staring down at a dying woman, and did nothing to help comfort her?

An animal-like groan escaped my throat as I pushed myself to my feet. I hated her for making me question my feelings. The right and wrong of them. I owed her nothing. And the painful, ugly death she was dying was exactly what she deserved.

Exhaling angrily, I strode to the bathroom for the cleaning supplies Paulina kept handy in a bucket. Grabbing a bottle of cleaner and a rag, I entered the bedroom again and gagged at the smell that seemed stronger in this part of the room where it had no place to escape.

Not caring about the cold that would rush in, I swept open the curtains covering the nearest window and threw it open, inhaling at the rush of cool, clean air, the nausea building in my throat subsiding.

"Oh! Lena, no!"

I turned to see Paulina rushing in and grabbing one of the extra blankets from the foot of the bed. She unfolded it and threw it over my mother before hurrying across the room and slamming the window closed.

"What are you doing?" she asked.

"It stinks," I said. "I was going to be sick."

"The cold will kill her," she said and I stared back at her with unblinking eyes.

Her own eyes filled with tears and her shoulders slumped.

"Give it to me," she said, reaching for the cleaner. "Go downstairs. Breakfast is ready."

Shame filled me. Not because of my mother, but because of Paulina, who had spent the last several years caring for my mother. She had sacrificed and endured, and if my mother lived long enough, she would no doubt put her body in front of her employer's to protect it should the Allies take the city. I knew she also carried guilt because of these things. For tending to a woman who had contributed to the imprisonment and deaths of thousands while hiding her own beliefs in order to protect and watch over Catrin and me until she felt she had no other choice but to stay.

"I'm sorry, Paulina," I whispered.

She sniffed and gave me a sad smile.

"Go," she said. "Before the food gets cold."

Two weeks later I was sitting at the kitchen table eating soup and what was nearly our last slice of bread.

"I'll go out today," Paulina had said, pushing the bread toward me when I'd argued we should save it for my mother.

"What if the baker doesn't have any more?"

"He always holds a loaf aside until end of day in case I come by."

I'd learned she paid him every week to do so.

The radio beside me was on and turned down low. We kept it like this all day. The volume down so we didn't have to hear the lies the German people were told by the news outlets, but the noise coming from it constant. It had been my idea. The house was so quiet, it helped fill the absence of sound.

At least a dozen times a day we leaned in close to the speaker and one of us turned the knob, watching the dial in anticipation as it neared the notch that sometimes brought in broadcasts from the BBC. It was traitorous to do so, and getting caught listening to it was cause for imprisonment…and even death. Oftentimes we only got static on that station, but every so often we got lucky. We just had to be very careful we didn't forget and leave it tuned there, should Lieutenant Schmeiden make one of his unscheduled house calls.

I had the radio tuned there now and as I took a tentative bite of my soup, a potato and leek concoction that so far my body hadn't rejected, I heard something about Belgium and reached over to turn up the volume a tick.

"Is something happening?" Paulina asked, entering the room.

I waved a hand to shush her and she quietly took the seat across from me, the two of us listening intently to the announcer report that Germany was heading into a new attack on Belgium.

"There won't be any of us left by the end of this," Paulina said with a sigh as she got up and went to the pantry to grab the cloth bag she used for getting groceries. "What a selfish, ignorant little man."

I turned the volume down, moved the dial back, and got to my feet, holding out my hand for the bag.

"Let me go," I said.

I'd rarely left the house since meeting Max to tell him I wasn't going with him, and had so far been able to keep Paulina at bay when she'd questioned my plans to reach out to his contact.

"It's not a good idea," she said, tightening her grip on the bag.

"Why not?"

"You could slip and fall on the ice and debris."

“Paulina—”

“I worry someone will recognize you,” she said, slapping her hand on the counter and making me jump.

“But… I haven’t been here in years. I barely look like the sixteen-year-old version of me that last lived in this house.”

“You look like her,” she said, pointing in the direction of my mother’s room.

She wasn’t wrong about that.

“I’ll keep my head down and wear a scarf over my hair. And a hat over that!”

She exhaled, peering at me.

“Please, Paulina. I need to get out of this house. I need fresh air and sunlight on my face.”

It was a beautiful, clear day. Cold, but the blue sky was calling to me. And the smell of my mother’s room was starting to invade the other spaces.

“I promise I’ll be careful.”

“What if someone stops and questions you? Asks to see your ID?”

“Then I’ll show it to them.”

I stared at her and she stared back.

Her shoulders slumped and I knew I’d won.

“Don’t talk to anyone,” she said. “Only the baker. Hand him the list. It has my signature on it and the address here. If he questions you. Asks why you’ve come instead of me, tell him Mrs. Holländer isn’t doing well and I couldn’t leave her side.”

I reached out to squeeze her hand. “I’ll be fine. I’ll be smart. I promise.”

Several minutes later I entered the stairwell, a scarf over my hair and one of Paulina’s raggedy old knit hats over the top. Instead of one of my father’s coats, she gave me one of hers.

“Nothing that says money,” she’d said, and gave me a pair of mittens that had seen better days.

Gasping at the cold just beyond our lobby, I hurried down

the stairs, careful to keep one hand on the banister in case I slipped, my footsteps echoing throughout the enclosed space. At the landing I paused, listening for anyone coming down behind me, and then opening the door into the grand lobby that used to be filled with the excitement of people coming and going, packages arriving, beautiful women in expensive clothing, men smoking and laughing loudly, the elevator steward smiling politely as he held the door and pressed the buttons, winking at me a moment before he disappeared.

It was odd how quiet it was now. Besides my mother, Paulina had told me only three other families had stayed. A family of four on the second, a couple on the sixth, and a family of three on the tenth.

"All moved in after you left," Paulina had told me. "So if you happen to run into them, they won't recognize you."

It was a small comfort.

A brisk wind whipped against my face as soon as I stepped outside. Ducking my head, I stayed close to the buildings to try and block it as I hurried to the address I'd been given.

The line out front was long, and though Paulina had told me I didn't have to wait, that I could in fact go straight to the counter, I would have felt guilty walking past all the others to the front of the line.

It took at least an hour to get to the front of the line. An expanse of time that would've been almost pleasant in springtime, but was miserable in winter, the wind cutting through my layers, my stomach grumbling at the smell of fresh-baked bread.

As I stepped forward, a small loaf of bread that had barely risen was placed before me. It looked dry. Old. And smelled of nothing. I slid Paulina's list across the counter and waited patiently as the old man on the other side scanned it, stared at me, and then turned away and disappeared behind a door.

My heart raced. Where was he going? Had I done it wrong? Was I in trouble? Who was he going to tell?

But a moment later he reappeared, a paper sack in his hands, a fresh loaf of bread peeking out the top, the scent of it nearly making me swoon.

"Here you are," he said, giving me a small, confused smile. "Didn't Paulina tell you to come straight to the front?"

"She did but..." I glanced behind me. "The line was so long and I felt bad."

"She pays extra for the fast service. Next time you don't wait. I don't want to make Paulina mad. It wouldn't do to anger my most generous customer."

"Of course. I'm so sorry. I'll be sure to tell her it was my fault."

He nodded then and turned his attention to the next person in line as I hurried to get out of the way.

"Gisela?" a woman's voice said.

I almost stopped, my step hesitating for half a second. I recovered by pretending to check the contents of the bag and kept going.

"Excuse me."

She was behind me. Following me. Her hand on my elbow.

I jumped, pretending to be surprised.

"Yes?" I said, my gaze moving across her face, trying to recognize her from my past. She looked familiar, but it had been ten years since I'd seen any of my old classmates. "Can I help you?"

"Are you..." She was staring at me, trying to see the young girl I'd once been in the womanly face looking back at her. "I'm sorry. It's silly. You look a little like a girl I used to know but..." She glanced at the people still waiting in line, watching our exchange curiously, and then at the soldier by the door.

"But what?" I asked.

"You can't be," she said, her shoulders sagging. "She died. A long time ago. I'm sorry."

Johanna. That was her name. She'd sat two seats back from me in the last mathematics class I'd ever taken in a German school. She'd been a sweet girl. Smart. Bookish. And friendly.

One of the only girls to reach out, to touch my hand the day Ruthie didn't come to school. But I couldn't know her now.

Life and war had aged her, etching deep lines into her young face, hollowing beneath her eyes, and drying her lips. I gave her a smile and reached out, touching her paper-dry hand with my own.

"I'm sorry about your friend," I said, and she nodded.

It wasn't a rare story. It was, unfortunately, an oft-told one these days.

"Are you..." I searched for something to say, not wanting to leave her just yet. Human interaction wasn't a given these days. Who knew if she had anyone at home to converse with. "Do you have a family?"

"I live with my mother and younger sister," she said. "My father and brothers were sent off two years ago. My fiancé the year before. We used to get letters from all of them, but..." She shook her head. "They stopped months ago."

I nodded.

"My sister and I were in The League, of course. They had us at two different camps. When our mother became ill, neither camp informed the other and we were both sent home to care for her. We never told, and no one ever came looking for us."

"And is your mother well now?"

"She is."

"Good," I said. "Well, I hope you hear from the rest of your family and fiancé soon. I should get home now. It's been lovely chatting to you."

I was about to turn away but stopped and reached into my bag instead. I couldn't tell what anything was, save for the bread, since everything was wrapped in brown paper. I grabbed one of the smaller items and handed it to her.

"Oh," she said, holding her hand up. "No. I can't take that."

"Please," I said, lifting the bag as proof and glancing at the tiny loaf in her hand. "We have plenty."

She sighed, looked from the item in my hand to my face, and then nodded.

“You are very kind,” she said.

“Stay safe,” I said, and then turned on my heel and hurried down the street for home, preparing myself to be admonished by Paulina for taking so long.

As I turned the corner I looked back. Johanna still stood where I’d left her, head bent as she hurriedly ate the food I’d given her.

37

CHRISTMAS CAME, Paulina and I doing what we could to make the day a tiny bit festive for one another. She had pulled out one of the many boxes of decorations from the attic the week before and we'd placed a few items here and there around the first floor, smiling as the flames coming from the fireplace danced off stained glass angels and stars.

As a girl, Christmas had been the one time of the year that life in this house had actually felt magical. My mother would hire a decorator to come in while the four of us, plus Nanny Paulina, went out for a day of meals, shopping, and dazzling the citizens of Hamburg with the perfectly coordinated outfits my mother had put together for us all. She'd be in a red dress with a white fur coat, my father in a charcoal suit, white button-down shirt, and a red tie that matched her dress, and Catrin and I would wear matching white dresses with full skirts, and red sashes tied into bows at our backs. Even our nanny would be outfitted to complement our festive attire, her usual uniform swapped for one in a deep forest green with red piping.

When we'd return from our adventures, the house would look like a winter wonderland that lasted until the second of January, when it would all come down and be tucked away once more, taking with it a small bit of my happiness every year. It was only during Christmastime that we got any kind of acknowledgment from our parents that wasn't pure scrutiny and dismay. They watched with interest when we opened our gifts, as if genuinely hoping we'd like whatever they'd had their assistants pick out.

I reached out now, my finger brushing a crystal angel hanging from a small gold metal tree. Firelight glinted off it, casting prisms of light around the room. I'd done the same thing when I was a girl when no one was around to reprimand me for touching the expensive ornaments.

"The lamb is roasting," Paulina said and I turned, a question in my eyes. "And the champagne is chilling."

I grinned at her joke.

We'd been reminiscing on Christmas dinners past as we'd decorated the previous week. It had begun in sadness, and then became a game that had at one point made us laugh so hard we both had tears running down our faces, remembering how over-the-top the meals had been. The guests. My mother's attire. At one point we grew so loud in our mirth, we woke my mother, who screamed down at us *"den mund halted!"* Shut up. We'd clapped our hands over our mouths and continued to snicker quietly. It had felt good to laugh so hard.

There was no lamb this year, of course. No elegant cuts of steak. No array of perfectly roasted vegetables. No trifle. But there would be small servings of chicken, roasted potatoes, canned green beans one of the residents on the lower floors had offered us, and for which we exchanged one of the muffins we'd received from the bakery that week, warm bread Paulina had browned and slathered in butter, and a small, dense cake whose lack of sweetness was covered with the addition of small chunks of apple throughout.

And there were three gifts. One for her, and two for me.

"Oh," I said, looking down at the two small gifts wrapped in some of my mother's expensive paper. "But I've only gotten you one thing."

"And I've only gotten you one." She held out one of the two boxes. "This one is for..." She looked to my stomach, which had just begun to show, but was still barely noticeable when I was covered in layers.

"Oh," I said again, my eyes filling with tears.

It was still strange to think I had a child growing inside me. In fact, I often tried not to think about it, beyond determining I was about four months along and still had plenty of time before worrying about the process of giving birth. My biggest concerns were getting stuck and having to have the baby here or the city being attacked again. And what if something went wrong with the pregnancy and there was no one to help? Sure, I was a nurse. But I hadn't trained in childbirth. I wouldn't know how to help myself if something went awry.

And then of course there was always the chance my mother might tell the lieutenant who I was. So far she had been asleep when he came, not even stirring when he slammed cupboard doors and drawers in her room. But Paulina had convinced her that there was danger for her in telling the lieutenant who I was. He might not believe her story that I'd run away and instead come to his own conclusion that my parents had sent me away in an attempt to save me. That they'd hidden me and they themselves were traitors. My mother may be in pain, but her pride in her status was greater. She would not be sent to her death as a traitor to her country, and so she promised to keep my identity a secret. For all our sakes.

Of course, her promise made our exchanges that much worse.

She knew she was doing me a favor and thus demanded my assistance over Paulina's more and more, screaming for me whenever she was awake, her broken voice sending shivers up and down my spine daily.

Nothing was good enough for her. When I ran a wet cloth over her shockingly fragile body the water was too hot. Too cold. My touch too hard, too soft. I missed a spot. I was too thorough. I smelled. I was inept.

"A nurse," she'd scoffed more than once as she eyed me always with disdain, her milky eyes sweeping from my face to my breasts to my stomach. "My daughter, the traitor."

I pushed the memory from my mind as Paulina pressed the gift for my baby into my hands. I peeled the paper away, lifted the lid of the box beneath, and gasped.

It had been my favorite dress when I was little, the pale blue fabric soft, unlike so many of my other dresses. There had been no petticoat to be worn under. No stiff material that felt like it was suffocating me as it scratched at my neck or arms. It was a dress for summers. For sunshine and walks in the park with my nanny. For falling asleep in after a big day of play. And I had worn it well past when I should've stopped, forcing my growing torso into the tightening bodice.

"Can't we find another?" I'd asked Nanny Paulina.

"Sorry, Miss Gisela," she'd said. "It was bought over a year ago. The store won't have it any longer."

And so, regretfully, I wore it for a last time and then folded it up and tucked it away in my closet for safekeeping.

Here it was now though, in my hands once more, the fabric as soft as I remembered it, and refashioned in not one, but two outfits—a dress with a rounded white collar, and a pair of overalls.

"Do you recognize the fabric?" Paulina asked.

I nodded, my eyes filled with tears.

"I remembered how you loved that dress." She sighed. "I

found it years ago when I was cleaning. When you told me you were pregnant, I knew I had to turn it into something your child could wear. Of course, we don't know if you're having a boy or a girl so…I made something for both sexes. I hope you like them?"

"Oh, Paulina," I said, my voice catching on a sob. "They're beautiful. Absolutely perfect. Thank you."

"I'm making a few other things, as well," she said, wiping away a tear of her own. "But I thought these were a perfect gift for Christmas."

I hugged her and she held me tight for a moment before letting me go and handing me the other gift at the same time I handed her the one I had for her.

When we'd decided to have a small celebration for the holiday, we'd agreed not to risk going out to find gifts at the few shops in town, but to shop the house instead. Nothing was off limits. But it had to be thoughtful and well-intentioned.

"Do not give me one of your mother's gaudy jeweled necklaces," Paulina had said, making me laugh.

"What about one of her furs?"

"Can you imagine if I went out in one of those to pick up meat from the butcher?" We'd laughed more and then looked out the window where huge snowflakes were coming down. "On second thought," she'd said.

And so there were no jewels or furs beneath the elegant wrapping paper. Instead, for her there was a beautiful knit scarf in a vibrant blue that had been gifted to my mother years before and shoved in the back of her closet because "Such a horrid color shouldn't be forced upon anyone." But it was pretty. And soft. And all Paulina's scarves were worn and old.

"I remember when she got this," she said, wrapping it around her neck and burying her face in it. "I'd thought it so beautiful, and then felt a fool hearing how she hated it. I clearly knew nothing about fashion if I coveted something she deemed so awful."

"My mother is a snob," I said. "You know that. What she really didn't like was that it wasn't a Vionnet or Lanvin."

"Well, her loss is my gain."

She pointed to my gift then and I pulled the wrapping away from a box the size of my hand. When I lifted the lid, I smiled. Inside was a crystal angel like the ones we'd hung in the living room.

"You've always loved them," she said as I pulled it from the box and held it up by its string, watching as it twirled, the light from the candles we'd lit and the fire sending tiny rainbows around the room. "Do you remember doing that for Catrin when she was a baby? I would bring you to her bassinet and she'd smile up at you. I don't even think she noticed the angel."

I sighed and dropped my arm.

"Part of me thought…hoped…today would be the day she showed up."

"I won't lie. I thought she would too."

"Do you think something has happened to her?"

Paulina shook her head. "If anything had, we would know right away. I promise."

We cleaned up the wrapping paper and then Paulina went to check on dinner while I climbed the stairs to my mother's room. She'd been asleep all day, not even waking when Paulina changed her soiled clothes and bedding. Paulina had called for me after, worried, and I'd checked her pulse and temperature. She was breathing, her irises responded to light, there was no fever, and her pulse was faint, but no different than it had been in the weeks before.

"Do you think maybe…" Paulina's voice had trailed off. "Maybe she won't wake up again?"

It would be a small mercy for all of us. But I didn't say that to Paulina, who I knew, despite my mother's many shortcomings, wretched ideologies, and propensity to ruin lives, cared for the woman who had employed her for decades.

"I don't know," I'd told her, taking her hand. "It's possible she's awake now, but tired in a way that won't allow her to respond to us."

I entered the room now and put a log on the fire, then moved to the diminished form of my mother, shifting bedding carefully so I could see if it, and her clothing, needed to be changed out.

"You should leave."

I nearly jumped out of my skin at the sound of my mother's raspy voice cutting through the quiet.

"I intend to," I said, pulling the bedding back into place. "Are you hungry? Would you like Paulina or me to bring you some broth?"

"She will never go with you."

I ignored her. There was no point in arguing.

"Your Kitty Cat," she whispered, "is no longer yours. She is mine. She is Germany's."

I pasted a smile on my face, ignoring her and picking up the water glass on her bedside table. "I'll have Paulina bring you some fresh water and broth."

It took everything I had not to slam the door after me when I left. But it would do no good. She would always have the upper hand, because she didn't care. And somewhere deep inside me was still the little girl who just wanted her mother to love her.

The scent of dinner filled the main floor and I inhaled, smiling as I descended the stairs. At least after my mother was tended to Paulina and I would share a nice meal, maybe partake in a bottle of wine from my father's collection, and perhaps even play a rousing game or two of cards.

"We need to warm up the broth," I said as I opened the door to the kitchen. "She's awa—"

I stopped, my eyes moving from the worried look on Paulina's face to the shocked one on the face of the young woman standing at the far end of the kitchen.

And then a name. One I hadn't heard spoken in ten years.

"Gigi?" she whispered.

I exhaled, my heart pounding in my chest, my knees so weak I had to reach for the countertop beside me.

"Hi, Kitty Cat."

38

"I DON'T UNDERSTAND," Catrin said, looking from me to Paulina and then back again.

But I couldn't speak. I was too busy staring at her. Taking in the young woman she'd grown into. The soft angles of her face, wide blue eyes, and elegant presence. I wanted to rush to her. Throw my arms around her. Tell her I was sorry and grab her hand, dragging her to the address hidden in my bag so that we could escape this place. This—

Home.

The word flashed in my mind and I suddenly remembered that before William, the only sense of home I'd had was when I'd been with Cat in our wing of the house. We were one another's sanctuary. It was only when I was with her that I felt I belonged.

But the way she was looking at me now…

"I don't understand," Catrin said, her voice harder now as she sank into one of the kitchen chairs and looked to Paulina. "Can you please explain what's going on."

"Of course," Pauline said, pulling the pot of broth from the icebox and setting it on the stove to warm. "But first, why don't you go say hello to your mother and bring her some water while she's awake."

She took a clean glass from the cupboard, filled it with water, and held it out to Catrin, who stared at it for a moment before nodding and getting to her feet.

She stopped beside me, her blue eyes, the same color as mine, skimming across my face. And then she leaned forward and kissed me first on one cheek, then the other.

"Willkomen zu Hause, Schwester," she murmured, and then disappeared out the door.

Paulina and I stared at one another in my sister's wake.

"You should go," Paulina said, her voice low. "Now. It's too dark outside to find your contact, but you could hide in one of the closets in the lobby until morning."

"What?" I asked, shaking my head in confusion. "Why? She just got here. We've barely said two words to one another. I haven't even told her—"

"She'll never go with you. I was stupid to entertain the idea that she might." She motioned toward the door, but I frowned and crossed my arms over my chest.

"Paulina—"

She moved toward me so fast I found myself backing up until I ran into the wall behind me.

"That young woman is not the same girl you knew, Gisela," she said, her voice a furious whisper. "She is dangerous. Conniving. She is *their* child. Do you understand me? *Theirs.*"

I sucked in a breath, tears hovering on my lower lashes. She didn't just mean Catrin was my parents' child. She meant Catrin was a child of the Third Reich. I nodded, a tear streaking down my cheek as I moved a hand to my growing belly.

"I just—I don't understand. She seemed fine. Why do you

suddenly think I'm in danger? Do you think she'd try and hurt me?" I asked.

Paulina stepped back, her eyes filled with sadness. "I don't know, fräulein. Is it worth the risk of staying and finding out?"

"She's shocked to see me alive," I said.

"I don't trust her."

I stared at her. I had risked everything to get here. To this moment. To see my sister and bring her to New York with me. And now, when I was so close to seeing it happen, was I really going to give up, turn around, and go back home without her?

I felt a small shift deep inside me. At first I thought it was emotional, and then I realized it was a physical shift. My baby. William's baby.

The kitchen door swung open and Catrin stepped inside.

"You can take the broth off the stove," she told Paulina. "She's gone back to sleep."

Paulina nodded and switched off the stove. "Did she see you at least?" she asked.

"For a moment. She looks…" Her voice trailed off as she looked from Paulina to me.

"It won't be long now," I said and she nodded.

"Well," Paulina said. "Our dinner is ready. Shall we eat?"

I pulled out another set of dishes from the cupboards and the three of us took our seats around the kitchen table.

"How long have you been here?" Catrin asked me.

"She arrived two weeks after you left for Berlin last month," Paulina answered.

I watched Catrin's mouth turn up in a small, almost irritated smile as she looked at our former nanny.

"Thank you, Paulina," she said and then turned back to me. "And what brought you back?"

"Well…" I glanced at Paulina and then to my sister again. "You. I learned you were alive and had to come."

"Where have you been for the past ten years? And with

whom? How did you leave?" She tilted her head, narrowing her eyes. "Was there ever a pen pal or was it all a lie? Who helped you?"

How many times had I had this conversation with her in my mind? How many times had I tried to explain, hoping my words were enough for her to forgive me for leaving, for lying, and for making her believe I'd died. I'd imagined having to plead with her, a young girl, to accept my apologies. I'd never imagined us doing this as adults. This was much harder.

I took in a long breath and exhaled, rubbing my eyes as I prepared myself, and then sitting back in my chair, a feeling of defeat resonating through my body. This was not going to go how I'd imagined it all those many years before. Catrin was not the same girl.

"It was all set up by our aunt and uncle," I said.

Catrin frowned. "The ones who died?"

I pursed my lips and saw understanding dawn in her eyes.

"Ah. They didn't die, did they."

"No," I said quietly. "They faked their deaths. A boat accident in the South of France two years before I left."

"I remember," she said. "You were devastated. You were a good actress."

I ignored the comment and continued.

"A few months later I got the invitation from my pen pal in California to come visit in the summer. She, as you might've guessed by now, was not a sixteen-year-old girl but an adult contact through the same organization our aunt and uncle worked for."

"And Mother's friend Alina?" Catrin asked.

I nodded. "She was in on it too." I let that sit with her for a moment before going on. "The plan, as it was explained to me, was to get me out first, then come back for you two years later when you were a little bit older and would understand better—and could keep secrets better. I only agreed to go because I knew you would follow."

"Why didn't they just take us both at the same time?"

"I don't know. I was never privy to the planning. I assume it had to do with opportunities that presented themselves. I just did as I was told."

"Why did you want to go in the first place?"

I sighed, my eyes wandering the extravagant room, faded by age and war but still beautiful. What I would say next would not sit well between us, but she asked, and so I told her.

"I hated them," I said, my voice soft but firm. "Hated everything about them. Hated what they were trying to force me to be. I didn't agree with what they believed in, and I could see what I—what we—would be forced into if we stayed."

She was quiet for a moment and then: "What happened next? After you left with Alina."

"We went to California, met up with our contact there, and were given paperwork with our new identities. We stayed a night in a hotel, and then in the morning we boarded a train for New York where we met up with our aunt and uncle, who also had new identities and a whole life set up in Manhattan. I said goodbye to Alina and she left. I never saw her again."

"And then?"

I exhaled, remembering.

"My and Alina's deaths were faked and I spent the next many months terrified and sad. I was so worried we'd be found out. Scared I'd be taken away, brought back, punished in ways I couldn't imagine. And I was bereft at the thought of possibly never seeing you again. Before and during the escape, I'd been sure I was doing the right thing for the both of us. But once I was there and settled, I feared I'd been wrong." I closed my eyes, thinking back to those first days. "I didn't leave my room for days. I was afraid of the city, which seemed so big and loud, the people brash and hurried. And while I knew the language,

I was tentative to use it, worried everyone who heard it would know where I was from and tell the police or try and harm me."

My sister looked at me with a frank expression, unmoved by my story and waiting for me to go on.

"It got better, of course," I continued. "Time passed, I got more comfortable and, while I wasn't told the plans for getting you to the States, I knew things were underway and I was excited to see you and have you with me." My eyes filled with tears. "And then we heard the news about the bomb." I stopped talking and swallowed a sob, the memory of hearing my sister had been killed still painful, no matter that she was now sitting before me. "I was devastated. And for a time, I hated our aunt and uncle, blaming them for things they weren't responsible for and couldn't possibly have foreseen. But I was angry regardless. And then again, time passed, the wound still stung but the three of us tried to move forward, until eventually life became a new kind of normal again. I went to school, graduated, became a nurse. And then I got a letter saying you were alive and...you can imagine my shock when I learned you were alive after all this time."

Catrin's smile was small and tight. "Yes. I can."

"I'm sorry, Catrin." I reached out and wrapped my hand around hers. She let me hold it for a moment, then slid it from mine and picked up her napkin to dab at her mouth.

"Did you...have you had a good life?" I asked, even though I was afraid to hear.

"Well, after the sister my world revolved around died, I was devastated," she said. "But our parents, as you know, found grieving to be a selfish endeavor, and so I was pushed into activities. I learned to play the piano, took painting classes, and was encouraged to join any number of clubs. After the bomb, I lived in the country for a time with an interesting family. The father took special interest in me, though he didn't express his interest quite like his eldest son did."

I inhaled, horrified as she continued.

"Things got a little better, though," she said. "I joined Bund Deutscher Mädel where I was bullied by the older girls for a time, and then eventually I was one of the older girls. I got top grades in school, was invited to parties, was introduced to the right boys, and eventually got a much sought-after job doing administrative work at an office in Berlin, where I now live. I have a lovely flat, a nice circle of friends, and a boyfriend whose boss does important work for the Führer."

She watched me closely as she said that last part and it took everything I had not to cringe.

Instead, I smiled and nodded. "It sounds like you've built a good life."

"I have. And I only intend for it to get better. Despite the growing rumors and fears about how this war is going, there are a great many plans in place to see the dream carried out in myriad of ways."

I swallowed and snuck a look at Paulina, but she was staring down at her plate, her interest seemingly piqued by the remaining potatoes on her plate.

I startled at the scrape of Catrin's chair against the floor as she pushed away from the table.

"While this has been lovely—Paulina, the dinner was wonderful as always—I must get to bed."

"You are staying?" Paulina asked, her eyes wide as she got to her feet.

"It is dark now so I don't have much choice," Catrin said. "And of course, my sister is home. How could I leave now when Gisela has returned from the dead? There is so much more to discuss."

Paulina shot me a look, but I was too busy staring at my sister to look back.

"I have errands to run tomorrow," Catrin said to me. "But perhaps we can have dinner together when I return?"

"I would like that," I said, my voice faint.

"Good. Then I shall say good-night to you both."

She was gone a moment later and I found myself staring at the seat she'd vacated.

"Gisela." Paulina's voice was soft.

I turned and met her eyes, seeing worry laced with fear.

"She's in shock," I said. "She thought I was dead and now here I am, very much alive."

"Gisela—" There was a warning in her voice now.

"Just let me talk to her tomorrow," I said. "Let me tell her my plan. Tell her about life in New York. Tell her about the baby and how she's going to be an aunt."

Paulina's hand was a vise around my wrist.

"Whatever you do," she said. "Do *not* tell that girl about your baby."

Paulina and I cleaned up the kitchen in silence. The dessert she made went uneaten, neither of us in the mood. The wine she'd chosen but never poured was dumped in the sink.

"Good night, Paulina," I said, standing by the door.

"We'll talk more in the morning," she said. "After she's gone."

I nodded, opened the door, and headed upstairs to my room.

From the end of the hall I could see light beneath Catrin's bedroom door. But as I passed by on the way to my own room, the light turned off.

I entered my room and stared through the door of the adjoining bathroom to her door at the other end. Turning on the light, I saw a small bag on her side of the counter beside her sink, a toothbrush and hairbrush laid out just so.

Hurrying, I washed my face and brushed my teeth. As I turned to leave, I hesitated, glancing back at the door to my sister's room and staring at the lock, the warning in Paulina's voice earlier still echoing in my mind. But there was no point in locking it. Catrin had learned how to unlock it from the other side using a hairpin at an early age. I was the one who taught her.

Sighing, I turned out the light and shut the door on my side, then climbed in bed and fell asleep.

39

I WOKE WITH a start the next morning, a feeling that I wasn't alone causing me to sit upright in bed, my eyes bleary as they searched the darkness.

But there was no one there, and as I lay back down, I realized I must've had a dream. A dream that Catrin had lain beside me in the night like she had when we were girls, her hand in mine, our breath becoming one. My eyes pricked with tears. I could still feel her hand in mine, as if it had been real. I could feel the imprint of her body beside mine. I wanted so badly to have my sister back. To be the girls we once were. But Paulina's words of warning the night before had startled me. Was I fooling myself? Had I come too late?

Unsettled, I swung my legs over the side of the bed and pulled my valise from beneath my bed, and then ran my hand along the lining until I felt my engagement ring. I closed the case and slid it back to its hiding place and then made my way to the bathroom. The door, which I was positive I'd shut the night before, was open just a crack. I stared back at my bed. Had it been a dream? Had she been here? Rather than be comforted at the thought, a shiver ran down my spine.

Turning on the light, my eyes went to Catrin's side of the counter where her belongings still sat, though moved slightly, as though they'd been used.

She was still here. There was still time.

"Good morning," Paulina said when I entered the kitchen, my gaze sweeping the room for signs of my sister. "She's gone already."

"But she'll be back," I said, a statement, not a question.

"She will. But Gisela—"

"I have to try, Paulina." My voice was firm.

"Please consider what you could lose," she said, her eyes moving to my stomach.

"I don't believe she would bring me harm," I said. "No matter how she's been brainwashed. We are still sisters. We are still bonded by our love for one another."

"You could come back. After. When things have settled. When it's all over. You could go to France and wait."

"Paulina…what do you think is going to happen? What do you think she'll do?"

Paulina's voice was quiet as she answered.

"I used to worry she'd become like your mother. Vicious. Unrelenting. Not hiding her disdain for others. But then I realized who she was becoming was much worse than that. She became like your father. A hunter. Quiet. Sizing up her prey before snapping its neck and dragging it into the dark. I don't know what they teach those girls in the League. I don't know if it was a combination of those teachings and being your parents' child that led her to become what she is. But I should've turned you away as soon as you got here. I just thought…hoped…" Her eyes filled with tears. "I wanted you to be right. I wanted the sight of you to shake her out of whatever it was they've done to her. If anyone could, it's you. But Gisela… I can feel her… watching you. Sizing you up. Taking your pulse. You are not safe here. She will attack."

"No." I shook my head. "No. I don't believe that. She's twenty years old. She's not like them. She may have some of them in her, but she also has me and our memories as sisters. Love and silly songs and holding hands…"

"I've heard rumors," Paulina said. "Rumors that she's turned in her own friends. Hannah… Lior."

I shook my head. "No. That can't be true."

"She's changed, fräulein. They changed her."

"No. And even if you're right, it's because of me. Because I left. But I'm back now. I can make it right. I can make her see…"

"Gisela—"

"No," I whispered, a tear making a path down my cheek. "She would never. She couldn't. She's a child still."

"She is not a child anymore, Gisela. She's made choices."

"Because she had no choice," I said. "I left her. She had no one to protect her. To show her what was right."

Paulina sighed and handed me a plate of toast. "You have a big heart, my love. But you are blinded by the guilt of something you were never responsible for. None of this is your fault. And you are putting yourself, and your child, at risk. For all we know, she could come back with an officer and turn you in."

I shook my head, angry tears making their way down my cheeks.

"She wouldn't," I said. "And I will not leave without talking to her. I must do what should've been done years ago."

Paulina opened her mouth to say more, but my mother's scream cut her off and after hesitating for a moment, she put down the kitchen towel in her hand and hurried from the room.

Catrin didn't return for hours, and every minute that passed served to make me more and more anxious, Paulina's words returning to me in waves. What if she was right and I was terribly and tragically wrong? But even as I thought it, I pictured her as a girl trailing behind me, reaching for my hand.

I passed the time by doing the chores I'd become accustomed to. Dusting rooms that never got seen, shining silver that was never used, and checking the pantry for ingredients we needed, should they become available.

In the late afternoon I checked in on my mother so Paulina could begin prepping food for dinner. I had just returned to the kitchen to help when I heard the front door open and close. Paulina's eyes met mine and she motioned for me to stand beside her, and then she stepped in front of me, busying herself at the kitchen island, her body creating a barrier in front of mine.

"Guten Tag," Catrin said as she entered the room.

"Good afternoon," Paulina said. "How has your day been, fräulein?"

I hadn't noticed the tone in Paulina's voice when she spoke to my sister. But I did now. It was formal. Tense. And wary.

"It has been good, thank you, Paulina," Catrin said. "How is my mother?"

"She is the same."

"I should go see her. Does she need fresh water?"

"Gisela just brought her some."

There was silence in the room and I could feel my sister's gaze on me. I set down the knife I was using and turned, meeting her gaze across the room, taking in the small smile on her face that didn't quite reach her eyes.

"And how was your day, sister?" Catrin asked, the words friendly, the undertone laced with something that made me feel ill at ease.

"Busy," I said. "Dinner should be done soon. Shall we eat in the kitchen again?"

"The dining room," she said, and then left to see our mother.

I didn't bother to look at Paulina. I could feel her fear from across the room.

Paulina set the table for two while I washed up and changed into a fresh sweater. Another of my father's, its bulk easily hiding my growing belly. When I returned downstairs, water had been poured in the crystal glasses, a bottle of wine opened, and my sister sat in the seat she'd occupied as a girl.

"This looks lovely, Paulina," I said as I took my seat. "Thank you."

"Of course," she said. "If you two need anything, I'll be in the kitchen."

We were quiet as we dug into our meal, and while I marveled at the succulent chicken and roasted potatoes Paulina had made for the occasion, our usual meals much sparer, Catrin seemed unimpressed by it all. She was clearly used to such luxuries still, the war seemingly having no impact on her life whatsoever.

"Why have you come really?" Catrin said finally, her voice curious. Measured.

"I told you," I said, frowning across the table at her. "For you."

"To see me? To…what? Pick up where we left off? Me at the front door, crying as you promised to return?"

I could hear the bitterness creep in, but I was prepared for that. I knew she would need more from me to truly believe that what had happened could not be controlled. But as I opened my mouth to explain further, she began to talk again.

"Have you come for their fortune? Because it's mine. They've left it all to me. And I cannot wait to see that smug lieutenant's face when he realizes it's not up for grabs."

I caught myself as my mouth dropped open, closing it quick and shaking my head.

"Of course not," I said. "I've never cared about any of that. I came to make things right and bring you back with me."

"Back? Back where?"

"To New York. To the life you should've been living with me. Your sister."

I watched Catrin sit back in her chair and delicately set down her fork. She lifted her chin, and when her gaze met mine again, it wasn't my sister's eyes I was looking into, but our father's.

"I have no sister," she said, her voice flat. "She died ten years ago. A car accident, I was told."

"Cat—" I shook my head and reached across the table for her hand, but she drew it back, her eyes still glued to mine.

"You didn't have to go, Gisela. That was a choice *you* made. For *you*. Those were *your* beliefs. I have my own." Her voice was hard now. "This world needs to be cleansed. The weak and undesirables must go. On top of their bones we will build a stronger world. A better world. And you would do well to forget the lies our aunt and uncle brainwashed you with as a child. You are too old to believe those stories now. If you want to be my sister again, then you will forsake those ideologies and remember who you are. A Holländer. A German. You will be a soldier for the Third Reich and do your duty. Or I will have no choice but to reveal you for what you are. A traitor."

Ice filled my veins as I stared into Catrin's eyes, searching desperately for some clue that the girl I once knew was somewhere inside. That what she said was merely the bluster of a young woman carrying years of pain and needed to let it out in the vilest way she could before we turned the page and began to heal together.

But there was no such girl. If she had ever existed, she was long gone now, buried deep beneath years of her indoctrination into Nazism.

A tear slid down my cheek. Then another, my hand drifting down protectively to my belly. At the last moment I caught myself, remembering Paulina's words. *Don't let Catrin know about the baby.* I understood now.

I jumped at the sudden noise of Catrin's chair scraping against the floor as she slid it back and stood.

"Shall we take our glasses of wine upstairs and visit with Mother?"

I had no idea what she had planned, but feared what she might do or who she might call should I say no. I nodded and stood, then picked up my wineglass with a trembling hand and followed her from the room.

40

I WAS SURPRISED to see the bedside lamps on, and realized Paulina must've turned them on when Catrin and I were finishing up dinner.

"Good evening, Mother," Catrin said, taking a seat in one of the armchairs near the fireplace. "You missed a most interesting dinner."

I could see our mother watching us behind half-closed lids, and I wondered what she felt, if anything, about her two once-dead daughters under her roof at the same time once more.

"Gisela thinks I should move to New York with her," Catrin continued, crossing one slender leg over the other, and bobbing it up and down as though this conversation was nothing but a casual chat between old friends. "I can't possibly abandon my post in Berlin, of course, but it's an intriguing thought—being the one to bring our ideas to Manhattan. Can you imagine?"

My mind immediately went to my aunt and uncle's many Jewish neighbors and my stomach turned over.

It was horrific looking at this young woman I'd once doted on. Had she always been this way and I'd been blind to it because I'd loved her? If I had stayed, would she still have turned out this way? Making it three against one in our household? Would I have had to leave eventually, unable to reconcile my relationship to them? Or, God forbid, would their influence and threats have turned me into whatever this creature was my sister had become? This icy, cruel woman with evil at her root.

There was a knock and we turned to see Paulina standing in the doorway, her eyes moving from me to my sister to our mother—and then back to me.

"Is everything okay?" she asked, still staring at me. "You've left your dinner."

"I lost my appetite," Catrin said. "But it was a lovely meal, Paulina. Thank you. You may go now."

I looked desperately at our childhood nanny, pleading with my eyes for her not to go. Trying to convey that she'd been right, and I knew it now—and was frightened.

"Of course," Paulina said. "I'll just clear the dishes then."

I listened as her footsteps receded down the hallway, the growing distance filling me with dread.

"I found something interesting today," Catrin said. "While you were helping Paulina."

I closed my eyes for a moment, preparing myself, and then turned to meet her stony gaze.

"Yes?"

"I thought it might help you with your decision."

To my horror, she pulled the cloth bag I'd been using when I left the house out from behind the chair and retrieved both passports from inside.

"One might think you are a spy," she said, opening first one, then the other. "Kate and Lena? How common of you, Gisela. You couldn't come up with something a little more exotic?"

I wanted to fire back, but we both knew she held all the cards, quite literally, in her hands.

"What do you want?" I asked.

"I told you. Your allegiance."

"And if I give it to you? To Germany?"

"Well then, I won't have to have you arrested."

"For what? I could easily say I was abducted, brainwashed, threatened..."

"These would say otherwise," she said, waving the passports back and forth. "Tell you what..."

And as I watched, she threw one of the passports into the fire.

"No!"

I spun and found Paulina once more in the doorway, her eyes filled with horror.

"Catrin—" she said. But her words stopped there. She would be putting herself in danger if she defended me. Her eyes met mine and I shook my head. I wouldn't let her do it.

"Congratulations, sister," Catrin said, getting to her feet. "You are German once more. No more American identity to hide behind."

I heard a noise from the other side of the room and glanced at my mother who was watching the whole thing from her bed in weary fascination.

"I thought we weren't sisters anymore," I said. "Didn't you say—" But my thought was cut off by the sound of someone knocking at the front door.

The four of us stared at one another, and then Paulina rushed from the room, only to return moments later with Lieutenant Schmeiden leading the way.

"Well, what do we have here?" he asked and I watched with curiosity as Catrin's demeanor changed from steely to something almost meek.

"Good evening, Lieutenant," she said, eyes downcast, shoulders slumping slightly.

"I see they've let you leave your post in Berlin again, fräulein," he said.

"My superior is aware of Mrs. Holländer's failing health, and my loyalty to her because of her years of sponsorship," Catrin said.

I glanced at Paulina, but she was too engrossed in the conversation to catch my eye, her hands deep in her skirt pockets as she slowly moved in closer, her gaze moving from Catrin to the lieutenant.

"Of course," the lieutenant said in a smooth, almost placating voice that set my nerves on edge. I got the distinct feeling there was no love lost between these two and began to feel like I'd somehow gotten myself trapped in a cat-and-mouse situation. But who was the mouse? And who was the cat…

"What's that in your hand?" Lieutenant Schmeiden asked Catrin.

My heart nearly stopped. My German passport.

She held it out and the room went still as he examined it, and then looked from me to Catrin.

"And why do you have fräulein Klein's identification?" he asked her.

At that, my mother began to cough, waving one hand while the other grasped at her throat.

"She's choking," I said, hurrying to the bedside and hauling her quickly but gently into a seated position. "Paulina. Her water."

Paulina was instantly beside me, helping me hold my mother upright. But even as we were trying to help her, she was pushing against us. Pushing us aside, her eyes trained on my sister, more intent than I'd seen them since arriving.

I looked over my shoulder at Cat and saw her jaw clench, seeming to physically restrain herself from whatever it was she'd been about to say. The fear I'd felt before intensified as understanding about the dynamics happening in the room became clear. We were in a web of lies, and one truth could undo it all in front of the anxious lieutenant, risking all our lives. What he wanted was dependent on me and my sister not existing as the next of kin to our mother. As far as he knew, we were acquaintances, and the estate was up for grabs as soon as our mother passed. Were he to find out we were her daughters, our lives would be in danger. Meanwhile, my sister hated me. Would she risk revenge by revealing the truth about me? By doing so, she didn't know if I'd reveal her in turn. If we were found out, our mother could be questioned. And then there was Paulina…who held all our secrets.

I felt my mother's body falter, the strain of sitting up too much. Carefully, Paulina and I laid her back down and then moved back to our previous spots in the room, the lieutenant watching our every move.

"Why did you have this?" Lieutenant Schmeiden asked Catrin again, holding up the passport and then handing it over to me.

I shoved it in my pocket and looked to Paulina again, worried about the soldier's focus on my sister.

"I wanted to know who this stranger was who's been taking care of my friend," Catrin said. "I was surprised to return yesterday and find fräulein Klein here. I was suspicious of her motives."

"But she is a nurse. Brought here by Mrs. Holländer's trusted servant. I would think you'd be happy to have help for your friend in her last days."

"Of course," Catrin said, sinking into herself as if trying to seem smaller. Insignificant and non-threatening. "I am very grateful."

The lieutenant began to move around the room. "It's you whose motives I question, fräulein," he said. "It is you who began showing up as soon as Mrs. Holländer arrived back in her lovely, expensive home, knowing what treasures you might gain for yourself once she's gone."

Catrin shook her head and I could see her calculating her next words carefully as Paulina moved closer to me, her arm brushing mine. I ignored her at first, and then her arm pressed into me, as though she were trying to get my attention. I looked over and met her eyes, which moved downward purposefully. Frowning, I followed her gaze, my heart skipping a beat when I saw what she had in her skirt pocket.

A pistol.

She stepped away from me again and I shook my head. This could only go very wrong. Paulina was trained in household affairs. Lieutenant Schmeiden was a soldier, trained in killing.

"No."

We all turned to look at my mother, who was shaking her head, her cloudy eyes wild in her sunken face.

"Not that one," she rasped, raising a shaking finger toward Catrin before turning it on me. "That one. That's the one you can't trust."

"Don't you dare," Paulina said, her voice shaking with anger.

In the many nights that would follow, fraught with fear, hunger, and pain, I would have nightmares about the scene that played out now.

Lieutenant Schmeiden turned to see Paulina pulling the gun from her pocket. He grabbed his own pistol and two shots rang out, echoing throughout the room. I gasped and ducked, staring in terror across the room at my sister. Her eyes met mine, her fingers wrapping around the long, iron stoker beside the fireplace as a thud shook the floor beneath our feet, and the sound of someone wailing filled the air.

My ears rang and my body shook as I realized what Cat was about to do.

"Cat, no," I whispered, taking a step toward her and watching in horror as she raised her arm and took aim at the lieutenant's back. But he turned just in time—and another shot rang out.

Catrin jerked, her eyes widening, and then the stoker clanged to the floor a second before her body followed.

I raced toward her and fell to my knees beside her. But she was gone, her eyes, so like mine, closed forever.

Catrin. Kitty Cat.

Holding in a sob, I got to my feet and took in the rest of the room. Paulina lay on the floor, a bullet wound to her forehead, eyes open and devoid of life, the gun lying beside her.

On the bed, my mother's emaciated body lay thrown back against the blood-spattered ivory satin headboard from a gunshot wound to her neck.

I knelt beside Paulina's body and closed her eyes, then stood and stared at the lieutenant to await whatever came next. I couldn't imagine he'd just let me go. As far as he was concerned, no one could be trusted with what he considered to be his. It wouldn't matter if I promised I wanted none of it. To him, it was all worth too much to risk.

He gestured toward the door with his gun.

"You may pack a small bag while I watch," he said. "Steal anything and I'll shoot you too."

I nodded silently and walked down the hall to my room as he followed close behind, watching as with shaking hands I filled a small cloth bag with underwear, a brassiere, socks, a pair of trousers and a sweater that had been my father's, and a few items Paulina had made for the baby. In the bathroom I grabbed my toothbrush and hairbrush, my eyes moving across the counter to Catrin's belongings still sitting where she'd left them earlier this morning.

I took my journal from the bedside table and slid it into the bag and then took a last look around my childhood bedroom, glancing at the space beneath my bed where my ring and the only picture I had of William was hidden, and then I turned and led the way down the hallway.

I paused when I reached my mother's room where she, my sister, and Paulina lay lifeless, guilt and bile rising in my throat. Had I never come, they'd all still be alive.

"Let's go," the lieutenant said, giving me a soft shove in the back.

Numb, I nodded and then descended the staircase, my eyes taking it all in as I left the apartment I'd grown up in for what I knew would be the last time, a bag of borrowed clothes over my shoulder, an ID calling me Lena in my pocket, and William's baby in my belly.

41

William

Seattle
2003

"DAD?"

I jumped in my seat and wiped a hand across my eyes before turning to stare up at Lizzie, whose own eyes looked down at me with concern.

"Are you okay?" she asked.

"Yeah," I said, my voice husky. I gestured toward the house. "How's it going?"

"Good," she said, drawing the word out, her voice carrying the tone of someone wondering what the heck was going on. "Are you gonna..." It was her turn to gesture toward the house. I'd sent Selene inside thirty minutes before to wander at will, telling my daughter and granddaughter to pay no mind. "A mystery was afoot." It was a phrase my wife had always used when she was trying to figure something out for one of her stories. It meant, "Give me a minute and don't ask any more questions. For now."

I smiled at my daughter.

"I still need a minute," I said. "Is she..."

"In the hall. Looking at the pictures."

I nodded.

"Okay, honey. I'll be right there."

She left and I turned back to the journal, my heart still lodged in my throat. Taking a breath, I opened it again, flipping to the page I'd found in the back where only two words were written.

"William. Forevermore."

It wasn't dated, and the way it was buried amid the blank pages made it feel like an acceptance. Maybe even a surrender. She hadn't known how things would turn out. She'd only known she'd loved me.

Wiping my eyes again, I got to my feet and went inside the house, giving Lizzie what I hoped was a reassuring smile when she shot me another concerned look.

"All will be revealed in time," I said in what she used to call my "wizard voice" when she was a little girl.

"Alright, oh wise one," she called. "But we're getting hungry and the lasagna is nearly done. Mom put extra cheese on it."

"Is she trying to clog my arteries?" I asked.

"Can't live forever, Old Man," Emma yelled from where she was sitting cross-legged on the living room floor, several boxes open in front of her, her ponytail now piled into a messy bun on top of her head. "But," she added, looking up, a worried smile on her face. "Please do."

"Can't get rid of me that easily," I said, giving her a wink before heading toward the hallway.

Selene was halfway down, a small smile on her face as she looked at pictures of Olivia and me on our wedding day, a newly born and angry-looking Emma, Lizzie in a leotard, a ladybug costume, her high school graduation gown. The family on vacation in California, New York, and Paris.

"You must miss her," she said, pointing to a photo of Olivia. It was her first official author headshot. I'd told her she was a babe and had immediately run out to buy a frame. She'd blushed profusely when I'd hung it in the middle of a then-bare wall. But I wouldn't let her take it down, so instead she'd added to it, thus creating what was now known as Memory Lane.

"I do," I said. "She was fun. Smart. Classy. But she could also be silly. And a little bit devilish."

She grinned, watching me as I spoke. Again there was something in her smile that I couldn't quite put my finger on.

"And you?" she asked.

"What about me?"

"Could you be silly and devilish as well?"

I pressed a hand to my chest. "Who, me?"

"Yes!" Emma shouted from the other room, making the both of us laugh.

I shrugged. "I suppose yes, I could be."

"Yes," she said, an almost knowing look in her pale eyes. "You could."

She pointed to the door to my left.

"Is that your office?"

"It is."

"May I?"

"You may," I said, standing back to let her enter. "I apologize for the mess."

But if she was bothered, she didn't let on, moving slowly around the room, taking in the silly signs, a homemade clay ashtray from Lizzie's elementary days, a picture frame made of puzzle pieces from Emma's. There were drawings in crayon that had faded over the years, and photos from every decade scattered about—from this one all the way back to my childhood.

She stopped in front of a black-and-white photograph. The

first ever taken of me in my uniform. We were supposed to keep a straight face, but at the last moment I couldn't help it, the corners of my lips turning up just slightly. Selene turned, the same smile on her face, and I froze.

"You're..."

But I didn't know what to say. I didn't understand. I blinked once. Again. But there it was, right in front of me this whole time. I hadn't seen it because I'd been looking for Kate. But it wasn't Kate I should've been looking for.

It was me.

I reached back, feeling around for my chair and then sinking down onto it.

"I don't understand," I whispered.

She sighed, her eyes conveying something I'd seen many times in my life. Surrender. But not the kind that leads to the end of a life. The kind that accepts whatever is coming next.

Her smile remained soft as she gestured to the sofa half-covered in paperwork and books behind her. I waved a hand. Yes. Please. Sit. And waited as she did so, catching a small stack of books as they slid toward her and setting them upright, before turning her pale eyes to me, her fingers laced in her lap.

"First, I'm sorry I wasn't forthright at the front door," she said. "I wasn't sure how to begin. Despite rehearsing in the car on the way over." She gave a shy laugh and then clasped her hands as she continued, a more serious expression on her face. "The woman you knew as Kate Campbell was born with a different name."

I frowned, and then remembered Selene mentioning another name when she'd arrived. Something Kate had alluded to having in the few entries she'd made in the journal I'd read, but had never stated outright. Perhaps because she'd been afraid what might've happened if it had gotten into the wrong hands. I assumed that was also why she'd only vaguely mentioned the places she'd stopped on her way to Germany, choosing descriptions over names, and feelings instead of facts about what was happening and who she might've met.

"Giselle?" I asked.

"Gisela Holländer," she said. "Born to Gerhard and Gabriela Holländer, two people who fully supported the Nazi ideology. And when I say supported, I mean funded, threw lavish parties, and mixed with the man himself."

The words sat between us as I tried to take them in. Absorb them. Have them make sense as I remembered the woman from my past who had haunted me ever since.

"I don't understand," I said. "How..."

My eyes darted around the room, memories, tarnished and blurry with age, forcing their way to the forefront of my mind.

"It's a long and complicated story," Selene said, empathy welling in her eyes, just as Kate's had so many years before as she'd worked over me, stitching me up so I wouldn't bleed to death.

I held up a hand. "I'm sorry. Can you just..." I stood. "I'll be right back."

I hurried down the hallway and found Lizzie and Emma standing at the kitchen island, a laptop open to our favorite pizza place.

"Old Man?" Emma said, looking up, taking in my face, and stepping toward me. "What's wrong?"

"Dad?" Lizzie reached out a hand, placing it on my arm. "Are you okay?"

"Can the pizza wait?" I asked. "I want you to hear this at the same time I do."

"Hear what?" Emma asked.

"I'm not really sure. I just...don't want to be alone."

The two women looked at one another and then nodded and followed me silently back to my office where Selene had cleared the sofa, making neat little stacks on the floor beside it. She stood waiting for us, as if anticipating a slightly larger audience.

"I know this is all very strange," I said, looking from my daughter to my grandaughter. "And I'm sorry for the secrecy. I just...wasn't sure where this was going. But now..." I motioned toward Selene. "This is Selene Michel. She knew an old friend of mine and is helping clear up a bit of a mystery. Selene, this is my daughter, Lizzie, and my granddaughter, Emma."

"I am so pleased to meet you both," Selene said.

The four of us sat then, Lizzie and Emma looking curiously from Selene to me, seeing the same thing in her that I had, but not realizing yet what I'd come to understand but couldn't quite explain. Yet. But finally, after a lifetime of wonder, I knew the answers were coming.

"Who is the old friend?" Lizzie asked.

"A woman," I said. "Someone I knew before your mother. The woman who saved my life during the war."

"Someone you loved?" Lizzie asked.

I inhaled. As I let the breath go, I nodded.

"Yes."

"Did..." Emma looked from me to her mother and back again. "Did Gran know?"

I smiled and chuckled. "Your grandmother was the one who helped heal me after I returned home, thinking Kate dead."

Emma nodded and slid her hand into her mother's. I met Lizzie's eyes and she gave me the same smile her mother used to give and then we all turned our attention back to Selene.

"Kate Campbell's name at birth was Gisela Holländer," Selene began, and then went on to explain the parents she'd been born to, the quality of her life—the extreme wealth, the apartment in the city, the country house, and the travel. The circle of friends they belonged to. The way she was treated by her parents, how she was expected to behave, the friends she was to surround herself with, the piano lessons, social graces lessons, extra tutoring to ensure she excelled not only in school, but understood politics. *Their* politics.

"She hated it," Selene said. "All of it. And her mother made no qualms about her disdain for her. And her sister."

I frowned. "I thought… Wasn't she an only child?"

Selene shook her head. "She had a younger sister. Younger by six years. Catrin. Cat. Kitty Cat. When you met Gisela, she was of the assumption that her sister had died years before. She learned she was still alive after you returned to the front."

"She sent a letter that said she had to go home," I said, remembering. "I thought she'd meant Manhattan. I thought she'd gone back to where she lived with her aunt… Victoria?"

"Victoria. Yes," she said. "Victoria was actually born Helene. Gisela was nine when Helene married a man named Elias Fuchs, a wealthy Austrian businessman who ran in the same circles as Gisela's parents. Elias was the only son of one of Austria's wealthiest couples, who had died years before, leaving him, their sole heir, the entirety of their fortune. What his parents didn't know when they were alive, was that he had been using his hefty allowance to help the opposition of their political leanings." Selene paused and took in each of us before continuing. "Like Gisela, Elias didn't agree with his parents' ideologies. Or those of the man they supported. He was secretly working against them, attending parties to gain knowledge, which he then passed on to certain friends he'd made. American and British friends. In Helene he met a kindred spirit, and the two of them worked together as part of an underground group that had existed since the First World War. No one would suspect the wealthy, sparkling couple attending parties at her sister and brother-in-law's bidding could be spies. So when they left on a long-planned vacation the year Gisela turned thirteen, there was intense shock and sadness within the group when their plane crashed and they died."

She went on to explain that they'd actually faked their deaths, setting them up to begin a new life in America, Gisela's knowledge of the plan, and how they'd sent for her, under false pretenses, two years later.

"When Gisela was fourteen, she began correspondence with a girl her same age," Selene said. "It was a program set up between her exclusive private school and one in California where the parents of the children quietly supported Nazism. Of course, Gerhard and Gabriela loved this. They had hosted several prominent European celebrities over the years, and the thought of getting in with Hollywood… Well. Gabriela was keen. And so they both supported the pen-pal relationship wholeheartedly. And when Gisela was invited to go visit her for two weeks the summer after she turned sixteen, they practically packed her bags for her, sending her off with a trusted friend of the family."

Selene shifted in her seat, suddenly looking uncomfortable and glancing worriedly from Lizzie to Emma to me.

"I understand this is a lot of information and I've come to your home uninvited," she said. "I—if you want me to stop at any time I can."

"Please keep going," Emma said.

Selene looked to Lizzie, who nodded, then to me.

"Can't stop now, kid," I said. "This group loves a good story."

She nodded. "Where was I?"

"The pen pal," Lizzie said, leaning forward, her elbows on her knees.

"The pen pal didn't really exist. At least not in the form of a sixteen-year-old girl. The letters were actually written by the woman in charge of handling the mail that came in and out of the school—and who was part of the network Gisela's aunt and uncle worked with. Using a code Helene and Gisela had made up during their many walks and talks, she sent letters filled with innocent-sounding details of her life by the ocean, browning her skin in the sun, and luxurious vacations with her imaginary parents. A month in France, a jaunt to Seattle, two weeks in

Hawaii…and a long, boring week in her grandmother's home on the Upper East Side of Manhattan.

"For two years Gisela exchanged letters with this imaginary girl, cementing a narrative. A history. Trust."

"What about the trusted friend?" Emma asked. "Did she know what she was getting herself into?"

"Indeed," Selene said. "In fact, there were a few people associated with the Holländer household who knew, as they'd been recommended for hire or introduced to the elder Holländers before Gisela was born. By her aunt Helene." She looked to me. "She had eyes and ears everywhere in that house."

"As soon as Gisela landed in California, the woman she'd been exchanging letters with handed her a set of papers. Inside was her new name, a new birthday, and a hometown listed as Manhattan.

"She spoke English, but with a heavy German accent, and so she didn't say a word on the train that took her cross-country to New York and her aunt Helene, now Victoria, and Uncle Elias, now Frank.

"She was homeschooled until she could speak without a trace of an accent," Selene said. "Then went to high school, made friends, and on the weekends she volunteered as a candy striper at a nearby hospital with her aunt. It was there she found her love of caring for others. And in the back of her mind… a mission.

"The three of them, Victoria, Frank, and Kate were a tight-knit group. At home they listened constantly to the radio. Due to Uncle Frank's job, still providing funds for spies overseas, they were privy to information others weren't about the war coming. After Kate graduated from high school, she immediately enrolled in nursing school. She was determined that if war should come, she would be able to help her fellow Americans. It was her way of trying to make amends for her country's transgressions."

Selene looked to me then.

"There was a program in Kentucky for additional training. Military training. For nursing while in flight. She was based first in the Pacific Theater. Then the European, where she met you on a flight to England."

I could feel Lizzie's and Emma's eyes on me, but I could only see Selene now.

"What happened in Germany?" I asked.

Once more, she reached for her purse. Another stack of letters, tied with a string, yellowed with age, bent from time.

She leaned forward and held them out to me. At the familiar sight of my name written in Kate's penmanship, I sucked in a breath.

"She wrote these to you. A few from her parents' home in Hamburg, but most were written from the work camp she was sent to after her mother, sister, and her childhood nanny were killed. She never sent them, thus the absence of postage. I imagine she didn't have a way to. The ones written in Hamburg were returned to her a few months after she arrived back in Manhattan." She stopped, taking a breath. And then, "The bottom one in the pile, I believe, will answer your question."

My eyes filled with tears, the weight of the letters in my hand growing, an ache I'd long since buried, building in my chest.

"Dad?" Lizzie said. "What question?"

But I couldn't answer. Not yet. Instead, I slid the letter at the bottom of the pile free from its binding, stood, and left the room.

42

Lena

Ravensbrück Concentration Camp
March 1945

DESPITE ALL I'D been through, there had been nothing in my life that could've prepared me for the scene that greeted me when I exited the military vehicle that brought me from Hamburg to Ravensbrück.

The first thing I noticed when the truck stopped was the stench. I gulped in a breath through my mouth as I stepped carefully to the ground, slipping and nearly falling on a patch of ice. Following the line of women in front of me, I rounded the truck, only to be faced with a large wooden cart filled with dead bodies.

"Oh," the woman behind me said.

The bodies, their arms and legs spilling over the sides, stared out in all directions with empty eyes, their mouths open as if waiting to inhale a breath that would never again come.

"This way," a woman in uniform snapped, and we hurried to obey, not wanting to end up like those in the cart.

I'd spent two awful months in a jail in Hamburg before being transferred to Ravensbrück. My crime, per Lieutenant Schmeiden, was theft.

"Caught her in the Holländer estate with another young woman who was carrying a gun. She shot Mrs. Holländer and the maid before I put her down."

One of the guards had chuckled. "Clearly they didn't know they were stepping on your turf."

The lieutenant had smirked in return. "I'm having it cleared out as we speak."

I didn't talk to anyone unless spoken to, my mind too full of what had transpired in my mother's bedroom, my heart broken for all that had been lost in a matter of seconds, my soul empty.

I moved when I was told to move, ate when I was told to eat, and when it was time to go, I didn't listen to where we were headed, nor did I question it. I just went. It was only through the other women murmuring to one another on the way there that I learned the name of the camp and noticed the scared looks on their faces. I had no idea where their fear stemmed from or if I should feel frightened as well. But even if I'd wanted to, I wasn't sure I could. The only thing I felt was numb. The only thought I had in my mind was an image of Catrin as she lay lifeless on the floor.

"Cat," I whispered as I followed behind the others to a long narrow building.

We were marched down several long hallways until we reached a room where we were told to strip down. We were sprayed, made to wash, and sprayed again, holding our hands up to ward off the water coming at our faces and bruising our tender skin. After we'd dried off, we were handed black-and-white striped uniforms. Our belongings were gone through, some items confiscated, others tossed in a bin. I was allowed to keep my journal and the clothes I'd brought. But others cried as small pieces of their lives were found and thrown into a bin like trash before we were then led to another room where different-colored triangle patches were handed to us to be sewn onto our sleeves. Mine was green.

There were twelve barracks for living in and the seven of us that had traveled together were dispersed among them. As I entered my new home and saw the crush of bodies inside, I wondered if I'd ever see the women I'd traveled with again. There were so many of us, I wasn't sure it was possible to see the same face twice.

"You're in the back," a woman with a worn face and shaved head said with a wave of her hand. "Come on."

I followed, trying not to blanch at the smell. It was hot in here. Humid. And smelled of dirty bodies and dirtier clothes. There were flies in the air and rats on the floor. I tried not to imagine the other things I knew must be there, though I couldn't see them. Things like disease and lice.

We squeezed between bodies and beds. So many beds. Bunks stacked three high, reminding me of the planes I'd worked on carrying the wounded. Reminding me of William.

The baby kicked inside me and I ran my hand over my belly. Without fail, should I think of William, a kick followed.

"This is you," the woman said, pointing to a middle bunk. She frowned and took in my belly, which was much more prominent in the striped uniform than it had been in my father's bulky sweater. "Hmm. This won't do."

"I can manage," I said, not wanting to bother anyone by making them move.

"We can do better. Not much, but certainly better than making a pregnant woman climb up to bed." Her eyes flicked over me. Friendly, but guarded. "I'm Zuz, by the way." She held out a red, calloused hand. "Zuzanna."

"Lena," I said, placing my hand in hers.

She showed me around then and introduced me to several of the other women, their names and colored triangle patches floating in and out of my mind as I tried to breathe in the acrid, humid air accumulated by so many bodies gathered in one enclosed space.

The population was mostly Polish, but there were women from the Soviet Union, Germany, Hungary, France, Czechoslovakia, the Benelux countries, and Yugoslavia too. A cacophony of languages filled the large building, our only saving grace to communicating the overlapping English we'd either learned in school or picked up from friends and family.

We ended up back at the bunks and the woman who was assigned the bottom was thankfully amenable to swapping. I was shown where to put my belongings, where to find the threadbare and stained towels for showering, and then I followed the crowd through the cold to another building where a small bowl of lukewarm soup with barely more than a couple of small potatoes was served for dinner.

Throughout the next week I was put to work doing physically demanding labor in the sprawling, near-frozen fields surrounding the camp. Digging, planting, building fences… My pregnant belly allowed me no mercy, but I kept my mouth shut, refusing to utter even a whimper as my body, now depleted of the meals I'd had access to only a few weeks ago, were reduced to rations that couldn't adequately nourish an adult body. Much less one carrying a baby. I was tired, exhausted…and starving.

"Can I have that?" a voice said.

I stared at my bunkmate, Agata.

"Can you have what?" I asked, looking to where she was pointing on my body and seeing nothing.

She reached over and pulled a thread hanging from the cuff of my sleeve.

"You want the thread?" I asked.

She nodded and I shrugged, holding out my arm and watching as she wrapped it around her finger twice and gave it a quick tug, severing it from my uniform.

"Thank you," she said, and then set it beside her with a small pile of similar bits of thread and fabric.

"What are you making?" I asked, noticing what looked like a small lump of fabric in her hand. She held it up and my eyes widened. "Oh! It's a doll."

She smiled and nodded. "One of the kids in the other barracks lost her mom two days ago. I'm making it for her." She pointed to my belly. "I could make one for you too if you like."

"That's very kind of you."

She shrugged. "Helps pass the time, searching for scraps, putting them together."

"What do you stuff them with?"

"Usually just more scraps. Sometimes hair."

My mouth went dry.

"Hair?"

"I was able to fill five dolls when Zuz first got here. She had a beautiful head of dark hair. She saved a handful for me when they shaved it off. Snuck it from the floor and stuffed it in her pocket." She glanced at my hair. "Yours is nice too. They won't shave you though."

"They won't?"

"Nah. They don't shave the Germans. Only the Poles and Czechs."

"Why?" I asked.

Her eyes met mine with a frank look. "Why do they do any of it?"

The following morning we were back out in the fields after a meager offering of food that would leave no one satiated. The number of hours we worked were cruel. The work backbreaking as the skin on our palms, fingers, and feet blistered, broke, started to heal, then broke again the next day until calluses formed. It wasn't an uncommon sight to see women lined up for the bathroom to rinse their bloodied hands in brown-tinted water at the end of a long day. I wondered what kind of infections we were breeding, and whispered at night to my baby how sorry I was that I'd brought him or her to this dreadful place.

"Please forgive me," I murmured before drifting off into a sleep filled with nightmares.

Catrin was never far from my mind. I went over the few interactions we'd had as I clawed with insufficient tools at the earth, trying to make peace and always failing. This wasn't how it was supposed to have turned out. The only person who was supposed to have died was my mother. Losing the sister I'd loved so dearly, and Paulina, the woman who had taken me in and given me shelter, and a friend when she'd been putting her own life at risk by doing so, had altered me. I didn't want to make friends with the women I bunked so close to and shared meals with. I didn't want to share any part of me with them. I wasn't even sure I wanted to survive. The only things that kept me going were the child inside me, and the thought that one day I might see William again.

The days began to blur into one. Each the same as the last. Wake, go through an endless round of roll call, and then get our instructions for the day by an *aufseherin*, the female guard assigned our barracks. They were the most unpleasant women I'd ever had the chance to be around. Save for my mother.

Aufseherin Elfriede Muller was the worst of the bunch, earning her the name the Beast of Ravensbrück. We avoided her at all costs.

These women were hard-faced with bellowing voices filled with cruelty that demanded, shouted, belittled, and sneered as we stumbled by, trying to keep our wits about us and look strong, praying not to be noticed and pulled from the group. Being "selected" was not something anyone wanted.

"What's it mean?" I asked Agata one night, lying on my bunk below hers.

"Being selected?" she asked. A doll appeared above me and I reached out to take it from her. "How's it look?"

I grinned at the little doll, no bigger than my hand with its skinny limbs, plain face, and body made out of someone's old blue-and-white polka-dot garment.

"She's perfect," I said, handing it back up and then waiting for her to answer my question. But when she didn't, a voice across from me did.

"They make it sound like a good thing," a woman called Brigitte said in thick, French-accented English. "Ah…you have been selected! You are so lucky!" She tsked and slid from her bed, her thin body barely covered by a black slip that had seen better days, her bones protruding through the thin fabric, her breasts, probably once full, now barely filling the cups of the gown. "But you pay attention. The ones they select, they are not strong. They are not pretty or smart. They are the weak. They tell them they are being moved somewhere better. But they are not."

"How do you know?" I asked.

"I hear things," she said, lifting the hem of her slip and scratching at a rash on her inner thigh. "The men. They talk sometimes. Give warnings."

The men.

Brigitte was one of many women who had either been chosen or volunteered to work in a brothel located just outside the camp, their "services" a reward for soldiers risking their lives for their country. They had been told, Brigitte divulged, that performing this job would get them early release from camp.

"But I have been providing my body for two years," she'd told me the first night we met. "And here I still am. One of the lucky ones not killed by their brutality and diseases."

Apparently, it wasn't uncommon for the women working in the brothel to get infected with a venereal disease that oftentimes killed them. Or if not the disease itself, a guard shooting them to keep it from spreading.

But as I watched Brigitte now, scratching at the raised, red rash, I feared her time with us was waning.

"You should get a cold damp cloth on that," I said, pointing to her leg. "It will help with the itching."

Her cheeks flushed and she dropped the hem of her skirt. "It is nothing," she said, and climbed back up onto her bunk.

I was knee-deep in a muddy trench the next afternoon following a rainstorm that had washed much of our work from the day before back into the areas we'd dug out. I was soaked, my back screaming with pain, my brain driving me to keep going, don't stop, don't look up, just a little bit longer.

"What was that?" the woman beside me said, stopping her work to stand and look down the line of bodies driving trowels into the ground.

"Don't stop," I whispered, glancing down the line the other way where Aufseherin Bösel was stalking back and forth, watching our progress from beneath a black umbrella.

"I think someone is hurt."

"They'll take care of it," I said, placing my hand on her arm. But now I was listening too, my nurse's training making it impossible not to help if I could.

Somewhere nearby someone was whimpering. I turned, trying to find where it was coming from.

"You hear it?"

"I do. Where is it coming from?"

There was a flurry of movement then as several women left their posts to help whoever was hurt. I looked back toward the *aufseherin*, but she had marched farther away to inspect another line.

"Dammit," I whispered, dropping my trowel and hauling myself out of the mud. "Stay here," I told the woman beside me. "I'll be back in a moment."

I walked as fast as I could, my feet sticking and slipping in the mud as I hurried to where a small group of women had gathered around one, the bright red of her blood staining her otherwise mud-covered dress.

"What happened?" I asked, pushing through and kneeling beside the woman. Her sleeve was torn and a deep gash ran up the inside of her arm. "How did this happen?" I looked around to the others and then moved into action, taking hold of the torn sleeve and ripping it free of the seam at the shoulder and tying a tourniquet around her biceps. "We need to get you to sick bay. Now. This needs to be cleaned and dressed."

"What is going on here?" a voice snapped.

There were gasps all around as everyone but me and the wounded woman scrambled to their feet.

"Elsa's been hurt," someone said.

"Show me," she said and Elsa lifted her arm, her dirty face tear-streaked, lower lip trembling. The guard looked at me. "Take her to sick bay and then come right back. Understand?"

"Yes, ma'am."

I stood and helped the young woman to her feet, the two of us stumbling as our shoes stuck in the mud, the rain blinding us as we went. We were a sight as we entered sick bay, our clothes dripping and filthy, hair plastered to our faces, her blood now on the both of us.

"What happened?" a serious-looking man asked, hurrying over.

"I was digging," Elsa said. "My hand slipped off the trowel and slid down the edge."

"Come," he said and led her away. A few steps in he stopped and turned back to me. "Are you coming?"

"I have to go back."

"Are you not hurt too?" He motioned to the blood on my uniform.

"It's hers," I said.

He nodded and began to turn away again when once more he looked to me. "Did you do this?" He pointed to the makeshift tourniquet.

"Yes, sir. I'm a nurse."

His eyes narrowed and then he did a quick glance around the rows of beds filled with patients. When he returned his gaze to me it dropped to my belly before raising to meet my eyes again.

"How far along are you?"

"I'm due early May."

"I'm not doing you any favors, you got yourself that way. But you'd be doing me one. We're short-staffed. Think you could get cleaned up and help out?"

My mouth opened and shut. I wanted to say yes. But I couldn't imagine Aufseherin Bösel letting me out of trench duty.

"I'm to be digging," I said.

He waved a hand. "I'll take care of it. Stay there."

A few minutes later he'd sent someone to inform the *aufseherin* that my expertise was needed in sick bay. Indefinitely. I was led to a storage room, given a clean uniform, undergarments, and a coveted pair of shoes. And then I was shown to the shower room where I was allowed a quick shower in tepid but clean water.

I worked as fast as I could, lathering my hair and face and body with soap. Scrubbing under my arms and between my legs, savoring every second before I turned off the water, dried, and dressed in the cleanest clothes I'd worn since I'd arrived.

"You'll need to attach that before you do anything," the doctor said when I exited the restroom, my dirty uniform in my hands. He was pointing to the green triangle attached to the sleeve of the soiled dress. I nodded and was pointed in the direction of scissors and sewing supplies.

Ten minutes later, green patch attached to my clean uniform, I was helping dress Elsa's wound, then moving down the line of beds, checking temperatures and injuries, cleaning scrapes and boils, and washing out bins filled with vomit.

My back still screamed, my feet still ached, my hands were sore…but I was clean, for the most part, dry, and I was doing something I was good at. Something that could help these women who came in tortured, terrorized, and scared. And I knew the care they received from me while I was tending to them might be the only kind words and touch they got all day. Maybe all month.

But there was something else I knew as well. Most of these women would die. Not from the infections or injuries, but from being too weakened to be of any use at the camp. The longer they stayed, the more likely they'd never go back to their barracks. And so as I checked each one, I made sure to give them my full attention, brushing my fingers across foreheads, holding hands, rubbing backs, and whispering words I hoped comforted them, and that they kept close to their hearts when they were eventually taken away, never to return.

43

"IT'S MAIL DAY TOMORROW."

I looked up to see Brigitte standing beside my bed, a piece of paper, envelope, and pencil in her hand.

I frowned.

"What do you mean?"

"We get to send one letter out a month."

I pushed myself up so I was sitting, my head bent under the bunk above me.

"And the letters…are mailed?"

She shrugged, the strap of her black slip falling off her shoulder. "I do not understand. Yes?"

"And do you receive letters as well?"

"Some do. Some don't. But it feels good, no? To write home?"

"I guess so."

I'd written as I'd felt moved to in my journal. Memories. Dreams. Moments I'd barely been able to find words for. After seeing the bags of mail waiting to be burned behind the post office in a city outside Hamburg, I'd only bothered to write a few more during nights I couldn't get to sleep right away. I hadn't intended to try and send them though, assuming it would be pointless. I'd merely tucked them in envelopes and stashed them in a drawer. I wondered if Lieutenant Schmeiden had found them. I could imagine him reading them aloud to his buddies and laughing.

"They check the letters," Brigitte said. "So be careful what you say. Anything private, keep it short and write it in urine."

I sat up, hitting my head on the bed frame above me.

"Excuse me?" I said. "Urine?"

She handed me the paper, envelope, and pencil and sat beside me, leaning close, her skin stinking of cheap perfume and sweat.

"It is a trick some of the women that were spies use. The urine dries invisible, but if heat is held under the paper, it shows up like magic."

"But how would anyone know to look?"

"I do not know. I have never tried it myself and have no secrets to share. But maybe you do?" She pointed to my belly.

I nodded. "Maybe."

She left then and I looked around, seeing nearly every woman around me sprawled in some position or another on her bed, writing on her one piece of paper.

I wanted to write to William, but I only got one letter a month and I had no idea how long I'd be here. With a baby on the way in this horrible place, I knew I was in danger of losing it without proper care, my own life…or both our lives. I also knew if the letter got to William, there was nothing he could do to help me.

But perhaps my aunt and uncle could.

And so I wrote a letter so banal and boring that no guard could find fault in it, with what I hoped were some well-chosen words my uncle might pick up on. The visit with my family had been lovely, but cut short due to death. I had gone to do my civic duty working in a camp with many other women for the good of our country. The baby grows strong. I was unsure of how long my time here would run, but I hoped to travel west again soon. I missed them. I loved them. I hoped to see them soon.

I signed it with my fake German name, Lena Klein, looping the end of the *n* around the bottom to circle the *K*. For Kate.

I stared at the letter for a long time, reading it over and over. Wondering if they'd pick up on my clues: I was working in a camp with many women. Would they know there were different kinds of camps? Hopefully this would lead them to look for one exclusively for women.

I hoped to travel west again soon. Meaning I'd gone east.

I was pregnant. That, if anything, would hopefully prompt some sort of action.

But was it enough?

I looked to Brigitte's empty bed and wondered if the urine tip was true. Why would she say it if it wasn't? But what would happen if one of the guards knew this trick and saw what was written? Would they merely toss it? Or would they punish us all in retaliation?

Too scared to risk it, I folded the letter, placed it inside the envelope, and addressed it to my aunt in New York. I had no idea if it would make it there, but at least I'd tried. Pushing it from my mind, I readied myself for bed, and the whispers and tears that always came with nightfall.

I jumped as someone banged on the door.

"I'll be right out!" I said, hurrying off the toilet where I'd been sitting for far longer than I'd needed to, but wanting to rest, if even just for a moment.

"Restroom breaks can be done during your lunch break," the doctor pushing past me said, his elbow ramming hard into my belly as he passed.

Rubbing my stomach, I hurried back and resumed my duties.

There were several doctors and nurses that went in and out of the two sick bays that were situated one right next to the other, making it easy for the staff to circulate and move supplies as needed. I had only been there three days when I took notice of the different setups. One sick bay was for the sick. The other, injuries. Injuries that I hadn't heard about or seen happen when I'd been out in the fields, or even in the barracks. And the injuries themselves were strange. I couldn't understand how these women had all gotten such terrible leg wounds.

"How did you do this?" I asked one woman as I inspected her red, swollen leg while removing the soiled dressing to replace it with a clean one. The wound had been sewn shut but was festering. And with a small bit of pressure, hot, putrid liquid squeezed out.

But she merely shook her head, her eyes half-closed, and looked away.

It wasn't until the last patient of the day that I got an answer. Her name was Jelena. A strong Yugoslavian woman with a crude haircut and dark eyes.

"Experiments," she whispered to me as I ran a wet cloth over her newly stitched shinbone.

"What do you mean?" I whispered back, looking around to see if anyone was paying attention to us. Luckily it was late and half of the staff had left for the night.

"They cut into our skin. With glass. Wood. Whatever they want. They put chemicals into the cuts. Sometimes bones. And then they sew it shut and watch if we heal…or fester."

I felt the blood drain from my face, glad I was already sitting because I was sure I'd fall otherwise, not just from the shock of what she'd said, but from the little nutrition I'd had in the past three weeks. I was all belly now, my arms and legs like sticks as my body gave nearly all I took in to grow the baby. It was dangerous. If I fainted, I'd be seen as weak. And the weak did not survive here.

Taking in a long breath, I continued to dab gently at her leg.

"All of you?" I asked, looking around the room. There were at least fifty women occupying the space. "Have you all been…"

"Most," she said.

I closed my eyes, a wave of nausea threatening to bring up the little bit still in my stomach. I couldn't afford to lose it, so I took deep breaths until the feeling subsided, then wrapped her wound and squeezed her hand.

"I'll see you tomorrow," I said.

"I hope you do," she said.

But the following day was chaos.

"What's happening?" someone yelled as the air around me compressed from a rush of movement from the women in the barracks, hurrying from their beds and throwing on clothes. Shouting and tearful cries, worry, fear…and hope.

"What's going on?" I asked Agata, who was lying in her bunk, pulling on her shoes.

"I'm not sure," she said, sliding from her bed to stand beside me.

"They're rounding us up."

We turned to see Brigitte, for once clothed in her uniform, black triangle on display.

"For…what?" Agata's voice trembled.

"Lord only knows," Brigitte answered. "Nothing good, I am sure of it. We are to gather our things and line up outside. Wherever we're going, we're not coming back."

The three of us stared at one another and then one by one we turned to our bunks and began packing our things.

It was early still when we stepped outside, the sun just beginning to rise, mist lying like a blanket across the fields.

"Line up!" the *aufseherin* shouted, stalking back and forth.

We moved like cattle, roaming around one another, moving down the line, spreading out, taking our places. But as I stumbled along, my gaze moved toward the two sick bays. Were they coming too?

I reached out and squeezed Brigitte's hand. When she turned, I pointed.

"I'll be back," I whispered.

"Lena, no."

"They'll need help," I said. "It's okay."

There were so many people milling about, no one noticed me hurrying to the medical buildings. But what I saw when I entered made me stop. Every single woman was still in her bed, no doctors or nurses to be found. I went to the next building and found the same. Stunned, I stepped back outside, staying out of sight as best I could, trying to understand what was happening.

A woman's voice in the distance could be heard calling out names. German names. Men were shouting, military vehicles starting up, driving toward the front gates.

"What are you doing here?"

I jumped, my hand reaching protectively for my belly as I turned to face one of the *aufsehrin*.

"I work here," I said.

"There is no need for that anymore."

"But..." I frowned and waved toward the building. "There are patients. Is there new staff coming?"

"No. No one is coming." Her eyes flicked down to my belly and back up, meeting my own with a dead stare. "You must decide. Stay, or go."

I glanced at the door to the building, running my hand in a slow circle on my belly, and then nodded.

"I'll stay," I said.

She gave me a curt nod, turned on her heel, and left.

It took most of the day for them to get organized but I didn't have time to pay attention, I was one woman caring for so many sick and injured, trying to make sense of notes made in charts, chemicals and medications administered, and women calling out to me in languages I didn't understand.

"She wants water," a woman told me as I stared, confused and near tears at a patient repeating a word I didn't understand.

"Water?" I asked and then mimed drinking to the patient, who nodded.

And then there was the matter of food. I had no idea how I was going to get food to these women while the commotion outside was still happening. If I was seen and forced into line, or worse, shot, who knows if they'd ever get fed. Most of them could barely get out of their beds.

By noon I was soaked in sweat, my muscles straining to keep my body upright, my stomach grumbling, and my wits at their limit as crying and anguish filled both buildings.

I needed a moment.

Cracking the door open an inch, I made sure no one was around before stepping outside. Still the voices filled the air. Shouting, herding, crying, names being called out. There was a gunshot. A scream. A herd of feet. I pressed my back to the wall and closed my eyes. Waiting for more gunfire, but there was none. After a few deep breaths of the cool, clean afternoon air, I opened the door and resumed my duties.

After a while I noticed the quiet.

"I'll be back," I whispered to a woman, leaving the damp cloth I'd been patting her skin with on her forehead.

Again, I peeked out the door before stepping outside. But there was no one around, the air eerily still.

I crept down the line of buildings used for barracks, looking around as I went, the quiet and emptiness sending a chill up my spine. Where had they all gone? I turned a corner and inhaled, stopping and placing my hand against the building beside me to steady myself. In the distance I saw them. All of them. Walking. The thousands of women who had lived at Ravensbrück, now being marched out in one long line, flanked by several military vehicles, guns at the ready should any of them try to flee. I feared where they were headed as I searched the crowd for Brigitte and Agata. But there were too many and they were already too far.

"Where are they taking them?"

I jumped at the voice behind me and turned to see Jelena leaning on a cane, her stitched leg red but not as swollen as it had been before.

"I don't know," I said.

"Do you think they'll come back?"

I met her gaze.

"I think we're on our own now."

44

"LENA?"

The women had been marched out a week and a half ago, the rest of us trying to survive on the rations left in the kitchen and my medical expertise. Two women had died the first night, their bodies unable to hold off the infections overtaking them anymore. Four more died the next day.

It had taken seven of us to move the bodies, placing them in carts and burying them in shallow graves where we'd once dug trenches.

I'd dragged a bed inside what had once been used as an office, but I rarely rested, someone always needing me. Always calling out. They were in pain, hungry, and scared.

As was I.

"Lena?"

"Over here," I managed, my voice strained as my belly tightened.

I'd gone to the kitchen to begin the process of getting food for everyone, a task that took nearly two hours as I loaded a cart, pushed it to the two sick bay buildings, went back and forth handing out what I'd brought, then went back for more. Usually, Jelena helped me, but today she'd stayed behind to tend to a woman delirious from pain.

This morning I'd woken to an aching back. Worse than usual, the pain spread around my hips and settled low in my belly. It wasn't until I began pulling items from the shelves that a feeling like nothing I'd known before took me to my knees.

I looked up through the strands of my hair at Jelena, who stared down, her eyes moving over me.

"The baby is coming?" she asked.

"I think so," I said and then bit my lip as another wave of pain ripped through me.

"Come," she said, kneeling beside me and putting my arm around her neck. "Back to sick bay. We need to put you on a bed."

I didn't know how she could take the weight of me with her leg still healing. But somehow she managed, limping us both all the way, pausing only when the pains of my contractions rendered me immobile, my entire body shaking afterward.

"The baby?" someone said as we entered the building and Jelena led me to my office bedroom.

"Stay here," she said. "I'll get supplies."

I was panting now, a moaning sound coming from me, low and mournful, my body working, pushing, tightening, stretching, all of its own accord as I kicked out and gripped the sides of the mattress.

How stupid I was to come to Germany. I was going to die here, and my baby with me. Even if we survived the birth, the lack of food, the high possibility of infection…

"Here we are," Jelena said almost cheerfully, her arms filled with clean sheets. She disappeared again and returned with gloves, a bucket of water, and scissors. Another trip and she had the familiar bottle of alcohol and a stack of gauze.

"Have you done this before?" I asked, my voice barely more than a whisper.

"In a manner of speaking," she said, looking away.

My heart ached as I understood. I wondered where her child was now. If he or she was still alive. If they'd one day reunite.

"Just let your body guide you," she said. "It knows what to do."

A tear ran down the side of my face as I nodded. I couldn't lose this baby. I needed this little being who had resided inside me, keeping me company, bringing me comfort, reminding me of William and hope and having a future beyond this hell I found myself in.

One of the other women knocked before poking her head in. Ema, another of the experiment patients whose wound had been left to fester, but by some miracle I'd gotten it under control, bringing down the fever she'd had, and the bright red swelling as well.

"Tereza and I are going to do the food run," she said, giving me a brave smile. "We'll make sure to bring some for you for after. You'll need your strength for the baby."

I smiled and nodded, then dropped my head back as another contraction came.

Two hours went by with no baby, my body drenched in sweat, exhausted, weakened by my efforts and lack of sustenance for the past month and a half. A couple of women came in and out, bringing Jelena more water, antiseptic, sheets, and gauze.

"I can't," I whispered for what had to be the hundredth time as I stared at the barren white walls.

"You can," Jelena said, her voice calm as she said the same thing she'd said each time I proclaimed I was giving up. "Try and relax. Let the body do its job."

"But I'm tired," I cried, my clothes soaked with sweat. "I just can't anymore. It's not coming. Please."

She wet a cloth and wiped my brow.

"Be strong, Lena. Be strong for your baby."

I whimpered, and this time when the contraction came, I gave myself over to it. I didn't try to resist, riding the wave of pain, crying out as my body pushed in a way it hadn't before, the pressure moving, heavy, *more.*

"That's it, Lena!" Jelena said. "Again!"

But I shook my head. That wasn't me. I didn't do that. It had just happened. And before I could catch my breath, it happened again, my body straining, pushing, a guttural, animal-like sound roaring from my throat until I was spent, my limbs going weak.

And then a cry rang out.

Somehow in my exhausted state I raised my head and then struggled to lift myself up on my elbows, staring at Jelena, who was smiling as she wrapped a clean sheet around something pink and moving, and then lifted the bundle toward me.

"It's a girl," she said.

And as I looked down at the baby on my chest, it was as though William were looking up at me, his pale blue eyes inside a tiny pink face.

I inhaled, and then I started to laugh and cry all at once.

"Oh," I whispered. "Hello there."

I was in awe as I stared at her, barely aware of Jelena still tending to me, my attention taken solely by the baby in my arms. She had no place being in this horrid camp and this terrible situation, and yet here she was, blinking, staring, confused.

Mine.

"What will you call her?" Jelena said, moving so that she was sitting beside us, staring with me at the tiny human with rosebud lips and a crinkled nose.

I shook my head. I had no idea. In all the turmoil since realizing I was pregnant, I'd never once given thought to a name, the idea that I'd actually give birth seeming like an impossibility. The thought of getting excited when so much could go wrong paralyzed me from giving the baby much thought at all. But now here she was. Perfect and beautiful and her father's daughter through and through.

I grinned and looked down at the precious life in my arms.

"I think," I said, running my fingertip over her downy-soft cheek, "I'll call her Willa."

Jelena fashioned a sling out of a sheet and that was where Willa lay, snug against my body every day while I hobbled about, checking on the injured while Jelena took over taking care of the sick, many of whom were better now and able to help with those who still needed care.

But with our food supplies running low, and a baby who got her nourishment from me, I could feel my energy waning with each passing hour. That combined with a lack of sleep, by Willa's third day in the world, I was beginning to forget things.

"You need to rest," Jelena said, her hand on my arm, steadying me as I restitched a wound that had needed to be reopened and washed out, then left open to heal before being sewn shut again. With barely any anesthetic left, I'd had to use it sparingly, making my shaking hands harder to mask.

"There's no time," I muttered, shifting to get a better angle and waking Willa, who shrieked her displeasure.

"Let me take her."

But I didn't want to hand the baby over. Jelena spent all day with the sick. If Willa got something, she most likely wouldn't survive it.

I whispered to my daughter as I continued to sew, breathing a sigh of relief when the wound was closed and the thread knotted.

Rising slowly, I gasped as my back muscles seized and eased myself back into the chair until the spasm passed.

"Lena," Jelena said, following me to the back where I washed my hands. "You need to leave her in her bed. You're not strong enough to carry her while you work."

But I didn't want to hear it. I was afraid to leave her. Afraid if she cried I wouldn't hear. Or that I'd fall asleep when I hadn't planned to, as I had earlier this morning when I'd sat for just a moment, and then woke with a start when one of the women shouted for help.

Every night now, I went to sleep with my stomach complaining about the lack of food. Every morning I rolled from my bed, trying to ignore the hunger, distracting myself with Willa, who had started to complain now too about the smaller portions of milk my body was producing.

We'd scavenged the entirety of the camp, looking through the officers' and guards' old quarters, hoping to find something left behind that could be consumed. But there was nothing. The rations in the kitchen were nearly gone, the bags of porridge dwindling fast.

Jelena and I talked often of leaving. Of gathering those who were able and having them help the others. But there were still so many of us. We wouldn't make it far, and we had no idea in what direction to head.

"Maybe just a handful of us could go," she'd said one night as we sat in my room like we did most nights now, after everyone else had gone to sleep.

"And if you're caught and sent back? Or...I don't know. What if someone gets hurt and you get stuck with no shelter and no food?"

The problem was, we had no idea what was waiting for us beyond the fences surrounding the camp. And we couldn't be sure the risk would be worth it.

Willa was three weeks old when Jelena found me listless in

my bed, my daughter screaming in my arms. I had tried to feed her, but while she suckled furiously at my breast, her angry little cry made it clear little was coming out.

"Here," Jelena said, holding out a bowl.

I stared at the steam coming off it and frowned.

"Sit up," she said.

I struggled to do as she said and didn't even complain when she took Willa in her arms so I could move easier. When I was upright, I reached for the bowl she'd left on the side table. It was heavier than usual and I stared at the portion size.

"It's too much," I said, but she shook her head, her eyes on my daughter as she rocked her.

"We lost three more last night," she said. "I didn't want to bother you with it. They're buried with the others." She looked at me finally. "I gave you their portions."

"Jelena—"

"Don't," she said. "You need it. For her." She looked back down at Willa. "So eat up. And today you stay in bed. Doctor's orders."

"But—"

"We'll make it through one day without you. I've already gotten a few of the others up and moving so that they can help out."

I sighed. I hated adding to the burden, but I was exhausted in a way I'd never been before.

"Okay," I said. "But just today."

The extra food helped, and a couple hours later I was able to feed Willa, who snuffled delicately at my breast, making me smile. A rare occurrence these days.

But the one day of rest was only that, and the next day I was back making rounds, checking wounds, cleaning injuries and rewrapping them, and trying to make everyone as comfortable as they could be.

I held hands, wiped brows, and tried to put on a brave face.

"Do you think anyone will come and save us?" was a question I got at least three times a day in the beginning. Now no one asked. No one believed we'd be saved.

Not even me.

So when a man suddenly appeared in the doorway the following week, all I could do was stare in fear and confusion while several of the other women screamed and scurried as far from him as they could get, gathering together at the far corner of the large room, their faces filled with terror.

The man looked at us incredulously, disappeared for a few tense minutes, and then returned with two more men, all three of them looking around the room as if trying to figure out what they'd walked into.

My entire body shaking, I stepped forward. I had tended to these women for weeks. I'd cared for them and tried quietly to protect them, and I wasn't about to let them down now. But as I opened my mouth to speak, I saw the insignia on the men's sleeves. My knees buckled and I reached for the arm of the woman next to me.

"I'm sorry we scared you," he said, his accent decidedly British, his step hesitant as he moved farther into the room, his arms up as if he himself were surrendering. "We are not here to harm you. We are here to get you to safety."

45

May 1945

THE HOSPITAL WE were brought to was a haven compared to where we had just been. Clean and bright and sterile. Not that I noticed much of it, my body and mind so weary and weakened, I was only able to stay awake for a couple hours at a time as fluids were pumped into me through an IV, Willa in a small bed beside me with her own bag of fluids.

I missed her nestling against me constantly. But the nurses reassured me as I stared down at her downy hair and pale skin, the pink returning slowly to her cheeks, that she was fine and that I needed to rest and regain my strength for the both of us.

At first we'd all been frightened to get on the trucks that had been brought in to transport us. We didn't trust anyone. Not the soldiers who brought us clean water and small portions of food, not the nurses and doctors who greeted us when we arrived.

We clung to our possessions, meager as they were, not wanting to hand over the uniforms we wore or the tiny trinkets we'd managed to hang on to. It was all we had in the world anymore. Giving them up was letting go of the last things we owned. But they were filthy, bug-ridden, and in the end, it was almost a relief to let them go. A last reminder of what we'd endured, gathered and burned and forgotten.

"Wait!" I said, reaching for the little dress Paulina had made my daughter out of fabric I'd worn as a girl. I held it to me, my fingers digging into the soft material. "Not this. Please."

The days were a blur. I was often confused, unsure whether it was day or night. Sometimes I didn't recognize my roommates, even Jelena who was in the bed next to me. Sometimes I forgot who I was, where I'd been, and where I needed to go. My mind had been plagued by the distraction of starvation, my body using whatever it could just to stay alive—so that I could keep Willa alive. I hadn't even realized how much I had changed until I was helped to the restroom and saw my reflection in the mirror, and then my legs as I pulled my gown up to use the toilet.

I was skin and bones, any evidence that I'd been pregnant only a month and a half before now gone, my stomach concave, my once full breasts depleted but still aching with the want to feed my child.

As the hours became days, and the days became weeks, I was taken on walks in a wheelchair into the fresh air. Sometimes alone, sometimes with Jelena limping beside me, Willa swaddled against my chest. Eventually, I began to take short walks without the wheelchair, visiting with the other women I'd survived with, Jelena and Willa and I forming what the nurses caring for us called a happy little tribe.

It was during a rare walk alone that I wandered past an open door and heard someone call my name, the voice familiar. I stopped and turned, my gaze meeting another across the threshold.

"Brigitte?" I said, my breath catching in my throat.

We began to cry at the same time as I moved as fast as my legs could carry me to her bed, my arms wrapping around her thin body as she wept.

"What happened to you?" I asked, sitting in the chair beside her.

She shook her head, her eyes haunted.

"They made us walk. Forever. No stopping. If we stopped we were shot." She looked away for a moment, gathering herself before she continued. "No food. No bathroom breaks. We were to just walk…until we couldn't anymore. They were walking us until we died. Women would just stop suddenly, one minute standing, the next on the ground. It was only if the guards stopped that we could, but we had to stay standing. If they caught someone kneeling…" She shook her head. "It went on for days. And then one day…they left. We were in the middle of nowhere, no town in sight. A trail of women dead behind us. We didn't know where to go or what to do. Some of us had just decided we'd go on ahead and try to find a town or a house…anything. And then the Red Army arrived."

"Agata?" I asked, but she shook her head.

I closed my eyes and said a silent prayer for my old bunkmate, remembering the sweet doll she'd made for Willa that I'd had to give up when I got to the hospital.

"I wonder what they'll do with us now," Brigitte said. "Once we're healthy enough to leave. Are we free? Do we get to go home? How do we get there? What if there's no one left?"

It was something I'd only just begun to think of myself, now that I was able to concentrate on more than my daughter and just making it through the day alive. How would I explain I wasn't the woman they had listed. That I wasn't German. Except that I was. If I said I was American, would they think me a spy? Would that hinder my ability to get home? To get in touch with my aunt and uncle?

I remembered the letter I'd written. Had it ever been mailed? And if so, had they received it? Were they looking for me? Had they figured out my hidden messages? And William…how did I find him now? Was he still based in France? Was he in England? Had he gone home to Seattle? Was he looking for me…wondering what had become of me when the letters stopped? Was he…alive?

I sighed and shook my head, squeezing Brigitte's hand.

"I don't know," I said. "Maybe all we have now is each other."

She asked about the baby then and I told her I'd bring her with me the next time I visited.

Two weeks later we began to meet outside, Brigitte brought out in a wheelchair, me under my own steam, Willa in my arms, Jelena charging ahead. The four of us would sit in the shade while Willa fed from my breast, dreaming of what our lives would be like once we left. Brigitte would go back to France, find her sister and parents, meet a nice man and fall in love. Jelena was desperate to get back to Yugoslavia.

"And you, Lena?" Brigitte asked.

"Home," I said, closing my eyes. "And William."

They thought by "home" I meant Hamburg. They'd asked once how William and I had met and I'd had to scramble to come up with a vague lie.

"Oh, you know," I'd said, waving a hand as if it wasn't that special. "He was a soldier stationed nearby my home. I thought he was handsome."

They didn't ask me to elaborate, it was a story told over and over again round the world. And they didn't ask what I'd do if I found out he hadn't survived the war, letting me keep my fantasy alive. Instead, they imagined having their own daughters, and got excited at the idea that maybe they'd become friends one day.

"They can be pen pals," she said.

"I had a pen pal once," I said, a secret grin on my face. But she was too busy imagining what our daughters would teach one another about their cultures to notice.

Eventually the women who'd made it to the hospital were well enough to leave, family members coming to collect them in some cases, others leaving of their own accord, a small bag of secondhand clothes they'd been given in one hand, a train ticket in the other.

Jelena was among them.

There were promises of keeping in touch, hugs, and a lot of tears, her hands shaking as she hugged Brigitte, gave Willa a last kiss, and then held me to her.

"Thank you, Lena," she whispered. "I will never forget you and your unfailing kindness and bravery."

My body shook as I sobbed. This woman had become my lifeline in our last weeks at the camp. She had delivered my baby. Her presence had saved my life in more ways than one. Saying goodbye felt impossible.

We watched her go, stepping onto a bus with several others, her face appearing in a window as she waved, the tears streaking down her face as the door closed and she was driven away into another unknown.

As more and more women left, the rooms becoming emptier, I grew nervous. I was still recovering, my body ravaged from malnutrition and giving birth. And I was scared.

"Have you sent your letter?" Brigitte asked me as we once more sat outside in the shade.

I'd written to my aunt, telling her where I was now, but I was scared to give the letter to the nurses to send. The war was over, but what if someone saw the address and asked questions? Was anyone still reading and censoring content? What if the letter was read and I was reported? What if it was found out that I was a German who had posed as an American for years? Would they make me stay here? Would I go back to jail? What would happen to Willa? Without my American passport to switch to at the borders, I would be seen for what I was, a German. And I couldn't imagine that would get me home to New York. I had no idea where I stood post-war in a country that was mine, but that I'd rejected.

"I wrote it," I said. "But I haven't sent it yet."

"Why not?"

I shrugged, averting my eyes.

"Lena..."

I nodded. "I'll send it tomorrow," I said.

"Promise?"

"I promise."

The following day I held the letter in my hands, flipping it over, reading my aunt's name and the address below.

"Is that for me?"

I looked up to see one of the many nurses entering my room. She smiled and pointed to the envelope in my hand. Hesitating, I stared down at the letter, then back at her. I nodded.

"We'll get it out in today's post," she said, removing it from my fingertips before I could have second thoughts. She glanced at the address. "Ooh. New York. I've always wanted to go. You have family there?"

I held my breath and nodded. "I do. The only family I have left. Besides Willa."

But if the nurse was suspicious, she didn't show it. "Well," she said. "Let's hope this gets to them soon then."

After tucking it in her pocket, she checked my vitals, moved aside as my breakfast was brought in, and promised to be back shortly with Willa.

"Would you like a room for just the two of you?" she asked as she took my temperature.

"Is that a possibility?"

"We just had a single clear out."

"I'd like that."

"Then it's yours. We'll move you after your morning walk."

It was early June when Brigitte left. She'd been sick when she arrived. Starved, and nursing a sprained ankle. But she'd made contact with her sister and as soon as the doctor said she was fit to leave, there was a train ticket in her hand.

"Write to me," she said, hugging me close. "And take care of this sweet girl of ours." She bent to kiss Willa's head.

"I will."

"Get home soon, Lena. Find a way. Even if you never hear from your aunt. Or go straight to Seattle. Get to your William."

I nodded and hugged her again.

On a stormy spring night, I'd finally told her the truth. Who I was. Where I'd come from. My childhood and how my aunt and uncle had saved me. The work I'd done to become Kate, the degree in nursing and subsequent service, first in the Pacific, then in England and France. Meeting William.

Catrin.

"It was stupid," I'd whispered. "Had I not gone..." I pictured my sister. As a girl. As a woman. Tears welled in my eyes.

"Erase those thoughts from your mind. What's done is done. You are alive. You have Willa. And soon you will have William again too. Things are looking up for us, my friend. Just keep looking forward. Keep looking toward the sun."

It was something she'd begun to say a lot. A sentiment found on a painting in her hospital room. "Look for the light. Seek the sun. Feel its warmth on your face."

I smiled and hugged her now again. I thought of the friends who had gotten me through so much. Tilly, Char, and Paulette in the Pacific. Hazel in England. Brigitte, Agata, and Jelena here. And another. The first. The one who had been with me at the beginning.

Ruthie.

But Brigitte was the only one I thought I'd keep in touch with. The others I felt so far from already. Time and distance and circumstance now separating us. I was excited to hear about

Brigitte's life. Where she'd end up living, what job she would find, what man she would love.

"Travel safe," I said.

"Get home, Kate," she whispered.

The next few days were lonely without my friend. We'd grown close during our time at the hospital and I felt adrift without her. There were others I could visit with, and sometimes did. But I mostly kept to myself. Just me and Willa, walking in the sunshine, playing on a sheet in the grass that one of the nurses provided, singing German lullabies Nanny Paulina used to sing to me.

It was a late June evening when I gathered the sheet we'd spent the past two hours lying on, me reading a book one of the nurses had loaned me, Willa gurgling happily beside me, kicking her tiny limbs at the sky.

"Time to go in, little one," I said, pulling her to me and sighing as her downy-soft head tucked beneath my chin. I kissed her, breathing in the scent of her, and walked slowly back to our strange home, smiling as we passed other patients yet to leave as well.

I turned down a corridor, then another, waving to the familiar faces as I walked past the many rooms.

"Someone needs a bath tonight," I whispered to Willa as I turned into our room and then stopped, not understanding for a moment what I was seeing.

"Kate."

I stood, my mouth open but no sound coming out as I stared at my aunt Victoria, her eyes filling with tears as she rushed toward us, taking both me and Willa into her arms.

I couldn't move at first, staring over her shoulder at Uncle Frank who was standing beside Willa's bed, his own eyes red with emotion.

And then the shock was gone and I was holding on to my aunt for dear life.

46

THE GOODBYES HAPPENED in a flurry, my one small bag, provided by the hospital, packed in minutes. Everyone wanted to say goodbye to Willa. To kiss what they called the "miracle baby," her birth and survival under such extreme and terrible circumstances inspiration for so many.

"Be well," they all called as I climbed into the car, Aunt Victoria beside me, Willa in my lap.

I waved from the window and then turned to face forward, not once looking back as we drove out of the hospital grounds. I never wanted to look back again. To wonder. To have regrets. I only wanted to look ahead.

We spent a week in a nearby hotel, Aunt Victoria procuring a pram and taking Willa and me shopping the day after we arrived. There wasn't much, so many of the shops closed, but there was enough to get us to our next destination, including a pair of men's pajamas.

And while we were there, Aunt Vic presented me with a small box tied with a white ribbon.

"What is this?" I asked.

Her smile was worried. "I'm sorry I didn't send them before but we had no idea where to send them—and then we heard reports that the postal system was a mess. I hope… I hope you aren't too mad."

She left me alone then and, my heart racing, I lifted the lid of the box.

Inside were letters. Letters from William. At first he'd written weekly, but after a while they were spaced out more, the words filled with weariness from the constant fighting, pushing forward, losing men, needing sleep…and worrying that he hadn't heard from me.

"I'm scared you aren't receiving these. Why else would you not respond? Unless… Please, Kate. Please write me soon. I am desperate to know you're okay."

My heart hurt as I raced through the letters, reading his pain, his worry, his loss of hope, until I got to the last one.

"I fear the worst now," he wrote. "I cannot imagine why you would not write. Even if you'd changed your mind about me, I know you would never be cruel enough not to tell me. And so I have to believe you have gone. I write this letter to the woman you once were. The woman I will always love. Goodbye, Kate. Goodbye, my love."

My heart was in my throat as I rushed from the room, the letter clutched in my hand.

"I need to get home," I said, choking on a sob as I shoved it at my aunt. "I need to get to Seattle."

I paced the room as she read it, my mind racing. How soon could we get to New York? How long would it take to get to Seattle? Would I bring Willa? Of course I would. He'd want to see her.

My aunt's voice broke into my thoughts.

"Oh, Kate," she said, passing the letter to my uncle as she got to her feet. "We'll go out first thing tomorrow and get some stationery so you can write him. And then we'll see about getting you both home." She pulled me to her. "It will be okay."

In the morning, stationery bought and Willa fed, I sat down to write to William, trying to explain that I had written, but feared my letters had been burned, never finding their way to him. But I was alive, and I loved him, and I was coming to Seattle as soon as I could.

I looked to Willa, asleep beside me in her bassinet. I wanted to tell him, but something so important. So precious. It had to be said in person.

We hurried to the post office, then returned to the hotel, where Uncle Frank told us to pack.

"I've gotten us rooms at a hotel in Paris," he said. "There's a train that can take us there this afternoon. We'll stay there a few days. At most a week." He held up a hand as I started to protest. "I am working at getting you an American passport. It could take a little while. Once we have it, we'll go to New York."

Aunt Victoria looked to me and I nodded and then hurried to my room to pack Willa's and my belongings.

And so we went to Paris. While Uncle Frank met with his contacts there, the three of us ladies took long leisurely walks by the Seine, stopping for crepes, buying baguettes to take back to our rented flat, and meandering in and out of shops. I ate, regaining some of the weight I'd lost, and I became stronger, both physically and mentally.

My new American passport arrived on our fifth day. I was Kate once more.

After a week in Paris, we boarded a plane for New York.

As soon as we were home I reached for the stack of mail on the entryway table. But there was nothing for me from William.

"Do you think he hasn't gotten it yet?" I asked my aunt. "Or maybe his parents moved?"

William had given me two addresses before he'd left for the front. One in France, and the other—his parents' address in Seattle.

"It's possible they moved," she said. "But who knows how the mail system is working between countries these days. I'm sure they're overwhelmed with getting letters in and out. Be patient, my love."

But I grew more anxious by the day, unable to concentrate or carry on conversations. I had resumed my friendships with Claire and Janie, whose husbands had returned from war, one with a bullet wound to the arm, the other with some shrapnel in his back. But while they cooed over Willa's pale eyes and hair—"She looks like an angel, Kate… She's the spitting image of you"—and asked questions about my eventual move to Seattle, I was barely able to remember the lie my aunt and uncle and I had come up with to explain my disappearance and my return with a baby on my hip.

"The simpler the better," Uncle Frank had said before launching into the idea while we were still in the hotel in Paris.

After they'd gotten word that I had stayed behind in Germany, they'd come up with a story in case things went awry or they didn't hear from me.

"When you got too far along in your pregnancy, you quit your nursing position and went to stay with family friends in a remote town in northern England. We didn't know about the pregnancy because you were embarrassed about having the baby out of wedlock and were waiting for William to rejoin you after the war so you could marry and then come home and tell us the happy news. But then you got sick and we had to go retrieve you. We met William, who then went home to Seattle to see his family and see about acquiring a house before you and Willa joined him."

"Can you remember all that?" Aunt Vic had asked.

"Of course," I'd said.

But as I sat here now, blankly staring back at Janie while I tried to come up with an answer to her question about if William had found a house yet, I was at a loss.

"Not yet," I said slowly, my mind scrambling to find an answer that sounded believable. "I'm going to go out there soon and help him look though."

"Just you?" Claire asked. "Or are you taking Willa too?"

"And Willa of course," I said, making it up as I went. "And Aunt Victoria. We're making a fun cross-country trip of it. I'm just sad Uncle Frank can't go, but he has to work."

"Well, I think that sounds lovely," Janie said. "And what about the wedding? Will it be here or there? Oh…you must have it here! We'll have such fun!"

I held back a sigh. The number of lies I was accumulating were staggering.

"I'm not sure," I said. "It's honestly the last thing on our minds right now. We just want to get me and Willa to Seattle and find a house. Then we'll figure out the wedding. But I promise, you two will be the first to know anything. After Aunt Vic."

"So, this upcoming trip to Seattle," Claire said. "Is that it? Unless you come back for the wedding?"

I nodded, not trusting myself to open my mouth again. Who knew what fable I'd tell next.

"We should have a little party then!" Clair said. "A proper send-off."

"Oh no…you don't have to do that," I said.

"It's done," Janie said, pulling an elegant pink notebook from her handbag and opening it to the calendar. "How about this Friday?"

And so Friday it was. A small elegant affair at the house that Janie and Claire organized with my aunt. Some of the neighbors came, a couple more women I'd known from high school, and Janie and Claire and their families. I tried to enjoy the evening, but it was hard when it felt like a farce, and by the end of the night, I felt as though my face might crack from smiling so hard to cover the pain.

The following morning made it all feel that much worse.

"Good morning," I said as I entered the kitchen, having followed the aroma of coffee brewing. Willa was still asleep and I'd snuck down quickly in hopes of having a couple minutes to myself before she woke and needed me.

"Good morning," Aunt Victoria said from where she was sitting at the kitchen table, the newspaper laid out before her. But there was something in her voice that made me pause.

"Is something wrong?" I asked.

She took in a long breath, held it, then blew it out, sliding an envelope from beneath the paper as she did.

"This was in the mail yesterday," she said. "With all the excitement about the party happening, no one went through it until an hour ago. It's..." She chewed her lip and then held it out.

I was confused at first by the sight of my own handwriting, and then I saw the crude stamp plastered across the front.

"Not At This Address. Return to Sender."

"It probably just means they've moved," Uncle Frank said, entering the room. "Something we considered."

"I need to go there," I said. "I can ask whoever lives in the house now if they know where they went."

"Kate..." Aunt Vic said and then looked to her husband. "I'll go with you."

On a humid day in mid-August, I boarded a train for Seattle, my aunt and daughter by my side.

Uncle Frank had booked two hotel rooms for us and, after the weeklong journey, we checked in and went straight to bed. In the morning I rose, dressed myself and Willa, and then met my aunt in the downstairs restaurant.

"You're sure you don't want us to come with you?" she asked. "I could hire a driver."

But I shook my head. I had no idea what I would find, and I wanted to be alone when it happened.

"I'll be fine," I said. "I'll be back as soon as I can."

She nodded and then smiled down at my daughter, who was happily making a mess of a banana in the high chair the restaurant had provided.

"Well then, I guess the two of us will do a little exploring, won't we?" she said, getting a slobbery, toothless grin in return.

"Wish me luck?" I said as I gathered my purse and sweater.

Aunt Victoria grasped my hand in hers.

"Whatever you find, you're going to be okay. I promise."

I nodded, not quite believing her, kissed the top of Willa's head, and then went out front to get a cab. After rattling off the last known address for William Mitchell, I sat back in my seat and closed my eyes.

The house was a large two-story with a tidy front yard and a Ford in the driveway. Taking a deep breath, I slid from the back seat of the cab and ran my hands down the skirt of the pale yellow dress I'd worn.

"Can you wait for me?" I asked the cab driver.

"Meter's running," he said.

I nodded, stared up at the house, and then hurried up the steps before my nerves got the best of me and knocked on the door.

"Hello there," the man who answered the door said. "Can I help you?"

He looked to be around forty, nice-looking, friendly…but definitely not William, and too young to be his father.

"I'm sorry to bother you, sir," I said. "But I'm looking for a William Mitchell."

He shook his head. "Sorry to say I don't know anyone by that name."

"Do you mind if I ask how long you've lived here?"

"Just about a year," he said.

I nodded. "The family that lived here before you. Their son is William. Do you happen to know where they moved to?"

"Sorry. Can't say I do. I know they sold the house because their son, William I guess, got injured flying in the war. They needed a house with only one floor for his wheelchair."

"That would be his brother. He was a pilot."

The man shrugged.

"You have no idea if they stayed in the area?" I asked.

"Sorry, miss. I never met 'em. They'd moved out before I even saw the house."

I sighed, masking my frustration the best I could. "Okay well, thank you anyways. Have a nice day."

He shut the door and I turned and stood on the porch, staring blindly toward the cab, unsure what to do next. This had been my only lead. Slowly, I walked back down the steps. When I reached the sidewalk I stopped, looking both ways for traffic.

"Yoohoo! Miss?"

I turned to see a woman in the next yard over, waving a gloved hand at me.

"Yes?" I called.

"You looking for the family that used to live there?" She pointed at the house I'd just been at.

"I am," I said, taking a step toward her.

"They moved," she said. "Just over a year ago." She put her pruning shears down and waved me over.

"Do you know where they went?" I asked.

"Sure do. The parents and their youngest son moved across town to a nice one-story home that's easier to get a wheelchair around in. Their eldest, William, moved just around the corner."

My lips parted, my breath caught between an inhale and exhale as I looked up and then down the street, wondering what corner he was around.

"Where?" I asked, my voice barely more than a whisper.

The woman pointed. "Take a right at the stop sign up there and it's the fourth house on the left. He—"

"Thank you," I said, cutting her off. "Have a good day!"

I hurried to the cab and jumped in the back seat, giving directions as I shut the door. A moment later we were off, my eyes staring straight ahead, willing the driver to go faster. At the stop sign we paused and then he took a right. I scooted across the seat so I was on the left side of the car, staring out the window, counting houses.

"Stop," I said, and the driver pulled off to the side of the road.

It was a quaint brick Tudor, the yard neat, the door painted white with a floral wreath hanging from it, the curtains in the front window open and welcoming. For some reason I felt suddenly afraid. I slid back to the right side of the car and placed my hand on the handle, but didn't open the door.

"Do you want me to stay again?" the driver asked.

"Yes, please," I whispered.

I took a breath, opened the door, and stepped out, facing the house but not moving. As I stared up at it, a car pulled into the driveway.

William.

And as I watched, he emerged from the car.

He was just as I remembered him. Tall and strong and so handsome. My heart nearly leaped from my chest as I watched him walk around the car. I was about to move from behind the safety of the cab when I saw him open the passenger-side door, his hand reaching down to catch a woman's. He helped her from her seat, a smile on his face as she emerged, the little pale blue hat on her dark brown hair perfectly matching her dress.

She could've been anyone. A friend. A cousin. But then he

did something unmistakable. He placed a hand tenderly on her belly, and then kissed her before leading her to the front door.

I wasn't sure how long I stood there. I didn't care that the meter was running. All I knew was that I was once again seeing glimpses of my life flash before my eyes. Precious moments I'd believed were leading me to something better—but instead had led to one crushing blow after another.

Ruthie.

Catrin.

And now William.

Each one beloved. Each one gone.

I crouched down and rested my forehead on the side of the cab.

"Miss?" the driver called.

"Sorry," I said. "I just need a minute."

I could still go. I could knock on the door. I could explain everything. But then what? I ruined the life he was clearly building with a woman he'd found after he'd thought me dead?

My breath caught, strangled on a sob, my body beginning to shake as the tears I'd held in for so long threatened to break free. I had waited for him. I had endured because of my memories of him and us. I had kept going, knowing it would all be worth it…because in the end I'd be with him again. But it was not to be. I would not go there now…or ever. I had to let him go.

Taking in a deep breath, I stood and steadied myself before opening the door and getting back inside.

"Please take me back to the hotel," I said.

"Are you okay, miss?"

I sighed and looked out at the little brick house.

"Not yet," I said. "Not in a long time. But I will be."

47

William

Somewhere over the Atlantic
2003

TRY AS I MIGHT, I couldn't sleep.

Lizzie sat beside me on one side, Emma across the aisle on the other. Both had been looking after me all day, from the moment they arrived at my house to pick me up, on the drive to the airport, as we went through security, to when we took our seats on the plane. But now, finally, they were asleep, and I was left alone with my thoughts.

It had been startling to hear from Selene that Kate had come to find me that day. It had been shocking to find out she'd been alive. Though shocking didn't quite cover the feeling. It was something more along the lines of devastating. I'd been so sure she'd died. There was no other explanation in my mind. I knew there hadn't been some other great love she might've gone back to. We had made plans. We were in love. I'd never been so sure of anything or anyone in my life. So the only thing that made sense was, she'd died. And in the chaos of war, when we weren't legally bound or blood relatives, there was no reason I'd have been told.

I'd ached for her. Mourned. Grieved for months. I became a danger to my platoon, putting us at risk when my mind had wandered, bullets whizzing past my helmet, missing me left and right…until one didn't. This time the damage would take more than a couple of months to heal, and with the war nearly over by all accounts, on February fourteenth, nineteen forty-five, I was sent home.

Except I no longer had a home. My parents had moved when my brother was sent home in a wheelchair, the stairs making it impossible to get to his bedroom.

I found a small apartment once I was released from the hospital, barely unpacked any of the boxes, threw a mattress on the floor, put a radio on the counter, and made do with one pot and one pan. I was isolated, sad, and angry. I'd lost friends. I'd lost the woman I loved. I didn't care anymore and it showed.

And then an old friend showed up on my doorstep.

"There's a group of us that gets together once a week," Bill said. "We have a couple of beers, talk a little about what we went through, what we saw over there… It helps. No one else understands."

"I don't feel like talking."

"You don't have to if you don't want to. It's really just a way to get us all out of our houses and remembering how to have friends when there aren't bullets coming at us."

I said thanks but no thanks. But the next week when he came by again, I couldn't find a reason not to. After that I was there every Thursday night. Sometimes I talked, sometimes I only listened. It didn't matter. It was just nice to not feel alone after a night of thrashing, the nightmares chasing me around my pillow.

After a while, a couple of women joined the group. One was the sister of a guy we all knew who'd been killed. She'd been close with her brother and had had a hard time since his death. The other woman was named Olivia.

A widow, Olivia's husband of two months had died almost immediately upon being sent to the front. He'd been friends with several of the men in the group, which was how she got the call to join. They knew she'd been struggling for a long time, her folks and several friends encouraging her to move on.

"I'm tired of people assuming I'm ready because of some timetable they've put on my grief," she'd said quietly the first night she came.

We all understood. We felt the same.

And then one Thursday I got off work early from the job I'd just started at an architecture firm and found her tucked into the corner of the bar we all met at, reading a book and scribbling furiously into a notebook.

I bought her a beer and she told me she was a writer.

"Or trying to be anyways," she'd said with a shrug. "I'll get there eventually."

I asked her what she liked to write about and she asked me what I liked to design. We started meeting before the gatherings every Thursday after that. We hadn't made a decision to, it just began to happen. But despite my interest in her as a person, and the fact that she was beautiful and smart and kind, I was still too broken by the loss of Kate to care about her in any way other than as a friend. And despite her husband dying years before, I could tell falling in love was the last thing on her mind.

Until the night we got caught in the rain.

The meeting had been canceled that Thursday, but I was antsy after work. I had no idea if she'd be there, but I went to the bar anyways.

"It's closed," she said as I walked toward her on the sidewalk outside the pub.

I frowned and stared at the handmade sign inside the window. Short-staffed. Closed Thursday, it read in messy handwriting.

The rain was pissing down and neither of us had an umbrella.

"This must be why the meeting was canceled," I said.

"It is," she said. "I saw it this morning and called Hal to alert everyone."

"Oh," I said and then met her eyes. She gave me an almost embarrassed smile, which surprised me. Olivia didn't get embarrassed. Every meeting she just talked about whatever was on her mind. Not ashamed to put it out there for the group to know. So to see her look shy was strange.

"I was hoping you'd come anyways," she said, staring up at me with her warm, brown eyes.

I could never explain what happened to my body and mind in that moment. It was like a salve being gently massaged into my heart. And Olivia was the salve.

We were shy with one another at first. Careful. Afraid of stepping into a relationship together. We felt guilt for the memories we were stepping around, treading ever-so-lightly, wary of thinking less about the ones we lost, and more about one another.

But we were also tired. Tired of being sad, of feeling we had nothing to live for, nothing to look forward to. And so we began to live for one another.

Lizzie shifted beside me and I glanced down at her hand in mine. When she was just a girl and scared at night, she'd climb into bed between her mother and me and hold my hand. As she'd drifted off to sleep beside me on the plane, I'd felt her soft hand slip into mine and I'd smiled and met her eyes, so like her mother's, and given her fingers a squeeze, saying in my head what I'd said when she was small: "You're okay, sweet girl. It's all going to be just fine."

It was a surprise when Olivia got pregnant. For the both of us. We weren't married yet, but had begun to talk of it here and there. And then she arrived at my apartment door one day, white as a sheet, and told me what she suspected. We went to the doctor the next day and had it confirmed.

"William," she'd said, her eyes wide, mortified. We'd been so careful.

But I'd smiled. "Wanna have a baby with me, Ollie?"

It wasn't something we'd ever discussed as we were still just trying to navigate being part of a couple again, but I wasn't upset.

"You're not mad?" she'd whispered. "I could—"

I pressed my finger to her lips. "I don't know what you're about to say, but don't. If you want this baby, let's have this baby. You and me. It will be the three of us. We'll be a family. You'll write books, I'll design us a house, and we'll be happy."

She'd grinned through her tears. "You're going to be the man I always write."

"I damn well better be!" I said and we both laughed.

And so our life together began. And it was beautiful and full of light and laughter, some funny fights, lots of family vacations, a few nightmares that still haunted our nights, but we were okay. We were just fine.

We were more than fine.

Selene met us at the airport like she said she would, but I felt myself looking around for someone else.

"How was the flight?" she asked as we followed her to her car, a soft breeze cooling the warm Southern France air.

"Good," we all said at once and she laughed.

The drive was easy, all of us staring out the windows, taking in the beauty of Nice. I'd told Lizzie and Emma how Kate and I had once talked about living here together if we decided Seattle didn't suit us as a couple. She'd been here often as a girl and had fond memories. Had always dreamed she'd lived here one day, and I'd been fascinated and willing to follow her wherever she wanted to go.

"It's so beautiful," Emma said from the back seat. "I already don't want to leave."

While the three women chatted, Selene pointing and explaining bits about her hometown, I grew quiet, my mind elsewhere.

"Dad?" Lizzie said, her hand on my shoulder. "You okay?"

I smiled over my shoulder, meeting her eyes and feeling the gazes of the other two women on me.

"I'm okay," I said.

It was strange being here. The place I always thought I'd come with Kate. Seeing what she'd seen every day of her life once she'd decided to leave New York.

Per Selene, after she'd seen me that day in Seattle, she'd gone back home to her aunt and uncle's place in Manhattan and felt adrift.

"She took a lot of walks around the city with Willa, but it felt too big. Too claustrophobic. And not where she wanted to raise her child. She began to dream of the South of France, remembering how much she'd loved it as a child. She broached the subject with Aunt Vic, who told her to think on it for a while, and maybe get back into one of the nearby hospitals—to see how she felt about nursing again. To see if it was something she still wanted to do with her life. As soon as she stepped inside, she knew it was still what she was meant to do. She worked for about a year, saving and making plans, and then when Willa was nearly two, the four of them went to France. Uncle Frank was ready to retire by then, and Aunt Victoria wanted a smaller, quieter life. They found a house for the four of them, until Kate could afford to live on her own, and they were happy, living out their days by the seaside."

"Did she ever marry?" I'd asked, feeling a small prickle of something related to jealousy at the thought.

But Selene shook her head. "She did not. She always said

she was content. She liked it being just her and Willa. She said it was all her heart could handle."

Kate had worked in a small medical clinic as the head nurse until she retired. She'd lived a mostly quiet life with a lovely group of friends who rotated dinners at one another's houses every couple of weeks, and evenings and weekends were spent with Willa and her aunt and uncle until they passed when both were well into their eighties. She was by Willa's side when Selene was born, was a collector of seaside paintings by local artists, helped in her community, and loved to work in her garden, a space filled with flowers in every color.

"She was magnificent," Selene had said as she sat on the couch in my office that day that seemed so long ago now, but was only the month before. "Happy, peaceful, knowledgeable, funny, and beautiful."

"She was stunning," I'd said, smiling as Lizzie looked to me, curious about this woman she'd never heard of.

Kate had passed peacefully in her sleep eight months before Selene showed up on my front porch asking if I'd ever known a woman called Gisela. She'd always been honest with both her daughter and her granddaughter about what had happened in her life, and why she'd made the choices she'd made. But while Willa had worried looking for her father might alter their life in a way that was hurtful, Selene had always been curious about me. And so, eight months after Kate had passed, she'd come looking.

"I knew it was you the moment you came to the door," Selene had said, reaching for her purse a last time. "She always said this was her most prized possession."

She'd pulled something out and handed it to me. As my fingertips touched the image, my heart began to race. We'd taken one photo together and I'd given it to her. I hadn't seen it since the day I left her in England. And now here it was in my hands.

"Some months after the war ended," Selene said, "a bunch

of boxes arrived at the apartment in Manhattan. Through their network, Aunt Victoria and Uncle Frank had been able to salvage some of the Holländer estate. Including a few of the belongings Kate had left behind."

I'd stared down at the couple in the photo, choking back a sob. It was the day I'd asked her to marry me. I'd borrowed a camera and remembered Kate laughing as I set the stand precariously in the field our tree grew in, watching it fall over twice before I got it to balance and then ran to stand beside her, pulling her close, her hair brushing against my cheek, her body rising and falling against mine.

"Forevermore," I'd whispered then before the camera flashed.

"Forevermore," I'd whispered again as I stared down at the photo.

We pulled up to a small two-story house the color of the fading sun, shutters on every window, a small yard filled with ornamental weeping trees and flowering shrubs in front.

"This was Kate's home," Selene said. "She was so proud of being able to afford it on her own. Loved puttering around fixing little things, decorating… Maman moved in after she passed as neither of us could imagine letting it go to anyone else. We had too many wonderful memories here."

She turned off the car and got out, Lizzie and Emma behind her. But I was slower. My heart beating hard in my chest.

I'd never known I had another daughter in the world, and I was afraid. Would she hate me for having another family? Would we like one another? Would she and Lizzie get along? What if this was it? Would we have this one meeting and then never see one another again?

"William?" Selene said.

"Yes?" I wiped my damp palms on my slacks.

She pointed to a little arched gate. "Through there."

I glanced at Lizzie, then Emma.

"You've got this, Old Man," Emma said, and I grinned,

took a breath, and nodded, turning toward the gate. They didn't follow.

As I pushed through, a little bell rang, announcing my arrival. The garden at the back of the house was somehow lusher than the front with layers upon layers of flowers and shrubs. It reminded me of something out of one of Olivia's books.

I followed a stone path as it curved gently through the grass toward a patio with a table and chairs and a bright turquoise umbrella, a slender woman with light brown hair kissed by the sun sitting beneath it.

She stood, the skirt of her pale-yellow sundress billowing gently in the breeze, a hesitant smile on her face. My face. My eyes. She was the spitting image of me. There was no doubt this was my child. Mine and Kate's.

"Willa," I said, my voice hoarse with emotion.

"Bonjour, Papa."

48

Nice, France
1950

"ICE CREAM?" Willa asked, staring at her cone, a drip making its way down the back of her pudgy little hand. She was always sticky. Always smiling, her pale blue eyes reminding me of another time, another place, another human I'd loved almost as much.

"Ice cream," I repeated, nodding at her pronunciation.

She spoke mostly French, something that happened when you lived in France, attended a French school, and had little French playmates. I did too these days, after struggling our first couple of years in the country. I was teaching her other languages too though. The language of my adopted home, and sometimes the words of the country I was born into as well. But not as often.

"C'est bon?" she asked, and I nodded.

"It is good," I said.

"Good," she repeated, her little pink lips puckering around the word before she took another lick of the gelato, some of it ending up on her nose.

We sat back then and stared out at the sea, the sun sparking off the gentle waves, another day nearly done.

The move here had been necessary, my heart needing distraction, my mind needing peace. I'd always had happy memories here and figured, why not make more? Why not give my child the life I'd always dreamed of having? And so I had.

There was love in our house. Laughter, messes, running, music...honesty. We made art, we made cakes, we stuffed our faces with cookies and walked to the beach, throwing ourselves into the water and squealing as we splashed one another before packing up our things and heading back home.

Most evenings we had dinner with Aunt Vic and Uncle Frank. Eventually we made friends and had dinners with them too. We took trips up and down the coast. Train rides to different cities, and sometimes different countries. It was a good life. Sometimes a lonely one, but I pushed those feelings aside. I'd made my choices and I was at peace with them. Proud of everything I'd been through, and coming out the other side with nary a physical scar...but a couple of deep emotional ones that ran straight across my heart. One for Cat. One for William. But while some scars turned hard, mine had stayed soft. Pliable. Marking me, but not ruining me. Altering me, but not changing who I was at my core.

I leaned over and kissed Willa's hair, watching as she gobbled up the last bit of her cone, and then turning once more to look at the blue-green water stretched out before us, the sky turning magenta and tangerine as the sun lowered toward the horizon.

Life was strange. Complicated. Painful. It was simple and precious. And it was beautiful. For those of us who got to live it. To experience it in all its many forms...we were the lucky ones.

Willa slid from the bench and held her hand out to me. I leaned forward and took it.

"What shall we do now, *peu d'amour*?" I asked.

Her grip tightened on mine as she pulled, a teasing smile on her lips, those soft denim-blue eyes reminding me always of the man I still loved. Reminding me if not for him, I would not have her. And I would not have come here, to the place I finally felt at peace.

"Rentrons à la maison, Maman," she said, and I smiled and got to my feet.

"A good idea, my love. Let's go home."

Author Note

SOMETIMES THE STORIES fall in my lap. Other times I have to seek them out, which is what I was doing when I came across Jane Kendeigh, the first naval flight nurse to fly to an active combat zone during WWII. As with my first two books, *The Flight Girls* and *Angels of the Resistance*, I was immediately inspired by the brave and selfless actions of this woman and her comrades, whose work and courage were left out of the history books I read as a schoolgirl.

This is not Jane's story. This is a work of fiction. Sometimes I've had to flub the dates a little to make the story work for me. Many times I used my imagination to fill in the gaps where I couldn't find the details I was seeking. But there are moments of truth in these pages. Facts interwoven in so that you, my dear reader, will know forevermore what this fearless group of women did for their country.

Resource for readers: Want to know more about the incredible nurses of WWII? Check out *No Time for Fear* by Diane Burke Fessler.

Acknowledgments

THERE ARE ALWAYS so many people to thank for a number of wonderful reasons I feel unworthy of. First and foremost, my readers, without whom I would not get to do this job I have always dreamed I'd get to do. Knowing you wait excitedly for my next books is beyond comprehension. Thank you. I hope I've entertained you, moved you, inspired you, and left you wanting to read more.

A ginormous thank-you to my agent extraordinaire, Erin Cox. Your belief in me from day one is something I will always cherish. I adore you. Thank you for your support and laughter. To April Osborn—as always, you saw what I was trying to say and made it so. Much. BETTER! Thanks for making my story shine once again. Nancy Fischer, you should have a platinum catcher's-mitt trophy to commemorate how many of my boo-boos you caught. Thank you for making me look smart. Leah Morse and Sophie James—you both are incredible at your jobs. I am so grateful for everything you do—for getting my book into the world and getting me to my readers and many incredible booksellers.

My book covers are stunning pieces of art thanks to the amazing work and genius minds at HTP Books. My eternal gratitude.

Writer friends are simply the best and I'd be lost without them. Jamie Pacton, Kate Quinn, Elise Hooper, the PNW lunch crew…your support is PRICELESS. The business of writing seems like it should be easy, but as we all know, many times it is not. Without all of you, I'd be lost. Thank you.

Dan Hanks. You are a partner like no other. I don't deserve you. Thank you for looking at my ugly words and calling them pretty. Also for the sticky toffee pudding and ridiculous nonstop road trips across the English countryside that restore my soul and refill my storytelling well. You put up with me so well.

And last but certainly not least, thank you to my children, Jack and Dylan, who somehow think I'm cool despite my terrible mom jokes, ridiculous morning songs, and bad dance moves. You are my everything. ♥